Advance Praise for The Relentless Heart

Much more than a coming of age story, though it is that, too, this book lays bare the hidden truths of the heart through a cast of well-drawn characters and intriguing action handled deftly and touchingly by the author. If you're a fan of classic family drama, "The Relentless Heart" will capture your imagination from the first page to the exciting and surprising end.

MARGARET GUTHRIE, Author *of The Quest and Exploring Cassy as well as other novels and poetry collections.*

I loved the story. It's really wonderful. I fell in love with the boys.

Ron Froehlich's debut novel explores how a tragic loss rips a family apart and how only the love and the indomitable spirit of a young woman puts the pieces of the family back together again. It is easy to root for Froehlich's vivid characters in an intense and charming story that will stick with you long after you've read the last page.

STEVE MITCHELL, Author of *Steve McQueen Would Be Proud* and *Throwing Grenades at Gilligan's Island*

I haven't been able to put it down.

The
Relentless
Heart

A Novel

Ronald L. Froehlich

ISBN: 1480283592
ISBN 13: 9781480283596
Library of Congress Control Number: 2012921458
CreateSpace Independent Publishing Platform
North Charleston, South Carolina

Cover Design by Joseph Stellato

For Elaine,

the *"Lilly"* in my life.

Acknowledgements

This book was written with the encouragement and assistance of family members, friends, people who are here and people who have gone ahead. Of special note are two very special friends in Colorado who provided valuable assistance and timely encouragement, both talented writers in their own right. I am forever indebted to Steve Mitchell and Margaret Guthrie. I'm also grateful for the thoughtful and extremely helpful comments of my advance readers who made invaluable contributions to the manuscript prior to publication. They are Rita Anderson, Ron Krajnovich, Jo Calhoun and Mac Smith.

Author's Note: At the beginning of each chapter there is a quotation, or epigraph, that provides continuity to the unfolding theme of the story. The first quote is by the 17th-century French physicist, inventor, writer, and Christian philosopher Blaise Pascal.

> ## The heart has its reasons of which reason knows nothing.

–Blaise Pascal

Chapter 1

Winter, 1950

Henry Goodwin, at age 34, stood a pudgy five-foot-seven and had a slightly spongy look about him, enhanced by thick, golden-brown hair, a round baby-face and blue eyes. Overall, his appearance was unremarkable. But when he stared into the mirror he saw himself as taller, thinner and handsome as a movie star, a fun-loving guy with enough natural charm and confidence to wrangle just about anything he wanted out of life. He also had a reputation for being the best joke teller for miles around.

"It's a talent the good Lord put inside my head when I was in my momma's womb," he always said when asked how he'd acquired his keen-edged tongue. Then he'd grin like a toothy chimpanzee.

At the moment he was standing at the bar in the Riverfront Tavern, cranking himself up to regale his drinking buddies with one of his dirty jokes. "Gather 'round, folks," Henry said, as he glided to the center of the small crowd and raised his hand to signal for quiet. "Gotta new one and it's a real jim-dandy, and I want you all to hear it."

In a low and commanding voice, he spun out the raunchy tale, word upon word, dramatically building to the apex, then he flung out the punch-line like bait on a hook and watched as the dour and long-faced farmers and townspeople burst into fits of rollicking, side-splitting laughter. He rocked back on his heels and beamed like a kid who'd gotten his first base hit—amazed that he had the power to incite such jovial responses.

Henry Goodwin of Belleview, Nebraska, a little farm town high on the bluffs overlooking the Missouri River, had just unleashed what he judged to be his best joke ever. He'd found the path to the human funny bone—and he'd learned how to tickle it. How great was that!

But the following night, the last thing on Henry's mind was telling a joke. His mind reeled as he stalked the vacant upstairs hallway of his house. He started to punch the wall but pulled back when his fist was inches from the hard plaster.

His ball-busting Mother-In-Law Lucille!

She had the nerve to ask him—no, make that order him—to wait in the hall while Lucille and his two sons, Paul, 11, and Arthur, 6, spent time in the master bedroom alone with his wife, Margaret, known to most everyone as Margie. His beautiful wife was down with a severe case of influenza. What ticked him off was that he'd meekly gone along with Lucille's demands. What did that make him—a wimp, a pleaser, half a man? The sick woman was his wife and those two boys were his kids. He had every right to be in that bedroom with them.

Lucille had backed him down before. In fact, she'd tormented him for the past 13 years, ever since he and Margie had gone against her wishes and gotten married. And over the years whenever any little thing went wrong in his family, whether it was a kid breaking an arm, having problems at school, or fighting, it always came back to being his fault. Now, with Margie sick, he was sure this was his fault, too.

Looking back, he felt certain the trigger for Lucille's "let's blame Henry for everything" began when he and Margie had been married three happy years and everything was going great. Paul was a two-year-old toddler and Arthur hadn't come along yet. One afternoon after work, Henry pulled into their gravel driveway singing along with Hank Williams' blockbuster hit "Lonesome Blues" on the radio. It was a warm evening and Paul was playing in the yard. In five minutes he and his young son would sit down with Margie to a tasty hot supper.

Hank Williams was wailing now. He glanced down to turn up the radio when he felt a slight bump to the right fender of the car.

"Oh, shit!" he said aloud. "What the hell was that?"

Paul lay on the ground, screaming bloody murder. Christ, the kid could hardly walk two steps without falling over, yet somehow he'd made it to the driveway—and he'd hit the little guy.

Hearing his cries, Margie flew out the front door and Lucille, who was visiting, followed on her heels. Margie, tall and agile as an athlete, reached the boy in three long strides. "Oh my God!" she cried, sweeping up Paul and examining him head to toe. She rushed him toward the house as Henry piled out of the car to follow. He'd almost made it to the porch when Lucille stepped in front of him.

"You stay away from him, you drunken sot," she hollered, coming at him with both fists flying. A striking woman with a hair-trigger temper, Lucille was big and broad-shouldered, with long silver-gray hair and muscular arms and legs weathered brown from long hours tending her acre-size yard and vegetable garden.

"How could you be so careless?" she demanded.

Henry fended off the blows, retreated to the car and crawled into the driver's seat, slamming the door in his mother-in-law's face. She banged on the window as he punched down the door lock.

By then the yard was full of neighbors and, to Henry's astonishment, a sheriff's squad car, siren blaring, pulled up in front. He must have been patrolling near by.

Raging, Lucille rushed to the deputy and yelled, "He's drunk, and he ran over his own child. Put him in jail. I'll file charges."

"Now wait a minute, lady," the deputy said, holding up his hand. "Calm down. Let's see how the boy's doing."

"Stay right here," the deputy ordered Henry.

He almost started after the man but thought better of it. Instead, Henry leaned against the left front fender, crossed his legs and waited. Glancing up at the neighbors, he offered an embarrassed, half-crooked grin. "Paul will be fine," he called out. "Just a little bump."

A moment later, the uniformed officer returned and with a piece of chalk he drew a long, straight line on the street pavement.

"Okay, walk that line," he said.

Henry negotiated the white line pretty as can be, without once wobbling, even though it was humiliating to do it with the gaggle of neighbors craning to eyeball his every step.

"You seem all right to me," the deputy announced, which didn't surprise Henry. He'd only hoisted one, maybe two beers with the boys after work, though later he'd heard some A-hole at the tavern had claimed it was more like four. That guy obviously had a problem. Anyway, the deputy left, and Paul was fine. After a dozen times of telling Margie how sorry he was, she forgave him with a stern warning not to let it happen again.

On the other hand, Lucille wasn't one to forgive or forget anything. For instance, he was certain the incident involving Paul all those years ago was actually behind her ordering him to stay out of the bedroom tonight. It was part of a long chain of her finding ways to keep him in line.

Lucille loved having control.

"Doc Mullen's due any time now," she said, when she had asked him to wait in the hall. "Send him right in when he arrives."

Checking his watch, Henry noted the physician was already 45 minutes late. A dozen or more of Belleview's citizens, like his Margie, also were suffering from fevers and chills, which in tiny Belleview made this viral outbreak epidemic in proportion. As such, he could understand why the doc was running behind. The old guy was well past retirement age, and even a younger man would be hard-pressed to keep up with all the house calls.

Tired of standing, Henry ducked into one of the other bedrooms and pulled a straight-back chair into the hall. He placed it several feet from the closed bedroom door where Margie lay ill and sat down. With little else to do, he began inching his way along the polished plank floor with the goal of reaching the bedroom without ever once getting up from the chair. It was a stupid game; still, it was something to do.

Almost there, Henry tipped the chair to one side and leaned in to eavesdrop on the murmurings coming from inside the bedroom. That's when the chair skidded out from under him. He crashed to the floor and cracked his head on the heavy oak door on his way down.

"Ouch!" he yelped, ears ringing and stars exploding in his eyes.

The door flew open and Lucille stood there, glaring a "what-a-dunce" look at him, the kind she'd perfected in more than 30 years as a public school teacher.

"Oh, come on, Henry, your wife's in there sick as can be and you're out here blundering around. Where's that doctor? He should be here by now. Go downstairs and wait for him there."

Her eyes were level and her voice hard and accusing. She marched back into the bedroom and quietly but firmly shut the door behind her, leaving him alone in the hallway.

Still nursing his head, Henry reset the chair. He sat down and crossed his arms over his chest. The hell with her, he was staying right where he was.

With a thump-thump of tired footsteps, Doc Mullen trudged up the stairs. They'd left the front door open for him. Haggard and, if possible, looking even wearier than he did the day before, he took a long time making his way down the hallway.

"Hello," he said, studying Henry with a clinical eye.

"Lucille's in there with my boys," Henry said, feeling a need to explain why he was alone in the hallway. "She doesn't want me in there with my own wife. That's not right."

Tall and wiry, wearing round spectacles with thick lenses and nearly bald, Doc Mullen lifted his shoulders, like he couldn't think of a sensible reply to Henry's remarks.

"I'll speak to her. She's obviously upset. It doesn't sound like Lucille, you know, asking you to stay out here by yourself."

He'd been Lucille's doctor and friend for years. The relationship had started when he delivered Margie way back when. In the ensuing years, the doctor had gone on to deliver his two sons. More than once, Henry had tried making friends with Doc Mullen but the guy always backed away, probably because he knew how Lucille felt toward her son-in-law, and he figured it'd be smart to keep his distance. Too bad. Henry liked to think he could get along with anyone. Course that was before he'd met Lucille.

The doctor knocked softly on the bedroom door. "Lucille, it's me. May I come in, please?"

Re-taking his seat, Henry began piecing together when it was that Margie had first come down sick. It was two days earlier when he and the boys sat waiting at the blue-checked, oilcloth-covered table for her to serve them breakfast. Margie reached up and touched her forehead. She seemed distracted, out of it, not really aware of her surroundings.

"Gosh, my head aches," she had said. "And I'm warm. Must be coming down with something. There's so much to do."

Then she coughed so hard she doubled over and had to reach for the counter for support. Paul, the older boy, rushed over to her. Henry knew it wasn't like his wife to complain.

"Hey, kids, don't' worry, she managed to say after catching her breath. "Eat up or you'll be late for school." Her words came out in hoarse whispers. "Henry, please bring milk when you come home for lunch. The milkman doesn't come till tomorrow."

"You'll be okay, honey," Henry said. "Wish I had your constitution. Always some darn thing wrong with me." He made a slight cough, like he was coming down with the same thing she had.

He returned at lunchtime and apologized for forgetting the milk. It was clear Margie had gone downhill since breakfast. Her eyes were yellow and glassy, and she had a sick-cat look about her. She moved like a sick animal, too—real slow, like every muscle hurt.

"You don't look so good," he said, shoveling in forkfuls of leftover goulash from the plate she'd placed before him. "Got any bread and butter?"

"Has to be more than a cold," she said, her voice trailing off. She placed a stack of sliced white bread and a small saucer with butter on the table before him. "Temperature's 102. Can you take the rest of the day off? The boys will be home at 3:45. I need to go to bed."

"Shoot, wish I could, honey. My afternoon calendar's full. The farm boys are on their way to town right now.

Hey, why don't you lie down for a couple of hours? A little nap and you'll pop up good as new."

He felt a twinge of guilt as he left the house but, heck, she'd be fine. Tough as nails, that woman.

After work, he stopped off for a couple of beers at the tavern. He accommodated the patrons with a new joke before leaving to make a final stop at the grocery for milk. He'd had a great day; made some sales. He whistled a snappy little tune as he walked in the door at 6:30. He immediately sensed something was wrong. The kids were at the kitchen table, still wearing their winter coats, hunched over with their elbows up on the table, working on homework. The house was cold.

Fiddling with the furnace control, he called out, "For Christ's sake, Paul, this place is freezing? Born in a barn, boy?"

"Mom's sick and hot all over. She asked me to turn down the heat. You're supposed to go upstairs right away."

Gnawing on his lip, Henry ramped up the heat 5 degrees, to 72, then, on second thought, backed it down to 70. Pushing out a heavy sigh, he removed his coat and walked up the stairs. The hallway light spilled a pathway into the darkened bedroom. Usually Margie had an apple-red complexion and a full head of vibrant brown hair. Today she lay drawn up in a tight fetal position, her nightgown sweaty, the covers pushed down to the foot of the bed. Her hair was limp, as though the strands were too exhausted to keep a curl. She looked up at him, her eyes flat, unfocused. He touched her cheek but retracted it immediately. She might be contagious. No sense him catching whatever the heck she had.

"Feeling any better, honey?" he asked softly.

"No," she whimpered. "Please call Doctor Mullen and my mother. I need her here. Have the boys had dinner?"

"I'll call them right away, and I'll make the kids a good supper. Don't worry. I'm here for you. Everything will be fine."

Lucille and Doctor Mullen arrived at the same time. Lucille first went to the boys to make certain they were all right and then followed the doctor up the stairs. Henry set out cornflakes and milk for supper.

"Don't sit there like a dumb bunny," he admonished his oldest son. "Make us some toast. You guys pitch in and help till your mother gets back on her feet. I can't do everything."

Without being told to, the brothers washed and dried the dishes, and returned every item to its proper place, exactly as their mother would have wanted.

"She okay?" Henry inquired when his mother-in-law came down.

"She's very sick," Lucille stammered. "It's a bad case of that awful influenza that's going around. The doctor gave her a shot—penicillin. He said someone should have called him earlier."

The realization that Margie was sick—really sick—rocked Henry. In their 13-year marriage, his wife had trucked through all kinds of trouble. Now with this talk of the seriousness of her illness, his stomach churned. He was scared.

Over the next two days, the doctor visited at least four times. "I've given Margie every drug I have to bring down her temperature," he explained. "Her fever won't break. She's congested and coughing, and growing weaker by the hour. I'd put her in the hospital but there's nothing we can do for her there that we can't do here."

"What are you saying?" Henry demanded, in an angry voice. "She was fine a few days ago. Now you tell me she's not getting better. You're a doctor. You're supposed to fix people."

Mullen turned and began rummaging in his black-leather medicine bag. Taking his time to gather his thoughts, he said: "I'm doing the best I can, Henry. Normally a person as young and strong as Margie shakes this type of thing off in a few days. There are other folks in town nearly as bad off. Pneumonia is a big worry. If her lungs fill with fluids, I'm afraid we could lose her."

"That's nuts. She's got a bad cold. That's all. You need to quit fiddling with that bag and do something."

Early Friday morning, as first light seeped in around the edges of the heavily curtained windows in the bedroom, Henry, Lucille and Doctor Mullen watched as Margie's body shuddered violently in a desperate struggle for air. Then she died. Stunned, Henry took a step backward. How could this joyful, vibrant, 32-year-old, a beautiful, spirited woman with great strength of character, a loving mother, someone who had shared his bed, slip from this world so easily, here one moment, gone the next? A nightmare.

The doctor went downstairs to summon the undertaker, leaving Henry and Lucille alone. Crumpling to her knees, Lucille grasped her daughter's still-warm hand and sobbed. He reached down to offer comfort then stopped. He'd never actually touched his mother-in-law and had no idea how she'd react if he did.

Henry's father and mother had died when he was a youngster. Their passing seemed natural. After all, in his eyes, they were old and worn out. Margie was young and healthy. They had two children. She was the glue that held his life together. He needed her.

Lucille dabbed a white, lace-trimmed handkerchief to her eyes and gently laid her daughter's hand alongside the body. His knees trembled as an overwhelming sense of dread swept over him. In a moment she'd stand, fix her eyes on his, and he'd wither under her glare. It made no sense to blame him. Margie's dying wasn't his fault. But she'd never see it that way.

He bolted down the hallway, taking the stairs two at a time. Grabbing his coat, he stepped outside into the fuzzy-gray dawning light. Sucking in the cold air, his mind began to clear. He stomped on the half-frozen ground and scratched up a handful of dirt. Squeezing the frozen pellets in his fist, he felt the soil turn warm and moist as he struggled to control a low rumble of raw emotion that bubbled inside. Margie was dead. He loved her, he truly did. This was no bad dream. He rubbed his hands together. The soil fell to the ground. Margie was gone. God rest her soul.

But he was alive.

Accept those things which fate binds you...do so with all your heart.

–Marcus Aurelia

Chapter 2

From the top of the stairs Lucille watched Henry dash out the front door. She considered calling out, then decided it'd be better if she and Doctor Mullen broke the sad news to the kids without him. Henry would only mess things up. Sensitivity wasn't one of her son-in-law's strong suits.

In the kitchen, the boys, in their winter underwear and rubbing sleep from their eyes, stood as Lucille searched for the right words to tell them that their mother had passed away and was in Heaven. Nothing she said seemed to register with the children.

"Come on," she offered, taking each by the hand and leading them up the stairs to her daughter's bedroom. "You'll want to say goodbye."

Lucille flipped the switch and flooded the room in harsh yellow light. She stepped aside to allow Paul and Arthur to gaze down on their mother's corpse. Neither spoke. Finally, tears splashed down the younger child's cheeks. She drew Arthur to her.

"It's all right, dear, go ahead, let it out."

Two hours later, after the funeral director and a helper had removed Margie's remains, Lucille drove the boys to her house. While they were off to themselves in the back-yard, she filled the teapot and sat down at the kitchen table to wait for it to heat up. The kids needed time alone to sort things out. As the older of the two, Paul was a good boy, mature for his age. He'd help his little brother. In truth, he'd do a better job consoling Arthur than his father ever could. She figured Henry at this very moment, even though it was before noon, was settled in at the tavern, feeling sorry for himself, with no thought whatsoever to the welfare of his sons.

As Lucille twisted the empty cup, her mind filled with disturbing images of Margie's naked body stretched out on a cold marble slab in the basement of Callahan's Funeral Home, stainless steel instruments on a table nearby ready to open the poor girl up, and drain the blood from her veins. Despite her best efforts, Lucille couldn't purge the awful images from her mind.

Dismally, she had first-hand knowledge of what the basement-level scene looked like. Two years earlier, at Mr. Callahan's invitation, she had toured the mortuary "for a behind-the-scene look at what goes on here," as the funeral director described it. She had convinced herself it would be educational to learn such things. Still, she didn't want to go alone so she harangued two schoolteacher friends into accompanying her.

"It'll be interesting," she told them. "Besides, it'll make poor Mr. Callahan happy to at last have found someone to take him up on his offer. He's been after me for years to tour his facility. We're teachers. We're supposed to know everything. Right?"

Callahan led the three nervous women into the basement, where it was dark and dank and reeked of mold and nose-stinging formaldehyde.

"Here is the embalming area, what we consider the most important and critical step in the process of preparing the deceased for burial," he intoned ominously.

One of Lucille's companions leaned forward and whispered, "This place gives me the creeps."

"Spooky, too," said the other, as she hugged herself and shuddered.

Callahan's face, in this light, appeared chalk-white, something that Lucille noticed right away. He led them to a large, hollowed-out marble table with a drain on one end, which stood stark and menacing in the middle of the empty basement. Two brightly polished metal shades dangled on twisted electrical wire and hung low over the embalming table. It occurred to Lucille this could be a scene from a hospital operating room—or a horror movie. Switching on the lights, Callahan flipped over a white towel, revealing the gleaming set of stainless-steel instruments, the tools of his trade: scalpels, heavy cutters, a saw, scissors, and sewing needles. He glanced up with a hint of mischief in his manner, as if he enjoyed revealing a side of himself that few people had ever seen.

"The deceased is placed here upon arrival," he said, indicating the hollowed-out table. "Excuse my indelicacy. It is at this point the clothing is removed, the body washed, and the veins are opened. Embalming fluid is infused, which forces the blood to drain from the body. Once the blood is gone, the veins are closed and the embalming process is completed. The cavity is suctioned clean and a special, sterilized packing material is used in those places where the body cavity may need support. In some instances, such as when an autopsy is required, the internal organs are removed and, as a consequence, even more packing material may be necessary to fill in the voids."

"Oh, my," said one of the teachers.

"Then the body and hair are washed again to remove any blood or chemicals," he continued. "We do restorations where needed, such as rebuilding features, masking sores and abrasions, that sort of thing. The final step is to apply makeup, trim nails and comb the hair and stage the casket. It is very important to surviving family and friends that the deceased appear as life-like as possible during the public viewing," Callahan said, as though he was stating the obvious.

The whistling of the boiling teapot returned Lucille to the moment. She shook her head, desperate to rid her mind of the image of her beautiful only child lying at this very moment on that awful stone table.

Her thoughts settled on an incident that had happened 14 years earlier when she and Margie sat at this very table arguing about her daughter's plans to marry a local boy, Henry Goodwin. They'd been at each other for weeks on the subject.

"You can do better, honey," Lucille said. "I've known him since he was five years old, and he thinks only of himself. He's vain and fancies himself a good-time Charlie, with those jokes that some people think are funny. They're really just trash."

Pushing even harder, with her voice rising, she added: "He's foul-mouthed and he craves attention, and he'll do anything to get it. Can't you see this?" she implored.

"The worse thing is he got 15-year-old Rebecca Johnson pregnant. Instead of stepping up like a man, he chose to spread lies about her. Claimed other boys, lots of them, had had their way with the child. Can you imagine? The poor girl had to go off to Omaha to have the baby."

"Now, Mom, you don't know if all that's true. Henry told me it wasn't him. I believe him. He's not like that."

"You're so young, so blind, dear. Can't you see what he's really like?"

"I don't care what you say. I'm going to marry him. He tries to cover up what's good inside. Lots of men are like that. I can change him. I'll make him into a better person."

"Bunk!" Lucille said under her breath.

In the end, she had to step aside and allow the wedding to proceed. Over the next dozen years, Lucille had never been so rash as to say to her daughter, "I told you so." She didn't have to. Margie long ago had accepted that Henry wasn't going to change for her, or for anyone else— not now, not ever. By then, though, they had the two boys and Lucille knew her daughter would never, *ever* break up her family.

Margie had suffered terribly as a little girl when her father, whom she adored, ran off with a neighbor woman.

Like it was yesterday, she could hear her husband coming home and saying, "I'm leaving you, Lucille. I've fallen in love with another woman. We haven't been husband and wife for a long time. We both know you never really loved me."

"Are you insane?" Lucille had screamed at him. "You can't walk out. What about Margie? Do you know what this will do to that child?"

"I do, and it breaks my heart. If I could, I'd take her with me but you'll never let her go. Margie will one day forget me and grow up to be a wonderful woman. This is the best I can do. I'm sorry."

"You're sorry! How easy is that to say. You're god-damn right you won't see her again. Now get the hell out and never come back."

As he pulled the front door shut, Lucille heard a noise coming from behind the draperies in the front room. Margie was there, crying. She'd heard every angry word that had transpired. Lucille gathered the child in her arms.

"What's the matter with Daddy?" she asked. "Why is he leaving? Make him stay."

Lucille put a soothing hand on the five-year-old girl's shoulder but she broke away and ran to her room. Later, sitting on the edge of the bed, Lucille chose her words carefully as she tried to explain that it wasn't her but her father who'd chosen to leave them. Margie shook her head back and forth and pounded on her mother's chest.

"It's all your fault!" she screamed. "You told him to leave. I heard you send him away. Please, please, find Daddy and bring him home."

Over the years, despite numerous attempts at reconciliation, Margie's loss of her father hung like a heavy curtain between mother and daughter. It was a barrier that never parted.

Lucille took the teapot, cup and saucer to the sink and began reviewing the promise she'd made to Margie a few hours earlier, just minutes before her daughter had died.

She'd been dozing fitfully in a chair pulled close to Margie's bed, and awoke to a soft, raspy whisper, like a rustling in the dark bedroom.

"Mom, Mom, wake up. I need to talk to you."

"What is it, honey. Do you want water? Are you in pain?"

"No, please listen. I can only say this once." Her voice was low, gravelly.

"Mom, you need to do something for me, and it's going to be hard. But I want you to promise you'll do it."

"Of course, honey. Anything. What is it?"

"If something happens to me, Henry will want you to raise the boys. I want you to tell him no."

"What! Don't talk like that. You'll be fine."

"Promise me you won't take the kids. And don't weaken because he'll beg and plead and try to make you feel guilty. I want Paul and Arthur to stay with their father. I want them to be a family."

"Honey, I *have* to take care of them. They're my grand-children. That man hasn't the sense to take care of a stray cat, let alone two children. He'll neglect them; they'll starve, or something worse."

"He won't. Henry can be a good father. But if you allow it, he'll take the easy way and push the kids on you. Then they won't have a mother or father. Please, Mom."

Lucille looked into her daughter's suffering face and recoiled. There is was: the same barrier she'd been trying to break down for years. Margie wanted Henry and the boys to be together, whether it made sense or not.

"I don't agree with your decision, honey. But I'll honor your request. I won't take the boys, even though I can raise them right. "

"I know you can, Mom. This is what I want."

Later in the day, when Henry came by to pick up the boys and the three of them returned to their house, Lucille lay in bed fully dressed as heavy shadows fell upon the bedroom. Tears slid down her face. She'd lost her only child, and with the deathbed promise she'd made, she'd relinquished all claims to her grandchildren. Her daughter had chosen Henry over her to take the children and there was nothing she could do.

She stepped into the bathroom and washed her face. Squinting into the mirror, she saw someone she barely recognized—an old and tired woman, with a tormented face and a broken heart.

The heart will break, but broken lives on....

–Lord Byron

Chapter 3

Two months had passed since Margie's funeral. At the time of her death, in the frozen dead of winter, the Missouri River was mostly ice-packed and quiet except for the occasional sighting of bald eagles with six-foot wingspans skimming the sky. Belleview was one of a dozen quaint little farm villages dotting the Nebraska side of the Missouri River. Now the ice had gone out early and the river was running full. From the high bluffs, spectators once again enjoyed the movement of grain and ore-filled barges moving up and down North America's longest river.

The spring weather also had raised Henry's spirits. But when his boss called him into his office he delivered terrible news, which only added to his run of trouble.

"C'mon on boss," he pleaded. "Don't do this. I need this job. My wife's dead and I'm trying to raise two young boys."

Sitting across from him was Barry Fister, a blustery, heavy set bald man with a face as red as his suspenders. Henry once considered the manager of the Farmer's Co-Op a friend. Now, as an emotion-charged fear raged within his chest, he struggled to comprehend what the man was saying.

"Sorry, Henry, but you know the farm economy's in the dumper, and it's squeezing our customers." The boss wouldn't meet his eyes. "Sales are off 25 percent, and, frankly, I don't see much improvement coming. The board told me to cut expenses."

"I understand," Henry said, his voice breaking. "But for crying out loud, lay off someone else, not me, not now!"

"You've missed a lot of work." Fister paused and took a white handkerchief from his pocket and folded it carefully on the desk.

"You know I lost my wife. My two boys rely on me now. I've been a good salesman, earned you a boatload of money over the years."

"Not recently," Fister answered brusquely. "Lately, even when you're at work you haven't been your old self. You've lost that spark."

"I'm still hurting from my loss. I loved Margie, depended on her. It's been devastating. Sure, I haven't been at the top of my game. I can pull myself together. Give me another chance. I'll work day and night. I swear."

Fister put the handkerchief back in his pocket. This meeting was over. "My hands are tied. The board wants to cut overhead. Today's your last day. You'll get two weeks severance pay."

Now, Henry sat on a barstool at the Riverfront Tavern with several of his drinking buddies. His mind was running as he tried to come up with a few jokes the guys hadn't heard before.

With Henry's popularity, the tavern owner had cut him a deal: he'd provide free beers and sandwiches as long as Henry hung around the tavern and entertained the customers.

Henry was taking a bite out of a ham sandwich as he listened to a half dozen men quarrel over whether the U.S. should enter another war so soon after World War II.

"It's only five years since we whipped the Krauts and Japs and all ready the politicians and generals are banging the war drums," said a gruff man in bib overalls. He had three fingers missing from his left hand, whether from the war or a farm accident Henry didn't know. He dared not ask. "Now they want to start something in Korea, wherever the hell that is."

Almost to a man, they were World War II veterans and, far as he could tell, not a single one was in a mood to fight again. Henry had missed the Big War with a farm deferment. As a consequence, several of the tavern regulars had from time to time referred to him as a yellow-belly draft-dodger, sometimes right to his face.

"The deferment wasn't my idea," he always protested. It was Fister at the Co-Op who'd gone before the County Draft Board and argued that his employee, Henry Goodwin, could better serve his country by staying at home and helping farmers raise bumper yields than carry a rifle in Europe. But nobody wanted to hear Henry's side of the story and, what the hell, he was tired of trying to clear up the point.

Tonight, a veteran named Joel broke away from the others and limped over on his artificial leg to where Henry was standing. He splashed a big swig of beer around in his mouth, swallowed, and said, "I've got no beef with a bunch of slant-eyes in a little Asian country that most people never heard of and could care less about."

Wiping his mouth with his sleeve, he continued: "Shit, if there's another war, send some others. I paid the price on Guadalcanal. Hey, how about you Henry? You finally ready to do your part—you draft-dodging bastard?"

Uh-oh, Henry thought, as he chomped down on the sandwich. This could be trouble. Joel leaned in close like he was going to say more. He was drunk and losing momentum. Henry grabbed the opportunity and side-stepped his way toward a table full of men and announced in a loud voice that he had a couple of new jokes, one about an old guy with an oversized penis and the other "about this super-endowed blonde who was cherry-ripe and ready for harvesting." Everyone bunched up to listen as Joel stumbled away. Soon talk of war disappeared and the laughter rang clear and sweet.

Henry wasn't concerned about the Draft Board calling him up to fight in Korea. At his age, and with two motherless young boys, there was no way that would happen. Who'd take care of the kids?

Besides, he had more pressing things to deal with. Of late, the landlord and the utility companies were after him for money. Good luck, he thought. He was nearly flat broke. Margie's funeral had taken a big chunk of his savings and there were no more Co-Op paychecks. He was in a real pickle.

He'd started looking for a new job when his severance check was spent, with the cock-sure attitude that he'd have no trouble finding a new, good-paying job. Unfortunately, the doors around Belleview slammed in his face and he couldn't fathom why, even as he watched other men take jobs ahead of him. It didn't occur to him that a talent for making people laugh didn't rank as a meaningful qualification when a boss was looking for a hard-working man to fill an important position. After nearly a month of trying, and not a single offer, he had to do something.

Only this morning he'd sat the kids down and announced they'd be leaving Belleview, the only home Paul and Arthur had ever known. "What about school?" Paul countered. "And Grandma, we can't leave her?"

"Grandma doesn't want you guys living with her," Henry said, his voice tinged with loathing. "Believe me, I asked, practically begged her, to take you till I find work. She said no. Hey kids, don't worry. I'm loaded with good, solid relatives on my side of the family. They won't mind a bit taking us in till I can land a job. Times are hard as hell for a lot of folks. There's no choice; we have to move on. And I don't want any guff from you, Paul, or whining from you, Arthur. My mind's made up. We leave on the bus in three days."

How could it be, Paul thought? His grandmother didn't want them? In only two weeks he'd have a birthday. He'd be 12, and a few months later, in August, Arthur would be 7 years old. Grandma wouldn't be there for either of these special events. Neither would Mom. He had no idea where they were going. After Dad left the room, Paul put his arm around Arthur; his little brother was crying again.

Henry visited the boys' school and explained how his family was leaving and they probably wouldn't be returning to Belleview.

Since it was almost time for summer vacation, and both Paul and Arthur were excellent pupils, the principal certified that they should advance to the next grades when they enrolled in a new school in the fall, Arthur to second grade, and Paul to the seventh.

Not surprisingly, as Henry's bus trip unfolded over the next few weeks, the visits to "welcoming kinfolk" that he'd promised the boys failed to materialize. So far, in three successive small-town visits, it took only a week or so at each stop for the host relatives to begin suggesting, in the plainest language possible, it was time for Henry and his boys to pack up and move along.

On this morning, the three of them stepped off a bus in Platteville, just south of the Minnesota border, for yet another opportunity to cozy in with relatives. From a pay phone, Henry made a call to his Uncle Carl, confirming that they'd arrived and asking if it'd be all right if they walked over to the house.

"Well, that'll be fine," Carl boomed. "It's only a couple of blocks. We'll keep an eye out the window. Emma's so excited she baked three pies this morning. They're lined up on the kitchen counter, ready to eat. Hope you and your boys are hungry. We're on Wilson. You remember the house, Henry. See you soon."

Finally, Henry thought, a relative who's actually excited about seeing them. His spirits lifted.

No question about it, Carl and Emma had always ranked as favorite relatives—or if not always, they sure did today. When he had spotted them in a pew at Margie's funeral, he wasn't a bit surprised that they'd made the effort to attend the services. They were good people. "We'd sure love to have you and your boys pay us visit sometime," Aunt Emma had told him at the luncheon following Margie's graveside services.

Now here they were in Platteville. Putting on a wide grin, Henry rapped boldly on the front door.

"Greetings, greetings!" Aunt Emma sang out, pecking Henry's cheek and smothering the boys with tight embraces. She was a petite woman, under 100 pounds, wearing a paisley dress with her gray-streaked hair pushed up and topped off with a bun.

Carl patted shoulders and shook hands. He was rail-thin, six-foot-two, and towered over his impish mate. On appearances alone, they made an odd couple; still it was clear from the affectionate touches and the loving looks they exchanged that there was something special about this match.

After depositing the luggage in a back bedroom, the elderly couple shooed them out the front door to tour the town. Beaming with civic pride, Carl steered them toward Platteville's Livestock Sale Barn.

"You're a country boy, Henry," Carl said. "You know how important a Sale Barn is to a small town. Saturday mornings this place is hoppin' with farmers bidding on cows, horses, sheep, and even ducks and chickens. Quite a show, and it brings in a lot of money to our town." He poked his elbow into Henry's ribs. "Smell the manure? Farmers say that's the smell of money."

This might be a great place for us to settle, Henry thought. Must be lots of jobs around here. Carl and Emma are nice folks, genuinely interested in helping. They could be like a grandpa and grandma and keep an eye on the kids while he went off to work. With every step through the towering Sale Barn, he felt better and better.

The town's architecture clearly reflected Platteville's Dutch heritage, including cobblestone streets and ornately rounded gables on the commercial and residential buildings. Everything was neat and orderly, carefully planned and thought out. "Well, shoot, this town's as pretty as the gingerbread village my Margie baked up and decorated for the kids last Christmas," Henry declared. "You folks must be real proud."

"Our little bit of heaven, ain't that right Emma?" Carl said, pleased to hear his nephew's comments.

Lunch was at the busy B&B Restaurant. Carl suggested the day's special: franks, beans, and a side of sauerkraut.

"You won't taste any better," he promised, licking his lips.

The boys, with Aunt Emma's encouragement, settled on hamburgers and fries. She smiled and commented, "An excellent choice, boys."

"Say, Henry, let's you and me take a little walk while they prepare the food," Carl said, standing. "I'd like you to meet some of the local folks."

"Sure," Henry said, sliding off the chair.

The first stop was at a red vinyl booth overflowing with four heavyset farmers dressed in various shades of blue-denim overalls. At a break in the conversation, Carl said in a gentle voice, "Excuse me, fellahs. This here is my nephew from Belleview, Henry Goodwin. He and his boys are visiting."

The men looked up, and one said: "Welcome to Platteville. Any relative of Carl's is a friend of ours." They all nodded in unison.

Henry appreciated his uncle introducing him to his friends, like he was proud to show him off. Carl was a straight-up guy.

Now back at Carl and Emma's house, Henry's aunt took him aside. "It must have been a shock having your wife pass so young," she said in a low, sympathetic tone. "I know Margaret loved these boys."

"We miss her, don't we guys?" Henry said loudly. Then he stepped forward and draped his arms around their shoulders. "Everything happened much too fast. She woke up early last March with a headache and slight fever. That was all—just a headache and fever."

"Oh my," said Emma, pressing her palms together as moisture filled her eyes.

Henry spent much of the following week in the front room sprawled out on an overstuffed chair while his aunt and uncle entertained the boys. He'd had a rough time since leaving Belleview and figured he deserved a little relaxation and a break from worrying. He talked to Carl about finding a job. His uncle seemed uncomfortable on the subject and pointed out things were tight around Platteville, too. "Everybody's seems to be pulling back."

When the boys weren't playing games, or hooting at Carl's corny jokes, they explored the town, played ball in the yard, and helped out with chores. At the moment, a laughter-filled, four-way card game was underway in the kitchen.

Unfortunately, this morning he'd overheard Carl saying to Emma, "When do you suppose Henry and the boys will be movin' on?" They'd only been a week in Platteville, seven days precisely, and Henry felt the noose starting to tighten again.

After supper, he followed Carl out to the front porch. As was his habit, Carl took out his pipe and lit up.

"Mind if I sit?" Henry asked, indicating Emma's matching rocker.

"Sure! Have a seat. Emma will be awhile. I swear, that woman would live in the kitchen and never come out if she could."

"Thanks. Um, Uncle Carl, I want you to know how much I appreciate your taking us in. Don't know what we'd have done. Everything just seems…well, difficult. First Margie dying, then losing my job, and then, well, you know."

Carl puffed out some smoke and looked out at the street. "How come you lost your job, Henry?"

Taken back by the direct question, Henry paused and finally said, "Well, it really wasn't my fault. My boss said business was slow and he needed to cut overhead."

Carl frowned.

"Bare in mind, though, that wasn't the real reason. Business was off some, no question about that. And with Margie's passing, I did take extra time off to look out for the boys. Plus, damn it, I needed time alone to deal with the shock from my loss. Work didn't seem so important at the time. When I started feeling better and got back into the swing of things, that's when the boss dropped the gate on me."

Carl took a deep pull on the pipe. "Margaret had family in Belleview. Couldn't they have helped?"

"Hell no!" Henry said, offering his uncle a "if-you-only-knew" look. "Excuse my language, but the only relative in town was Margie's mother, and she didn't mince words in telling me they were my kids, and it was up to me to take care of them."

"Don't want to second guess," Carl said. "Wasn't it risky leaving your hometown with no clear place in mind of where you were going? Seems you'd been better off staying put, you know, near friends and neighbors, and people from church who'd be happy to lend a hand."

"Not really," Henry replied, now on the defensive. "I had some buddies I thought I could count on, but not a single one bothered attending Margie's funeral. To top it off, after losing my job at the Co-Op, those guys disappeared quicker than the savings in my bank account."

"That so," Carl said, removing the pipe from his mouth, this time knocking it against the porch railing. He dug in his pocket for a bag of tobacco.

"As far as the church," Henry added, "I've never been keen on organized religion, even though I sure do believe in the Lord. The minister came by once to check on us. I must have said something he didn't like, 'cause he never returned. From the day we got married, Margie knew my feelings about religion, so she handled the churching with the boys."

"Well, bless her," Carl said. "She did the right thing. Young people need to learn about the Savior."

As he kept his eyes on Uncle Carl, he could see the man take a turn, like he was thinking his nephew wasn't as solid a guy as he had first thought. Well, screw him! He hadn't walked in his shoes. It wouldn't hurt to remind the old coot what he'd been through. Christ, he had to try something.

"Uncle Carl, surely you remember how Pa was killed in that tractor rollover on our farm."

"Yeah, I do remember that heartbreak."

Henry continued on, not skipping a beat. "He was tilling along a steep hillside when the tractor rolled. He was still alive when I found him but he died before we could get him to a doctor. I was 12. Mom and me alone couldn't run things on the rented farm, so we moved to Belleview. Four years later, would you believe it, she went and died of cancer."

"Yep, real sad, a double tragedy, especially for a boy as young as you at the time."

"Orphaned at 16. I talked a store fellow into hiring me and finished high school and then the Lord put me in the right spot to meet Margie. She was 19. I was 21. That's when I took the job at the Co-op and started making good money.

"Don't want to burden you, Uncle Carl, with all this trouble. I wanted you to know how the boys and I are feeling like Gypsies, with no place to call home. You folks have been lifesavers. Can't imagine how we'd have managed without your help. Hope to pay you back someday."

Carl had feelings for people in trouble, Henry thought. Certainly his story would soften the old man's kind heart.

It was all to no avail. The next morning at breakfast, Carl cleared his throat. "We've enjoyed your visit, Henry. Your boys are real gems."

Henry noticed his uncle's voice broke as he spoke. He kept glancing at Emma. "The thing is, we haven't visited our son in Kansas City for some time. We're leaving at noon Monday and be gone a week. It just...er...doesn't seem right leaving you folks here on your own. Isn't that right, hon?"

Uneasy at being called upon, Aunt Emma knitted and unknitted her hands. She finally spoke: "One of our grandchildren is getting married this fall. Wish you'd have given us more notice before you came, dear, so we could have made other arrangements."

Not for one minute did Henry buy into this cock-and-bull story. Still, he forced a smile onto his face. Obviously, his sob story hadn't budged the old man an inch. Platteville was turning out like all the other visits.

"Oh, heck, I understand perfectly," Henry offered. "You've been very generous and we sure appreciate your hospitality."

Arthur kept his eyes on the food on his plate. Paul rose and walked into the front room.

"Shoot, we'll mosey on down to Floyd and Wilma's in Elk Point," Henry said, his voice rising with false cheer. "You remember, Carl, how I told you Cousin Floyd invited us to drop by. I'm hoping there's work in Elk Point. It sure won't hurt to take a look down that way."

Henry picked up his fork and began eating. "I'll call him later."

You've a good heart. Sometimes that's enough to see you safe wherever you go."

–Neil Gaiman

Chapter 4

Monday morning everyone rose early so Henry and the boys could board the 8:30 a.m. bus. Emma's final breakfast was something to behold: sausages, eggs, hot biscuits with butter and strawberry preserves, pancakes, and tall glasses of cold milk for the boys and plenty of coffee with rich cream for the adults.

"Well, this is a great send-off for you fellows," Uncle Carl said, as he surveyed the table and paused to gaze lovingly at his wife. "You've out-done yourself this morning, dear."

Henry kept piling more on his plate, and the boys did the same. The luggage waited on the front porch. Aunt

Emma embraced Paul and Arthur and shook Henry's hand while studiously avoiding eye contact with her nephew. At the bus stop, Henry muttered a grudging "thanks" when Uncle Carl stepped ahead of him and paid the driver for tickets to Elk Point.

The bus left on schedule and headed south to the small north-central Nebraska town of Elk Point where Cousin Floyd had lived all of his life. It was the first day of summer. For the past two hours the driver in the khaki cap pushed the rig south. Somewhere along the road the muffler blew. Henry could hardly hear himself over the rumbling roar.

"Sorry 'bout the racket, folks!" the driver called out as passengers boarded at each of the many small-town stops along the route. "We'll get that darned noise quieted down at the terminal in Omaha tonight. Don't worry about exhaust fumes. Everything's sealed good and tight under there."

Henry struggled to break through the black cloud of despondency that enveloped him. Platteville at first seemed like the answer to his prayers, and Aunt Emma and Uncle Carl a lifeline. It had all blown up.

He brushed a finger across his forehead and flicked the droplets of sweat onto the worn, dirty carpet under his feet. He stared trance-like out the bus window at the mile-after-mile of flat cornfields, neatly laid out in horizon-bending rows of green corn shoots. This was the Corn Belt, the richest and most productive soil in the world.

He'd worked fields like these as a kid. Now, as sweat drenched his body, he pushed up from the seat and stood in the aisle, his underwear and pants sticking to his legs. Anything for a little relief!

"Man!" he heard the guy in the seat ahead of him say to his female companion. "It's a barnburner. Temperature's already in the nineties, just like yesterday and the day before. Can't wait till we reach Omaha."

Henry had read somewhere that GM was producing fancy new buses with air conditioning; this old beater, however, was a long ways from a cool ride. It felt like he was on a hot pancake grill—and he was the pancake!

Paul and Arthur slept across the aisle. How they slept in this heat was a mystery to him. The good news was that Paul finally was taking more responsibility for his younger brother. Now, maybe little Arthur would tug on his brother's leg and leave him alone.

Licking his lips, Henry rubbed his damp palms on his pants. The money was running low. On top of that, he worried what he'd find at Cousin Floyd and Wilma's. When he called yesterday, something in his cousin's voice made him uneasy. He guessed it involved Wilma. Henry had met her briefly at Margie's wake and she struck him as the ultimate sourpuss, with nothing good to say about anything or anyone.

The bus rolled down Main Street in Elk Point, past the limestone three-story Lucas County Courthouse, an imposing edifice with a pure white dome on top gleaming in the bright, late-morning sun. While not as quaint as Platteville, Elk Point was the county seat, and the town appeared to have a larger, more prosperous business district.

The driver eased the bus to a stop along the curb in front of the Baylor Hotel, the screech of the air brakes and the noisy muffler drawing everyone's attention. The town square bustled with shoppers, mostly women, browsing from shop to shop, pausing every now and then to call out a cheery hello to a passerby.

Whoever had designed the Baylor Hotel had given the brick, double-story building a touch of elegance by equipping it with impressive10-foot-tall, brass-trimmed entrance doors. A restaurant occupied the left side of the first floor, with the guest reception desk on the right. From his high perch in the bus, Henry spotted a young waitress weaving her way through the tables with a pot of coffee. She was pretty and with a slick figure, too.

* * * * *

Paul woke up and nudged Arthur awake, and asked, "We here, Dad?"

"Yep, this is it, Elk Point," Henry said, rushing to be the first one off the bus and out of the stifling heat. "Gather your stuff, boys," he called over his shoulder. "I'll see about the luggage."

Paul stepped off the bus and blinked into the bright sunshine. Now 12 years old, he was a tall, good-looking kid who could easily pass for 16. Shading his eyes with the flat of his right hand, he surveyed downtown Elk Point. The town didn't seem a lot different from the others they'd visited since leaving Belleview? Aunt Emma and Uncle Carl's place had been their favorite stop by far. He and Arthur had hit if off with the elderly couple but even before Dad announced they'd be moving on, Paul predicted that Platteville was too good to last, which soon proved to be the case.

Placing his toes on the edge of the curb, he stretched his arms wide and drew in deep gulps of fresh air. He'd inherited his mother's tall, lanky stature, prominent nose, classic chin, high cheekbones, and natural athleticism. Like her, Paul's movements were agile, quick and confident.

On the other hand, Arthur had his father's soft body, round face and delicate facial features. The most obvious trait he'd inherited from his mother was her expressive, sparkling blue eyes. When Arthur was a baby, neighbors and friends commented on how the two of them had perfectly matched blue eyes. Some described them as "happy" eyes because, in the right light, they actually seemed to dance. It was an entertaining little show, watching Arthur and his mother light up a room as they joyously took in everything around them.

"Well, isn't that the darndest thing?" Paul overheard one lady say.

No question about it, Arthur had his appealing moments. But in Paul's view, the kid was a major pain in the butt. Lately, he'd begun to think God must have put his little brother on earth solely to make his life miserable.

Arthur also was a well-oiled talking machine, a chirping little bird. He'd run on and on, talking all the time, saying nothing that could be of any possible interest to anyone. And since Mom died he'd gotten even more verbose. It was like running off at the mouth had given his younger brother some control over his life at a time when everything and everyone kept pushing him along at a pace he didn't like.

Dad was of little help. Without warning Arthur would burst out crying and run to him for comfort. He'd shove him off, saying, "For Christ's sakes, Paul, do something. I can't stand all that sniveling."

"What can I do? He's homesick and misses Mom."

"Hell, I don't know a damn thing about kids, especially a bawl-baby like him. You handle it. I've got my own problems."

Having Arthur dumped on him was a royal pain. Still, if he didn't look out for him, who would? More than once Paul had the feeling that his mother was watching him through Arthur's bright eyes. Cripes, he thought, it's like the whole family's ganging up on me.

The bus driver stacked the bags and packages on the sidewalk in front of the hotel. Meanwhile, Arthur sat on the edge of the curb, engrossed in digging dirt out of a crack in the sidewalk with a twig. His father stood beside the driver, talking loud and fast.

"It's not my fault I can't find a job," Henry said. "The paper says there's more than a million able-bodied men are out of work. Almost as bad as the Great Depression; that's what they say."

The bus driver offered an occasional uh-huh as he continued to stack packages, trying to be polite as Henry rambled on.

"My father worked WPA. You know, off and on during the Depression. If he hadn't, we'd have starved. President Roosevelt did some good with that program. They should bring it back, don't you think?"

"Yeah, I expect so." The harried man slammed the side luggage panel down and locked it. He walked fast, almost at a trot, to the bus door.

"Good luck to you and your boys!" he yelled as he grabbed the chrome handle inside the bus and yanked the door shut. A moment later, the big transmission ground into gear and the bus rolled off with the hole in the muffler sending out a rumble that could be heard all around the square.

Paul knew times were tough. That's all Dad crabbed about. Even at his age, Paul knew the difference between the rich and poor. Rich folks drove nice cars and lived in snazzy houses, had pretty wives, and kids who smiled and laughed a lot, like they hadn't a care in the world. Rich guys walked ramrod straight, like they were hot stuff, while poor folks kept their eyes to the ground, hoping maybe to find a dime.

More than once Paul had told his younger brother when he grew up he planned to be rich, "not some sorry loser without two nickels to rub together."

As the bus pulled away, Paul's gaze swept the square. The shoppers poked around, pausing to look into store windows, strolling under the protection of the covered sidewalks. It was all so nice. The younger women wore colorful straw hats and freshly pressed light summer dresses that fluttered in the late-morning breeze. He noticed the older ladies kept pushing down their skirts, while the younger ones didn't bother. He kind of liked that.

An overly sensitive heart is an unhappy possession on this shaky earth.

–Johann Wolfgang van Goethe

Chapter 5

Henry dragged his feet in the dusty road as he and the boys walked toward Floyd and Wilma's house. He didn't know what he'd find ahead.

To take his mind off his troubles, he remembered happier times when he was a boy and Floyd's parents would drop his cousin off at the Goodwin family farm for two-week summer visits. Floyd's first visit came when they were both eight years old.

On steamy summer days, the boys would rush around to complete the morning chores, including milking, shoveling cow manure, pitching down fresh hay from the hayloft and feeding the pigs. They'd finish by gathering eggs and delivering them to Henry's mother in the kitchen.

Afternoons were all theirs. They'd plop down in the shade of the open hayloft door, hoping to catch a cool breeze. Henry would suck on a stalk of hay, pretending to smoke it like a cigarette, and Floyd would do likewise, because his cousin always did what he did. Conversations usually centered on one thing—the fact that Henry detested life on the farm.

"All Pop does is crab about the weather and the price of crops," Henry told his cousin. "I'm sick of busting my butt and not even a thank you. Now Pop wants me to start working in the fields, says I can drive the tractor, like that's a big deal."

"I like the hard work around here—you bet!" Floyd said. Then he stood and posed like Charles Atlas, his arms lifted high and wide, his biceps bulging. "Don't ya' think I'm lookin' more and more like a tough ole' farm boy, and I feel great?" Floyd asked, waiting for Henry to acknowledge the changes in him.

"You actually like it here on the farm?" Henry asked, not believing what he was hearing.

"Yep. I like it here on the farm, I sure do. My family's a bunch of goofballs. Most of them hardly know how to read and write. They're peculiar that's for certain. Fact is, unless your Pop lets me, I'll never get a chance to drive a tractor. Think he will?"

Henry shook his head. Floyd was such a dumbbell.

Like most farm people, Henry and his folks lived for Saturday nights, when they headed for town. It was a chance to have a little fun and meet with people. In the summer when

Floyd was at the farm, the two of them would squeeze into the front seat of the pickup with his parents and they'd pull onto the gravel road to join a caravan of farm folks headed for Belleview, four miles to the east. By six o'clock, cars and pickups took every parking space on River Street. The men got haircuts, sat outside stores, talked crops, and complained that John Deere charged too much for new tractors.

"Those tractors are pretty dear," Henry heard one farmer complain.

"Yeah, that's true," his father replied to the man's statement. "But you know Deere does make reliable farm machinery, and that green paint looks good out in the field." Henry's dad took a lot of pride in his own Deere tractor, which he always kept in a shed when he wasn't working with it in the fields.

The ladies sat on benches and on borrowed chairs in front of the stores, knitting and talking about the latest polio outbreak and how the children were doing in school. Gossip was always on their lips. Henry had learned early on that women loved to talk more than men.

Sitting on a step with Floyd in front of a group of the women, Henry listened as one lady said in a confidential manner, "Olive's daughter moved to Omaha to work for one of those insurance companies. She's living all alone in an apartment in that big city!"

"Well, I declare," Henry's mother answered. "What must her family be thinking, allowing a young girl like that to move away on her own?"

It was standing room only in the town's tavern, and the loud laughter spilled out into the street. Occasionally, a couple of young studs feeling their juices stumbled out of the bar and duked it out. If they were lucky, Henry and Floyd caught a glimpse of the dust-up before the fist-fighters tired, shook hands and returned to the bar.

After two or three summers had passed, Henry and Floyd had grown big enough to sneak away from the grownups and meet up with other farm and town kids in the alleys behind the stores to smoke cigarettes and palaver among themselves.

The boys talked mostly about cars and girls, and sometimes girls and cars.

"I get plenty of tit-petting from Dorothy Schneider, you can believe it!" one guy bragged.

A chorus of "that's a lie" greeted the kid's story, but the bragger wouldn't back down. In the end, it was Buster Ledbetter who quieted everyone with the most outrageous claim of all.

"Down by the tracks, there's this girl, I ain't saying who she is…." Buster paused for effect. "She'll go all the way."

"What's her name?" someone asked.

"I'm not telling. Keepin' her for myself."

Cousin Floyd's summer visits to the Belleview farm ended the year Henry's father died in the accident and he and his mother had to move from the rented farm property to a small house in town.

More than 20 years passed before the cousins got together again, this time at Margie's funeral. At 250 pounds, Floyd stood well over six feet tall and he looked like a runaway train as he rushed up to Henry at the funeral reception and thrust his face so close that Henry had to turn away from the rank smell of coffee and chewing tobacco on the man's breath.

"Really sorry, old buddy, about your wife passing," Floyd said. "How you holding up?"

"Okay. Got to be a rock for the boys."

"Gosh, you know, you're like the brother I never had," Floyd declared in a loud voice, flinging an arm around Henry's shoulders. "Those were great times we had on the farm, and what about those Saturday nights in Belleview? Man, I never had so much fun in my whole life. Say, have you met my wife Wilma?"

A thin, bony woman stepped in front of her husband. Half a foot shorter than Floyd, she had black curly hair and dark blue veins popping up on her hands. Her head was small, horse-shaped, and she had coal-dark eyes and a tiny mouth. To Henry, she looked more like a varmint than a woman. He and Floyd were both in their mid-thirties. Wilma looked older, at least 50. Henry doubted she was that old. She'd probably spent a lot of time in the sun when she was growing up; her skin was as brown and deeply wrinkled as a dried-up apple. There was something scary in the way she looked at him with those dark eyes, like she was challenging him to say or do something.

"Pleasure meeting you, Wilma," Henry said, taking her hand. "I'm sure my Margie's looking down from above appreciating the fact that so many good people like you traveled so far to be here today."

Wilma forcefully withdrew her hand. From the scowl on her face, it was clear she was forbidding him to ever touch her again. At the same time, she looked as tightly wound as a new spool of thread. Hoping to ward off trouble, Floyd pressed closer, stepping between his wife and Henry and said, "You guys come visit us in Elk Point, stay a while, you know, after you and the boys get to feeling better and you're up to traveling. We have a lot of catching up to do. Your boys are welcome. We've got two of our own, about the same ages as yours."

Wilma stiffened, and Henry figured she was about to detonate. She must have thought better of it and instead wheeled around and walked away.

Floyd raised his eyebrows at Wilma's behavior and said, "The wife doesn't like funerals much. Now, like I was saying, we'd love to have you guys pay us a visit."

Later, Henry learned from a know-it-all relative that Wilma had had her spirit broken early on in life. She'd grown up in Elk Point, the oldest of 10 kids. Even as a little girl, she declared she'd only marry a man with money—and plenty of it. It didn't turn out that way. The relative's theory was that Wilma had tricked Floyd into marrying her. She'd been bedding down with a rich kid and gotten herself pregnant. With the whole town talking and the rich boy going off to the university, Wilma laid down for Floyd and told him the baby was his. After the wedding, Wilma turned bitter, harsh and mean as a skunk. At least that's what the relative reported.

There is no instinct like that of the heart.

–Lord Byron

Chapter 6

When Henry made the call to his cousin from Uncle Carl's in Platteville, Floyd suggested that he and the boys plan to arrive at his house in Elk Point during the lunch hour or after 5:30 on Monday. "I'll be home from work at those times and I'd like to be there to greet ya'."

Glancing at his watch, Henry saw it was 12:15. He prayed Floyd was there. He sure didn't want to knock on the front door and face Wilma without his cousin's hulking presence there to shield him.

There were two boys playing in the front yard of what Henry judged to be Floyd's place. The small white bungalow had green shutters and was shaded by a huge, leafed-out Dutch Elm. A sun-bleached Ford sedan with rust rimming the wheel wells sat in the driveway.

The bigger of the two boys ran up the front porch steps and yelled through the screen door, loud enough to be heard half-a-block away, "Dad, they're comin'!"

Floyd stepped out onto the small porch, wearing a white, sleeveless t-shirt and a baggy pair of brown trousers. He wiped his palms on his trousers. Behind him stood Wilma, thin and sinewy, chin uplifted, nose to the sky, like she was sniffing something bad in the air. Fear gripped Henry's bowels.

Floyd shook Henry's hand and mussed Arthur and Paul's hair, saying in an unnaturally loud voice, "Glad to see you fellahs. Have a good trip? Sure is hot, eh."

Then Floyd's voice lowered, as if he didn't want Wilma to hear. "Say, Henry, mind to step around the corner of the house for a word in private."

Making the turn with Henry right behind, he yelled back: "You kids get to know each other. That's my son Harvey, the tall one, almost 14, and the other is Bob. We call 'im Bo. He's 9. We'll be right back."

Once out of sight, Floyd said: "Hey, good to see you, ole buddy."

"Yeah, same here."

"Uh, before we go inside, I wanted to tip you off that Wilma's...um...you know, I guess you could say she's having a bad day."

"Sorry. If there's a problem, we can move on."

"No, no! Won't hear of it. Truth is, most of her days are bad." He faked a laugh to cover up his nervousness.

"She's been raggin' on me about the house being too small to accommodate you and your boys. There's plenty of room. This house is bigger than the one I grew up in, and, what the hell, Wilma's folks raised nearly a dozen kids in a ramshackle shack half this size down by the creek with the kids runnin' nearly naked like wild Indians in the warm weather. When I pointed out this little fact to her she damn near snapped my head off."

"You sure it's okay? Don't want to cause you and the missus any trouble."

"Right as rain, old buddy. I pay the bills and wear the pants 'round here." He swelled up, even as Henry saw the fear in his eyes. "Still, it might be smart for you and your kids to keep a distance much as you can. She can be bothersome sometimes."

As it turned out, everything Floyd warned about Wilma was the god's truth. Mean and contrary didn't begin to describe the woman. She hated him, and Henry had no idea why. He tried to win her over. He'd tell her a joke, a clean one, and she'd give him a look of disgust, like he was crazy.

The day they arrived, he promised Floyd it'd be a short stay. Three weeks later they were still there, much to Wilma's consternation. And as the days dragged on, her mood and tongue grew ever sharper.

She slammed a plate of runny noodles on the table before Henry and sneered, "Got a job yet? You even tryin'?"

It wasn't long before Henry noticed that when Wilma handed the plates around the table, the portions on his and the boys' invariably were smaller than those she served to her family members. She was trying to starve them out. Wilma looked at him, daring him to say something. He never did. What was the point?

Henry's one shot at finding a job came from a chicken-processing operation west of town. When he applied, the foreman, short-handed and desperate for help, walked Henry around the plant. Along a rubber conveyor belt, a line of men and women methodically gutted and plucked feathers from the dead chickens that passed in front of them. Henry gagged at the stench in the afternoon heat, throat-burning vomit crawling up his throat. Through an open doorway, he spotted a mess of guts and chicken waste parts fermenting under the sun in a field down-wind.

"Start you tomorrow," the foreman declared, obviously eager to start a new person on the line.

"I surely do appreciate the offer," Henry responded. "I'll need to think about it and get back to you."

Once outside, Henry stepped behind a tree and everything came up in a ripping explosion, followed by dry heaves until he thought his own innards would pour out.

He never breathed a word to anyone about the job interview. If Wilma learned he'd turned down an offer, she'd have him and his sons out the front door faster than you can say Jack Robinson.

The days passed and Wilma's hostility grew. One time she walked past him carrying a black frying pan, and Henry swore she'd whack him on the side of his head if given half a chance. He once dreamed she came into their room with a long knife and stabbed both of the boys in their bed, and she was headed right for him when he woke up in an awful sweat.

Still, what could he do? There was no money and no place to go.

He walked in the front door late in the afternoon and heard Wilma and Floyd: "They're eating us out of house and home," Wilma screeched. "The grocery money's gone by Wednesday. Our kids go hungry to feed those slackers!"

"It's un-Christian to turn them out while they're down on their luck. They're blood relation. I used to stay with Henry's family for weeks at a time. No one ever made me feel unwelcome. Besides, I've talked to him. He says they'll be moving on soon."

To stay out of Wilma's sight, Henry began spending afternoons at the town's only beer joint, Lilly's Tavern, a half-block east of the Baylor Hotel. He'd arrive after the lunch hour and order a 15-cent draw and nurse it all afternoon. Sometimes, he'd be the only customer, except on Tuesday and Thursday afternoons when he could always count on the half dozen old-timers who'd gather around a table in the corner and play nickel-dime poker.

He learned Lilly's Tavern took its name from the lady bartender who worked the day shift. She tended to stay at the far end of the bar, and pretty much ignored him. Using the word "lady" to describe the barkeep wasn't quite right. She was overweight, but a real babe, with striking blond hair, tall, big-boned and with a nice set of boobs and near-perfect facial features. He kept stealing looks at her. Take off the pounds and she'd win a beauty contest hands down. The poker players called her Lilly. Putting two and two together Henry concluded she was the boss, though she seemed awfully young to own her own bar.

"Say, Lilly," Henry said, in an attempt at conversation. "That's your name, isn't it, Lilly?"

"Yes, it is," she answered formally. "May I help you?"

"Oh, I'm just trying to make some friendly talk. Awfully quiet in here, and I was wondering if you'd like to hear a joke I heard from a fellow."

"Sure, why not," Lilly said, moving down the bar to hear him better.

"Know why a chicken doesn't wear pants?"

She raised a hand, and spread her fingers, and gave a shrug, like she hadn't a clue.

"Because his pecker is on his head."

It was an off-kilter, silly thing, and a very lame joke. Still, on a long, monotonous afternoon it was Henry's best idea to break the ice. At first she wrinkled her nose, and then she covered her mouth and began to laugh, and laugh harder, until tears streamed down her face. She bent over and held her sides.

After that, things loosened up between them and Lilly began spending more time at his end of the bar. He noticed she brightened when he walked through the front door, like he was her lifeline from the dull everyday events in Elk Point. He cranked up the joke telling and the charm. Now and then he'd bitch about Wilma but mostly he kept the small talk on the light side. He never mentioned the boys.

"You know," she said, "I haven't laughed so hard in years."

Henry took this as a sign to move the jokes to a racier level, which she didn't seem to mind. With an attractive young girl paying such rapt attention, Henry was in his glory. Wilma seemed far away and unimportant during the hours with this new friend.

The night bartender showed up at his usual 4:30 hour, and that was the time Lilly left for home. Henry, his stomach growling, would drain his glass and head back to Cousin Floyd's for supper. During those meals, he never breathed a word about Lilly. He ate fast and left the table before Wilma could attack. Once he did try to make light conversation with her.

"Say, Wilma, you know any of those old guys who play poker at Lilly's?" he asked innocently. "Seem like nice enough fellows."

"Nobody I know plays poker!" she said, contemptuously. "And I don't approve of gambling. With two young boys and no money, and living on others' charity, you shouldn't either."

"Now, Wilma, I don't play cards myself. I'm only asking if you know those fellows, since y'all have lived here a long while. Didn't mean any harm, and sure didn't mean to cause any heartburn."

"I don't get heartburn," she fired back, giving him a look that could kill.

Chapter 7

Slowly, thought-by-thought, Lilly began to consider Henry as a possible paramour. Her belly tingled from the daring idea. Physically, he was no dreamboat, and he was older, but she supposed he might be called cute. He seemed in pretty good shape, at least compared to the men with the beer bellies who frequented the bar. He'd lost his wife recently and she'd heard he and his sons were living with his cousin Floyd and his wife Wilma.

From the tone of the stranger's words, it didn't sound like a happy arrangement. He had come to Elk Point looking for a job and hadn't had any success. She wasn't surprised. There were few jobs in the area, what with farm prices so low farmers could barely cover seed and fertilizer costs let alone make a profit.

"I'm a crackerjack salesman. I can sell anything to anyone if given the chance," Henry boasted. "I made great money at the Co-Op in Belleview. When the farm economy began to tank, the boss had to cut overhead, and he figured I was dispensable."

They started flirting, harmless stuff in her mind. More than once she'd bend over to retrieve a dropped cloth or to pick up a napkin and she could feel Henry's eyes checking her out. Blushing when she rose up, he'd grin, not in the least embarrassed to be caught staring at her. She never said anything; fact is, she liked the attention.

"How're the boys doing since they lost their mother?" Lilly asked him one day. She hadn't met Henry's kids but more than once she'd watched them through the tavern's front window weave their way along the sidewalks, dragging a burlap sack partially filled with empty bottles that they had picked up to redeem at Pierson's Grocery for two cents each. Why wasn't their father out there with his kids, searching for bottles instead of sitting here hour after hour sipping on a beer?

The boys tugged at her heartstrings.

"Yeah, they're good kids," Henry said. "Their mom raised them right. Like me, they leave Wilma's early and stay away as much as possible. Kids are adaptable. They take hikes, and pick up pop bottles. They're fine."

She didn't respond to his high-handed remarks. It occurred to her if she had any sense she'd stay far away from this man. He was bad news. But there was little else going on in this town and, frankly, she was bored to tears.

"So what's your plan?" Lilly asked. "Sounds like your days at Wilma's are numbered."

"Sheesh, I don't know, Lilly. I've got a little money but not enough for bus tickets to another town, even if I had a place to go. My problem is I've run out of relatives to visit. Christ—and believe me I'm not one to feel sorry for myself—I'm beginning to think the Lord has it in for me. I can't imagine what I did to bring on all this trouble. I'm desperate for a break."

Lilly made sympathetic noises but inside her heart truly went out to the boys. They didn't deserve what was happening to them, especially so soon after losing their mother.

Lilly had her own problems. She burned to get on with life. Running a tavern in Elk Point for the rest of her life left her feeling dull and hollow inside. Frustrated with a lack of a love life or, to be truthful, any sex life at all, she felt her life slipping away—and she was only 21 years old. Her single romantic experience to date involved a fumbled attempt at sex with a second-string football player in the back seat of a car when she was a senior in high school. That messy encounter had left her virginity intact. The only reason she'd been in the back seat with the football player in the first place was because her super-loose girlfriend was stretched out in the front seat with another boy. She was along for the ride, as was the dull-headed football guy she'd been making out with in a prone position in the back seat.

The problem was her weight. In high school, the only attention she got from the boys was when one of them made a snide remark behind her back about her weight. She overheard one dork refer to her as a fat cow. That really stung!

Now this Henry guy had come to town, and he had her head spinning. Glib and easy with the jokes, he had two kids, and with 13 years of marriage, he obviously had plenty of bedroom experience, certainly a lot more than that dopey football player. But what was her next step? She was trying to lose weight but it was slow going. She didn't want to scare the guy off. For now she'd have to content herself with imagining what it'd be like to lie down with a man who knew what he was doing.

"Say, Lilly, how'd you come to own this tavern at such a tender young age?" he asked her one day. "Someone said you also own the café next door."

"Oh, it's a long story and not very interesting. I'd rather listen to your jokes," she said, irritation in her voice. This man was being overly nosy. He had no right to pry into her affairs. Besides, he'd probably be moving on one of these days and he sure didn't need to know her business.

Henry was seated at one of the tables and picked up a copy of the local newspaper and began reading. Lilly busied herself behind the bar washing and rinsing dirty beer glasses in the bar sink before stacking them in neat rows on a clean white towel spread across the bar. She began remembering.

Lilly's Tavern used to be known as Big Ed's, taking its name from her father, Ed Swenson, a big man, with a big heart. Her dad ate, smoked and drank too much. He was only 51 when he passed from a massive heart attack.

Thoughts of her father still hurt. He'd been an ally in the many fights she'd had over the years with her mother, Phyllis. Her mom was one of those people who rarely smiled and was all business. She ran the café and managed the finances for both businesses. Ed stayed out of her way, and out of her reach, spending his time running the adjoining tavern. A jovial sort, Ed enjoyed mixing it up with the customers. He was famous for pouring a full glass of beer. Half the town showed up for his funeral. He was that well liked.

It really bothered Lilly that only six weeks after burying her husband, Mom took up with a local farmer named Elliott Nelson. She started wearing lipstick and eye shadow and dressed like a 20-year-old: tight skirts, low-cut tops, even spiked heels. She looked ridiculous. On top of that, she lost all interest in the businesses; for example, these days it was rare for her to even drop by the café. She left it all to up to daughter. Lilly heard via the grapevine that Phyllis and this Elliott guy were seen at the Elks Club dancing real close. One woman swore she'd seen her mother in Elliot's pickup in a parking lot making out like horny teenagers. It was only a few weeks later when Phyllis came skipping into the tavern, looking girlish and all aglow, to make the pronouncement that she and Elliott were getting hitched and relocating to Phoenix. Lilly begged her to give it more time. Mom said no, the clock was ticking and she was going. The next day Phyllis visited a local lawyer and signed the café and the adjoining tavern over to her.

"The businesses are all yours now, honey," she declared. "You deserve them. You've worked hard."

Yeah, Lilly thought, I sure as hell have worked hard, and, wouldn't you know it, for one lousy dollar to make it legal, her mom had off-loaded a lifetime of drudgery, hard work and long hours right smack onto her daughter's back. Thanks a lot, Mom!

Her parents first came to Elk Point from a farm in Minnesota when they were kids, Mom 19, and Dad barely 21. They purchased the café and adjoining bar with no down payment and a promise to make regular payments for five years to the man who'd run the businesses into the ground. As it turned out, they paid off the debt in only three years.

Looking back, it seemed she'd lived her whole life at the restaurant, always under her mother's watchful eye. Only a few days after she was born—she'd be an only child—Phyllis brought her to work and Lilly spent her first days in a crib parked in the hallway leading to the bathrooms. By the time she was seven, Mom had taught her to run the cash register and make change. With her blond curls and round blue eyes, the waitresses oohed and ahhed and told her she looked like a little princess all dressed up and so pretty as she sat high on the stool behind the register, smiling and taking in the money from the departing customers. Lilly adored the attention.

But when she turned 15 and started high school, Mom crashed her world by banishing her to a beat-up commercial dishwashing sink in a small alcove off the back of the kitchen, away from the customers, away from everybody. She felt like Cinderella, isolated, utterly betrayed, and no longer the pretty princess who had once sat high on her stool in front of the big cash register.

"It's time you learned there's more to running a restaurant than a smile and a nice dress," her mother told her. At that moment she hated her, and in the years ahead she come to passionately hate washing the dishes and the pots and pans that arrived in an endless flow to her sink area. She gagged as she scraped off chunks of food, gravy and squashed-out cigarettes butts. At night, she'd go home and peel off layers of dead skin from her hands. Her nails turned crinkly and a sickly yellow. Mom kept her captive in that back room for the next four years, forcing her to wash dishes right up to the night before she graduated from high school.

She missed everything—sleepovers with girlfriends, Friday-night football games, hanging out at the drugstore.

Unlike other girls her age, she never had a regular boyfriend. She grew increasingly unhappy and took most of her meals at the restaurant, usually eating by herself at a small table in the back of the kitchen, devouring meat loaf, pork tenderloin sandwiches, potatoes and gravy, and desserts, sometimes two pieces of pie at suppertime. The Sunday afternoon she walked across the stage to pick up her high school diploma she weighed nearly 190 pounds. A couple of days later, her mother showed her the pictures she'd taken at the ceremony. Lilly cringed. She looked like a fat turkey dressed in a black robe, topped off with a mortarboard.

Finally taking note of what she'd done to her daughter, Phyllis promoted the new graduate to assistant manager, and Lilly resumed her perch behind the cash register. It didn't seem like nearly as much fun now. Then Big Ed died and once she turned 21 Mom made her manager of the tavern. Not long after, Phyllis and Elliott took off for Phoenix, and she was left holding the bag.

Lilly frowned and finished washing the glasses. She turned and straightened the liquor bottles behind the bar that didn't need straightening.

Henry came over. "You sure have a long face, pretty lady. Something wrong?"

"No, I'm fine," she said, offering him a bright smile.

"So you like this place, huh?" she asked.

"Yeah, it's great. I always wanted to own a bar. This place has lots of potential."

"Maybe I'll give it to you," Lilly offered, but the sudden look of raw greed that came over Henry's face shocked her. She added, "Hey, relax, I'm only kidding."

Henry sipped his now warm beer.

"Fact is, I'm not a happy camper. A while back, I promoted the cook at the restaurant to manager, and he's running the cafe for me now, while I spend my daylight hours here. This is all temporary until I can make some decisions."

He looked at her, up and down. "Really? I had the impression you liked it around here, this being your home for so long."

"It's okay. But I'm ready to do something different."

He stared at her chest. She blushed.

"Well, here's Russ, the night bartender. I need to get going. I'll see you tomorrow."

"Yeah," he answered. "Look forward to it."

That night, Lilly stood naked in her room before a walnut-framed, full-length mirror, a daily routine she'd been following as part of her weight-loss program. She saw a tall, robust young woman and now, thanks to a herculean effort, someone who weighed a much more manageable 160 pounds. She'd lost more than 25 pounds; her ultimate goal was to get down to 145.

In her favor, her natural, radiant skin had a glowing effect on her long blond hair, her teeth were strong and straight, and she had shapely buttocks, and firm breasts, which were almost perfect in size and shape. There was still some fat on her stomach, and her arms and chest were too big for the lower part of her body. A scattering of unsightly black moles dotted her torso. There wasn't much she could do about them.

Overall, she looked better and felt better than she had in a long time. She recognized her improved outlook was due in large part to Henry. The flirting and his smooth conversational style were things she enjoyed. She also liked the dreams she was having at night. She touched her right nipple, and it sprang up rock hard. A tingle of excitement coursed through her body. She was ready for something new.

But what?

There never was any truly great and generous heart...not also tender and compassionate.

–Robert Frost

Chapter 8

At Bottman's Standard gas station, Frank Bottman sat at his desk and plowed through paperwork, a job he detested. Frank was 56 years old, six-foot-two and, thanks to a lifetime of hard labor, barrel-chested. He had the rugged head of a prizefighter and arms as bold and knotted as the exposed roots of an ancient giant oak. His bright blue eyes were warm and friendly and his thick bushy eyebrows ran wild and tangled over the bridge of his nose.

Over the years he prided himself on being fair and honest with everyone he met, and particularly with those who traded with him at the station. He also had the reputation of not giving a person the time of the day if anyone tried to pull a fast one, or failed to keep his word.

He glanced up to check for vehicles pulling up to the pumps and spotted two boys crossing the drive and headed toward the station's front door. He'd seen them before, the big one in the lead and the little guy always trailing behind. They were in the habit of wandering the downtown area, shuffling their feet, walking aimlessly as they killed time, like they had no place to go and were in no hurry to get there.

Clara, Frank's wife, had heard about the nomadic family and she told her husband that the boys' father had brought them to Elk Point on a bus a few weeks earlier and they were staying with Floyd and Wilma Weber. The kids were motherless and their father was out of work and hanging out at Lilly's Tavern. It wasn't a good situation, far as Frank could tell.

Clara also reported Wilma was telling anyone who'd listen that Floyd's no-good cousin and his two sons were eating them out of house and home.

And to make Wilma even madder, Floyd refused to make them leave, so they kept staying, day after day, no end in sight.

"Hi, kids," Frank grunted. "Help you with something?"

"How much you get for Baby Ruths and Coca-Colas?" the bigger boy asked. His voice was challenging, and he seemed to have a chip on his shoulder. It was tough to guess the kid's age; he was good-sized, and good-looking, maybe 15 or 16. Slid in behind him was the little shaver, his brother. He looked scared and hungry. Frank put him at maybe 5 or 6.

"Well, it depends. Normally, I get 5 cents for the candy and 10 cents for a bottle of pop. Sometimes I charge more, sometimes less."

The big guy's head snapped up. Frank figured the kid was thinking: What the hell? This old guy charges different prices to different customers?

"Hey, relax! I'm joking," Frank laughed. "The price is the same here as everywhere else. A nickel for the candy and a dime for the soda. But here's the deal. I'll give each of you a free Coke and candy bar today. I do that for all my new customers. But when you want a treat, you gotta come here, not to the grocery or drugstore. I need the business. Got it?"

"Yeah, guess so," Paul said, and then, remembering his manners, stammered, "Thank you, mister."

After that, Bottman's Standard became the boys' hangout. Frank liked the company. He had four children of his own. The three girls had moved out of town and had families of their own. The boy, John, wasn't with them anymore.

Lately, nothing much excited Frank. He went to work and came home for supper, day after day, staying in a routine, not straying much because it was easier to go through the same motions. Interestingly, this older boy, Paul, reminded him of his son John. He was big like John, and he had the same quiet and steady manner about him.

It was common knowledge around town that the two boys left Floyd and Wilma's house before breakfast each day, dragging an old gunny sack behind them, searching in ditches, behind buildings, and in garbage cans for discarded beer and pop bottles, which they turned in at the grocery store. Some thought it was disgraceful and one or two even suggested someone ought to do something about it. But no one did. Typically, the boys kept searching until they had collected enough bottles to buy lunch, which usually consisted of candy bars and pop. That wasn't the best food for growing boys so, at Clara's urging, Frank began bringing extra food from home in his lunch bag: a spare sandwich, apples, and cookies.

Frank emptied the bag on his desk the first day.

"You kids help yourself," he said. The little guy, Arthur, dove right in; the older brother stepped back and folded his arms. He was too proud to take food.

"I got plenty of apples," Frank urged. "Wife and I have two big trees in the back yard. If you guys don't eat 'em the worms will get 'em."

Frank nodded toward Paul. He shook his head and mumbled, "Thanks, but I'm okay."

Frank didn't press. At Paul's age he wouldn't accept anything from anybody either, unless he'd earned it. He admired the kid's brass—he was just like his son John.

Once he got comfortable around Frank, Arthur, the sweet-natured younger boy, talked and talked—a born yakker if Frank had ever met one. He complained a lot, too. The weather was too hot or too cold, and no matter when he'd last eaten, the kid was always hungry. This embarrassed his big brother. Frank understood. Both boys were in a tough spot and deserved some slack. For Christ's sake they'd lost their mother and, from what he'd heard, the old man was as worthless as tits on a boar hog.

Paul was the strong, silent type, rarely speaking unless spoken to or asked a direct question. Frank could tell he carried a lot of anger inside. When he learned Paul was only 12, he could hardly believe it. He sure as hell looked and acted older.

Paul gravitated to the back garage and began hanging out with Frank's two mechanics, Chuck Ahrens and Dave "Smitty" Smith. Both were in their mid-twenties, and single with thin and wiry builds; neither weighed more than 125 pounds. Chuck, a redhead with freckles all over his face and arms, assumed the role of boss, even though Frank never bestowed him with the position, while Smitty, who was always smeared with grease from face to boots, was the clown. Both kidded around and teased a lot. However, when it came to getting the job done right, they were serious as hell. Frank had taught them to work hard and to never pad the clock when they worked on a job. He wouldn't put up with any bullshit.

He'd hired the mechanics out of high school and under his direction they'd become skilled auto, truck, and tractor mechanics, to the point where Frank had hung up his overalls and turned all the mechanical work over to them. He'd had enough grease-ball work to last a lifetime.

Chuck and Smitty welcomed Paul's help, and even outfitted their volunteer assistant in a pair of overalls, complete with a grease rag to hang out of his back pocket. He did what they asked: brought them tools, bathed carburetor parts in gasoline, fixed tires, loosened rust-frozen bolts, and did the grunt clean-up work that they hated to do themselves. Paul never complained. Frank noticed he thrived on hard, physical labor and working with his hands.

With Paul as their captive audience, the crowing mechanics delighted in recounting the intimate details of their previous nights' sex lives with their two super-hot girlfriends. Each tried to one-up the other on their use of "special tricks" to bring their respective girlfriend to screaming climaxes.

It all seemed harmless to Frank. What these guys were saying and doing with Paul as an audience was a lot like the streetwise way he'd learned about sex as a kid. He hadn't been much older than Paul at the time either. Hadn't done him any harm.

But one day the backroom wrench-boys took things too far when they jumped all over the news that Paul's father was in the habit of hanging out at Lilly's Tavern.

"Shit, that Lilly's a damn good-looking babe. She's got a little extra beef on her, but I always say the bigger the woman the bigger the fun," Smitty said, grinning and looking directly at Paul. "You're one lucky stiff. She's hot. Ever get a peek up her skirt?"

Paul's face turned bright red.

Frank charged into the garage yelling, "Knock that crap off! It's one thing to lie about your girlfriends. Lilly is a respectable young lady, so don't be talking about her that way. Besides, she's way above your class. Keep your mouths shut. Understand?"

Frank was pissed, mostly at himself. He'd let it go too far. The station owner knew Lilly and her family. They'd traded with him for a long time. It was disgraceful to hear Smitty talking about a nice young girl like that.

Back at his desk, Frank realized it was time to make Paul a part of his crew with regular pay.

"How'd you like a real job here, you know, one that pays?" Frank asked him.

"I guess it'd be okay. Money's okay."

"Think your old man would go along with it?"

"He doesn't give a damn what I do."

"I'll ask anyway."

Around four that afternoon, Frank took a chance that Paul's father might still be at the tavern. Sure enough, he found him at the bar. Lilly was at the other end checking on some paperwork. Henry's appearance surprised Frank. He'd heard stories about this fellow being a big flirt, a ladies man, a real bull-shitter around town, so he expected the tall, handsome type, like in the movies. This guy was of medium-height and tended toward plumpness. Hard to believe women would tumble over him.

"Say, you wouldn't happen to be Henry Goodwin, would you?" Frank asked, taking a stool next to him.

"Yeah," he replied, his voice guarded.

Lilly made her way toward him. "Nothing for now, thanks. Can't stay long. Just have a minute." He swung back toward Henry.

"I'm Frank Bottman. I own the Standard station down the street. Your boys are there a lot."

"Yeah. That's what they say," Henry replied, and then his face grew stern. "Say, they haven't been a problem, have they? I'll chew their butts off."

"Not at all. We're all getting along great. Your oldest boy has been doing a good job helping out in the back shop."

"Pleased to hear it. If either of those rascals causes any trouble, Mr. Bottman, be sure and let me know. I'll take care of it right away."

"I'd like to put Paul on a work schedule until school starts, and, later, schedule him for a few hours after school and on Saturdays. I'd pay him—say 50 cents an hour."

"Well, that sounds fine. He's sure big enough to work."

"He's smart and real good with his hands," Frank added, finding it strange to describe the boy to his own father. "I can find a few things for his little brother to do.

You know sweeping, picking up the driveway, emptying trash, that sort of thing. I'll pay him a little something. Seems like he wants to stay close to his older brother."

"Well, heck, this sounds like a fine opportunity. I'll talk to the boys tonight and let 'em know it's fine and dandy with me. You be sure and let me know if either of them gives you any trouble."

That night, lying awake in bed, Frank thought about John. He'd planned to pass the business on to him, just as his father had passed the Standard station to him. A telegram from the War Department in the spring of 1944 crushed that dream forever. A military policeman in London, John and his squad were sent to a bar to break up a bar fight. During the confusion, a coward crept up behind his only son and cut his throat.

Frank's hands trembled when he read the telegram. Clara ripped it from him, read it, and collapsed on the floor.

Others in Elk Point had lost sons, husbands and brothers in the war; still Frank never expected anything to happen to John. Now his son was dead, and not on a battlefield in Europe but slaughtered like a farm animal in a London bar.

Clara turned to family members and the church for consolation. Frank turned inward. At first, he wouldn't even allow Clara to bring up his son's name around the house. He was the boy's father. Fathers looked after their children, protected them. Blindly, he'd allowed himself to be caught up in the swell of patriotism after Pearl Harbor. He'd actually encouraged John to join up.

On April 25, the casket arrived on the train on a rain-drenched morning, exactly two years from the day church members had gathered in the spiral-capped Methodist church and sang *Onward Christian Soldiers* as a send-off for John who was going off to war.

Now, with the church overflowing with mourners, The Reverend Clay, dressed in black mourning cloth, began preaching on how God only knows why terrible things happen to young men with such promise. Frank heard the man's voice, not the words.

At the graveyard, Army Honor Guard rifles barked out a military volley. A uniformed soldier stood on a nearby hillside, at rapt attention, a trumpet pressed to his lips. Clouds obscured the late-morning sun as the trumpeter played, "Day is done, Gone the sun."

Frank stood at the edge of the open grave. His body shook. One of his son-in-laws stepped forward and grabbed his arm, which saved the grieving man from tumbling into the grave on top of his son's casket. He eased Frank down on to his knees. Frank stayed there, sobbing uncontrollably. Clara came forward and knelt beside her husband and wrapped him in her arms, comforting him like a child.

Don't lose your heart, just keep going, keep at it.

–Mark Ruffalo

Chapter 9

Henry was hurting. He walked into Lilly's Tavern, grumbling to himself. There was stubble on his chin, his hair was a matted mess and he needed a bath. He plopped down in a heap on a barstool. "My beer, please," he said, his voice low, discouraged.

"Problems with Wilma?"

"It's always Wilma," he groaned. "She's been riding me all morning. School's about to start, and the crazy woman is taunting me about whether I'm going to enroll the boys in school or not. It's like she's daring me do it."

"Sounds like she won't stop pushing," Lilly said.

"I've had it!" Henry snapped as he gulped some beer. "She's the most hate-filled woman I've every met. Hell, I should pack up and head back to Belleview. Maybe the boys' grandmother will take us in."

Henry slammed his mug on the bar. "Shit, that won't work! Moving in with that woman would be like going from the edge of a cliff to tumbling into hell."

"Maybe I can help."

"Don't see how. Far as I can see, I'm screwed."

"Russ, the night bartender, wants to retire. Job's open. Interested?"

Henry leaned forward, a look of sheer joy spreading across his face. "Hire me and I'll be the best bartender this town ever saw."

"I'm thinking you'd be good at it, too. People seem to like the stories you tell."

She leaned back and nodded, like she'd made up her mind. "Okay, the job's yours. Doesn't pay a lot. I can throw in the back storage room of the tavern at no charge for you and the boys to stay. At least you'll be out of Wilma's house. It's a mess back there, filled with junk, old beer signs, discarded furniture, you name it and it's probably in there somewhere. Everything needs a good scrubbing. There's a working sink in the back. I know where to find a used refrigerator and stove. We can probably find enough furniture in my parents' attic; you know beds, kitchen table and chairs. And if business picks up, so will your pay."

"Thank you. Thank you. You're saving my life. I can't wait to tell Wilma to go to hell. How can I ever repay you?"

"Just don't leave my customers thirsty," she said, giving him an encouraging smile.

On his first day on the job, Henry rushed around like a teenager fired up on Coca-Cola. In the days ahead, he dressed better, shaved regularly, and entertained the customers with funny stories. Lilly's Tavern became the place to meet with friends, even to bring along the wife or girlfriend. As business picked up and the cash register rang more often, as promised, Lilly rewarded Henry with a pay raise. With no place else to go, he'd work as many as 12 hours a day. She always made certain he took time off to make the boys supper. For the first time in her life, she had time for herself. The arrangement was working out perfectly.

She used some of her spare time to help Paul and Arthur get settled. She helped them enroll in school, and they shopped together for school shoes and clothes. Meanwhile, Paul and Arthur had stopped scrounging for cans and bottles and worked exclusively at their jobs at Bottman's. She worried about them; still, it wasn't really any of her business.

One thing that irked her was Henry's growing popularity with the bar's female customers. Young or old, married or single, the ladies flocked around her single bartender, batting their eyes, casually bumping and rubbing against him, vying for his attention. More than one inquired about when he got off work. It was all part of doing business, Lilly told herself. But that was before the incident involving "Sweet Tits" happened and set the town buzzing. This local divorcee of about 40 had come by her unusual nickname because of her bawdy behavior and huge breasts, which she always led with, especially in her dealings with the opposite sex.

One busy evening when Lilly was at home, the Double-D-size gal, after tippling several beers, cornered Henry and in a lusty voice described in precise detail what she'd do if she ever got him into her bed. The description she laid out was so graphic and vulgar that the salacious details quickly became the talk of the town.

Whether Henry had taken Sweet Tits up on the offer Lilly didn't know. However, the mere offer of the lady's favors was enough to spike her bartender's notoriety to lofty heights in the small town.

Several of the town's upper-crust ladies, those who fancied themselves as keepers of the town's morals, demanded that the mayor shut down Lilly's Tavern. Nothing came of it. As it turned out, the mayor happened to be in attendance the night of Sweet Tits' grand offer, and had found it hugely entertaining.

It was embarrassing having the episode occur in her bar. After all she'd been born and had grown up in this town. She suspected Henry had had a part in encouraging the lusty woman's bawdy behavior. Henry flirted with every woman he encountered. That made Lilly feel something else she didn't like—jealousy! She and Henry still flirted and teased, and she was hoping for possibly more.

Now she had competition. She considered saying something to him about keeping his distance from the female patrons. She never found the right moment to bring up the subject.

Henry, smug and cocky, thanks to all the attention coming his way, bragged at the bar that Elk Point was a nice place but he was destined for bigger things.

"I'm going to California," he'd tell folks. "I've got friends begging me to move out west. Factory workers are drawing down nearly $100 a week with overtime putting together airplanes for the war in Korea. Hell, they say even the women are earning that much. I figure I'll put back a few bucks this winter, then head west with the boys, work at a factory and save some money and open a bar of my own. That's the way people get rich, you know, owning things, not dragging their butts around working for someone else."

Lilly was surprised when Henry's travel plans reached her ears. Did he know of her desire to leave Elk Point? Working late one night to square up the bookkeeping, she watched Henry lock the front door after the last customer had departed. He began turning chairs upside down on the tables in preparation for the nightly sweeping. She closed the checkbook and said: "Hey, let's take a break. How about a beer, on me?"

"Heck, yes," he answered. "Best offer I've had all night."

The neon Hamm's, Budweiser, and Falstaff signs hanging from chains on the walls and in the windows provided a warm, soft hum as they sat across from each other in a vinyl-covered booth, tucked away toward the back, and hidden from outside view.

"What's this I hear about your moving to California?" Lilly asked, arching her eyebrows. "Don't you like us?"

He swallowed a swig of beer and offered an apologetic look. "Oh, you know me, I like to blow smoke and show off when I'm working. Always trying to be the big shot. Doesn't mean a thing. I wouldn't quit on you, Lilly, not without plenty of notice, that's for sure."

"Hey, I'm not putting you on a spot. It's just that I'm considering moving to California myself."

"Really? You'd leave Elk Point?" he asked, as he leaned foreword and placed a hand over hers. "I always thought you liked it here in your hometown."

She removed his hand. This wasn't the time or place. She wanted to talk about California.

"Yes. I'm very serious. I've been dreaming of going west since I was old enough to thumb through all those movie and fashion magazines."

"Well, doesn't that beat all? I've got this close friend in Los Angeles. His name is Zeke. We graduated high school together in Belleview. I ran into him in Belleview the summer before last when he was back home visiting his mom. We had a couple of beers and that's when he said I'd be a damned fool if didn't get out to California soon as possible, even said I could stay with him till I find my own place."

"Why didn't you take him up on the offer?"

"Margie was still alive, and I had a good job, and with the boys depending on me, moving across the country seemed like too much hassle to even think about. It's different now. I'm ready to go. There's a big world out there."

"Nice of Zeke to extend the invite."

"Yeah, he's a peach, one of the best. My problem is I don't have a car, and there's no way I'm boarding one of those damn buses to travel that far, especially with two kids in tow."

"I've got my mother's car, and it's nearly brand new."

Henry straightened, his interest on high alert.

"You'd lend me your car?"

"No, but we might all go together in my station wagon."

"Are you serious?"

"Maybe," she said, a small smile playing on her lips. "We'll see. For now, let's just think about it."

A gentle heart is tied with an easy thread.

–George Herbert

Chapter 10

It was Christmas morning, 1950. Paul and Arthur were on holiday break from school. Arthur, now seven years old, was in second grade, and Paul had started junior high. They ate cornflakes at the small table next to the sink in the back room. Dad's snores threatened to drown out the squeaky, static-filled sound of Christmas carols coming from the old tabletop radio that Lilly had donated. "It stinks awful in here," Arthur whined. The back room always smelled of sour beer, cigarette and cigar smoke. It was tolerable when they could open windows and doors. Now, with cold weather and everything shut tight, the odors and staleness hung heavy over everything, and there was no way to bring in fresh air.

"Not much we can do about it," Paul offered.

Paul knew complaining never helped anything. He knew this as well as he knew his old man wouldn't be climbing out from under his pile of blankets for several more hours. He'd worked last night. Lilly was off to Phoenix to visit her mother and Elliott. He and Arthur would spend this Christmas day alone.

Gray light filtered through the small window in the side door as Paul peeked out and watched snowflakes swirl in the winter air. The town had four overhead traffic lights, one on each corner of the square. The light visible from the window swayed back and forth in the gusts of wind. Paul wondered if the cable might snap. Except for a skinny mongrel dog, downtown Main Street was as empty and as cleaned out as their cornflake bowls, not a soul or a car in sight.

"Let's see what we can find," Paul said, unfolding the gunnysack. These days they rarely looked for bottles. Today, though, it'd give them something to do.

They pulled the collars of their thin coats up around their necks and ventured out into the frigid December morning. After scrounging around for more than an hour, their total find consisted of three pop bottles worth six cents.

"Wait here a second," Paul called out. "I'll check behind Garner's Hardware."

Sure enough, next to the garbage can, frost glistening like diamonds on the brown glass, Paul found two six-packs of empty Hamm's beer bottles, a treasure to behold.

Mr. Garner must have treated the help to liquid holiday cheer before sending them home on Christmas Eve.

"Whoop!"

He grabbed the treasure and, a six-pack in each hand, rushed to show off the find to Arthur. With spirits high, the boys headed back to the tavern, arriving shortly before noon to find their father still sleeping.

"Should we wake him?" Arthur asked. "I'm hungry."

"Nah, let him alone. I'll make lunch."

Arthur's eyes squeezed shut and a tear trickled down his cheek. Here comes the waterworks.

"C'mon, Arthur, don't start bawling," Paul admonished, his voice not unkind.

Christmas had been their mother's all-time favorite holiday. Once Thanksgiving was out of the way, Mom turned her full attention to Christmas. He remembered her humming "Have yourself a merry little Christmas" as she went about decorating the house. By the first day of December, Christmas cookies by the dozens would be ready by the dozens for the season. He and Arthur were allowed one each per day, until Christmas morning, when they could eat their fill.

A holiday highlight was when the three of them hiked downtown to the Boy Scouts' Christmas tree lot, located just off River Street. They'd pick out the best tree and drag it home. If it was snowing, that'd be all the better.

Christmas Eve in Belleview traditionally started with church services at seven at the Presbyterian Church. Dad always begged off, saying he had to stay home and guard the presents in case burglars were working in the neighborhood.

After church Mom played the piano and they all joined in the caroling, even Dad, with Arthur warbling at the top of his lungs in an irritatingly high-pitched voice. Paul remembered gritting his teeth and poking his brother in the side. Mom always went to the little squirt's defense. "Oh, Paul," she'd say, "let him have his fun. Besides, I think his singing is wonderful. He's so happy."

Christmas morning they opened presents, and by noon, through some holiday magic, the dining room table groaned under the load of ham, turkey, and all the fixings. Grandma Lucille arrived, bringing two home-baked apples pies and a half-gallon of vanilla ice cream. She always brought the desert.

That's the way it used to be, Paul grimaced, as he looked at his father lumped up in bed.

A week earlier, Lilly had departed on the bas to Arizona. He'd overheard her say to Dad: "Make sure things are special for the boys. It'll be hard for them—the first Christmas without their mother."

She'd done her part and left behind a tantalizing pile of presents, one for Henry and a dozen neatly wrapped packages for the boys, with instructions that the gifts were to be opened on Christmas Eve, and no sooner. Now the open gifts stood in separate piles on the other side of the kitchen table: games, puzzles, adventure books, balls and a bat, and, their favorites, two stacks of comic books, one for him and one for his little brother.

Paul cranked the opener around the edge of a can of Campbell's chicken noodle soup as Arthur watched, his sniffling a sure sign that he was going to break out crying again. Paul poured the boiling soup into two bowls, and the boys broke handfuls of saltine crackers into the yellow broth and squiggly noodles and ate the soggy mess. Afterwards, they read comic books. At about three, Arthur crawled under the blankets and went to sleep.

At 4:30, just as it was turning dark outside, Henry woke up.

"Hey! How come you didn't wake me? I'm starving."

* * * * *

Lilly returned to Elk Point on Dec. 28, her arms and face reddened from the Phoenix sun. She looked rested and was in a happy mood. Arthur ran and embraced her like she was his own mother.

"How was Christmas?" she asked.

Paul remained silent and Arthur's lower lip trembled.

Her lips tightened into a grim line. "I'll be right back," she said. "You boys wait here."

Henry was in the bar. Paul and Arthur hid behind the curtain that separated the bar from the living area and listened.

"I've never seen such long faces. What in the hell happened?" she demanded.

Paul was surprised to hear Lilly talk to Dad like that.

"Oh, give me a break. I worked my tail off Christmas Eve and didn't finish cleaning until well into the morning. I gave everything a good shining."

"We agreed you'd close early so you could spend time with your sons."

"That was the plan until a couple of guys showed up and had no place else to go. I felt sorry for them, so I stayed open till almost midnight. They spent a lot of money."

"You felt sorry for them? What about your own kids?"

"Hell, Lilly. The boys played with the presents you gave them. I made a good supper Christmas night. You don't see a woman around here to help, do you?"

She looked at him steadily and said, "That's baloney!"

She returned to the back room and told the boys: "Be dressed and ready to go tomorrow at 10. We're going shopping in Norfolk."

The next morning they rushed out and piled into Lilly's station wagon, an almost-new 1949 Chevrolet. They both admired the car.

The vehicle's heater sent out a comforting flow of hot air. Paul thought he was in heaven.

"Wow, does that feel great," Arthur said, putting his face directly in front of one of the heater vents. "I could live in this car."

As Lilly drove the 27 miles to Norfolk, she chatted non-stop about the visit to Phoenix and the warm, sunny weather. She commented on the older citizens who were pouring into the retirement enclave to escape the cold and snow up north. And, wonders of wonders, she went on and on about her mother's backyard swimming pool.

"I'd have dived right in but I didn't have a swimming suit. I thought about buying one but decided to wait until I lose a few more pounds."

At Norfolk's Coast-to-Coast store, she steered them to a double rack of bicycles.

"You kids want bikes?"

"Sure it's okay?" Paul asked.

"You bet! Any color, any size. My treat. You'll want some accessories too—baskets, extra reflectors, whatever you like."

In a daze, the boys walked down the aisle examining the two-wheeled vehicles in every color and model. Paul wanted red and Arthur, after much thought, chose blue. The store manager suggested the appropriate sizes and Lilly arranged to have the bikes delivered to Elk Point the following day.

At Sears-Roebuck, she helped them select two sets of school clothes each, plus dress-up clothes for Sunday school and special events. Lilly remembered Arthur telling her their mom always took them to church and Sunday school, so maybe Lilly would start doing that, too. Sunday was their father's sleep-in day. They chose new winter coats, hats, and gloves. Paul's new gloves were lined with white wool. He swore he'd never felt anything as soft and warm. "Wear your Sunday clothes out of here," Lilly suggested. "We're going to a fancy place for lunch and want to look our best."

Paul's head swung like a pendulum on his neck as they walked into the dining room of Norfolk's Commodore Hotel. A double-row of brightly lit crystal chandeliers hung on gold-plated chains from the ornate ceiling. Huge gilded mirrors reflected hundreds of tiny Christmas lights, casting a festive glow everywhere. The table was draped with a crisp white tablecloth and set with sparkling glassware, china, and heavy silverware. A bouquet of colorful flowers sat in the center. Arthur touched a petal. "Gosh, these flowers are real, and it's wintertime."

They dined on roast chicken, mashed potatoes, gravy, cranberries, and green beans, sprinkled with almonds. Dessert was apple pie and vanilla ice cream, the same as Grandma Lucille used to dish up on Christmas Day.

Paul noticed the other guests were all dressed up. Several men stole glances their way and Paul guessed it was because Lilly was the prettiest girl in the room.

The Granada Theatre matinee was a double feature, with Roy Rogers and Dale Evans starring in one movie, and Gene Autry and his sidekick Smiley Burnett in the other. They walked out into the cloudy late afternoon grayness. Paul smiled. He hadn't felt so good in a long time.

On the drive home, Arthur fell asleep in the middle of the front seat. The station wagon merged onto Highway 17. Lilly turned on the headlights and she and Paul rode in silence as they advanced through the moonless night toward Elk Point. Using a fingernail, Paul scratched out an image of a woman's face framed with long, flowing hair on the frosted side window. He drew a series of short, straight lines to simulate sparkly eyes. He kept his face turned, not wanting Lilly to see the tears on his cheeks.

Great tranquility of heart is his who cares for neither praise nor blame.

–Thomas Kempis

Chapter 11

Paul stepped through the curtains into the bar to talk to his father. It was against the law for kids to be in a place that served beer and liquor but no one ever said anything.

"Dad, they say on the radio a big storm's coming tonight. Could be a blizzard. The fuel tank on the space heater reads half full, and the can is empty. Should I go for more?"

"Nah, there's plenty to get us through," Henry said, as he pointed at the blue sky through the window. "Look outside, son. It's 50 degrees and sunny. Those weather guys are wrong most of the time. We'll be fine."

Today was New Year's Eve, and the grocery would be closed tomorrow. Paul took two dollars from the food-money jar and walked to Pierce's Grocery to purchase extra milk, bread and a few other items, including a package of cookies. After all, tonight was special. They'd be ringing in a New Year—1951.

While working his way down a crowded aisle, he overheard a farm lady leaning on a cane.

"My hip's screaming," she commented to her friend, a knowing look on her face. "Sure sign a blizzard's comin'."

Her friend, wearing a red bandanna that pulled back her gray hair, replied, "I brung up some fruits and vegetables from my root cellar just in case."

"Smart idea," the first lady said, rubbing her hip. "Don't want to get caught short. Remember the blizzard of '43? It took two weeks before we could dig out enough to get to town for supplies. Our family liked to starve."

The next morning, New Year's Day, Paul and Arthur were sleeping soundly when Henry poked his head from the blankets and yelled, "Get up, Paul! Christ, it's freezing in here. Take the fuel can to Bottman's. I'm not moving till this place warms up."

Paul crawled out of bed and tip-toed across the icy floor and glanced out the back door. The new bikes leaning against the back wall were already half buried in a snow drift.

So much for his dad's prediction about the forecasters being wrong about a blizzard coming, Paul thought.

The old tavern building rattled to its foundation. Paul grabbed his pants and shirt from the floor and climbed back into bed, dressing under the covers. He swung his legs over the side and pulled on socks, shoes, and over-boots. His breath billowed white in the frigid room.

"I'm going, too," Arthur declared.

"Hurry up!" Henry urged while keeping his head close to the blankets.

The wind pressed against the back door as Paul struggled to open it. Finally, they staggered into the storm, each gripping a side of the wire handle on the five-gallon fuel can. The temperature was 19 degrees. Three blocks ahead the tall Standard Oil sign shimmered like an apparition in the blowing snow.

They hadn't gone 100 yards before Arthur began complaining, "I'm freezing. Let's go back. Please."

"We can't. Hold your mittens to your face."

Why in the heck had he allowed his younger brother to tag along? All he did was whine, Paul thought, as the empty can whipped back and forth, banging painfully against the boys' legs.

"Ouch!" Arthur yelped, letting go of the can.

"Keep walking," Paul urged. "We're almost there."

Paul was certain Frank would be at the station. He operated the only place in Elk Point for folks to buy fuel oil for home heaters and gasoline for vehicles. Frank wouldn't let the town down, no matter how bad the weather might be.

He glanced at the courthouse and saw the massive building standing solid in the storm, like an impervious, disinterested bystander, its windows frost-covered. That building didn't care what happened around it; nothing could hurt it. Surrounding the courthouse, the wood-framed, retail stores quaked in the wind, the signs swayed, chains screeched, shingles flapped, the entire downtown holding on for dear life. When he grew up he wanted to be like the courthouse, able to stand tall and firm against anything the world threw at him.

The brothers stomped into the gas station office, their noses running and faces stinging. The snow they brushed off their coats fell onto the concrete floor and immediately melted into small puddles. Still upset at his father for not allowing him to fill the can yesterday, Paul angrily banged the empty can on the concrete floor.

Frank looked up, annoyed. He'd been sitting quietly at his desk, catching up on paperwork.

"That wasn't necessary," he admonished, indicating the can on the floor. "Why in Sam Hill are you out on a god-awful morning like this anyway?"

Paul was about to retort with a smart-ass reply, then reconsidered. It wasn't Frank's fault his father was a dumbbell. Besides, Frank was his boss.

"The heater is out of kerosene. Here's 50 cents," he said, sliding two quarters across the desk. "That should get us three gallons, right."

"Something wrong with your old man he couldn't get out of bed and come down here himself?"

Neither boy responded. Paul moved closer to the space heater, which hissed and ticked in the corner. Heat waves rolled off of it. He felt certain that if he reached out he could actually touch the wavy air.

Arthur stripped off his coat and hat and sat in a chair across from Frank, his mouth running at top speed, as he commenced to relate every detail concerning the trip they took with Lilly to Norfolk.

"You should see our bikes, Frank. Paul's bike is red and mine's blue. Blue's better. We ate at this ritzy hotel and they had real flowers on the table in the middle of winter."

As Arthur moved on to recount the plot of the two films, never once pausing to take in air, Frank calmly and patiently nodded and smiled. How the old guy put up with his little brother was a mystery to him.

Slouched in a straight-back chair next to the heater, Paul dozed off.

Forty-five minutes later, Frank said, "Seems like we're through the worst of it."

Paul shook himself awake. "We need to go. Dad's waiting,"

Frank pulled on a heavy parka and carried the kerosene can outside, where he pumped a generous three gallons. The snow had stopped and the wind had fallen to a steady, more moderate pace. The sky remained a drab gray. Paul carried the heavy, nearly full fuel can on his own with his two hands, drawing the can in close to his chest. Arthur jumped and veered ahead, hiking bravely and brashly through the high snowdrifts heaped along the way.

The boys stumbled through the door and Henry sat up in bed.

"About time," he shouted. "Get this place warmed up."

Paul unscrewed the cap on the tank at the back of the heater and lifted the heavy can and began filling the tank. His hand slipped and the kerosene gushed out and spilled onto the wooden floor. Adjusting the angle, Paul took careful aim and slowly and steadily filled the tank to just below the brim. He placed the fuel can a few feet from the heater and primed the start button. Reaching in with a stick match, he held it until the oil caught fire and the flames spread. Satisfied, he closed the metal door.

"Ouch!" he yelled. The match had burned down to his fingers. Paul dropped it. With a whoosh, the floor surrounding the heater burst into flames.

Panicked, he yelled, "Cripes, Dad! There's a fire. Come quick!"

"Goddamn it! What the hell did you do?" Henry bellowed as he jumped up and grabbed a straw broom and pounded at the flames, at the same time yelling to Paul to call the fire department. The fire licked and crackled across the dry floor so fast and wide it blocked Paul's path through the doorway to the bar and the telephone.

"Arthur!" Henry screamed. "Run to Lilly's. Tell her to call the fire department." He gave his younger son a rough push toward the side door.

Barefoot, Henry stepped forward to move the fuel can away from the expanding fire. Suddenly, the floor under his feet burst into flames and he hopped up, screamed and scrambled back to his bed. Stunned, Paul watched as his father sat on the edge of the bed and tenderly examined the bottom of his feet, oblivious to the expanding fire around him.

Paul tugged at him. "Dad! Dad! We have to get out of here! Please, get up! Move! We'll burn alive!"

Henry looked at him and blinked through uncomprehending eyes. Paul kept tugging. The room filled with black, acrid smoke. Now they were both coughing and struggling for air, tears streaming down their cheeks. In a desperate, last-ditch effort, Paul grabbed both of his father's arms and pulled him toward the side door just as two men rushed into the room. They lifted Henry by the arms and legs and carried him outside. Paul was right behind.

"Get him around to the front," one of the men said. "This whole building is a goner. You all right, son?"

Paul watched as the fire licked at the new bikes leaning against the back wall. "Yeah, guess so."

A woman brought two blankets and they laid his father down in the middle of Main Street, a safe distance from the blaze, which had spread and jumped to the roof of the next-door restaurant.

"I heard the best thing for burns is to pack 'em in snow," said one of the male rescuers.

"Better wait till the doctor comes before doing any-thing," the blanket-lady replied. "Might do more harm than good."

Sirens blared and emergency lights flashed. Curi-ous residents crowded the street. The volunteer fire chief barked out instruction as many of the ill-trained volun-teers stood around talking to the crowd that had gathered, instead of snapping to.

"You fellows get moving. Direct those hoses on those other buildings," the chief ordered. "We can't save these two buildings but we sure don't want to lose more."

One fireman unspooled a hose and remarked, "An hour earlier with that howling wind we'd of probably lost the entire block."

Lilly and Arthur arrived on a full run. She knelt beside Henry, who laid swaddled in blankets, only his bare feet sticking out into the snow on the street. Paul thought he looked like a newborn baby, and blubbered like one, too.

"Did anyone call the doctor?" Lilly called out. "Are there more blankets?"

"I tried to put the fire out, honest I did," Henry said. "Oh, God, Lilly, it hurts so bad. I saved Arthur. I shoved him away from the fire and out the door."

He lifted his face close to hers. "It was Paul's fault. He dropped the match."

Paul's back straightened; most everyone standing around had heard his father's words.

In less than 15 minutes, the fire reduced the tavern and the restaurant to a smoldering mess. The two smoke-scorched brick foundations now held a tangle of charred lumber and still-burning shingles. Sparks flew into the cloudy morning sky. Cases of bottles filled with beer and stacked in the storage area went POP, POP, POP in the intense heat, like a string of firecrackers going off. Long, thin icicles formed along the water-drenched rooflines. With the wind now died down to almost still, a heavy, dark cloud of smoke rose lazily into the early-morning sky and hovered there, in no hurry to go anywhere.

Arthur tugged at his brother's leg. "Paul, Paul, what's going to happen? Is Dad going to die? Who's going to take care of me?"

"He'll be okay. His feet are burned, that's all. They'll fix him."

The doctor arrived and examined Henry's feet. He was a young guy, fairly new to Elk Point. He'd bought the medical practice from old Doc Powell, who'd moved on to a retirement home in Omaha. The town was still getting used to this young kid, who didn't seem old enough to shave let alone be a doctor. He did have an attractive wife who played the organ Sunday mornings at the Episcopal Church, so that was in his favor.

Paul eased forward and saw a clear, yellowish liquid oozing from the burns on the bottom of his father's feet. There was the smell of smoked pork in the air.

"The burns aren't too deep," the doctor told Lilly. "They're painful but he'll be all right. I'm sending him to Norfolk. They have better facilities there. He'll probably be in the hospital for a few days."

Cousin Floyd and his family arrived. Floyd stooped down. "Hey, Henry! We're real sorry. I heard the doc say you'll be okay. We're praying for you, buddy."

He hustled back to Wilma, who stood with their two sons in front of the crowd, a tight, self-satisfied look on her face.

"Don't even think about having them back in our house," Wilma sniffed. "I told you they were trouble. We're lucky they didn't burn our house down."

"Hush. People can hear."

"I don't care. Lilly took them in. They're her problem now, not ours."

Frank arrived, and after checking on Henry, walked over to Paul and Arthur.   "I'm sorry, Frank. The fire got away from me," Paul said. His eyes gleamed with tears.

Frank reached out and gathered the boys in close to him, circling his arms over their shoulders. "It's okay, guys," he said reassuringly. "An accident. Nobody's fault. Your dad's going to be fine."

It was the first time Frank had ever physically touched the boys.

The doctor hailed a fireman to bring over a car. "Get him to the hospital in Norfolk," he said, and then hurriedly packed his bag, like he couldn't wait to wash his hands of the entire matter and return home to enjoy the holiday with his family.

Lilly stared at the charred remains of the bar and restaurant. Walking over to Frank she said, "Well, there goes Mom and Dad's lifetime of sweat, worry and hard work. Poof, gone in a few minutes."

"Yeah, things like that sometimes happen, and not a damn thing any of us can do about it," he replied.

She looked into Frank's face, and there was a sadness and pain in his eyes. He was remembering a loss of his own.

Frank shook his head, and said: "Sorry for this fire, Miss Lilly. The good news is the boys are safe and it looks like their father will be okay." He patted her shoulder and turned and walked back to the boys.

A kiss makes the heart young again and wipes out the tears.

–Rupert Brooke

Chapter 12

She had no choice. She had to move the boys in with her. They'd lost everything: clothes, schoolbooks, the few toys they owned, even the new bikes. She settled them in an upstairs bedroom in her parents' two-story, Victorian-style house with a wraparound front porch.

Arthur admired the neatly made twin beds and gushed, "Gosh, Lilly. This is the first time I've had my own bed in a long time. Thanks a lot."

She gave the boy a hug and a kissed the top of his head. A warm feeling spread over her. She was becoming very fond of this young man.

Later, she filled the claw-foot white bathtub with hot water and distributed soap, shampoo, washcloths, and towels to her young guests. Arthur climbed in first. Paul said he'd use the same water when it was his turn. Lilly insisted on filling the tub with fresh water.

"Water's a thing we've got plenty of," she assured him.

One goal Lilly had set for her guests was to fatten them up. Living on Wilma's starvation rations, both had lost a lot of weight, especially Arthur, who resembled an inmate who'd escaped a prisoner-of-war camp. She could count every rib on his skinny torso.

She helped them shop for replacement clothes. They'd be back in school in a few days. They made another trip to Norfolk to shop, and filled in their wardrobes with local rummage-sale items. Sensing their deep disappointment at losing the bikes, she promised new ones in the spring.

Fortunately, the fire proved a blessing in one respect. Lilly collected just under $7,000 in insurance money, considerably more, she estimated, than if she'd sold the properties on her own before leaving for California. With the farm economy down, people weren't paying up for anything.

While the boys were in school, she drove the station wagon three times to visit Henry at the Norfolk Hospital, where he'd been a patient for more than a week. During the visits she'd made friends with several hospital staff members and learned that Henry had been, to put it politely, a "difficult" patient.

A nurse took her aside and related how Henry had traumatized one of the hospital's high school volunteer

Candy Stripers. "She's the nicest young lady, always a beautiful and cheerful smile," the nurse said. "As a courtesy, the young girl delivered the daily newspaper to Mr. Goodwin's room and accidently bumped into one of his injured feet. Well, you wouldn't believe what happened. He called her all kinds of names, ordered her out of his room. Can you imagine a grown man doing something like that?"

The nurse crossed her arms and said. "Well, I'll tell you our head nurse set him straight, told him we'd discharge him immediately if anything like that ever happened again." Lilly kept quiet about what she'd heard from the nurse but tucked the incident away in her mind for another time.

The day of his release, she parked the station wagon in the hospital's circle drive. An attendant named Max helped Henry out of the wheelchair and into the back seat of the Chevy. Max was a decent fellow, helpful and courteous. He and Lilly had hit it off during her visits. This morning, though, Max wasn't himself. He hurried around and there was a frown on his face. Normally a talker, he was quiet today. He folded the wheelchair and stowed it in the back of the station wagon and then turned to leave.

Lilly went over to him. "Is everything okay, Max?"

"Fine," he responded, even though he didn't sound like he meant it. She looked at him in a questioning way. Max took her aside and whispered, "Sorry to say this. Everyone here is glad to see this fellow go."

Apparently, Henry's encounter with the Candy Striper was only one of several troubling incidents. Henry played the nice guy to the doctors but he'd throw tantrums at the nurses and other hospital workers who changed the dressings on his burned feet and delivered his meals. As they drove away, Henry started talking. "Whew, I'm glad to be out of that place. It was the worst—horrible food, crabby nurses, and people interrupting my sleep all night long. I tried to cut the staff some slack, but I'll tell you this, Lilly, that hospital will never get any more of my business."

Considering he hadn't paid a dime on the bill, and likely never would, Lilly found his comments over the top. Rather than make an issue of it, she changed the subject.

"What's your preference for dinner your first night back?"

"I get to choose?" he said, his eyes lighting up. "I'm partial to beef, maybe pot roast with potatoes, onions, and tomatoes, all cooked up together. Margie used to make a delicious pot roast supper like that. Oh, yeah, and lots of fresh bread and sweet butter! Man, I can taste it now."

"Do the boys like that sort of a meal? From what I've seen they avoid onions like they're poison to the tongue."

"Never heard them complain. Course their mom made all the meals."

She spent nearly two hours preparing the food. When they sat down to eat, Henry glared at Paul and taunted,

"Guess we'll never know for sure what happened to get that blaze going, will we Paul?"

Paul squirmed and Arthur clammed up, which wasn't like him at all. The boys pushed the food around on their plates, piling all the onions to one side, and finally left most of the pot roast on their plates untouched. Henry, on the other hand, ate two over-sized helpings, a half-loaf of bread, and drank nearly a quart of milk.

Lilly dismissed the boys, "Don't worry, kids. I'll take care of the dishes tonight. Get busy on your homework."

After they left, Lilly turned to Henry. "You said the boys liked this kind of meal."

"I said I liked it; don't really know what they like. Kids can be real picky. Don't worry about it."

"And what the hell was the point of bringing up the fire? Paul feels awful. You make him feel worse. If you'd hadn't laid around in bed like a lazy bum that morning instead of sending the boys for the fuel oil, that fire might not have happened. Did you ever think about that?"

Taken back by the outburst, Henry lit a cigarette, a habit he'd picked up since taking up bartending. He sucked in a deep drag and exhaled a nearly perfect smoke ring. "Yeah, you're right. I need to keep my big mouth shut."

Lilly stood and began clearing the dishes, anger welling up from deep inside. What kind of a person acts like that toward his son?

Love cannot endure indifference. It needs the oil of another's heart.

–Henry Ward Beecher

Chapter 13

While Lilly worked at the sink, Henry pivoted his wheelchair around and headed to the safety of the front room. She loaded the dishes into the soapy water, gave them a rough scrubbing, and lined them up in the dish-drying rack. She finished the pots and pans and slammed them into the metal pull-out drawer under the stove. The sound of metal-on-metal resonated throughout the house.

Climbing the stairs to her bedroom, she laid down across the bed, feeling like a fool and wondering how she'd gotten into this muddle. She was a healthy, 22-year-old, full of energy and with a tidy fortune in the bank, by her standards. If she wanted to she could leave tomorrow for California and not look back. But no, she was stuck here playing nursemaid, cook, laundress and surrogate mother to near-strangers living in her house.

Wilma had the right idea to send them packing, she thought. Henry and Paul could take care of themselves. Then there was Arthur—poor little guy. She couldn't turn that wonderful child out.

She rose and opened her hope chest, something that always made her feel better. One by one, she removed the items and smoothed out the fabrics into neat piles, arranging her trousseau in a special order that she found comforting.

The Lane chest had been a gift from her parents on her sixteenth birthday. It came with a booklet that detailed a list of items a bride-to-be should collect for her special day. Over the years, as Lilly collected each item, she carefully checked them off the list: linens, tablecloths, sheets and pillowcases, dinnerware, candlesticks and, most importantly, an all white, silky-to-the-touch nightgown with pretty little ruffles sewn along the front. She'd admired the gown in a magazine ad. It was advertised as the perfect garment for a bride's wedding night—tasteful, yet alluring. When it arrived, she lovingly placed it inside her hope chest, vowing not to wear it until her wedding night. Now, holding it close, smelling and feeling the silky fabric, she imagined the look on the face of the handsome, kind man who'd be her lifelong companion, his eyes shining with love and admiration, as she stood before him, wearing this very gown.

"Lilly. Lilly, it's me!" Arthur's voice coming from the hall interrupted her thoughts.

"Come in," Lilly called, as she began to repack the chest.

The boy opened the door a crack and peeked into the bedroom. "Dad wants to talk to you downstairs."

The front room served as a makeshift bedroom so Henry wouldn't have to climb stairs on his bandaged feet. It was close to the downstairs bathroom, which also had a bathtub. He slept on a rollaway bed that she and Paul had hauled in from the garage where it'd been stored for years under an old sheet.

"Please tell him I'll be down in a few minutes. Get ready for bed, honey, and don't forget to brush your teeth."

She found Henry in Big Ed's wingback chair, his bandaged feet propped up on the matching footstool. Her throat tightened at seeing him in her father's favorite chair.

"Lilly, please take a seat," Henry said as he motioned toward the couch across from him, like she was the guest. "I want to apologize for my bad behavior."

Henry punched up the sincerity in his voice. Lilly wasn't buying it. Here comes the snow job, she thought.

"The person you need to apologize to is your son. You must take some sick pleasure in embarrassing him. That fire wasn't his fault and you know it."

"Sorry. I can't tell you how many times I wish I could take back hurtful words. Stuff just enter my head and comes out of my mouth. I'm always in trouble because of it."

"Jeez, grow up and think before you speak. Nobody has the right to put others down."

"I'll talk to Paul in the morning, you know, smooth things out between us," Henry said, and then he switched gears. "The reason I wanted to talk is to convey my thanks for taking us into your home. I can't imagine what would have happened to the boys while I was in the hospital. You've been an angel."

Henry looked at her and something softened. He seemed genuinely sorry, contrite. Was this all bull-crap again? Without her food and shelter, this guy would be in big trouble. She should throw him out right now. Yet something held her back. Henry had a way of getting to her. She never realized how important it is for a woman to have a man show an interest in her. While far from perfect, he had this appealing part, the way he looked at her, the way he caused her to blush with pleasure, the way he could make her laugh. He saw something special in her. She felt it in the lower part of her body. He wanted her.

Okay," she said, "let's move on. For heaven's sake, use your head. Set a good example. Your boys need a father they can look up to."

The household settled into a routine. The boys attended school and Lilly did laundry, made meals, and looked after Henry. Lilly would run his bath for him, and then leave him on his own to hobble in and climb over the edge of the tub.

One morning she heard a pitiful cry coming from the bathroom.

Lilly, Lilly, can you help," Henry called. She went to the door.

"What's the matter? Did you fall?"

"No. I'm stuck in this tub. My feet are killing me. The bottom is slick. I need you to grab onto while I step out. Just throw me a bath towel and turn your head. I'll cover up."

"All right," she said cautiously. "Stay covered up." He sat in the bathtub, all wet and soapy, with his hands cupped modestly over his crotch. She noticed without clothes, he seemed to be in decent shape. His eyes watched her, an odd expression on his face, like he knew what she was thinking. She turned away.

"Take my hand," she said, handing him a large white towel. "Stand up, and I'll put an arm around your waist. Go slowly."

The towel was wrapped and tucked in around his waist as he raised his left leg to step out. His right foot slipped on the tub bottom. Lilly tightened her grip around his waist. The towel fell into the tub and they stood there, her arms around his warm, wet body, supporting him.

"Oh, shit," Henry cried out. "Sorry."

Now naked and on the dry bath rug, Lilly averted her gaze from him. Without a word she turned and left the bathroom. A wave of thoughts flashed through her mind. She couldn't shake the image of Henry's naked body.

Henry started helping out around the house, even began treating Paul with more respect. While she made supper he'd hobble into the kitchen on crutches and set the table, all the time keeping up a lively conversation. It was a pleasant time.

The easy-going Henry had returned. He was telling jokes, and she laughed and laughed, like old times. While neither brought up the bathtub incident, the encounter hung over them and both felt the tension building.

A few days later, an hour or so after the boys had gone to bed, she finished bathing and washing and drying her hair. In her bedroom, she pulled a fluffy white robe over her naked body. She heard Henry in the hallway. He had healed enough to move upstairs into her parents' former bedroom. Hearing the bathroom door click, she walked to her door and cracked it open slightly. Even as she did it, her mind kept saying don't do it. She couldn't stop herself. She retreated to the chair in front of her makeup table and mirror.

Moments later she heard Henry shuffling back toward his room. He paused before the partially opened door.

"Lilly, you in there?" he asked softly.

"Yes."

He pushed the door open wider and looked in. "Mind if I come in a minute? Want to ask you something."

"Okay," Lilly answered, as she reached up to close the top of her bathrobe. She was trembling as blood rushed to her veins.

"It's nothing, really. I thought you'd like to know the bathwater's running slow out of the tub. Probably needs a plunger. If you have one, I could work on it tomorrow."

"I'm sure there's one somewhere. Probably in the basement."

Henry was also in his robe, or rather her father's robe. He took another step and was closer. She glanced up and saw him in the mirror, standing a few feet back. He looked clean; his wet hair slicked back, and smelled wonderful, like he'd put on a masculine cologne. The thought flitted through her mind that she'd never known him to wear a fragrance. Her eyes grew wide. She felt hot all over.

"God, you look terrific," he said with some urgency.

In two steps he was standing over her. She turned and tilted her chin up and looked at him. This wasn't the man of her dreams. But she couldn't stop. Something powerful had taken hold of her, and she felt herself slipping away on a wave of feelings, both emotional and physical.

Henry bent down, touched her cheek and kissed her. Her lips parted, as his arms swept around her and he pulled her into him. A strong current rushed through her. They both stood.

"I want you," Henry murmured. "I dream about you all the time."

Later, after he'd left to go to his room, she laid alone She'd done it and she wasn't sorry. It wasn't happening again. The next day, though, after the kids left for school, they sat in the kitchen having coffee. He was telling jokes. She was laughing. When he reached over and lightly brushed her cheek with his finger, she didn't push it away. She had abandoned all self-control, surrendered her good sense to the guilty pleasure of her body. They continued making love.

"You're so beautiful, so sexy, Lilly," he'd say. "I love you, sweetheart."

"Sure, I like you, too" she offered, "Just don't get carried away." She needed Henry to know she was in this for the sex, and nothing else. "We need to keep our distance when the boys are in the house. I don't want them to know about this. So, please, watch what you're saying and doing around them. You understand?"

"Okay," he said. But I really don't see it as a big deal. I'm not ashamed of anything."

"It matters to me. It matters a lot," she replied firmly, looking him right in the eye.

One night in her parents' bedroom, Lilly lay naked along side Henry. Something—a noise, a movement—caused her to glance toward the door, which was warped and stood slightly ajar. She swore she saw a pair of eyes peering through the crack. Was it Paul or Arthur? Maybe no one. She hoped so. Only her imagination—and sense of guilt—running wild?

Next morning at breakfast, trying to act like nothing had happened, she chatted nervously about the day and reminded the boys to take their lunches. Nothing seemed out of line. Good, she thought. Surely she'd been wrong. What a relief.

At suppertime a few days later, she stood at the stove browning fried chicken in the heavy cast-iron skillet. It was Paul's favorite meal. The boys stared at the frosted cake with 13 candles that Lilly had made for Paul's birthday.

Arthur waved a finger over the two-layer chocolate cake, pretending he was about to take a finger and swipe a sample of the frosting. Paul pushed the hand away. "Don't do that! It's my birthday, not yours."

Henry wandered into the kitchen and stepped close behind Lilly, peeking around for a look at the chicken. "Hmmm. Smells delicious."

His hand slid to the bottom of her skirt, and he started lifting it up. She shoved him away.

"Goddamn it! You screwing her right here?" Paul exploded.

Lilly stiffened and her eyes widened.

"I know what you've been doing. I saw you," Paul spat out the words. "You're a whore."

"Whoa, wait just a minute," protested Henry. "Don't talk to her that way! And don't use that kind of language in this house. You're getting too damn big for your britches."

"Who's gonna stop me?" Furious and out of control, Paul stood eye-to-eye with his father, his hands balled into fists, like he was going to punch him. Then he screamed at Lilly, "What about my mom? How can you do this?"

She stood there, shivering, her face flushed. She couldn't look at the boys. There was nothing to say. Paul had seen them. He knew.

Paul broke out crying and ran out the back, slamming the door behind him.

"Go after him. This is big trouble," she said.

"Oh, hell. He'll be fine. He needs a little air. I've never seen a kid with such a bad attitude. Going to have to knock it out of him one of these days."

Faith is knowledge within the heart, beyond the reach of proof.

–Kahlil Gibran

Chapter 14

Paul crossed the driveway in the gathering darkness, his hands jammed in his pockets, his shoulders slumping. A chilling, early-spring wind yanked at the coatless shirt. He opened the door and silently shuffled across the office floor to the space heater, turning his back to Frank Bottman as he warmed his hands.

"Hungry?" Frank asked, as he waved a brown paper bag. "Still got half a sandwich and an apple. You're welcome to them."

"Nah," Paul said, keeping his back to his boss.

"Anything I can help with?"

"She's a whore!" Paul snapped, and then it came out in a rush. "She's been screwing my dad. They think they're getting away with something. I saw them in bed. I hate her, and hate him, too."

"Slow down. Who're you talking about?"

"You know, Lilly, pretty little Lilly, the one who everyone thinks is so great, including you. Just because we live in her house doesn't mean she can screw my dad. He's a patsy to fall for her act. She's got Arthur wrapped around her finger. I ain't dumb. She pretends to care for us. She's all goody-goody but what she really wants is to fool around with Dad. How can she do that to Mom?"

The news that Lilly and Henry were going at it didn't surprise Frank. Heck, they were living in the same house, and things happen. Paul was an impressionable kid, and seeing them together in bed had to be a shock. The boy had worshipped her; now he had to feel betrayed.

"Keep in mind, Paul, adults sometimes make bad choices. Doesn't mean your father has forgotten your mom. I'm sure he still loves and misses her."

Paul didn't buy it. "They're in cahoots. And they both blame me for the fire."

He doubted the boy's accusations. However, he understood why he might think that way. He also knew that as Paul got older and more experienced he'd probably see things differently.

"I can't go back there tonight," Paul pleaded. "Can I stay at the station? I'll sleep in your chair."

"No," Frank said firmly. "You need to go home."

Back at the house, Lilly finished the dinner. She mashed the potatoes and made gravy from the drippings and loaded a serving platter with chicken. Henry hadn't let Paul's outburst affect his appetite. He ate like he hadn't had a meal in a month, smacking his lips, dabbing with a paper napkin as chicken grease dribbled down his chin.

Nothing fazed this guy. Disgusted, Lilly barely touched her food, and she noticed Arthur only picked at his meal. The boy had to be concerned and confused about why his big brother had stormed out of the house.

"What's happened to Paul?" he asked. "Is he coming back?"

"He's working something out," she said.

"Are we still having cake?"

"Yes, of course, and we'll have more tomorrow when Paul's here."

Arthur helped her clean up the kitchen. Henry had offered to help. She shooed him away. Afterwards, she laid out Arthur's pajamas, helped get him ready for his bath, and spent a half hour reading him a story. When he fell asleep, she went downstairs and found Henry reading the newspaper, his feet again propped on her father's footstool. At that moment, she hated him and herself.

"Shouldn't you go find your son? It's his birthday."

Henry rustled the newspaper and turned a page. "When he's hungry, he'll come home, like boys always do."

"I warned you to keep your hands to yourself."

"Sorry."

"That's it for us."

"Oh, come on, Lilly! This is nothing, a small thing. Everything will be fine in a few days.

He reached out a hand, hoping she'd take it; she stepped back. She'd made up her mind.

"No, it's never happening again. Count on it."

She climbed the stairs and returned with the remainder of the box of condoms she'd purchased at a pharmacy in Norfolk. With a pair of scissors, she sliced each of the rubbers in half, and watched as Henry's face fell.

Looking down at the sliced-up condoms piling on the floor, she knew her escapades with her houseguest were over. She liked sex, liked it a lot, now that she'd had a taste of it. But without protection she felt certain she wouldn't go anywhere near him, even though the urges would almost be overwhelming.

It was nearly nine when Paul returned.

Lilly looked up and said, "Dinner's warm in the oven."

Ignoring her, he moved toward the kitchen.

Sighing, she picked up a basket of clean clothes and walked up the stairs.

Wherever you go, go with all your heart.

–Confucius

Chapter 15

Henry began spending afternoons at the VFW Hall, drinking beer, playing pool and keeping a low profile. Around the house, Lilly remained cool. The plans for California were still in place. They'd leave once school let out. Meantime, Lilly pushed the cook who was out of work because of the fire to purchase the burned-out lots and rebuild the restaurant.

"This town needs a family cafe, and you're the perfect person to start a new one and run it," she advised him, a beefy man with faded anchor tattoos on his forearms. He'd been a cook in the Navy, a fact he reminded Lilly of often.

She sweetened the discussion by offering a reduced price if he purchased both lots. With his Navy pension, he could well afford to make the purchase.

A week later, he stopped by the house. "It's a deal," he said as he shook her hand. "Your mother did a great job building up the business."

Lilly had worked beside her mother all of her life and justly felt she had a part in the business success. She brushed the slight aside. She and the cook settled on a price of $1,600 for both lots, and that money, along with the insurance payout, was now safely in the bank. She'd cleared her decks in Elk Point except for her mother's house. That little chore had also been laid on her.

Paul was an on-going concern. When they bumped into each other in the house, she'd try to make conversation. He'd ignore her, and when he did say something it was smart-alecky and rude. Still, she kept trying to reconcile with him. She'd bite her lip and never respond to any of the mean things he said to her. She deeply regretted having been caught in bed with his father. She kept putting herself in the boy's shoes. How would she feel if something like that happened to her?

Arthur remained a dear. It was obvious that Paul hadn't said anything to him about the bedroom incident. She appreciated that. The boy helped her clean the house from top to bottom, and they made up games as they worked, singing and laughing, even throwing water at each other as they mopped floors and washed windows.

"You're a little dynamo the way you fly around here," she said. "You'll make some young lady a very nice husband."

Arthur grimaced and then smiled. She gave his tummy a friendly tap.

Moving from room to room, childhood memories flooded her mind. It was sad to have to sort through a lifetime of personal items: toys, dolls, pictures, clothing, and then to have to discard so much. She did ship two large boxes to a holding address in Los Angeles. Everything else, except what she could fit in the back and on top of the station wagon, had to go, including her hope chest.

She approached a neighborhood mother with a 12-year-old daughter, and asked: "I was wondering if Linda would like my hope chest? It's in lovely shape. I don't have the room to take it with me. I'd like her to have it." Lilly watched the girl's eyes bulge as she opened the chest and saw what was inside. Her father helped the pre-teen carry it to their house.

She donated her wedding night silk dressing gown, along with bags of other clothes to the church for their annual rummage sale. It was time to cut all ties with Elk Point. She was an adult now and on her own. Even though Prince Charming might one day show up in Elk Point, he wouldn't find her here. Her new address would be California. Her mind raced with the feel-good yet scary thoughts of the many changes she'd have to make to fit in there.

"What's the matter?" Arthur asked as they worked together. "You're crying."

"Oh, nothing. Moving is hard, don't you think? I guess you know all about that, huh?"

"Yeah," he replied. Lilly was surprised at the depth of understanding she saw in Arthur's face, far deeper than what one might expect from a child his age.

Mr. Crowell, a local used furniture dealer, made a low-ball offer on the furniture her parents had gathered over a lifetime, including what Lilly considered some very expensive antiques. She called her mom in Phoenix for advice.

"Oh, go ahead and sell it, honey," Phyllis told her. "I don't want it and you can't take it to California. I've learned when you've made up your mind to leave a place, it's best to do it fast and clean."

After she hung up, Lilly wondered when Mom had become so relaxed and philosophical. She used to fuss and worry over everything. It must be something in that Phoenix water—or that new hubby of hers.

A week later a young couple with three children, all under five years old, made an offer on the house for the full asking price. Lilly made another call to Phoenix.

"I'll split it with you, even-steven," Phyllis said. "Elliott is loaded and I'm feeling generous. Use your share to get a good start in California, hon'. I'm so happy for you."

Spring came late to Nebraska in 1951, bringing cloudy days and dismal, bone-chilling weather into May. Even the crocuses hung back in the flowerbeds, wary of what might happen if they showed their heads. Arthur, with his inexhaustible supply of high spirits, kept Lilly going through the long days. His incessant talking drove some people to distraction. She, however, found the lad charming and engaging, and she loved the playful back-and-forth teasing that went on between them. She'd never known a child with such a tenderness of heart.

They spent hours together in the kitchen; a bowl of popcorn at the ready, poring over maps and brochures related to the cross-country trip they were about to begin. They even concocted a covert smile and special wink to use on the trip, secret language only they could recognize and use.

"It's ours alone," Lilly said, poking him gently on the shoulder. "Not even your dad needs to know."

They visited Elk Point's pubic library and took turns reading travel books to one another. She marveled at Arthur's quickness and insightful sense of humor. He'd make an observation about this or that, and she'd burst into uncontrollable laughter. In this respect he was a lot like his father.

He read like an adult, and a smart one. He had an uncanny ability to remember everything he'd read. He could quote entire paragraphs, word-for-word. Lilly never tired of testing his skill.

"You must have one of those photographic memories," she told him one day. "That's pretty special."

At a teacher conference at Elk Point Elementary, Arthur's teacher reported that he was the brightest child she'd ever had in her classroom. "He's gifted, and with the proper training, he's going to do something very special one day."

Paul was always on her mind. She dreaded the idea of traveling 2,000 miles trapped in a car with a sullen, hostile teenager. She and Arthur's "Great Adventure Across America" would be a disaster with him constantly at them. She remained hopeful that he'd soften toward her, even as the calendar marched steadily ahead to the departure date.

As for Henry, he also had become worrisome. He wouldn't get moving. It was like he was stuck, and couldn't make a decision. She wondered: Was he still pouting over her no-sex policy? Was he thinking he'd be better off taking Arthur and Paul and traveling to California without her?

She nagged him to call his buddy in California and alert his friend that he and the boys would soon be on their way to Los Angeles. She wanted confirmation that Zeke was still willing to take them in to his house. Henry came up with all kinds of excuses to put off making the call, which made her suspicious. "Call him," Lilly kept saying. "We're leaving in 10 days."

Finally, she stood at his elbow as he picked up the phone.

"I don't have his number," Henry said, sounding a little put out. "I'll have to call his mother in Belleview."

"Well, quit dragging your feet and call her." She was determined to settle things once and for all.

The mother provided the number and even asked Henry to tell her son to call her. Lilly noticed Henry's hand shook as he connected with the long-distance operator and gave the number in California.

"Hey, buddy!" Henry yelled into the heavy black telephone receiver. "This is Henry, Henry Goodwin."

Lilly put a finger to her lips, signaling for him to lower his voice. While it was a long-distance call, he didn't have to scream. Zeke was yelling, too, and Lilly heard every word of the two-way conversation.

"You remember the summer before last at the tavern in Belleview?"

"I guess so," his high school friend replied.

"You said it'd be smart to pack up and move out there, what with all the jobs in the airplane industry opening up. I'm thinking about doing that in a couple of weeks."

"Yep, there are jobs here. A fellow has to work hard, though. Otherwise they'll send him packing."

They chatted about the weather and Belleview, and Henry mentioned he'd just talked to his mother in Belleview. "She sounds fine. Wants you to call her." Henry still yelled.

"Yeah, I need to do that. Hey, my wife's calling for supper. I gotta go. Ring me up when you get out here. Maybe we'll get together for a beer."

"Yeah, you bet. I appreciate this, and I'll give you a call."

He hung up and glanced at Lilly. He wore a shame-faced look. His high school buddy had brushed him off like yesterday's dust.

Now she had no choice. It was up to her to get them all to California.

A man is relieved...when he puts his heart into his work.

–Ralph Waldo Emerson

Chapter 16

"**A**s I see it, they're your family," Frank told Paul as they stood talking in the gas station office. "In my book, you go where they go."

Much as the thought repelled him, Paul had to face the possibility he'd soon be leaving his job at Bottman's and traveling to California in Lilly's car.

"Yeah, but I've been thinking. Maybe I could stay here and work at the station this summer. I can move the junk out of the back room and set up a cot."

"Now Paul…" Frank began.

"You know I'm a good worker," Paul persisted. "I'll hop a bus this fall and join them out there before school starts. By then, Dad will have thrown Lilly out. I'm sure of it. Can I stay here, please?"

Frank hesitated, "I can use the help. Still I'm wondering if this is the best thing. What would your old man say?"

Paul's lip curled. "He'd celebrate—one less kid to worry about."

"Let me run this by Clara. I'm not sure how she'll feel about this."

That evening at the dinner table Frank pushed aside his meat and potatoes. He wasn't that hungry. He told Clara about Paul.

Her forehead furrowed in worry as she searched her husband's eyes. "I can't imagine why a boy would want to split off from his family."

"It's just for the summer while his dad and little brother get settled in California," Frank offered, nothing in his voice suggesting he wanted the boy to stay.

"I heard Lilly's going, too."

"Yeah, with Paul there'd be four in the car, plus all their stuff. Paul's a big kid. He'll take up almost a full seat himself."

Frank hadn't told Clara about the sex thing involving the boy's father and Lilly Swenson. He figured she knew, though. She was linked in pretty tight to Elk Point's grapevine. Heck, she even knew how many Nehi Grapes he drank every afternoon.

Clara's face softened. "I think it's wonderful how you've gone to bat for that boy, but I won't have Paul sleeping in a dirty gas station all summer."

Frank's shoulders visibly slumped. "Of course, you're right, dear."

"We have a perfectly nice empty bedroom in our house. And he'll go to church every Sunday while he's under our roof. This town's full of hooligans and trouble-makers. The minister will keep him on a right path."

Frank smiled and pulled the dinner plate in close. His appetite was back. He could hardly contain himself that his wife had agreed to allow Paul to live with them for the summer. He had feelings for the kid, no question about that. Sometimes he'd watch Paul and a flood of memories of his son John would wash over him. The two could have been brothers. They were that much alike.

When he told Paul about the arrangement, the boy winced. He didn't like anyone dictating what he did, especially when it came to attending church. After thinking about it, though, he decided to go along with whatever Clara asked. He'd do anything to keep from going to California with Lilly.

"We'll need a signed note from your dad in case you get sick or hurt," Frank said. "His signature gives us permission to have you treated by a doctor or hospital. It's a legal thing."

That evening, Paul announced his plans at suppertime.

"Sure this is what you want?" Henry asked.

His father could barely conceal his excitement.

Henry continued, "Frank and his wife are good folks, and they'll take care of you. It's gotta be your decision, though."

"I'm the one who suggested it to Frank," Paul said, glaring at Lilly. "It's my idea to stay here. Frank says there's always a job here for me."

Henry went on to paint a rosy picture about how this plan would probably be in all of their best interests. "You'll make some money, and I'm sure Frank can use your help. It'll give us more room in the station wagon. I'll send you a bus ticket to join us in the fall."

Arthur burst out crying. "We can't leave without Paul. We stick together! That's what Mom always said."

Paul put his arm over his brother's shoulders. "It's just for the summer. It'll be fine."

Arthur continued to cry, so Lilly took him under her wing and guided him out of the room.

The next day Henry walked to the gas station and signed and dated a form that allowed Frank and Clara to make medical decisions. "Please extend my regards to Clara," Henry said. "And if the boy gives you any trouble, call me right away."

The night before the family's departure, Lilly packed two bags for Paul. Henry carried them out to the front porch where he gave Paul 20 dollars, money he'd borrowed from Lilly.

"Now, son, you do whatever Frank and Clara say. No trouble, you understand? We'll write as soon as we have a permanent address and a telephone number."

Henry shook his oldest son's hand and pulled him in for a tight hug. Paul stood still, his arms hanging from his sides. When Henry returned to the house, Lilly noticed the man's eyes glistened.

Arthur rushed past his father out onto the porch. He wrapped his arms around Paul's knees. Paul bent on one knee and stroked his little brother's hair. He talked quietly until Arthur nodded and returned to the house, sniffing and wiping his nose on his sleeve.

She watched Paul pick up his bags and walk down the street. It was a sad thing separating a kid from his family, she thought. But he knows the score. He can take care of himself. He'll be fine. They'd see him again in the fall.

The way is not in the sky. The way is in the heart.

–Buddha

Chapter 17

"**A**rthur!" Lilly stood over the boy's bed and gently shook his shoulder. "Wake up, bright eyes. Time to go."

She'd worked hard to prepare for this day. Volunteers from the church would arrive at the house Monday to clean out all the personal items left behind: clothing, bedding, kitchenware, tools, much of which was already boxed up and ready. The used-furniture guy arrives on Tuesday. She'd arranged to have the utilities turned off late next week, and a trusted neighbor would keep a close eye on the place once they'd driven away. The family who'd purchased the house planned to move in on the first of July.

Arthur stretched and shook himself awake. Then, realizing that this was the special day, his face brightened and he gave Lilly a huge smile. He leaped from the bed and pulled on the clothes he'd carefully laid out the night before.

"This is it!" he yelled, prancing around the room. "California, here we come!"

Downstairs at the kitchen table, Henry finished his toast, cereal, and coffee and rubbed the crumbs from around his mouth with the back of his hand.

"I'm ready," he declared. "Let's go. I'll drive."

Arthur's non-stop chatter infected Lilly with excitement. Her heart pounded in her chest. They were finally on their way, leaving Elk Point for the Promised Land. The music and lyrics of Bobbie Troup's traveling song ran through her head. She couldn't count the number of times—it must have been in the hundreds—she'd stood at the kitchen sink at the restaurant and sang along with Nat King Cole's version of the catchy tune blaring from the radio:

> *If you ever plan to motor west*
> *Take my way that's the highway that's the best*
> *Get your kicks on Route 66.*

She'd read that Route 66, the "mother road" made famous during the mass migration of people from the southern Great Plains during the drought in the 1930s, began in Chicago and uncoiled 2,400 miles through eight states to the shores of the Pacific Ocean at Santa Monica. Now, she, Lilly Swenson, who'd never traveled more than 50 miles from home until her recent visit to Phoenix, would travel that famous road. What a kick.

The night before, she dreamed she was in a car, the windows open and the hot desert air blowing her thick, blond hair away from her face. Ahead stretched the blue sky over a broad desert vista dotted with red, blue, yellow and violet wild flowers, dancing forward in the breeze, as if urging her onward. Unlike many of her childhood dreams, the ones that had left her wrung out and anxious, Lilly woke up with a happy heart and the sure conviction that she was meant to go to California.

In the station wagon's front seat, Arthur sat in the middle while Henry drove and she and Arthur tracked the route on the map as they traversed the Lincoln Highway. The first night they stayed in motel just west of Omaha. They traveled west along the Platte River Valley the next day and shared a lively travelogue about the sights and history of the places they passed. A memorable stop was at Buffalo Bill's ranch in North Platte, where they saw their first real-life buffalo, in fact a huge number of the shaggy beasts, one of the largest herds in the United States. Once into Wyoming, the Rocky Mountains loomed large, standing in stark drama as a jagged dark line on the horizon.

As they approached closer, Lilly noted how the purple snow-capped mountains appeared cool and serene against the sky, gracing the scene before them like cardboard cutouts. At the peaks and in the dark shadows of the mountain crevasses, snow spilled down like vanilla frosting lapping over the edges of a chocolate cake.

"Quite a sight," Henry remarked. "I've seen pictures. The real thing tops them all!"

He seemed equally thrilled to be on the road. They turned south at Cheyenne, drove right through the middle of Denver and stopped at a motel south of the city. Once again, Lilly paid for two rooms, one for her and the other for Henry and Arthur. The next day, they veered west onto U.S. Highway 50 near Colorado Springs for a visit to the Royal Gorge. Crossing into New Mexico, the station wagon merged onto Route 66. Billboards announced the state capitol of Albuquerque, 35 miles ahead. Once through the dusty, Spanish-style city of tan, sun-bleached adobe homes and buildings, traffic thinned. Henry punched the accelerator, hoping to reach Gallup before dark. Whenever they passed a Route 66 sign, Arthur would burst into song and Lilly and Henry would join in:

> *If you ever plan to motor west*
> *Take my way that's the highway that's the best*
> *Get your kicks on Route 66.*

Then they'd laugh and hoot.

"In the desert now, a land of vast skies and striking sunsets, tumbleweeds danced across the highway, sometimes in such great numbers Henry couldn't dodge them all. Every hour or so he'd pull over, climb under the car and yank out the Russian thistle that piled up under the vehicle's undercarriage.

After one such cleanup, Henry brushed the dust from his pants as he slid back into the driver's seat. "Well, that's something we don't experience in Nebraska," he observed.

"Wow, an ocean of sand. Does it ever end?" Arthur said in awe of the expansive, table-smooth desert that stretched beyond the eye.

"No cornfields here," his father remarked. "Only scrub grass, cactus, lizards, snakes, and plenty of sand. Looks like the biggest sandbox in the world!"

"Hey, Arthur," Lilly said. "Bet you didn't know camels once roamed this part of the country."

"Can't be! Camels? You mean with real humps on their backs?"

"Yep. One of those library books we borrowed said the U.S. Army brought camels here to the Southwest in mid-1800s to use as pack animals. Regrettably, the camels were too stubborn or, as some said, too dumb to be trained, and it frustrated the soldiers to the point they turned them loose to wander wild in the desert. Keep your eyes peeled. We might see one roaming these parts."

He tried to keep watch but the flat desert landscape eventually lulled him to sleep. Lilly's eyelids grew heavy as well. She remembered reading somewhere how sailors on long sea voyages sometimes fell into a stupors after leaning for hours at the ship's rail, with no land in sight in any direction. Now, fighting to stay awake, she understood how a lack of a point of reference could cause a person to fall into a trance and maybe drive off the highway and into a ditch. She looked over at Henry. He seemed all right.

She liked it that Henry did all of the driving. She could enjoy the passing scenes and discuss things with Arthur. As they continued west, the desert changed. Through the passenger window, Lilly saw jagged rock formations, tall, wide-limbed saguaro cactus and blooming desert flowers. Spotted along the highway were wide, dusty pull-offs where Hopi and Navajo Indians had erected teepees, with tables out front, overflowing with Indian-made pottery, handmade blankets, beaded turquoise jewelry and stone arrowheads. Signs advertised ice-cold Cokes. Indian children gathered along the edge of the road, waving and yelling at passing cars, urging the drivers to pull over and shop.

"I want my picture taken with an Indian chief," Arthur begged. "I'll send it to Paul. He'll go nuts."

"Okay," Henry said. "Make it quick."

Lilly gave Arthur a quarter and he ran up and down the line of squaws and Indian men trying to choose the right subject for the perfect photograph.

"Lilly! Bring the camera!" Arthur yelled. "This is the one."

Arthur trembled as he stood alongside an old Indian dressed in leather britches and a light brown vest decorated with colorful line-art drawings of elk, deer, snakes, birds, and horses. The feathered headdress trailed from the top of his head down his back until it nearly touched the ground.

Looking through the camera lens, Lilly saw a fierce Indian warrior. One of his hands rested on a sharp, stone-headed tomahawk hanging from his belt. How many scalps had he taken with that!

Lilly called out to Arthur to smile. He stuck out his tongue. A split second before she took the picture, he sucked in his tongue and put on a look as stern as the chief's. Fighting back giggles, Lilly nearly dropped the camera. The sight of the boy mimicking the Indian was outrageous!

That night they found a motel near the Grand Canyon.

The next morning, gathered at the canyon's edge, they gazed in wonder into what a travel brochure described as "one of nature's most spectacular scenes, carved by the mighty Colorado River over a period of 17 million years, and stretching for 277 miles, 18 miles at its widest point and more than a mile deep in places."

"That's a helluva big ditch!" said Henry.

"It certainly is," added Lilly. "It feels like we've been dropped into a different world, a place like nothing we've ever seen before or could ever have imagined."

She bought tickets for mule rides to the bottom. Henry refused to go down.

"Are you chicken, Dad?" Arthur asked.

"The only way I'm going is if I'm pushed. I'm not stupid."

As Lilly and Arthur bounced on the mules down the narrow, twisting path to the canyon floor, the lead wrangler told tall western tales about the canyon. They made camp along the Colorado River, at a place called Bright Angel Trail where Arthur removed his shoes and dangled his bare feet in the river's icy, snow-fed water.

Following a cowboy lunch of beans and ham sandwiches, he asked the wrangler how the trail got its name.

"Well, there're several stories going around," the gnarled horseman answered in a distinct western drawl. "The one I put most stock in has it that Bright Angel Trail was named in 1869 by an explorer fellow named Major John Wesley Powell, a one-armed, honest-to-god Civil War hero.

"The U.S. Government hired the major to make a map of the Grand Canyon. With 10 men and 4 boats, Powell embarked on the Green River in Wyoming. Three months and hundreds of miles later, the crew finally arrived right here at this spot in the canyon.

"It was a plumb awful trip. They ran out of food, even lost one of the boats and a couple of the men died. The worst thing was they almost all died of thirst. They couldn't drink the river water because of the runoff that turned the river muddy red. In a letter to his wife in Iowa, one of the explorers described the water as 'too thick to drink and too thin to plow,' or at least that's the story that's been told."

"Wow," said Arthur, his imagination fired up.

"When the major and his boys arrived right at this spot we're sittin' on, the river was running clean and fresh just like it is now. They drank their fill and agreed this place should forever be known as Bright Angel Trail because an angel must have brought them safely here.

"Now that's the story most people put stock in, but I gotta tell you I've heard other stories, too, so I'm not certain what's the gospel truth," the wrangler said.

"Who needs other stories?" Arthur piped up. "I like yours best!"

With all the side trips and tourist stops, the travelers spent nearly two weeks on the road before finally driving into the City of Los Angeles. It was, of course, a sunny day.

Faith means living with uncertainty...letting your heart guide you like a lantern in the dark.

–Dan Millman

Chapter 18

Lilly, with Henry and Arthur on her heels, rented a small house a couple blocks off of Sunset Boulevard, one of L.A.'s busiest and longest thoroughfares. At $45 a month, the rental seemed expensive by Elk Point standards, but the bungalow was clean and well-furnished, right down to dishes, pots and pans. Lilly took one of the small bedrooms while Henry and Arthur shared the other. She'd delay looking for a job for at least a couple of weeks in order to help Arthur get settled in the new neighborhood. Besides, she had no idea what kind of job to look for, other than she knew it wouldn't be tending bar or waiting on tables.

Soon after they arrived, Henry called Zeke. The former Nebraskan didn't even have time to meet him for a beer. At Lilly's urging, Henry applied and was hired on at the Lockheed aircraft factory to work on the fuselages of fighter planes. A nearby bus connection took him to and from the job. From day one, all he did was bitch about the dirt and noise and the "wetbacks, niggers, and Southern white trash" working along side of him.

"Jesus Christ!" he lamented at the supper table for the third evening in a row. "I'm at that bus stop in the dark and work all day inside that windowless factory and don't see the sun till I get back on that bus at suppertime. They make me work 10-hour-days, and the factory floor is a hellhole. Nobody speaks a language I understand. It's all gibberish. What the hell are they doing in our country anyway?"

"Oh, come on, Henry! Give it a chance," Lilly said, incredulous that he wanted to quit after less than a week on the job.

"Easy for you to say, sittin' around here all day long. I've got responsibilities, including taking care of you and Arthur."

"What? Whoa, just one minute, mister! I'm paying for everything and taking care of the house and Arthur. Exactly what is it that you do?"

There was a soft knock at the door. Henry took advantage of the interruption to huff out of the room.

A meek voice called through the screen door. "Hello! Hello in there? I have something for you."

A tiny, dark-skinned woman stood on the porch holding a pan, her black hair framing a beautiful, friendly face.

Lilly opened the door. "Hi. Won't you please come in?"

"I wanted to give you time to get settled before I stopped by," said the woman, who handed her a pan of tamales, ready for the oven. "I'm your next-door neighbor, Maria Garcia. I live over there."

She pointed to a house that looked a lot like the one Lilly was renting. In fact, all the houses on the block looked alike: white, two-bedroom bungalows, on cement slabs, with small front porches, blue shutters, matching shingles, tiny front and larger back yards, with dried-out patches of grass mixed in among the green weeds. The sound of children's voices was everywhere.

Lilly introduced herself and Arthur and the two women drank coffee and talked for more than an hour.

"My husband brought me and the kids here from Texas," Maria said. "He works at the Lockheed aircraft factory. It's a wonderful job. He likes it here so much better than Texas. He gets higher pay."

What a contrast, Lilly thought. She guessed Maria's husband took the same bus as Henry, only instead of being bitter and angry, he wore a smile and was grateful for the job.

Maria had three children: Sophia, 13; Carlos, 8; and Juanita, 3. She turned to Arthur in a reassuring way, "I'll ask my kids to introduce you around. There's lots of nice kids in the neighborhood, lots of fun!"

"Wow, that'd be great," Arthur replied.

Maria, who seemed to be in her early thirties, smiled shyly and continued, "Please. I don't want to, how do you say it, be nosey, but what is your husband's name?"

Lilly hesitated. She didn't want to shock her new neighbor with their unconventional living arrangements. Still, it was best to be up front right from the start. "Uh, well, to be honest, Henry's not my husband. He's Arthur's father. I'm renting this house and Henry and Arthur share one of the bedrooms while I have the other. I'm helping till his father gets on his feet, saves some money, you know, so he can find a place of his own. His full name is Henry Goodwin."

"Oh, yes, I see. That is very kind of you."

Before Maria departed, she invited Lilly to the weekly coffee attended by the neighborhood mothers and other ladies. "It's tomorrow morning at 9:30 at my house. I hope to see you there. I have to go home now to clean." She turned her hands, palms up, as if asking for understanding. "Everything is such a mess."

Five minutes later Maria's boy, Carlos, was at the door, asking if Arthur could come out and play. Arthur ran all afternoon and didn't return until suppertime, sunburned and talking non-stop about his new friends.

"That's wonderful!" Lilly said. "Feel free to invite them over any time."

Lilly rummaged in her new closet to find something appropriate to wear to the coffee get-together the next day.

There were four dresses on hangers that she'd brought with her. All were too big. Until she could do some shopping, she'd have to wear them for now.

It was exciting making new friends.

Over the next several days, with time on her hands, she began taking long walks every morning and evening. She watched what she ate and as a consequence dropped more pounds. Even after she went to work, she vowed to keep up the exercise and diet regimen.

With Maria willing to keep an eye on Arthur during the day, she began scanning the employment classified ads in local newspapers. One item that caught her eye was sponsored by a business school called the California Institute of Business, or CIB. The school offered a concentrated secretarial program with the promise to help students find good-paying jobs after graduation. That afternoon she called and scheduled an appointment.

In preparation for the school visit, she visited a beauty salon down the street that had been recommended by the ladies she'd met at the neighborhood coffee. She was met at the door by a puppy-dog friendly beautician who excitedly exclaimed, "Everyone in this city wears their hair shorter, except for a very few of the Hollywood starlets. Short hair is all the rage with the working crowd. It's so easy to care of. Want to try it?" she asked, taking Lilly by the arm and reaching up to feel her long blond hair.

Lilly had worn her hair long since junior high. With some trepidation, she accepted the girl's recommendation and took a seat. Pleased with the results, she handed her new beautician a dollar tip, and made a second appointment with her. She also took the young gal's recommendation and had her nails done professionally at the shop—a first for her. Visiting Bontel's Department store, she counted out more than half a month's rent, nearly $30, for a classy outfit, consisting of a dark navy blue, below-the-knee wool skirt and an all-white, long-sleeved blouse with ruffles in front and buttons up to the neckline. On her walk to her appointment at the business school, she couldn't help admiring her reflection in the storefront windows. Looking good, she thought, like those models in the newspaper ads, the young ladies who were all decked out in what was judged the season's most fashionable office wear. With her new look, she could pass for any one those misses; now all she needed was a job.

Offering her hand to the admissions lady, she said, "Hello, I'm Lilly Swenson."

Mrs. Lewis was a handsome if somewhat severe-looking woman in her forties, with wide hips and graying hair, which she wore in a tight bun.

She got straight to the point. "Miss Swenson, first we need a copy of your high school diploma. Our tuition is $28 a week, or $250, if paid in total in advance for the 10-week program. Attend classes faithfully, and do satisfactory work, and you'll receive a certificate from our school, which I believe you will find quite valuable in your career."

Lilly handed over her diploma and Mrs. Lewis pushed a stack of documents and information pamphlets across the desk.

"We're very particular at this school," she said, as she gave Lilly a frank once over. "We enroll only serious young women who will reflect well on our school. Will you make us proud?"

Smiling brightly, even though she considered this woman a tad over the top, Lilly nodded and signed the formal admission documents. She wrote the $250 check with a certain sense of satisfaction that she had the means to take care of herself. She walked out of the gleaming white two-story brick building into the bold California sunshine, excited and eager to begin her new life.

Arthur hugged her and did a little jig upon hearing Lilly's good news. He was especially pleased to learn Maria would watch out for him while she attended classes. He loved Maria; in fact he loved the entire Garcia family. They were a happy bunch, full of laughter and fun. He'd giggle when he heard them mashing Spanish words with English.

"I'm learning Spanish," he told Lilly with pride in his voice. "The kids help me."

It was too bad that Lilly and Arthur's good spirits didn't spill over into Henry's world. As the three of them sat down at the table for supper, Arthur went on and on about Lilly's plan to go back to school.

"Yeah, that's great for you," Henry snapped, as he stabbed his fork at the food on the plate. "You'll be attending a nice clean school, learning new things, while I'm stuck in that hellhole at Lockheed."

Lilly noticed Arthur had finished his plate and suggested he go outside and play. He didn't need to see his father throwing a fit.

"Pretty soon you'll get all fancied up and go to work in a nice office. Meantime I'm still be sweating my balls off in that crappy factory. That's okay though—you're the one with the big wad of cash in the bank, right?"

Lilly slammed her fork on the table. "Henry! Grow up." She was mad enough to spit.

He swallowed the last bite on his plate and, puffed up with defiance, stood and declared: "I'm going out."

Good riddance, she thought. She knew he'd head to Kelsey's Bar & Grill, a popular neighborhood watering hole three blocks down the street. That's fine. Just so he left the house and left she and Arthur in peace.

* * * * *

At Kelsey's, Henry took a drink from his bottle of beer and checked out the crowd. The piano player banged out show tunes as he tired to compete with the sound of dozens of noisy conversations. Everyone was either laughing or shouting, many doing both. The men wore business suits and ties; the women were done up in long dresses and high heels, like they'd come directly from the office. A few of the ladies had on two-piece suits. Almost all of the men and women appeared to fall somewhere between

20 and 30 years old. They were tanned and fit, and on the make.

The men bragged about their great jobs, fancy cars, big paychecks, and sun-filled weekends on the beach. Flirting and smiling, the women pressed in close with any man who'd pay the slightest attention. What a classy, fun-loving bunch of blond and fair-skinned Californians these were, Henry thought. I belong here! I'm one of them. God damn it, they just don't know it yet.

In the dew of little things the heart finds its morning.

–Kahlil Gibran

Chapter 19

Paul had been after Frank for permission to work alone and close the station a couple nights a week.

"Come on. I'm here anyway," Paul coaxed. "There's no reason for you to drive down here at nine o'clock at night to lock up. Don't you trust me with the keys?"

Frank unclipped his ring of keys from his belt loop and tossed them on his desk. "Now that I think about it, I'd just as soon be in bed by nine. You'll close Tuesday and Thursday nights on a trial basis. Keep in mind; Clara wants you home for supper most nights. She worries you're not eating right."

The first evening Paul closed, he shut down the pumps and turned off the lights at exactly 9:01 p.m. Twisting the key in the lock, he heard the satisfying click as the bolt slid solidly into place. Then he ambled down the middle of empty Main Street toward Frank and Clara's, taking his sweet time. The wide-open night sky blazed with starlight, deep and intense. The heavens glittered like tinsel on a Christmas tree. To Paul, the beauty of what he saw overhead was like seeing the universe with new eyes. A while back he'd read a magazine story that reported a flying saucer with space aliens had crashed a couple of years earlier in the desert near Roswell, New Mexico. It was said the Federal government hushed up the whole deal. Still, local authorities continued to claim they'd found bodies of weird-looking creatures near the crash site. With his eyes glued to the sky, Paul thought it was fun to think about such things.

Ever since he'd been left in Elk Point, a huge weight had lifted from his shoulders. No annoying little brother, no Lilly, and no dad. Perfect!

Staying with Frank and Clara had been great, even if he did have to attend church on Sundays. Frank didn't go to church and he wouldn't say why. Chuck in the garage told him the boss hadn't attended regular services in years, ever since his son John was killed during the war.

One Sunday morning as he and Clara walked home from church she hooked her arm in his like he was a grownup and asked him to give the church youth group a try. She'd asked before and he'd begged off.

"They're a terrific bunch and have loads of fun," Clara said. "It's a chance to make friends, meet kids your own age. Please try it, just once, for me."

Paul couldn't dodge the request this time. She'd been so nice.

"Okay. I'll try it, but if it doesn't work out...."

She gave his arm a squeeze and Paul shook his head. He wondered what he'd gotten himself into.

The minister met him at the door wearing casual slacks and an open-collared shirt. Paul was used to seeing the man in a formal black robe, standing in the pulpit, delivering booming sermons on teachings from the Bible. Now, he seemed younger, relaxed, more down to earth, like a regular person.

The Reverend Miller shook his hand and smiled, "Clara said you might drop by. Follow me up these stairs and I'll show the youth meeting room. Nice evening, isn't it?"

"Guess so," Paul mumbled, feeling shy and uncomfortable.

He was introduced to Annie Hemphill, the 14-year-old current leader of the Sunday-night junior high group.

"Mind introducing him around, Annie?"

"Sure!" she said, offering Paul a bright smile and giving him a firm, enthusiastic handshake.

Annie made a big impression on him. She wasn't the cutest girl on the block but he liked her grown-up style, which he considered rare for an eighth-grader. She didn't seem silly and giggly like a lot of the girls he'd seen in the school hallways.

Annie kept the meeting moving, minimizing the talking out of turn and the horseplay. She asked for volunteers to visit homes of elderly church members.

"We rake leaves, clean up gardens, that sort of thing," she said, looking into Paul's eyes.

After at least a full minute of no one stepping forward, three kids raised their hands, two girls and a shy boy, the youngest one in the group.

"We're also going to need a skit for the Christmas program," the leader reminded everyone. "We can talk about that next week."

At the end of the meeting, everyone formed a circle and joined hands. Annie led the closing prayer, nothing too heavy, just a heartfelt "Thanks to God for the wonderful church and the opportunity for fellowship." She mentioned Paul's name specifically, saying how happy they were he had visited.

Annie walked him out to the front door steps. He stuck his hands in his pockets and kicked a pebble as she locked the church door.

"My Dad's waiting right over there," she said, motioning toward a dark sedan with a man in the driver's seat. "I hope we'll see you next week, same time, same place."

"Yeah, maybe," he replied.

When the car drove off, Paul kicked himself.

Yeah, maybe? Was that best he could do? How ditsy was that! Annie had the effect of making him feel like a little kid. He was nearly six-feet tall now, with broad shoulders and muscles bulging under his shirt. He'd never thought much about girls. But she seemed different.

Later, lying in bed, he couldn't get the girl out of his head. She was tall, which pleased him, and had developed a woman's figure. She played softball in the summer and girls' basketball in the winter. So she was an athlete, like him. There was something about her, something in her eyes, in the way she talked, her confidence. She looked every person right in the eye, including him, which made him feel special. Had she ever kissed a boy? She'd be in ninth grade in the fall, a grade ahead of him. Maybe she'd let him kiss her.

Before falling asleep, Paul decided he'd attend the next meeting. He was sorry it was a whole week off.

On the nightstand next to his bed was a stack of travel postcards and letters, including an impressive photo of Arthur with an Indian chief. His brother had written about their terrific trip west and how California was such a great place. He'd already made lots of new friends. He wrote that Lilly was doing great. He never once mentioned their father. At first Paul thought the omission was unusual but he later decided it probably wasn't so strange after all.

There were two letters in the stack from his father. The first had arrived shortly after they'd reached Los Angeles. It contained their new address and a telephone number that Paul could use in an emergency.

The second had arrived yesterday. Dad wrote that he had a job in an airplane factory that he hated. He hoped to find a different job. The end of the letter contained the real news:

Paul. Things are tougher here than I thought. Everything is taking longer than I planned. I know I promised I'd bring you out here before school starts. Now I'm hoping you can stay with the Bottmans a while longer. Frank and Clara are great people. You couldn't be in a better place.

A lot of times, I'd give anything to be back behind the bar in Elk Point. I didn't know how well off I had it. Things will start looking up here. I'll be sending for you. You can count it.

Love, Dad.

The next morning Paul put the second letter in his back pocket and carried it around for two days. He liked Elk Point just fine. He didn't want to leave. But it still hurt that Dad didn't care enough to send for him. Was he still with Lilly? Was he trying to get rid of her or were they shacked up together? Is that why he didn't want him out there?

Wednesday morning, Paul walked into Frank's office and asked if he could stay longer in Elk Point. "Dad says he's having trouble finding a job he likes. He's short on money and says his job stinks and that it might be first of the year or even longer before he can send me a bus ticket. He can't be specific on a date right now."

"Hmmm," Frank said. "Sounds like it's not the walk in the park he thought it'd be in California."

"Yeah, surprise, surprise," Paul said sarcastically. "I don't know what his problem is. It pisses me off that he always breaks his promises. What the hell, I never really expect much from him. If I can stay here, Frank, that'll be great. If not, I'll have to look around for another job."

"You don't have to do that. You're always welcome here. Clara's taken a shine to you, and as far I'm concerned, you're an all-right fellow, part of our family."

Frank took off his cap and took a swig of his first Nehi Grape of the day. "Listen, buddy. Don't be too hard on your father. When he gets on his feet, he'll send for you."

Glancing up at his boss, Paul's legs began shaking. His feelings were getting away from him. He couldn't find the words to say what he felt about this man—finally he'd found someone he could trust.

"Thanks, Frank," he said, getting words out. "I appreciate it."

"I know you do, son. Now get back to work."

Thursday night after closing the station, Paul sat in Frank's worn and cracked black leather office chair. There was enough illumination from the streetlight coming in the window that he could re-read his father's letter. When he finished, he struck a match, held the letter at arm's length, and set it ablaze, then dropped it into the oversized ashtray on the desktop. The letter flared, twisted and crumbled into ashes.

His heart was like a sensitive plant that opens... in the sunshine.

–Anne Bronte

Chapter 20

You're going to be eight years old. Let's have a party, a big one!" Lilly said over breakfast. "Invite all the neighborhood kids. I'll bake a cake and Maria says she'll help."

"Wow! Super!" Arthur exclaimed. "Wait till I tell everyone. They'll go bananas."

Her business classes would be over in two weeks. Meantime, Henry continued to denounce the "goddamn unfairness of my job" every chance he had.

"Keep your foul mouth to yourself," Lilly cautioned.

He continued to pay the weekly six dollars Maria charged to watch his son while he worked and Lilly attended classes, even though he grumbled almost daily about the cost. Lilly had had enough. She threatened to hand over the babysitting responsibilities to him if he said another word, so he shut up. Henry had become so unpleasant to have around that she and Arthur always breathed a sigh of relief when the grouch headed for Kelsey's after supper. He usually didn't return until after nine o'clock. By then, Arthur had gone to bed.

The bond between Lilly and Arthur grew ever stronger. A couple times he'd slip and call her mom. While she had growing feelings for the boy, she sure as heck wasn't his mother, not by any stretch. Still, the thought that Henry one day might take him away scared her to death. The more she saw, the more convinced she was that this man had no idea how to be a real father.

Every couple of weeks the postman delivered a letter from Paul. Arthur always asked her to sit beside him while he read the letters "in case I need help with a word," which, of course, he never did.

Paul's M.O. was to scrawl a few words on a scrap of paper and include a tidbit of local news, a comment about work, the weather, and assurance that he was doing fine.

Arthur loved the letters, no matter how skimpy and banal the contents. It kept the connection going. For her part, she scrutinized his every word, hoping to find a clue that he'd softened toward her. She never found one.

"Let's invite Paul to my party," Arthur said. "He can meet all of my new friends. It's almost time for school to start anyway. He'll come early if we ask him."

Lilly had misgivings. A few days earlier she asked Henry when he planned to bring Paul to Los Angeles. He nearly bit her head off. "Mind your own damn business," he stated. Then he clammed up.

Henry's outburst caused her to wonder what he was trying to hide.

Arthur pestered her to where she decided there'd be no harm in helping him prepare a letter of invitation to his brother in Elk Point.

Dear Paul:

As you know, my birthday is August 17th. We're having a huge party to celebrate! Please, please come! I'm inviting Eddie, Mike, Sally, Juanita, Carlos, Sophia, and a bunch of other kids.

Dad's going to be here, although he says he can't stay for the whole thing 'cause he's so busy. We're having chocolate cake and chocolate ice cream, plus Kool-Aid — as much as anyone wants!

My friend Maria is going to tie a piñata in a tree so we can whack it till it breaks. A piñata is big paper donkey filled with candy. When it comes apart, all the candy flies out and we kids rush in and pick it up. It's loads of fun.

I sure miss you, Paul. I hope to see you at my birthday party.

A week later, Paul sent a funny birthday card to his brother with a note scribbled inside, and a crisp new dollar bill as a present. He wrote:

Sorry I can't be there. I'm real busy at work. Have a wonderful birthday. I'll be enrolling in school here in Elk Point this fall. Hope to see you next year. Have fun at the party!!!

"It'll be okay, honey," Lilly said, holding him close, as Arthur folded up on the coach.

So there it was. Henry had broken his word and asked Paul to stay in Elk Point. What an ass!

The night before the party, she and Maria had put the finishing touches on the cake. Arthur wanted the cake sprinkled with Red Hots, his favorite candy. The next morning he bounded out of bed, exploding with excitement. The party didn't start until four in the afternoon. Meanwhile, the kid was driving her crazy with his constant questions and antics. Finally she ordered him out the door to play with friends. "Don't come back until three o'clock. That'll give you time to get a bath and put on clean clothes."

At precisely four o'clock, 14 kids showed up. Maria was already in place. She and Lilly watched as they ran inside and outside the house, front yard to back, screaming their lungs out. At six o'clock everyone gathered around a picnic table in the back yard as she and Maria served the ice cream and cake. His tummy full, Arthur began opening birthday gifts. He was so pokey the kids started yelling at him.

"Come on! We haven't got all night," yelled Carlos. Soon chaos erupted, as several other partygoers jumped in to help with the present opening.

Henry was there, standing off to the side, taking an occasional nip from a bottle concealed in a brown paper bag. Lilly was tempted to rip the bag from his hand. He did join in singing Happy Birthday. He was teetering and way too loud. When Maria handed Arthur the stick for the piñata, Henry stepped forward and declared he'd take the first whack. Arthur's face fell.

Lilly stepped in front of him. "It's the kids' party, Henry. Let them have the fun."

"Oh, what the hell," he answered, a boozy grin on his face. "I'll just take one little swing."

"No you won't, "Lilly declared, taking the stick from him. "Why don't you leave?"

Henry's face turned red and he stepped toward her like he planned to grab the stick back. She raised the wood pole and took a threatening stance. "Okay, sure, Lilly, you're right. It's the kids' party. I'm getting the fuck out of here." He turned and walked to the front yard and headed toward Kelsey's.

"Here you are, Arthur," Lilly said, giving the boy the stick. "Go ahead."

"Hit it, hit it hard!" shouted the kids as he swung the heavy wooden pole at the piñata. CRACK! CRACK! CRACK! The colorful paper-mache donkey finally burst and candy flew everywhere.

"Whoopee!" Arthur yelped. He ran to Lilly and Maria and gave them hugs. "Let's do this every year," he declared, grinning up at the two ladies.

They laughed and assured him, yes, a party might very well be an annual event.

The next morning, a Sunday, Henry appeared at the breakfast table more hung over than usual. Arthur wasn't up yet so Lilly decided to say what had been bothering her.

"Paul sent a note to Arthur saying he was staying in Elk Point. Did you have something to do with that?"

Henry's head jerked up from his coffee in surprise. He raised the newspaper in front of his face and said, "I told you it's none of your business. If you must know I wrote and asked him to hold off coming for now."

She walked over to the sink and dropped the dirty Mel-Mac dishes with a clatter. "You didn't say a word to me or to Arthur. School starts in just over two weeks. Arthur has been counting on his big brother being here."

"Hey, I'm not ready to take on another kid," he growled, frustration in his voice. "Besides, Paul's got a smart mouth and bad attitude. He'll cause trouble, and you know it. He saw you naked in bed with me. You remember that, don't you?" He folded the newspaper in half and placed it on the table.

"Paul's fine with Frank and Clara. They're good people, and he's happy. So what's your problem?"

Taking a moment to keep from flying at him and pounding on him, Lilly replied in a controlled voice: "The problem is, he's your son, and you made promises. Now you're breaking them. Doesn't that bother you? Margie wanted you to be together. Now you do stupid things like this. What kind of a father are you?"

Henry stood, knocking over his cup and spilling coffee on the floor. "Don't you dare mention my poor dead wife's name. Not ever! You don't know anything about how we loved each other. And get off my back. He's *my* son. This isn't your business."

He stormed out the door, leaving Lilly alone in the kitchen.

There are many paths. Be sure to take the one with a heart.

–Lao Tzu

Chapter 21

"How ya doing, fellah?" said the assertive and loud female who dropped uninvited onto a barstool next to Henry at Kelsey's. She introduced herself as Gladys Walberg.

"Pleased to meet you. Gladys. My name's Henry, Henry Goodwin. Seen you around. I always thought you were one of the prettiest gals in the joint," he said, grinning and pouring on the bull.

"Well, that's kind of you to say. I like to keep myself up."

She reached up and pushed back her thick, black hair that was piled high and surrounded her triangular face, which was heavily powdered with makeup. Her ruby-red lipstick matched the color of her slithery silk blouse. She was tall, maybe five-foot-ten, with an hourglass though slightly thick figure. The buttons on her blouse strained to contain her ample, bullet-shaped breasts. Not caring that Henry noticed, Gladys, every couple of minutes, checked out her reflection in the big mirror behind the bar.

"Say I heard a good joke. Would you like to hear it? I should warn you it's a little off color," Henry said.

"You bet, and the dirtier the better," she challenged, elbowing him in the side.

When he finished, she nearly tumbled off the barstool. "Tell me more,' she said, choking on her laughter. She dabbed her mascara with a bright red handkerchief.

"Boy, you've got a real smooth tongue there, sweetie. You're one hell of a jokester, I'll tell you that."

Close up, under the makeup, as best he could tell, Gladys looked to be in her early to mid-forties, her eyes dark and shallow, impossible to read. She asked his age and when he told her 36, he could almost hear the click-click as she did the calculations in her head. She didn't volunteer hers.

As the evening advanced, Gladys told him with a certain satisfaction how she'd dumped her last husband in a quickie Reno divorce.

"He couldn't keep up with me. I wanted to have fun; he wanted to stay home." She pulled out a cigarette and Henry nervously fumbled in his pocket for a lighter, finally pulling it out and holding it to her cigarette. "Looking back, I don't think he even liked girls, if you know what I mean."

She winked, as if to say, unlike her ex, she was certain Henry liked girls just fine.

Gladys also worked at Lockheed, in an office on the top floor of the company's brick-red building. It sure looked like she spent a pretty penny keeping herself in fine figure, what with the fancy clothes, trendy hairdo, makeup and nails. She hinted that she'd made out damn good in the divorce. She owned her house free and clear.

One trait this lady couldn't hide with makeup was a cackling, shrill laugh that reminded Henry of a braying donkey. Every head in the bar turned when she cut loose.

It was embarrassing but he decided to put up with it. Since the falling out with Lilly, it had been a long dry spell since a woman, any woman, had paid him the slightest attention. Now the sun was breaking through; opportunity sat right next to him. She was exactly the tonic he needed and from what he'd seen, she was hot and ready for anything. Besides, she owned her house. And it was close by. How convenient was that?

She'd already touched his arm and now her hand rested lightly on his thigh. He ordered a third beer and she had another whiskey sour. Other guys at the bar kept shooting looks their way and Henry knew what they were thinking. It made him feel good about himself for the first time in months.

She saw him staring at her chest so she batted her eyelashes. She reached up with her fingers and spread the fabric even wider. "I leave the top button undone. Gives me a sporty look, don't you think?"

Henry raised an eyebrow and observed, "Yeah, real sporty."

Gladys touched his shoulder and slid off the stool. "Excuse me, sweetie. I'll be right back."

Henry watched her take long strides toward the ladies' room, weaving through the crowd, the dark seams of her nylons running up the back side of her long legs before disappearing under her short, tight black skirt.

She was a rough cookie on the edges, no question about that but she had a way of moving her backside that drove him crazy. She bragged how she could out-drink and out-cuss any man in the bar, including him. Before the evening ended she made him a believer.

The brassy lady downed a total of four whiskey sours and the only visible effects he observed was her slurred language and that the braying was even louder. She finished every phrase with a flourish of cuss words, like "I'll be goddamned" or "ain't that one big pile of shit."

"Henry," she said teasingly, as her hand inched up almost to his crouch, "it's been a long since I've had a real man in my bed. I'm due for some relief. The guys in this bar look like a pretty limp bunch to me, if you know what I mean. Sort of like that fairy-boy I married. He couldn't get it up if he used both hands. Plus, and I'm telling you this confidentially, he had the smallest prick I ever saw hanging from a man."

Soon they were kissing and groping each other and, thanks to the alcohol, not in the least mindful of others in the bar. Finally the bartender sidled over and said, "Excuse me, you guys. Better take that stuff home."

"Oh, that's a good idea," Gladys cooed into Henry's ear. "Let's go to my place for coffee or something." She offered up a wicked grin and rubbed her foot along Henry's leg.

Henry arrived back at Lilly's well past midnight, smelling of whiskey and beer and Gladys. He stumbled to his room trying not to awaken anyone.

From then on he and Gladys were inseparable, and it didn't take long for his new lady friend to start obsessing about the *woman* living with him.

"You say her name's Lilly?"

"Yeah, Lilly," Henry said, thinking fast. "I brought her to California from Nebraska to watch my youngest boy while I work. There's nothing between us. She's a kid."

Gladys' brow wrinkled. "Really? I'd like to meet this kid some time."

On Saturday night a week later, Henry practically stumbled into Kelsey's. He was an hour late. Gladys was boiling.

"Where you been, pal? Think all I have to do is wait on you?"

"Lilly's so damn ungrateful," Henry complained. "She blew her stack, like I'd murdered my own son or something."

Wanting to show concern, Gladys leaned in close and held Henry's hand, as he related how upset Lilly was that he had asked his oldest son, Paul, to stay a while longer in Elk Point.

"You know I can't deal with a second kid out here right now, Gladys."

"You're right to be upset, sweetie," she said, patting his shoulder.

Henry's anger faded when he noticed Gladys had undone two buttons on her blouse this evening, thus doubling her "sporty" exposure. Leaning in close, he caught a whiff of her perfume and felt her hot whiskey breath on his cheek.

"Well, sweetheart," Gladys breathed, "it's Saturday night and there's no work tomorrow." She ran a finger along the outline of his chin. "We can play all night if you like."

"Oh, I'd like!" he said, as he reached and squeezed the inside of her thigh.

Does this path have a heart? If it doesn't, it is of no use

–Carlos Castaneda

Chapter 22

Lilly was reading a manual on how to improve her typing skills. She lifted her head at the sound of a knock at the front door. Since it was only half past eight, and a little early for Henry to be returning, she was surprised when she saw him through the screen door.

"Arthur still up?" he said in a low voice.

She straightened and her eyes narrowed. Henry never knocked; his normal style was to barge right in. "Yes, he's almost ready for bed."

He walked in, a guilty grin on his face. Behind him, practically pushing him along was Gladys.

"Lilly, I'd like you to meet my friend, Gladys Walberg. We met at Kelsey's."

The woman had a hard, worn look around the eyes, and glittered with cheap costume jewelry—an oversized, gold-colored necklace, three-inch earrings and fingers overrun with garish rings of all shapes and sizes. Even though Gladys was about the same height as Lilly, she was broader in the shoulders and considerably bigger up front. She looked fifty, maybe a tad older, and chewed gum in a hard, intimidating way. She walked right up and stopped inches from her. Lilly backed away or they might have bumped noses. She didn't want trouble. If Gladys wanted to stake a claim to Henry, she'd help her fill out the papers. She extended her hand and smiled. "Welcome to our home."

"Glad to meet ya," Gladys said, snapping her gum. She nodded toward Arthur, who had just padded in wearing pajamas. "This your boy?"

Henry piped up, "Yeah, that's Arthur, my youngest. You remember my other boy, the older one, is still in Nebraska."

For a moment, she wondered whether Henry had told Gladys about their relationship in Elk Point. He liked to brag when it came to women. Forget it, she told herself. What do I care what this barracuda thinks!

She indicated for the guests to take a seat on the sofa, and then turned her attention to Arthur. "Please say goodnight, honey, you have to get up early tomorrow."

Disappointed, Arthur left the room without a word, pausing only to give a goodbye wave.

"I've got some great news," Henry said, sounding like he was delivering a well-rehearsed speech. "Gladys and I have hit it off. She's healing from a divorce from a guy who treated her rotten. And, as you know, I'm still grieving from Margie's passing. We're both coming off rough times. Now that we're good friends, we're ready to take the next step."

He placed a hand on his girlfriend's upper leg, as if displaying ownership.

"Yeah, that's so true, baby," the girlfriend said, snuggling up and bumping Henry on the lip with one of her dangling earrings. "You and me, we're a perfect match, ain't we?"

"I'm moving in with her at her place, so we can get to know each other better," Henry said, rushing to finish what he had to say. "I've quit my factory job and in two days I start as head bartender at Kelsey's. Isn't that great? With tips, I expect to earn as much as I did at Lockheed. You know I'm a great bartender." He waved his hands as he talked, his eyes darting from Lilly to Gladys, like he was trying to gauge the impact of what he was saying.

Lilly nodded. He'd put it all on the line with this new girlfriend and his new job. But where did Arthur stand in this?

"Problem is, I'll be working a lot more hours, especially nights and weekends at Kelsey's."

Lilly sat back in her chair and crossed her arms and waited for the song and dance.

"Gladys works in the office at Lockheed and puts in a lot of overtime. Arthur will be alone quite a bit, and he won't know anyone in Gladys' neighborhood. We're wondering if you'd keep him here, where he feels safe. It shouldn't be for long, just till we get situated. Isn't that right, Gladys?"

Lilly couldn't help but notice the shocked look on his girlfriend's face. Was this the first time she'd heard about a kid moving in with them? She rolled her eyes and turned away. Henry was at it again—putting distance between him and his boys, first dumping Paul in Elk Point and now Arthur on her. She fought to keep her emotions under control. Just let him hang himself, she thought.

Henry continued talking rapidly, as if sprinting to the finish line. "Of course, I'll still pay Maria for babysitting during the day because I know you're attending school. And for good measure, I'll throw in an extra $10 a week to cover expenses for Arthur's school clothes, shoes, a little spending money, that sort of thing. I'll pay that directly to you, Lilly."

"What about Paul?" Lilly asked, her voice insistent. "Is he staying forever in Elk Point?"

"No, of course not!" Henry answered defensively. "At the moment he's fine in Nebraska. When Gladys and I establish ourselves on a more permanent basis, the boys can move in with us, can't they, Gladys?"

His glittering companion pressed her lips together and stared at her lap. Her face flushed a deep purple. She didn't say a word.

Lilly paused and thought. Really, what choice did she have? Arthur wouldn't have a chance with these two. God only knows what would happen. Gladys was more than welcome to Henry but not to Arthur. She'd fight them both tooth and nail if necessary, even as she doubted that would be necessary. It was perfectly clear from Gladys' scowling reaction that she had no interest whatsoever in having kids underfoot. What was Henry thinking?

"So, what do ya think, Lilly? Is it okay with you?" Henry asked, looking for affirmation of his grand plan.

"I'll keep Arthur," she said.

Words of thanks poured from him as he hustled Gladys toward the door. "How about I come back tomorrow and talk to Arthur? I'm sure he'll be okay with this; he likes it here."

Lilly closed the door and took a few deep breaths. Adios, she thought. And good riddance.

The next afternoon, she and Arthur sat at the kitchen table waiting for Henry to arrive.

"Does this have something to do with that lady who was here last night with Dad?" Arthur asked.

"Everything is fine," Lilly said, taking his hand. "Your father wants to explain some things to you."

Ten minutes later Henry arrived and took a seat at the kitchen table. He wouldn't look at his son. Lilly leaned against the refrigerator and listened. He talked about his new job at Kelsey's, and asked Arthur what he thought of Gladys.

The boy looked to Lilly. "Don't know. Guess she's all right."

"Gladys and me are real close, not like your mother and I used to be," he explained. "I'm going to be living at her house. Lilly wants you to stay here, you know, close to Maria and the neighborhood kids."

Once again the boy looked to Lilly, like he wanted to see that this was true. She kept her face blank, not yet willing to let Henry off the hook.

"Nothing's going to change, son," his father went on. "It'll be better all around for us for now. I'll visit you all the time, I promise. Later, you and Paul and me will get our own place. Sound okay, son?"

This time when the boy looked to Lilly, she smiled and nodded.

Happy that everything seemed settled, Arthur said, "Sure, guess so. Can I go play now? The kids are waiting."

After he scooted out the back door, Lilly turned to Henry, "I visited with the principal at Arthur's school earlier today and learned if he's living with me, and you're not in the house, I'll need papers making me his legal guardian. It's the law. I've talked to a lawyer who can handle the paperwork. The three of us need to go before a judge and sign papers. And this needs to be done right away. School starts next week."

This news momentarily caught Henry by surprise. However, he quickly recovered and Lilly could see the wheels turning in his head. If he said no, then he'd be stuck with Arthur and that that would create a real complication with Gladys. She knew he didn't want that.

"Oh, sure," he answered. "If it's the law, that's what we need to do. Besides, it's only a formality. He'll always be my son."

Two days later they met in a courtroom with the dark-haired, scuffed-shoed lawyer Lilly had hired to draw up the papers. The attorney led them before the judge to certify the legal change.

"You understand what's happening here with you signing this paper?" the judge asked Henry. "You're turning over your legal rights to this lady, Lillian Swenson."

The judge looked at Arthur. "And you, son, Lillian Swenson will look out for you now and you'll have to mind her like she's your mother. You understand?"

"Yes, sir, I do," Arthur answered formally, exactly as the lawyer had instructed him to say.

"I understand as well, Judge," said Henry, also using the lawyer's words he'd been given. "I'm willing to do this because this is in my son's best interest."

With the papers signed and notarized, the clerk handed Henry a copy, gave one to Arthur and a third to Lilly. Before parting outside the courthouse, Henry promised, "I'll be over to see you soon, son. I need to go. I'm late for work."

The judge's comments about "like she's your mother" rang in Lilly's ears. In the eyes of the law, she was now legal guardian to an eight-year-old boy. Talk about life's surprises. The main thing is Arthur was safe. That alone eased her mind.

On a Sunday, only two weeks after they'd gone before the judge, Lilly was ironing and Arthur was outside playing with the neighborhood kids when she looked up and spotted Henry coming up the sidewalk.

"Lilly," he called out from the screen door. "It's me. We need to talk."

Oh cripes, now what? She put down the iron and walked to the door.

"Can I come in?" he asked.

Standing inside the door, Henry wrung his hands and cleared his throat. He was having difficulty getting started. "I've really screwed things up," he began. "I thought Gladys and I had a good thing. It's not working at all. She kicked me out."

"Sorry," Lilly said, not a bit surprised. She had figured this relationship was doomed from the start. She decided to play along, and said: "Gladys seems like a nice person, although I suppose having gone through a recent divorce she's probably not really sure what she wants."

"The big problem as it turns out is she doesn't want anything to do with my boys. She doesn't even want me to visit Arthur." He paused, a guilty look on his face. "That's why I haven't been over here to see him.

"On top of that, she doesn't like to cook, and she's a terrible housekeeper," Henry continued, clicking into his whining mode. "She wants me to do the cleaning, even the toilets. I told her straight out I don't do that sort of thing. That got her going."

"Um, couldn't you arrange to share chores?" Lilly asked.

"Naw. She's pure lazy. She goes out every night partying while I work 10-hour days, usually till well past midnight at Kelsey's. I come home exhausted. She's seeing another guy, too. I'm sure of it. We had a fight and, can you believe it, she blamed me? Told me to get out and wouldn't even let me stay till I found a new place."

Out of patience, Lilly stared him in the eye. "This is an interesting story. What do you want from me?"

"I've got my stuff out in the old Ford. I've no place to go. I'd appreciate it if you'd let me move back in here. It'll give me a chance to reconnect with Arthur. I sure miss him."

She sighed. Same old Henry.

"Sorry," she answered. You made your choice. You're welcome to visit Arthur. Call ahead before you do, though. This is a busy household."

Henry started to say something but stopped. Anger was building in him. This was something new. She decided to try to move him along, even if it meant she had to physically shove him out the door.

"Now wait a minute," Henry sputtered. "I've got a right to see him any time I want. That's what the judge said."

"That's true. Still, you don't have any right to move into my home. I make the rules here. You're welcome to visit your son. That's all."

"I'll tell you this," he replied defiantly. "I sure as hell can't afford to pay rent on an apartment plus pay child support and babysitting fees. Either I move in here, or I stop paying you and Maria."

"Keep your money. I know you make enough to take care of your son. If you choose not to, that's your decision. You have to live with yourself. Now get the hell out of my house and out of the neighborhood or I'll call the police."

Shaking, she banged the inside door closed behind him and locked it.

Moments later, she calmed down. Arthur was hers now, and that single fact made her smile inside. Far as she was concerned, what had just happened between she and Henry was probably best in the long run. Now she and Arthur could begin to make a life for themselves, without having to worry about him.

From what Paul wrote in recent letters, it appeared he had settled in for the long term with Frank and Clara. Henry was the odd man out. He'd made his messy bed, now he could wallow in it as best he could. It was not her problem.

"The heart is an organ of fire."

–Michael Ondaatje

Chapter 23

Paul had begun eighth grade in Elk Point and the first week in school wasn't going well. He had the country boy right where he wanted him, in a left-arm headlock, his most effective hold. He pounded his right fist into the kid's face and blood gushed from his nose. A dozen or so classmates kept urging the trapped boy to break loose. That wasn't going to happen. Paul had him locked in with no hope of escape. Like a wave, the crowd surged forward.

"Come on, get him!" yelled one of the trapped guy's buddies. "He's a pussy!"

Paul looked up and gave the big mouth a warning stare. The lippy kid looked like he was about to pee his pants. He slipped away into the crowd.

Paul continued to punch until the boy blubbered, "Please! I give up. I give. Let me go!"

With a shove, Paul sent the wounded kid stumbling toward his friends. They scrambled to make way, stunned that their warrior had lost the fight so decisively.

For a moment, the onlookers shuffled around, uncertain what to do. Two boys walked over to comfort their battered friend. Everyone else began moving away in small groups. None dared to look back. Paul's reputation as a tough guy, someone not to be messed with, was now set in stone.

The next day the principal called Frank. "I understand you and Clara are looking out for Paul Goodwin. He's had some trouble. Can you come by the office?"

"What's the problem?"

"A fist fight with another boy. I've already talked to them. The other kid got the worst of it. He swore to me he's through with fighting. But Paul wouldn't make any such promise. He thinks the rules don't apply to him. He won't take responsibility. I'm not tolerating this sort of thing at my school."

The news surprised Frank. Then again, it didn't.

Paul stood before Frank's desk, his head hanging.

"What the hell happened?" Frank demanded. "You start school, and the next thing the principal's calling. What's the deal?"

"I didn't want to fight. The other guy's buddies egged him on," Paul said, a sorry look on his face. "A bunch of them followed me out of school and the one kid kept poking at my chest, calling me a chicken and then clucking. I told him to knock it off. He didn't so I pushed him back. He jumped at me and I kicked his butt. I guess word got around and the principal called us in and gave us both detentions. That's why I'm late."

Frank nodded. Paul did have an attitude. He wouldn't take any blame for what had happened. But the principal didn't know Paul carried around a lot of baggage, mostly pent-up anger, and that had an impact on how the kid was thinking right now.

"Fighting's not the answer," Frank said. But even as he said the words he recognized there are times a fellow has to establish himself at school, especially when the bullies come around. That's what he'd taught his son John. Of course, his fatherly advice hadn't done John a bit of good.

Principal Conrad "Rooster" Smith sat at his desk when Frank arrived for his appointment. Conrad, a gruff, no-nonsense type was mostly bald except for a wisp of red hair standing straight up in front, hence the moniker "Rooster." Though a good customer at the station, Frank had never once seen Conrad crack a smile while he waited for his tank to fill and for Frank to clean his windshield. He also couldn't recall a time when the school boss ever made an effort to engage in friendly conversation with him. The thought of the diminutive principal chewing out Paul, who towered over the half-pint, brought a smile to

Frank's lips. Still he needed to proceed cautiously with this man. If Rooster got the idea anyone was challenging his authority, he'd lower the hammer on Paul and he didn't want that to happen.

"Well, Conrad, I'd take it as a personal favor if you'd cut the boy some slack. He's had a rough time, first losing his mother and then his father abandoning him here in Elk Point. He says it won't happen again."

That evening Frank didn't mention the fight to Clara or the meeting with the principal. No sense getting her all worked up.

Only a week later, Conrad called again about another fight on the school grounds, also involving Paul. "We need to talk," the principal said grimly. "I'll have the boy here in my office at 9 o'clock tomorrow morning. I'd like you to be here, too."

Frank was mad as hell when Paul showed up after school. "For Christ's sake. Principal Smith's says he's going to the school board to have you expelled."

Paul's shoulders dropped. "The kid said he was going to even the score for my beating up his buddy. I told him I couldn't fight; I even apologized, said I was sorry. He wouldn't back off. He swung and I ducked and socked him hard with one shot to the nose. That was the end of it. What was I supposed to do, stand there and take a punch from him?"

"Don't know. I wasn't there. Guess we'll sort it out tomorrow."

The next day Frank found Paul sitting alone on a hardwood bench in the principal's outer office. Neither acknowledged the other. In a moment, the secretary motioned for them to enter the office.

"The principal's in there with Coach Faraday," she said.

Frank knew Luke Faraday. He'd graduated three years earlier from the University of Nebraska where he'd been a star end for the Cornhuskers and helped to take the team to a Big Seven Conference championship in his senior year. "Luke, Luke, Luke" was the rallying cry on the lips of football-crazed Nebraska fans from Omaha to the Wyoming border.

When Faraday applied for a teaching and coaching job in Elk Point, the school board members couldn't believe their good fortune. As it happened, Faraday's wife had been born and raised in Elk Point and now that she was pregnant she insisted on living near her mother.

In his first year, Coach Faraday led the Elk Point football squad to its first-ever winning season. When he wasn't coaching, he taught eighth-grade math, which was where he first encountered Paul. Impressed with his size and the way he moved, Faraday approached Paul about going out for football.

"Sorry, I work at the gas station and don't have the time. Thanks for the offer."

Faraday called Frank, hoping he'd intervene.

"Don't want to get your hopes up, Coach. Paul's got a mind of his own and besides he might be moving to California any day now. That's where his family lives."

Faraday was 25 years old, a fair-haired, good-looking fellow, with a prominent chiseled nose, squared-off jaw, and a consistently serious look on his face. Most people were surprised that the star football player was only five foot seven. They expected someone taller. What wasn't so noticeable immediately was the fact that Faraday was well muscled, from head to toe.

When they entered the office, Frank tipped his head to Faraday and took a seat across from Principal Smith. Paul took a seat next to him.

"I asked the coach to join us," Principal Smith said. "Hope you don't mind."

Frank and Paul nodded.

Principal Smith got down to business. "Normally, with a second fight, I'd go right to the school board and recommend at least a month-long suspension."

"Suspension?" Paul blurted. "That's not fair. I have a right to defend myself."

"I'm not splitting hairs with you, young man. The other guy said you sucker-punched him."

"That's a lie!"

Coach Faraday raised his hand as if to settle things down. "Say, if you fellows don't mind, I'd like to take Paul outside for a little talk. That okay with you, Paul?"

It was a beautiful fall morning, a little breezy, sunny and warm. Falling leaves soared and tumbled like runaway kites as the coach and the boy sat down on the front steps leading up to the red brick, three-story consolidated school building.

"I've been talking to Roos...I mean Principal Smith," Coach Faraday said, grinning in spite of himself. "If you come out for football he'll waive the suspension."

"I don't care," Paul fired back. "I've got my job at the station. That's how I earn my living."

"With a suspension you'll miss a lot of school work, and they may hold you back."

"Law says I can quit school at fourteen."

"You're too smart for that. Besides, I talked to Frank. He says if you go out for football, and stick with it, he'll give you plenty of hours on weekends and holidays."

That evening, Paul walked over to Annie's house. He hadn't kissed her yet but sometimes they held hands. Her parents seemed okay. One time her dad asked him out to the yard to throw a football around. He enjoyed it.

"Coach Faraday said if I put forth the effort I could be the backup quarterback to Dan Wetzel next year," Paul said. "Gosh, he's a great player. Can I do that?"

"You can do anything you put your mind to," Annie said, taking his hand. "My dad was a quarterback in high school and it was one of the best experiences in his life. Go out for football, and he'll be one of your biggest fans and, of course, you already have me."

"Your dad played football?" Paul asked.

"Yes, right here in Elk Point. And Mom was a cheer-leader, and they dated all through high school."

She paused and with her brown eyes wide open she held Paul's eyes with hers. "You know Coach Faraday is a good Christian man. He thinks a lot of you."

"He doesn't know me."

"I do, and you're a wonderful person." She squeezed his hand. "Go for it, Paulie."

The most beautiful things in the world cannot be seen or touched...but are felt in the heart.

–Helen Keller

Chapter 24

O nce Lilly had her business school certificate in hand, the fussy Mrs. Lewis kept her word and arranged an interview with Performance Arts, one of Hollywood's leading talent agencies. "It's a plum opportunity," the woman said. "If they hire you, consider yourself a very lucky young lady."

Lilly skated through the interview and was told to come to work the following Monday. At the moment she was seated at a desk in a large open room with dozens of other young women, most with their heads down, clipping articles from magazines and newspapers. With razor-cutter in hand, Lilly leafed through stacks of local and national publications in search of any mention or photos of the agency's actor and actress clients.

The clippings were hard evidence that Performance Arts agency staff members were doing their jobs keeping the agency's high-profile clients in the public eye. Lilly could spot, slice and file a clipping before most girls opened a magazine or newspaper. A hard worker who buckled down to the task, she found the work repetitious and boring. On the plus side, she loved the opportunity to work in a professional L.A. office setting, surrounded by young people her age. She all ready had two new friends, Lois and Susan. The first day she arrived they went out of their way to welcome her into their group.

One of the agency bosses, Account Executive Thelma Rice, recognized Lilly as someone with potential and took an immediate liking to the Nebraska transplant. She made a habit of swinging by her desk to offer encouragement. A dozen or so years older than Lilly, and wise for her years, Lilly admired the woman's "let's-get-it-done" personality, her honey-colored hair, brown eyes, and trim, five-foot-three figure. Her facial features were soft as a child's but as Lilly would soon discover if Thelma didn't like something or someone, that perky, friendly face could turn in a flicker. Then watch out!

Over Caesar salads in the lunchroom one day, Thelma groused that despite her best efforts, a *Time* magazine editor in New York had blown her off when she pitched the idea for a major magazine story about the soon-to-be-released musical *Singin' in the Rain.* The movie, considered by insiders to be an Oscar contender, starred Gene Kelly, Debbie Reynolds and co-starred Thelma's client, Donald O'Connor.

Thelma explained that *Singin'* represented O'Connor's potential breakthrough into Hollywood's big leagues. To date, the song-and-dance man's most significant movie success had him starring in a series of B-grade movies about a talking horse named Francis.

"I've seen outtakes from *Singin'* and, in my opinion, Donald has a good shot at winning an Oscar for best-supporting actor," Thelma said, as she picked at her salad. "But unless I nail down a major publicity break, his chances of winning are slim to none. In this town, the "buzz" that precedes the release of a major new film matters a lot in terms of influencing how members of the Academy vote. It'd be a real shame if Donald missed out because I failed to convince *Time* to do the story," she said dejectedly.

Lilly listened and wondered how she might help. She was fascinated with all this inside Hollywood intrigue.

Thelma pushed her salad to the side and continued: "This is Donald's chance to move up to A-list status in Hollywood. New York magazine editors are an elite bunch of know-it-alls who think working stiffs like me should bow down and kiss their ass whenever they wave a finger. And I'll do it if it helps my clients. It's damn frustrating to deal with those prima donnas."

A couple of days later, on a hunch, Lilly carried a clipping from the *Chicago Post's* entertainment section to Thelma's office.

"Say, Thelma, I found this feature story from years back about Donald O'Connor growing up in a well-known theatrical family in Illinois." She handed the clipping to her. "According to the story, he learned to dance and sing as part of a family vaudeville act. The O'Connor family was a headliner until the Depression closed theatres all over the country. It got so bad the family sometimes had to trade performances for food and a place to sleep."

"Really!" Thelma said. "I never knew this about him, and Donald's been my client for three years." She turned her full attention to the clipping, glancing up as Lilly kept talking.

"Well, it gets more interesting—and sad. His older sister, Marjorie, was killed in a car crash at 13, devastating the family. A few weeks later Donald's father was singing and dancing on-stage and died of a heart attack. Donald's plucky mother kept the family act going for a few more years. Donald found his way to Hollywood, and picked up some bit parts before the Francis movies. The photograph in the newspaper shows him as a scrawny kid of 10 hoofing his heart out onstage in Peoria."

"It's heartbreaking!" Thelma exclaimed.

"I'm wondering if the *Time* editor saw this clipping, he'd soften up and do a rags-to-riches piece," Lilly suggested. "Readers love that sort of thing, don't they?"

Thelma thought for a minute. "You may be on to something here."

Thelma airmailed the clipping to New York. Two days later, the *Time* editor was on the telephone begging her to set up an interview and photo session with Donald O'Connor.

"That newspaper story brought tears to my eyes," the editor told her. "My boss wants an exclusive. It could be a cover story."

Thelma rushed to Lilly's desk. "Thank you, thank you!" she said, embracing her new friend. "It worked! We have our *Time* story. They want an exclusive—and it's all because of you."

Embarrassed, Lilly replied: "All I did was clip an item from the newspaper."

"No! That clipping turned things in our favor. That makes you a genius in my book, or damn close to it."

Lilly's success rocketed through the office grapevine. Funny thing, though, it didn't sit well with the two co-workers who had earlier befriended her, Lois and Susan.

A few days after Lilly was singled out for the high praise, she was in one of the women's private bathroom stalls when she overheard the two young women plotting to plant a story around the office that she, Lilly, was having an after-work encounter with one of Performance Arts' department managers.

"She's like that, you know," said Lois. "You should see the way she flirts with Fred. He's married. She doesn't care. She'll do anything to get ahead."

Hurt and not knowing what to do, Lilly went to Thelma.

"I'm not surprised," her friend told her. "This building is filled with wonderful people. But like in every place, there are a few bad apples, including those two phony friends of yours."

"Why are they after me?" Lilly asked. "I didn't do anything to them. Should I confront them?"

"No, leave it to me" Thelma replied. "Keep in mind, you need a thick skin to survive around here. Don't let a couple of back-stabbers get to you."

The next day two desks sat empty where the offending ladies had once sat, a stark reminder of what happens if you cross swords with Thelma.

When Lilly expressed her appreciation, her friend said, "Hey, forget it. Those little beauties have caused trouble before. They were long overdue to get their butts kicked."

Within the week, Thelma moved Lilly to an up-front desk location and gave her new duties. She enjoyed a direct view of the office elevator, and the comings and goings of celebrity clients like John Wayne, Glenn Ford, Kim Novak and, her personal favorite, Grace Kelly, an up-and-comer. Real movie stars! But her star-struck days didn't last for long. She soon found herself so busy she rarely found time to glance up from her desk when the elevator door opened.

She'd worked at Performance Arts nearly two months and hadn't once caught a glimpse of agency founder and owner, Michael Paulson. Word was he spent most of his time these days in Washington, D.C. trying to put out fires resulting from Senator Joseph McCarthy's communist witch-hunt hearings, which were ruining the reputations and careers of dozens of Hollywood actors, directors and writers, including several who were valued clients of the agency.

Thelma told her Mr. Paulson was due back in the office any day now. Lilly was excited at the prospect of finally catching a glimpse of him. The big boss enjoyed a reputation as a Hollywood mover and shaker, as well as a lady's man. Gossip columnists considered him one of Tinseltown's most-eligible bachelors. Lilly understood why. The photographs she'd seen of Paulson in movie magazines and newspapers showed a man handsome enough to be a leading movie star himself.

The heart knows what it wants, and it often makes no sense

–Jonathan H. Ellerby

Chapter 25

A week later Lilly stood next to Thelma and watched her give Donald O'Connor's hand a vigorous shake as she enthused: "Donald, we loved the *Singin' in the Rain* screening. It has Oscar written all over it."

They were assembled in one of the agency's conference rooms, and Thelma and a cadre of other staff members stood ready to brief the actor on what he could expect when the *Time* magazine people arrived from New York next Thursday to conduct interviews and take photographs.

"Donald, please meet one of our newest staff members, Lilly Swenson. She's the one I told you about."

"Thank you so much for your excellent work," O'Connor said, his voice barely audible. I very much appreciate it."

Lilly had seen one of the Francis movies and was surprised at the actor-dancer's shyness. He hadn't seemed bashful while cozying up with that talking horse. Also, to her surprise, Michael Paulson walked into the conference room to greet O'Connor and to congratulate him on the new role. Then he retreated to a seat in the back of the room where he sat quietly while Thelma and the others talked O'Connor through every step of the two days he'd spend with the *Time* crew.

Lilly glanced at Paulson and their eyes met. She blushed, embarrassed at being caught. He nodded, smiled, and took a deep drag on his cigarette. Lilly turned back to Thelma.

She tried to concentrate on what Thelma was saying but her mind kept returning to the man in the back of the room.

He was gorgeous. His smooth-shaven face was clear and robust, and he was blessed with classic features: a straight nose, full lips, a strong, prominent chin, and wide-set dark brown eyes, reflecting intelligence and confidence. Tall and slender, and graying at the temples in a distinguished way, he looked to be in his forties—a very young and fit forty. Lilly loved his natural graciousness and poise, the sound of his deep, warm voice and the way he carried himself.

Following the meeting, Thelma made a big production out of introducing the two of them.

"Mr. Paulson, this is one of your newest employees, Lilly Swenson."

"Now, Thelma, you know I like everyone to call me Michael," he said, looking directly into Lilly's eyes and offering her his hand.

"Thelma's a big fan of yours," he said. "I hope you're enjoying working here."

"I am. Thank you," Lilly said, glancing over at Thelma who grinned broadly at both of them.

The next day Mr. Paulson showed up at her desk, making small talk about the weather and progress on the *Time* project. Eventually, he got around to asking her to dinner. She hesitated. She still felt the sting of the incident with those two women. The last thing she wanted was gossip swirling that she, the new girl, was doing it again, only this time Lilly was dating the Big Boss! She could hear people saying: "Well maybe those two fired girls were right about her. She is a slut on the make."

Indicating all the work piled on her desk, Lilly nervously shuffled papers and said something about having too much to do, plus responsibilities at home. "Thank you so much. I don't have time to think about dating. I hope you understand." She offered up a weak smile.

"Well, another time, then," he said, disappointment on his face. "Doesn't have to be right away. I'd love to show you some of the town. There's a terrific restaurant called Palmas overlooking the Pacific Ocean that I'm sure you'd enjoy. The seafood's to die for, and the sunset from the patio is stunning, the best in Southern California."

"Sounds wonderful. If I may, I'll take a rain check."

"Sure, that's fine. We'll talk again," he said.

After he'd departed, Lilly regretted not having said yes. She'd wanted to go out with him in the worst way. It sounded heavenly. She liked him, really liked him. He was so handsome, and the spitting image of the man she'd dreamed of marrying as a little girl.

She was hesitant to mention to anyone that Michael Paulson had actually asked her to dinner. Yet, a few days later over lunch with Thelma, she couldn't resist.

Thelma nodded in understanding. "I'm not surprised."

"What do you mean?"

Thelma lit a cigarette, leaned forward and lowered her voice. "You know about Michael's reputation with the ladies, don't you?"

Lilly nodded.

"You're a beautiful woman and Michael has his eye on you. You could be his next target. At the end of the evening after a few drinks, well, you get the idea."

Lilly shook her head. "He doesn't seem like that at all. He's nice, thoughtful…"

"…and very fascinating," Thelma said. "I know from experience."

"You?" Lilly couldn't hide her surprise.

Thelma laughed. "You're shocked. Six years ago when he hired me I fell under his spell and it got serious. For two years we were an item."

"What happened?"

Thelma shook her head wryly at the memory. "I fell in love."

"You fell in love? Then why…?"

"…with another man," Thelma interrupted. "We've been happily married for eight years. No kids yet, but you never know."

Lilly sat back in her chair. "How do you and Michael get along now? I can't imagine."

"We get along just fine, honey. We both moved on. We're good friends, and a great business team."

"So how do you know he's still chasing women, taking them to bed?"

"Who do you think calls me in the wee hours baring his soul after yet another meaningless encounter? Yes, Michael. We have a connection. We talk for hours, especially after he's downed four or five drinks. He likes his booze, to a fault. It's his one weakness."

Lilly nodded. "I don't think I should go out with him. I sure don't want to end up like all the others, forgotten after one night. Besides, people in the office will talk."

"Don't be ridiculous! Michael's a catch and don't you forget it. Just one piece of advice: if he drinks a lot over dinner and then asks you to his place for a nightcap, refuse! In the morning you'll thank yourself."

A day later, she almost collided with the man of her dreams as she rushed down an office hallway.

"Sorry," she said. "I need to slow down. I'm so clumsy."

"No problem," he replied, chuckling, and pretending to check his body for damage.

Lilly was impressed that he knew exactly what to say to put her at ease.

"Say, if that dinner invitation is still available, I'd love to accept," she managed to get out.

Two days later, Thelma helped her select a long, close-fitting black dress for the occasion, fashionable yet under-stated.

"Black sets off that golden mane of yours. You'll knock his socks off, honey!"

In his powerful black Mercedes sedan, Michael drove Lilly to Palmas where a waiter led them to an isolated corner on the patio. It was a perfect evening, with the sun starting its descent. With Lilly's permission, Michael ordered dinner: house salads, sea bass, and wild rice, complemented with a bottle of California chardonnay. After dinner, the waiter brought snifters of Courvoisier, a carafe of coffee, and a silver plate of delicate Swiss choco-lates. Then Michael ordered a Manhattan.

"How did a beautiful woman like you find your way to L.A.?" he asked. "You don't appear to be the starry-eyed type looking for a big break in the movies."

Lilly blushed at the implied compliment and talked about growing up in a small town in Nebraska, working in a restaurant for her mother and father, the sudden fire that destroyed the two businesses, and finally making a break for California. She didn't mention her brief relationship with Henry.

"And, oh yes, I'm the guardian of a wonderful eight-year-old boy," Lilly said. "He's the one who keeps me so busy when I'm not at the office. His name is Arthur. His mother died two year ago and his father isn't able or, to be more correct, seems unwilling to care for him. So I'm living in this small house with a young boy, surrounded by great neighbors, including my neighbor, Maria, an angel, if ever there was one. She keeps an eye on Arthur during the day."

Her date listened to her every word as he sipped his drink. She wished she could read his mind. He was quite a bit older. Still, as Thelma pointed out, this is Hollywood. A lot of older men team up with younger women. Besides he wasn't *that* old. Could they have a future? She watched him light another cigarette.

"And I must say," Lilly continued, "when I was growing up in Nebraska I never in my wildest imaginings pictured myself seated in a place like this, and enjoying such a wonderful dinner, with the Pacific Ocean roaring far below. Thank you very much."

"I'd say Performance Arts is lucky to have you," Michael said, ordering his third Manhattan. Thelma wasn't kidding. Michael liked to drink. She'd read in one of her clippings that the cops had picked him up at least twice for drunken driving.

With her date prodding her to talk more about Nebraska, she opened up about the challenges she faced gaining weight and missing out on all the dates and fun of high school.

"Now you're raising a little boy on your own," Michael said. "I'm impressed. Say, this place is filling up. What say we drive over to my place for a nightcap? I live in an historic older place in the Hollywood Hills. Hope to remodel it one of these days." His voice was slurred, and she could tell the booze was taking hold.

Lilly's radar activated. This was exactly what Thelma had warned her against. She should refuse now! He seemed to genuinely care about her and her struggles. What would it hurt? Besides she was curious. One drink at his place and she'd call a cab and go home.

In the parking lot, she suggested they take a cab. Michael insisted he was fine. Despite reservations, she got into the car.

The house was a mansion, glorious in its day but now rundown and neglected. Still, in her eyes, it was an impressive place. After all, famous people had once lived here.

He asked her to take a seat on a small couch near the fireplace, and then excused himself. He returned with a Manhattan in each hand. He handed her the drink and drew her close, his hot breath on her neck. She melted in his arms, his hard body against hers. This is what she always wanted...BUT NO! Thelma's words rang in her ears. She'd made one mistake with Henry—she wasn't about to make another with this man as his hands roamed over her body.

"Please, stop that!" she exclaimed, pushing him away. She raised her hand to slap him but by then he'd pulled back. "Call me a cab. I'm going home."

"Oh, come on. I'm sorry. Let's finish our drinks."

"No, I need to go," she said, her voice rising. "Right now. Please!"

Without a word, Michael called a taxi and she waited on the front porch. She guessed he'd stumbled off to bed. Now she'd done it, messed up her chance to begin a relationship with the man of her dreams, and to add to her misery she'd probably lose her job.

At home, Lilly tossed and turned. She couldn't sleep. The clock said 1:30 a.m. Ignoring the late hour, she rang up Thelma. Her line was busy. Who was she talking to at this time of the night?

The next morning she arrived at work with a heavy heart and a sickening headache. The ache between her eyes dissolved when she found a dozen long-stemmed roses and a note from Michael on her desk. It was an apology. Relief flooded over her.

A moment later, Thelma appeared at her desk. "We have to talk, honey, but not here."

Her friend, and now confidant, invited her over to her house after work. Thelma's husband was at a ballgame with some buddies so they had the place to themselves. They curled up on the couch with cups of tea.

"You made an impression on Michael."

Lilly grimaced, "Yeah, I'll bet."

"Yes, it was Michael on the phone when you called last night," Thelma confided. "He talked and talked. He feels awful and wonders how he can make it up to you."

"He feels bad! You're kidding. I slapped him, well, I guess I didn't actually slap him, even though I sure wanted to take a wallop at him!"

"So I hear. It was exactly the right thing to do. Let me tell you about Michael and the kind of man he is. Maybe then you'll understand."

The two women settled in and Thelma told Michael's story.

"Your date last night grew up in Newark, New Jersey, where his father was a lab technician and his mom a first-grade teacher. He has one brother, Bob, who lives in Boston where he's an oncologist, married with two great kids, a girl and a boy. There are no sisters.

"Michael's mother was a force in the boys' lives. On many weekends, before they became rebellious teenagers and refused to participate, she'd dress them like dandies and, even though money was tight, the three would traipse off to New York City to visit museums, attend Broadway shows, symphonies and opera productions. Mom wanted her boys exposed to the finer things in life.

"Thanks in large part to her constant encouragement and help, Bob and Michael managed to win scholarships to top colleges. Bob, the more practical of the two, attended

Harvard and breezed though his undergraduate years and went on to medical school. Michael attended Dartmouth with plans to major in English and creative writing. His goal was to pen the Great American Novel. That didn't work out and his first job after college was as a crime reporter for *The Newark Chronicle.* He loved reporting even though the pay was dismal. One evening over a couple of beers, he hatched a plan with two fellow reporters to go out on their own. They quit the newspaper and moved across the river and opened an ad agency in Manhattan.

"Unfortunately, this is where the guy made his first misstep. He married a young lady he'd met in college. It didn't turn out well. His golden-girl bride had all the essentials to achieve success in New York: looks, ambition, family money, and connections. After a month-long European honeymoon, she became a fashion editor at a national women's magazine, while Michael resumed a 60-hour-a-week schedule at the ad agency. They made good money. She spent most of it on hair, nails, shoes, clothes, cosmetics, and beauty spas. The topper, though, was that she demanded Michael squire her to an endless succession of designer shows, parties, and special events.

"The marriage lasted barely a year. There were no children. They're still friends, and stay in touch, but infrequently.

"So, did Michael ever marry again?" Lilly asked.

Thelma shook her head. "No. He's dated lots of women, some of the most beautiful in the world, as a matter of fact. He told me during one of our late-night talks he'd like to marry again and have a family. He's waiting for the right girl to come along." Thelma looked right at Lilly.

"After the divorce the war started and Michael spent the next four years in uniform as an Army captain traveling the United States with Hollywood celebrities, encouraging people to buy War Bonds. In the process he made friends with several Hollywood biggies who said they'd vouch for him if he came to California. When the war ended he moved to L.A. Thelma rose from the couch and put her teacup in the sink. Lilly followed and placed a hand on her friend's shoulder.

"So what do you think?" Lilly asked. "About Michael and me?"

"That's up to you. He's interested, if my conversation with him last night is any indication. And he did send you those flowers. He's likes you, likes your Midwest values and your spunk. Not a lot of girls draw the line with him the way you did," Thelma said.

"I didn't actually slap him. But I nearly did."

"Well whatever happened, you've moved up to the A-list."

All grand thoughts come from the heart.

–Luc de Clapiers

Chapter 26

Michael and Lilly had been dating for over a year. For the past six months he'd been spending most nights and weekends with her and Arthur at her house. There were no more late-night calls to Thelma, and he'd cut way back on his drinking. The Manhattans were gone, replaced by an occasional beer and sometimes a glass of wine at dinner. He didn't want to screw things up. They loved staying home, and both liked to cook and took turns fixing meals. The neighbor kids now considered Michael one of the gang. For one thing, he was the best pitcher around and, as a result, practically every night after he and Lilly finished cleaning up the kitchen, one of the kids would bang on the back door and urge Michael to come out and play ball. Invariably, he did.

"The kids are wearing me out, and Arthur is the biggest offender," Michael said one Saturday afternoon as he stepped into the kitchen breathing heavily, his face wet and a blotchy red. He pulled out a chair and sat at the kitchen table and lit a *Camel* cigarette. Coughing and huffing to clear his chest, he finally regained his breath. "We've been tossing that ball around for a good hour and those kids won't let me quit."

Michael, at 43, prided himself on being in good shape. Lately, though, he'd been feeling his age. On the other hand, he hadn't had so much fun in years.

"And you haven't found a way to shut Arthur up, have you," Lilly observed with a laugh. "It's wonderful how you guys have hit it off. He beams when you're pitching. You're a hero at a time when he needs a man in his life to look up to."

"Well, I assure you, it's two-sided. That boy is a burst of sunshine. Makes me feel good to be around him, that's for sure."

"Hey, soon as you catch your breath there, how about starting the salad?"

"Absolutely," he said, stepping to the sink and washing his hands under the running faucet. He watched her work at the counter, adding spices to a pan of spaghetti sauce. A pot of water came to a boil on the stove. A sense of inner calm came over him. He hadn't felt so comfortable and happy in years. And it was because of Lilly and Arthur. They'd become inexpressibly dear to him.

Lilly glanced over at him. "Penny for your thoughts?"

"Have I told you how much I love you?" he answered.

"Not today! I've been waiting."

"Do you have any idea how much I enjoy this home life?" he asked. "But I have to tell you Arthur's been complaining that we never go out any more. He says we're turning into real bores. Our last outing was on his ninth birthday. Maybe we should plan a trip to the zoo or the beach? Just for a day. Far as I'm concerned, if I never attend another movie premiere or celebrity party, it's fine with me."

"Easy for you to say. You've had your good times," Lilly answered, wearing a pouty face that Michael knew wasn't for real. "What about me? What girl wouldn't love 'putting on the ritz' and attending a gala party, or dining privately with Kirk Douglas at his home, or rubbing elbows with Tyrone Power on a yacht?"

He leaned back and crossed his arms. "You choose the party, the time and place, and we'll go. My bet is in an hour you'll beg to make a mad dash for our safe and sane little hacienda just off Sunset Boulevard."

"I may surprise you and drink, dance and party till dawn," Lilly chided as she moved over to stand in front of him. "Would it bother you if I ran off with one of those handsome leading men?"

"Yeah, it would. You're the only girl for me, and always will be. I think you know that, don't you?"

"Isn't that nice," she said, rubbing the back of his neck. "I remember in bed last night you made a lot of promises."

Once supper was over, and Arthur had gone out to play, she raised the same question: "When are we going to see this house of yours?" She'd been after him for weeks on the subject, even though she knew the answer.

"Hey, come on. I told you. It's dangerous there," Michael protested. "You've seen the architect's plans. You know how much work is being done. There's a construction crew of 30 over there. Last time I nearly got bonked on the head with a falling brick. Besides, I want to surprise you with the full effect when it's finished. Trust me, you'll be the first to take the Grand Tour."

Re-construction on the old house had begun two months earlier. Michael had owned the property for just over six years, buying it at a distressed-sale price two years after he'd arrived in Los Angeles. He recognized the potential in the three-story, brick Tudor-style house, which was built by a Hollywood silent-film star in the early 1910s. The house had great bones. He especially liked the two-acre site, which sat high and provided a sliver of a view of the Pacific Ocean on clear days.

When he moved in, the first thing he did was patch the leaking roof. He always planned to launch a major renovation but with the demands of work he'd never gotten around to even contacting an architect. There didn't seem to be any rush. He lived there alone except for a daytime housekeeper named Myrna.

Now, with Lilly and Arthur in his life and—dare he hope—the possibility they'd one day be a family, Michael was embarked on a top-to-bottom re-do, and, with Lilly biting at his back, he was pushing the crew hard to finish up. Michael also approved adding a luxurious California-style swimming pool, bathhouse and patio off the back, and a championship-style tennis court on the side-yard, complete with lights for night games.

He contracted with one of California's most respected landscape architects to convert the over-grown yard into a green, leafy showplace, accented with fountains, stone-walls, flowerbeds, trees and shrubbery.

The tennis court was Michael's secret weapon with Arthur. He'd played the game since he was a kid in New Jersey and was skilled enough to make the Dartmouth college team. Several trophies gathered dust on a fireplace mantel in his bedroom. He hadn't played the game even once since starting Performance Arts, and he missed it. Now, with a tennis court soon to be on the property, he couldn't think of a better way to build a closer relationship with Arthur. He hoped one day the kid would love tennis as much as he did.

In the meantime, he and Arthur were following the skyrocketing career of a local L.A. tennis player, a young Mexican kid named Poncho Gonzales. Poncho had learned to play tennis on the weedy public courts of East Los Angeles. He was a natural, and when he combined his native talent with an aggressive, charge-the-net style of play that he'd developed on his own, he was a force to be reckoned with. From the first serve, anyone who played

Poncho soon learned it was to be a *mano-a-mano*, take-no-prisoners contest. The best players in the world couldn't stand up to the onslaught from this former juvenile delinquent from a barrio in Los Angeles.

The sports writers made him into a national hero, a poor Mexican kid who had forever changed the white-shorts, country-club game into a sport that was anything but gentlemanly. Arthur, always rooting for the underdog, worshipped Gonzales.

In late fall of 1953, workmen put the finishing touches to the house and its brand-new amenities. Michael invited Lilly to view it on a Saturday morning.

"It's nothing fancy, like some of the movie stars' homes," he said, as he escorted her across the threshold. "I hope you like it."

Lilly stepped into the vaulted, three-story high open foyer, with bright sunshine streaming through upper, east-facing windows. In what seemed like a very long pause, he waited nervously for her to say something.

Slowly turning in a circle, she said, "Nothing fancy, you say? Sure looks like a mansion to me! So different from that night when you brought me here and I had to put you in your place," she said, tapping him on the shoulder. She walked from room-to-room, her heels clacking on the gleaming marble floors. "God, Michael, it's beautiful."

"Will you marry me?" he asked. "I've spent a fortune here. And it was all for you."

This wasn't the first time he'd proposed. Lilly had put him off, suggesting it was too soon. "I'm not sure Arthur's ready to have his life turned upside down again," she'd say.

Now, with Michael standing before her, looking so proud, anticipation glowing on his face, she stepped into his arms.

"Of course, I'll marry you. Now we need to work on getting Arthur used to the idea of moving here. He loves Maria and her family. It's going to be hard for him to leave his friends and the old neighborhood."

"That's why I built the swimming pool and the tennis court. Shameless bribes. What kid could resist?"

"And am I also being bribed?" she asked, her voice low and sensual, as her gaze scanned the expansive dining room with its glittering chandeliers and a gleaming table with seating for 20 guests.

"At the moment, I'd like to see my new bedroom. I'm feeling a bit faint," she said laughing softly. "I need to lie down. Kindly lead the way, Sir Galahad."

Keep love in your heart. A life without it is like a sunless garden.

–Oscar Wilde

Chapter 27

"Oh my gosh!" Arthur gushed, using one of his favorite expressions, as he and Michael walked along the edge of the sparkling swimming pool.

"You're rich, aren't you?" he said, reaching down and running a hand through the water. "Paul would love this place. He wants to be rich some day. Is that a tennis court over there?"

"Sure is," he answered, throwing an arm across the boy's shoulders. "Use the pool anytime you like, and invite your friends over. They're all welcome."

"You're kidding! All my friends can come here? They'll go nuts."

"We can play tennis anytime, day or night. I had them install lights. How's that sound to you? Hey, and get this, maybe we'll have Poncho Gonzales over to give us a few lessons."

"Noooo. Poncho right here? Do you even know him?"

"Met him a week or so ago. He's a new client of Performance Arts. Seems like a great guy. They say his mother gave him a 51-cent racquet when he was 12 years old and he mostly taught himself to play by watching other players. Incredible story, and apparently true. Could happen to you," he said nudging the boy.

A week later Lilly and Michael sat Arthur down in Lilly's kitchen to tell him that they planned to marry.

"I want you to stand up with me at the wedding ceremony," Lilly said. Arthur's face lit up.

"And we're all going to move into the new house," Michael offered.

His face fell.

"No way!" Arthur flared. "I'm not leaving. This is where all my friends are—school, Maria, all the kids. You can't make me!"

He stomped to his feet and ran outside bawling.

When he returned for lunch, Lilly revisited the subject. "I know you're attached to your friends. Michael says they can visit anytime."

"Let's continue to live here. Michael likes it fine here. He plays ball with of us and we have a great time."

"We're both concerned about the neighborhood. This used to be a safe place but there's a lot more crime. The police can't stop it."

Arthur looked down at his shoes and used his fists to wipe the tears from his eyes.

"Did you hear about poor Mr. Ackerman, the elderly gentleman who lives down the street? He was walking home from the grocery and a gang of kids beat him up. And school's getting bad, too. Wasn't it last week you told me some kid tried to steal your lunch money?"

"I'm fine," Arthur said, trying to sound brave. "I can take care of myself, and besides we kids stick together."

"Please, honey, just think about it. Even after we move, Maria says you're welcome at her house. Talk to her, see what she thinks?"

The boy waited until Maria was alone on her front porch shelling peas into a bowl. He trudged up the porch steps.

"You think we should move, Maria?"

"Um, I heard you might be doing that. I understand a wedding is in the works. That's exciting."

"Gee whiz, I don't want to go. Why should I have to move?"

"Oh, honey, we'll miss you," Maria said, taking one of his hands. "You're always welcome here. You know, sweetie, it wasn't easy for my family to move here from Texas. I was scared and the kids cried and threw fits. Sophia didn't speak to me for a week. In the end, it worked out best for our family. And think about this: if we hadn't moved to Los Angeles we'd never have met you and Lilly, and wouldn't that be a shame?"

A few days later, a Saturday, Lilly and Michael loaded up eight of Arthur's friends, including Maria's children and they all drove to Hollywood Hills. As they jumped and splashed in the pool, Michael's housekeeper, Myrna, brought out trays of snacks and drinks.

After the pool party, Arthur begged Lilly, "Let's move in right away. Michael and I can play tennis every night."

Arthur threw himself into tennis, practicing every day and reading every tennis book he could put his hands on. Evenings and weekends, Michael taught him technique and etiquette. Saturday mornings, he took lessons from the resident pro at a nearby private sport complex.

Five months later Michael and Lilly were married in a style that proved to be a non-event by Hollywood standards. She was 25; he was 44. No announcement was made to the press. After a few weeks had passed, an eagle-eyed reporter spotted the official notice of the marriage license application while sorting through courthouse records. The next day a two-paragraph story appeared in the *LA Chronicle* followed by a bigger spread in the *Hollywood Reporter*. The coverage was paltry compared to what the media types would have headlined if two of Hollywood's top stars got hitched. However, as Lilly pointed out, no self-respecting fan magazine gave a whistle about an agency mogul marrying a small-town Nebraska girl like her.

Thelma, now the head of the writer/director division, and her husband, Harold, witnessed the proceedings in a courtroom in downtown L.A. Arthur stood up with the couple as the judge, Malcolm Lubben, a friend of Michael's, conducted the civil ceremony. At Michael's urging, Lilly kept her maiden name of Swenson.

To Lilly, keeping the Swenson name seemed disrespectful, temporary and tawdry, like the bride and groom were taking the marriage out for a test ride. Besides, the sound of "Mrs. Michael Paulson" had a nice ring to it. Thelma sided with Michael.

"In this town, it's smart to keep your maiden name, especially if the woman is earning her living in the entertainment industry," Thelma counseled. "Everything in this town is about personalities and name recognition. Women stand on what they've done, not on the shoulders of some man who's liable to do who knows what. Men are nuts!"

"Keep in mind, honey, this isn't the Midwest, certainly not Nebraska. Here, people like Marilyn Monroe will always be Marilyn Monroe, no matter whether she's married at any given moment or not, or even the number of times she waltzes to the altar. Marilyn's a brand name, like Coca-Cola or Christian Dior. When Michael advises you to keep the Swenson name, don't argue. He knows what he's talking about."

"That's ridiculous. I'm no Marilyn Monroe and never will be."

"Probably not. But you never know what might happen in 10, 20 or 30 years."

* * * * *

Henry was one of the few people to have read the tiny story about the application for a wedding license in the *LA Chronicle*. He wrote down Michael's home address, which was printed in the story. On one of his rare days off, he drove his old buggy to the Hollywood Hills address where Lilly now lived with her sugar daddy. His eyes followed the long curving driveway to the three-story house on the hilltop. Morning light glinted off the leaded windows and the manicured lawn glistened from the dew. The grass ran right up to the front door, like a lush, green carpet.

"Well, I'll be damned," he murmured. "So this is where she's living with my son while I hole up in a crummy apartment. She has all this and I'm living like a pauper. He lit a cigarette and kept his eyes focused on the house.

Seething with resentment, he promised: "She'll pay, somehow, someday."

A white sedan with "Security" stenciled on the side crept past. Henry caught the movement from the corner of his eye. The driver, in a khaki uniform and a billed hat, gave Henry's old Ford a long once-over. He pulled to the curb about 20 yards ahead and sat there, his head turned, watching him.

Henry started the motor. He didn't need trouble. He watched the private cop write something in a notepad, probably his license plate number. Henry gunned the engine, dropped the clutch, and left two black rubber stripes on the pristine white cement street. Flying past the guard, he lifted his left hand and gave the guy the finger. He let out a sigh of relief when the car didn't follow.

If we learn to open our hearts...anyone can be our teacher.

–Pema Chodron

Chapter 28

One of the special things Lilly loved was watching her two men play tennis. Sometimes she'd even shag errant balls, and she always called out encouragement from the sidelines. Slim and lithe, and growing taller by the day, 11-year-old Arthur flew around the tennis court, making up for a lack of experience with youthful liveliness. He needed more work on his shot selection, and practice on his serve. Michael was certain the boy one day would be an excellent player.

"He has the perfect physique for the game, combined with a fiercely competitive spirit," Michael pointed out.

During a practice match, Michael sliced a ball past Arthur before he could even lift his racket. Afterwards, Arthur approached the net and shook Michael's hand.

"Will I ever be as good as you are?" the boy asked, discouraged.

"Sooner than you might think," Michael said, struggling to catch his breath.

They continued to follow Poncho's career, and during the course of one of his tournaments, Arthur watched the Mexican sensation serve and volley and then rush forward to slam the return cross-court like a canon shot. From the look on Poncho's face, you'd think his opponent was his mortal enemy.

"Is he supposed to do that?" Arthur asked.

Michael shook his head. The people who enforce tennis rules say there's nothing to prevent him from the playing the game his way."

"He's out to win, and I like that," the boy stated emphatically.

A few weeks later, after another Gonzales match at the Los Angeles Tennis Center, Michael surprised Arthur with a trip to the locker room. Poncho greeted Arthur like they were long-time tennis pals. A photographer snapped a picture of the adoring boy and the tennis star. Poncho later autographed the photo, writing: "Never back down, kid! Your buddy, Poncho Gonzales."

Arthur would cherish the photograph for the rest of his life.

* * * * *

The school principal at Arthur's school, a crew-cut former college football player who'd made a name for himself as a UCLA running back, invited Lilly and Michael to attend a meeting in his office. When she asked what it was about, he said: "No problems. Matter of fact I'm confident you'll be delighted with what I have to say."

The principal and another man greeted them when she and Michael arrived. The principal seemed like a nice guy, always smiling, positive. He filled the room with his outgoing personality. The other guy was quiet and he had a steadiness about him, more the technician than the people person. His name was Mr. Thomas, and he represented the educational testing service that measured student progress with achievement tests. His firm also, when requested, calculated student IQs. Arthur was already in the principal's office, sitting in a chair next to the man's desk. He wore a puzzled look. He glanced at Lilly and she looked back, shaking her head, like she didn't have a clue about what was going on either.

"First, I want to congratulate this young man," the principal said. "He's achieved the highest scores ever by a student in this school. In fact, he ranks at the top for sixth graders in the entire Los Angeles School District, which, as I'm sure you know, is the largest school district in all of California." He made this statement with considerable pride in his voice.

"What do you think of that?" the principal asked, placing a firm, congratulatory hand on Arthur's shoulder.

"It's okay, I guess. All I did was answer the questions best I could."

"What it means is that your intelligent quotient, or IQ, is in the upper three percent of all students at your grade level in America," Mr. Thomas injected. "That's very special."

"And it also means we're extremely proud to have you in our school," the principal added.

Driving back to the office, Lilly said, "Can you believe it? A genius in the family! His teachers always said he was bright. Now we learn he's *really* smart. Wonder where he gets it from?"

"Perhaps his parents infected him with the genius bug," Michael said.

"I'm sure it didn't come from Henry, although I must say Henry is a walking encyclopedia of dirty jokes," Lilly said, wryly. "My money's on Margie. From what I heard, she was one smart cookie. God rest her soul. And his grandmother must have had a lot on the ball. She was a school teacher."

"It's a big responsibility having a child prodigy," Michael said. "I suppose behind the motor-mouth, he's powered by a heck of big brain. I'll have to start paying closer attention to what he says. He's always asking questions, then answering them himself. Who knew he was a freakin' Einstein!"

"Should he stay in public schools?" Lilly asked.

"I'd say he deserves to be challenged. A college friend heads up a top-rated prep school in San Francisco. Should I call him?"

"I don't think so. I can't see him going off all alone to a school hundreds of miles away. Besides, we want him here, don't we?"

"Absolutely! There are excellent schools in this area. I'll put out some feelers. Meantime, he starts junior high next fall.

Michael shook his head in wonder. "Did you notice the way Arthur took the genius talk in stride, like it wasn't anything to make a fuss about? What a kid!"

It is strange how often a heart must be broken before the years can make it wise.

–Sara Teasdale

Chapter 29

As Paul's hand crept toward her breast, long-time girlfriend Annie Hemphill's hand intercepted it. A vice-grip. How could a girl be so strong?

We've been over this so many times," she said, sitting up in the seat and straightening her blouse. "I thought you understood."

"Please, you're leaving for college tomorrow," Paul begged. "What am I supposed to do?"

They were parked on the blacktop at the town cemetery, located on a hilltop overlooking downtown Elk Point, a popular necking spot for high school kids. He moved away from Annie, and leaned his shoulder against the driver's side door. "Most of the other guys are getting what they want as often as they want," Paul said. "I'm supposed to be the big jock around town and I'm getting scratch."

"Sorry. I can't help what the other girls are doing. This is the way the Bible tells us to live our lives."

Paul drove her home and they kissed goodnight. She promised to write every day and he agreed to do the same, though he cautioned, "I'm not much of a writer." Annie's mom and dad planned to drive her to Lincoln where she'd begin her studies in pre-med at the University of Nebraska. Meantime, in Elk Point Paul had already started fall football practice. Classes for his senior year started next week.

Driving away, Paul got mad all over again. It wasn't right for him to be the only one missing out. It was her fault. How could she be such a prude?

The days flew by and Paul was so busy with school and football he hardly had time to think about Annie, let alone write letters. As the starting quarterback, everyone in Elk Point figured he'd lead the team to another conference win, and possibly a state championship at the playoffs in Omaha.

And that's how the season unfolded. Elk Point ran the table, winning all of its games, and secured a second consecutive conference title. Next Friday night, they'd play for the small-school state championship. The town was jubilant. Everyone planned to be in Omaha for the big game

Meanwhile, it was Saturday night and Paul and his friend John Ellsworth, also on the team, were in a party mood. They scooped the downtown business district in John's father's new Ford sedan. The local movie house had let out and crowds of teenagers gathered on the sidewalk, talking and laughing, trying to decide what to do next.

John pulled the Ford to the curb and yelled: "Hey, Linda! You girls wanna ride?"

John had dated Linda Crowley a couple of times and he knew she liked to make out. With her was another cheerleader, Nancy Bain. During timeouts, Paul had watched these varsity cheerleaders strut their stuff before the cheering crowds. They looked great, really sexy.

The girls piled into the back seat. Grinning and slapping Paul on the thigh, John pointed the car toward the cemetery, the same spot where he and Annie had parked the night before she'd left for Lincoln.

According to local folklore, a distraught young lady, jilted by her cavalier lover, leaped to her death from this overlook. However, when the local newspaper editor interviewed the cemetery superintendent for an April Fools Day spoof about the legend, the man in the overalls chuckled. "Shucks, worst thing could happen to a girl plunging off of here might be a nasty grass stain on her backside."

John edged the car as close as possible to the drop off and shut off the engine. At John's suggestion, Paul

stepped out and Linda took his place up front. Paul duti-
fully moved to the back seat with Nancy.

He'd known Nancy Bain since junior high and had
pretty much ignored her over the years. Annie took all of
his attention. Recently, though, he'd started to take more
interest in the locker room talk when the guys started bragging about the "easy girls" they were dating. Paul recalled
one conversation when Billy Simpson took him aside and,
in a confidential tone, told him: "Nancy's smokin' hot,
buddy, and she'll do it, and that's a fact, especially with
you. I heard she wants a piece of you, man."

When Paul first shared a class with Nancy in seventh
grade, she was skinny and flat-chested. Now, she ranked
as one of the cutest, most popular girl in the senior class.
In the winter, she wore tight sweaters and skirts as short
as school rules allowed. In the summer it was close-fitting
pullovers and short-shorts, reaching barely below the
crotch.

"I'm really excited about Friday's championship
game," Nancy said as Paul scooted in beside her. "The
cheerleaders are staying overnight at the hotel with the
team. Won't that be a hoot?"

She slid toward him and snuggled close.

"Yeah, sounds like fun," Paul said, not making any
moves.

In a moment, though, she was all over him, breathing
hot air on his neck. He couldn't get Billy's "she wants a
piece of you" out of his head. Annie's face popped into

his mind. Guilt seeped into his conscience. Nancy moved closer and they kissed. He slid his hand under her sweater and was dumbfounded when she didn't push him away. Instead, she squeezed closer. He lifted her bra and massaged her breasts. Her nipples swelled and hardened. She released a low moan and shoved one of her legs between his and pushed up. He reached under her skirt. She stopped him there.

"Sorry, Paul," she cooed. "It's not a good time. I'm having my monthly."

Paul jerked back like he'd stuck his hand in a bonfire.

Not the least embarrassed, Nancy sat up, smiled and brushed back her hair. She lifted her sweater and carefully placed each breast into its proper bra cup, giving a little shake to make certain everything was in its proper place before pulling down the sweater. She didn't mind that he kept his eyes on her every move.

"It's great we're able to get together tonight," she said, moving closer to him. "I understand Annie's off to college. Maybe we could go out sometime?"

Leaning forward, she called into the front seat, "Hey, John, hate to be a spoil sport. If I'm not home by ten, Mom will have a cow."

After dropping the girls off, John said, "Christ! I was this close to getting into her pants. How about you?"

"She's on the rag.

"Too bad, man. Hey, the cheerleaders are staying in the same hotel in Omaha. What say after the game we have a little party, just the four of us? I'll bring some whiskey. My dad won't miss it."

"Sounds okay."

"I'll set it up. Wooee, buddy, we're in for a good time!"

As it turned out, Elk Point trailed the Albia Cowboys by four points in the fourth quarter of the championship game. This was the team nearly everyone had predicted Elk Point would bury. But Albia's coaches had a lot of experience, and had won state championships nearly half a dozen times over the years. You had to figure the coaches would have their team ready for tonight's game. With less than 15 seconds on the time clock in the fourth quarter, it was do-or-die for Elk Point. Paul yelled "HUT!" and Harvey Jones, Elk Point's 240-pound, farm-boy center, placed the ball perfectly into his hands. Paul dropped back three steps, squared his shoulders, and threw a 30-yard spiral to Jerry Basel as two Albia linebackers crushed him to the ground. Paul popped up and his eyes narrowed as he focused on Jerry in the end zone. The pass had gone high. The clock read zero.

"Shit," Paul said aloud. He looked to the Elk Point side of the stadium and saw the air go out of the spectators. Elk Point was supposed to win. It hadn't turned out that way.

Following the second-place trophy presentation on the football field, two yellow school buses took the coaches, players, and cheerleaders to the Howard Johnson just off Dodge Street for the Booster Club post-game buffet dinner. Coach Faraday declared how proud he was of everyone. He did his best to paint a good face on the situation to help the locals deal with the disappointment. Paul was sorry. It was a shame they'd lost; still it wasn't a life or death matter. The other team outplayed them.

"Let's have our senior quarterback Paul Goodwin come forward," Faraday declared. "This guy's one heck of a football player and we're sure going to miss him. Give him a big hand."

The buffet wound down and students and parents broke into small groups. John slipped Linda a piece of paper with the boys' room number on it. A half hour later there was a knock on the door of Room 317. Linda and Nancy stood side-by-side in the hallway.

The two couples slow-danced around the room as the radio murmured in the background, the only light coming from the half-open bathroom door. Paul sipped a whiskey and Coke as they danced, and the room swirled faster. Nancy had quickly polished off two drinks. She leaned her head on his shoulder and whispered, a tease in her voice: "You know that little problem I told you about in the car, Paul? Well, I'm good as new. What say we leave these two alone and head down to my room?"

She grabbed his hand and tugged him toward the door.

Paul hesitated. He'd never cheated on Annie and he felt one hundred percent certain she'd been true to him. But what the heck. She was wrapped up in studying for

midterms, too busy to even attend tonight's championship game.

He followed Nancy unsteadily down the hallway and
was amazed how quickly she sobered up. She opened
the door with an efficient click and, once inside, pushed
against him and unbuttoned his shirt and loosened his belt
as he passively stood against the wall. Shirtless and with
his pants bunched around his feet, Paul watched Nancy
remove her blouse, skirt, panties and bra as quickly as
a shopkeeper undressing a mannequin. Naked, she lay
back on the single bed and beckoned. Paul stood frozen,
uncertain what to do next.

"Here, take this and put it on." She handed him a rubber.

He fumbled trying to get the damn thing on. Nancy
helped him with her long fingers. It was too much!

"Sorry," he said, mortified.

"No problem, kiddo," Nancy said.

Paul lay next to her and tried to catch his breath.

"Oh, man," he said aloud.

Nancy examined her nail polish and sat up in bed.
"You'll do better."

In a few minutes, he did just that.

"Hey, know what? My parents will be gone Saturday
night till after midnight. It's their night to play cards with
the Millers. Come on over. It'll be just you and me. We'll
have some fun."

Despite the team's loss, locals jammed downtown Elk
Point the next afternoon, Saturday, with horns blaring and

drums pounding. The Elk Point High marching band led a parade around the town square. Wearing their jerseys, the players stood on a flatbed hay trailer as a John Deere tractor pulled them slowly around the square. The crowd roared.

"Damn!" said Billy, who stood next to Paul. "Never saw so many people in town. We're heroes, ain't we?"

"Yep, I guess. Although we'd be bigger heroes if we'd won," Paul replied.

Booster Club members rode floats and rained handfuls of candy for the gangs of little kids and the occasional adult who ran along the curb. The bouncing cheerleaders led the cheers. Nancy flounced her long hair and waved. He didn't acknowledge her. His mind was elsewhere.

He remembered being on Main Street five years earlier when he and Arthur battled the blizzard and carried the empty red fuel container to Bottman's. No crowds, no cheers, only his little brother whining about the cold and snow. Then came the flames and the black smoke and his father hopping around on feet that were blistered from the flames. Even today, with the crowd roaring, the memory of his father's words blaming him for the fire turned his face red. A tear streaked across his face.

"Paul! Paul!"

Paul shook himself back to the moment. It was Annie, home from Lincoln, pointing and waving at him from the sidewalk. Her parents were there, too.

"See you at the drugstore!" she yelled

He waved back even as his stomach began churning. After the parade completed its rounds, Paul broke off from his teammates. Lowering his head slightly, he lifted a hand and gave the excited kids packed into the drugstore a finger wave as he walked to the booth where Annie waited with two girlfriends.

She jumped up and wrapped him in her arms. "Hey, there, Mr. Football. Congratulations. You're the town hero, now and forever."

"Well, I'm sorry we lost," he said, taking a seat. "Coach always said, no matter how good you are, there's always someone who'll do better. He was dead-on right this time."

"Oh, he's a stick-in-the-mud," Annie declared. "You're the best—always will be!"

Paul hadn't seen her in nearly eight weeks. Now, sitting in the drugstore where they had hung out for years, there was something different about her; she was more grown up, older around the eyes, like she was dealing with important stuff, things he didn't know anything about. One day she'd be a medical doctor. Since she'd been a little girl, she'd wanted to grow up to help people and work with the church as a missionary in foreign lands.

"Want a Coke?" she asked, sliding over to make room for him.

He took a seat and noticed Nancy Bain and a couple of other cheerleaders come bopping into the drugstore.

She hadn't spotted him yet. "No, don't think so. It's really noisy here. Let's cut out," he said.

They drove around until dark before parking at the curb in front of her house. They started making out. Paul slipped his hand under her blouse. As usual, she removed it.

"Please," she said, knowing he'd be upset. "I know it's not fair, Paul. You're here, and I'm in Lincoln and college classes are taking all my time and energy. I rarely find time to write to you anymore."

"I've noticed," he said, gripping the steering wheel and staring into the darkness, feeling pleased yet guilty that he'd found what he wanted with Nancy. Still, it didn't feel right.

"This is your final year in high school," Annie said. "You deserve some fun—you know, like going out with other girls, enjoying yourself. I can't be here, and next fall you'll be off to college in a different place, and we'll be even farther apart."

"Hey, what's happening here? Are you dumping me?"

"Of course not!" she said, looking hurt. "We've been together since junior high. Neither of us knows what it's like to date other people."

Uh, oh, Paul thought. Had Nancy Bain been blowing off her mouth around town? Had word reached Annie about the party in the hotel in Omaha? His face heated up. He hoped not.

"In Lincoln, when I have a little free time, I hang out with a bunch of friends, guys and gals," she ran on. "We talk, go to movies, and eat together in the cafeteria. It's interesting. They come from different backgrounds, like Chicago and Denver."

What the hell, Paul thought. She's too busy to write but has time for new friends, including some guys.

They talked a while longer. Things had changed. The comfortable way they used to toss out words to each other was gone. Now, there didn't seem much to say at all. Paul sat there, hands in his lap, eyes turned down. Finally, in an awkward movement, they came together and kissed, a kiss that startled him in its intensity. They both knew this was a goodbye kiss.

He drove away and tears clouded his vision. She was right. The distance between them was a problem, and it would be an even bigger problem next year when they'd be at different colleges. He'd be in Iowa; she'd be in Lincoln. He remembered her being there for him when he'd gotten in trouble over fighting at school. She'd pushed him to study and earn good grades. He couldn't recall a single instance when she'd let him down. Now she was moving on. One day she'd be a doctor, and a darned good one. Would they have anything in common? Was this the last time they'd be together?

Be still my heart; thou hast known worse than this.

–Homer

Chapter 30

Lilly stood on the open front porch of the house and reveled in the feel and taste of the ocean breeze that blew her hair away from her face. With the sun nearly down, long, willowy stratus clouds separated into creamy streams of muted oranges, reds, and gold as they rode the western horizon. She felt that God must have crafted this sunset especially for her as a fitting finale to a perfect day. Spreading her arms like she was about to take flight, she looked to the sea, and a sense of peace enveloped her.

Arthur had finished grade school and junior high, and now at 13, soon 14, would start prep school at the elite Los Angeles Academy in the fall. He'd grown to almost six feet and, thanks to tennis, was in peak physical shape.

Along the way, he'd matured into a handsome, confident young man.

The sky faded to dark and a full moon filled the sky as Lilly walked around the house and sat down on the green, park-style bench just inside the fence surrounding the tennis court. She tucked her legs under her, seeking warmth from the chill of the night. Under the lights, Michael and Arthur were going at it hard, the tennis ball a blur over the net. During each point the two exchanged wisecracks.

"Lucky shot!" Michael called out.

"Yeah, right!" Arthur retorted. "You mean that ball that landed right on the back line, or the one I hit, swear to God, so hard and fast it flew by before you could blink?"

"Hey, hey, you two. Be nice, and hold it down," Lilly admonished. "The neighbors will call the cops."

The good-natured ribbing continued.

Lilly had noticed for some time the trouble Michael was having keeping pace with Arthur, who as usual was showing no mercy as he forced her struggling husband to run from side-to-side to keep the ball in play.

Soon, Michael raised his hand to signal a break. Gasping for air, he stumbled over and collapsed alongside Lilly, his face flushed bright red and his white shirt soaked with sweat. "Cripes," he sputtered before several ragged coughs took his breath. Regaining his composure, he said, "The little rascal is too fast and too good. I need to shape up or I'll never beat him at tennis again."

Michael's breathing problem stemmed from a long smoking habit. Along with millions of other young soldiers, he'd gotten hooked on nicotine while serving in the Army.

He always claimed he was fine and asked her not to worry. However, his breathing problems had worsened to the point even Michael could no longer dismiss the coughing and shortness of breath as simply a result of aging.

She clipped articles from newspapers and magazines that linked heavy smoking to lung cancer and left them where she knew Michael would find them.

Of course, the tobacco companies denied the connection between their product and cancer, even going so far as to conduct their own "scientific" studies, which, surprise of surprises, found no link between smoking and threats to good health. In fact, the tobacco crowd concluded that smoking was actually beneficial, especially for people looking for a way to relax after a hard day at the office, or to enjoy a cocktail, or to share a smoke with a partner after a romantic encounter. Lilly's lip curled when she saw these outrageous advertising claims on television and in the newspapers.

What caused Michael to finally get serious about his own health was a call from a producer friend who reported that the Hollywood grapevine was buzzing about Humphrey Bogart. The word was the super-star had lung cancer and was dying.

Bogie wasn't a client. Still, Michael knew him and considered him a friend. Both he and Lilly loved his movies and his devil-may-care lifestyle, on and off the screen. Michael, like millions of other men, admired the sophisticated way Bogart dangled a cigarette from his mouth, and the way he handled women with feeling and masculine confidence.

"Bogie hasn't been seen around town much, and for a guy who loves to party, that's way out of character," the producer said. "Word is the studio's delaying the start of his next movie. People say he looks thin and haggard and can hardly stand up."

Bogart died two weeks later. Lilly and Michael attended the funeral. Bogart was 56 years old. One reporter showed some gumption and wrote a story about the disturbing pattern of tragic deaths involving A-list actors and others in the entertainment industry, and the fact that nearly all were heavy smokers. The reporter didn't actually use Bogart's name in the story. However, with the star's death so fresh on everyone's minds, the connection was clearly intimated.

The news story concluded: "Within the past few years, the Grim Reaper has locked in on Hollywood with a diabolical plan to strike down the enclave's most beautiful and talented celebrities. Is there a cause-effect relationship between smoking and lung cancer? You decide," he wrote.

She and Michael later learned the newspaper publisher fired the reporter along with the editor who allowed the story to be printed. The tobacco companies wielded significant power with the media, thanks to their multimillion-dollar advertising budgets. They took swift action whenever an unfavorable story hit the newsstands and airwaves.

After Bogart's funeral, her husband tried different ways to free himself from the addiction, including a week-long retreat advertised as a sure-fire path to smoke-free living. He tried tapering off, even went cold turkey—several times. Finally, after a particularly harrowing coughing fit, Michael told Lilly he'd had his last cigarette, and he flung his cigarette package into the wastebasket. He also agreed to see a lung specialist. The appointment was set for the following week.

"I'm going with you," she said.

She got no argument from Michael.

The mouth obeys poorly when the heart murmurs.

–Voltaire

Chapter 31

With the neighborhood in a downward spiral, the husband-wife owners of Kelsey's sold the bar and grill and invested the proceeds in a new place closer to downtown. They named it The Metropolitan Club.

The business was an unqualified success. That was of little consolation to Henry. It galled him that his former bosses didn't offer him a job when they moved to the more upscale location. He had to accept a proposal from the Filipino immigrant couple that had purchased Kelsey's.

"You be our manager," the new Kelsey's boss lady said. "You make lots of bucks here. You see!"

Unfortunately, the number of the customers who frequented Kelsey's plunged. Nothing was the same. Instead of the young, stylish Hollywood types, the customer base now consisted of down-and-out street people, and a colorful cast of pimps and prostitutes and other shady characters. Business was so slow even the kitchen was closed except on weekends.

Around Kelsey's neighborhood, iron bars went up on windows and doors, entire buildings were abandoned and homeowners put up "For Sale" signs as the cops beefed up patrols.

"A fellow could get killed around here," a once-loyal Kelsey's neighborhood patron told Henry. "I'm scared to even drop in for a beer."

With fewer customers, and practically no tips, Henry worked longer and harder for a slimmer paycheck. His earnings fell to where he could barely cover apartment rent and car payments, let alone buy groceries. Eating out or taking a dame on a date was a thing of the past.

The whores and pimps who sat on the bar stools and stayed for hours at a time, rarely ordered more than one drink. To pass the time, the ladies begged Henry to tell jokes.

"Nobody tells them better than you," said a middle-aged prostitute with a prominent mole on her left cheek. "I about snapped a bra strap when you told the one about the fellow catching his donger in his zipper. Cracked me up, honey."

The night ladies were a randy collection with neglected teeth, unkempt hair and a bizarre and revealing dress code.

They punctuated their third-grade vocabularies with a wild set of curses and catcalls. Henry found a few were likable, with big hearts and sympathetic stories to tell. He'd sometimes share his woeful tale with a select few of them through clouds of cigarette smoke as the ladies dallied and kept an eye out for the next john to appear. More than once he was offered a complimentary screw to lift his spirits. He always said thanks, but no thanks.

To provide a line of security, and to offer some sense of protection, Henry went to Sears-Roebuck and purchased three major-league baseball bats and spaced them within easy reach behind the bar. By God, if somebody came after him, he'd defend himself.

His days were reduced to a dismal routine of work and sleep. The two-room, walk-up apartment he occupied was a pigsty. Dishes and empty food cartons overflowed the sink and buried the counter. If he dared opening the fridge, the stench of rotting food and spoiled milk drove him back.

For years he'd kept live-in girlfriends to handle cooking, laundry, cleaning and to share his bed. Nowadays, he had neither the energy nor the money to keep that routine going. At night before going to bed, he'd wash the next day's socks and underwear in the bathroom sink with a bar of hand soap and hang them on a towel rack to dry. In the morning he'd rummage through the piles of dirty laundry that lay stiffening in a corner for a presentable pair of pants and shirt to wear to work that day.

Henry was behind the bar and Kelsey's was deserted except for a bum who'd panhandled some coins and was spending the money at the bar, and a tough-looking couple sitting silently in a back booth drinking bourbon and water.

Feeling low and abused, and certain that his life had hit bottom, Henry looked up to see Mac, his long-time bookie, walk through the door followed by a towering black man. "Hey, my man, how they hanging?" Mac asked. There was no friendliness in his voice.

Henry's stomach tightened. The big Negro was the enforcer, someone he'd heard about. The giant had a pocked face, creased and riddled with bumps and scars, like he'd been a boxer. At six-foot-four, he was as wide in the face and as frightening as the bulls Henry's father used to keep on the farm.

"Doing fine," Henry said, cautiously. "How about yourself, and who's your friend there?"

"Oh, him? This here's Lonnie, one of Dutch's boys."

Lonnie stared off to the side, his squared-off shoulders slumping and hands hanging loosely at his side. He had an odd, disquieting look, like he was bored with the whole scene.

"Yeah, I've been busy," Mac said. "Lots of guys falling behind on their obligations."

As usual, Mac was dressed like a well-heeled gent slumming an afternoon away. Today he wore a patterned suit with sharp creases in the slacks. The tie was a muted red and his black shoes gleamed like freshly polished mirrors.

He could be a great guy as long as everything went his way. But if a guy fell behind on his payments, Mac was one tough SOB. In flush times when Henry placed a bet, Mac jotted it down in a little book he kept in his inside suit jacket. Then, likely as not, he'd order a drink and shoot the bull for half an hour, leaving a nice tip on the bar.

Today there would be no drink, no shooting the bull, no tip. Henry owed Mac a bundle—more than $700.

Sweat swamped his armpits and his throat went dry as he spread his hands wide on the back of the bar and pushed down hard to control his trembling body and pounding heart. He had personal knowledge of two guys on crutches that had reneged on bets. Henry watched Mac remove the spiral notebook from his pocket, flip through the pages and stop. He paused and looked up at him, and his mouth turned down into a frown.

"Says here you owe Dutch $780 with interest—and there's been no payment for more than two weeks. That's not good."

"Yeah, Mac, you know how it is. They advertised the damn mare as a sure thing. Then she breaks a leg comin' out of the gate. Stupid nag."

Henry's eyes flicked back at the baseball bat behind the bar. Could he get to it in time?

"Dutch says you need to catch up," Mac said as he leaned in close. "You're a good customer, so I can give you a little leeway. The boss needs something now, you know, some good-faith money. Let's say $300."

"I'm... er...I'm a little short," Henry pleaded. "School's started and the kids needed clothes and shoes and other stuff. I get paid Friday. I'd sure appreciate it if you'd give me till Saturday."

Henry didn't see Mac's soft nod that brought the black bruiser lunging forward at startling speed. Lonnie grabbed him by the tie and pulled him close. Staring into his vacant eyes, he saw the man's yellow cracked front teeth, smelled the cigarette smoke and the sour stomach. He kept pulling on the tie, which forced him against the bar's sharp edge.

"Shit, Mac. Call him off. Please! You'll get your money."

The muscles on Lonnie's neck bulged angrily. The man could kill him with a slight twist of his arm. How had he gotten in so deep? Lonnie yanked tighter and tighter. Henry gasped. He couldn't breathe.

"Have $300 by five o'clock Saturday," Mac growled, his eyes black slits. "You understand?"

He motioned for Lonnie to step back.

Coughing and blinking back tears, Henry wrenched at his tie and finally loosened it enough to croak, "Saturday's more than fair."

"Don't even think about skipping out. We'll find your sorry ass." Mac smiled, a malevolent smile that gave all smiles a bad name. "And don't even think about that baseball bat."

After they'd gone, Henry loosened his tie and tossed it on the bar. His hands shaking, he poured a shot of bourbon and swallowed it in one gulp, and then poured another. He'd promised Mac $300 but this week's paycheck—maybe $80 at the most, wouldn't come close to covering the payment.

The only person with that kind of money was Lilly. He hadn't seen or talked to her since she'd sent him packing from the house that night years ago. He'd thought about calling and making an appointment to visit Arthur a couple of times. Something always came up. Meantime, she'd married her rich boyfriend. Still, what choice did he have? Mac wasn't kidding about turning Lonnie loose. It was either find the money or spend the rest of his life on crutches.

"Good afternoon. This is Performance Arts. To whom may I direct your call?"

"Yeah, I need to talk to Lilly Swenson."

"May I say who's calling, please?"

"Sure. Tell her it's her old friend, Henry Goodwin. She knows me." Henry waited on the phone as the minutes ticked away. What was taking her so long?

The phone clicked and Lilly snapped: "What do you want? How did you get this number?"

"It's in the book, sugar."

He knew she'd take the call. He could make trouble. He'd thought about it and figured those papers he'd signed in front of the judge weren't worth a tinker's damn. He was the father, Arthur's only living parent. That meant a lot under the law. By God, he had his rights, too, and he'd raise hell, that's for sure.

"We need to talk. It involves Arthur. Should I come to your office?"

"Arthur?" she asked skeptically. "What about him?"

"Tell you when I see ya."

Furious, she took a deep breath. "All right, I'll meet you at the little café on Monterey, around the corner from our office building. You know the place?"

"Yeah, I'll find it. What time?"

"Ten o'clock tomorrow morning. And this better not be some stupid trick to try to get money out of me."

Morning sun streamed through the café's windows. The waitress set two cups of coffee before them.

"So what is it?" she asked as she took a sip of the steamy black liquid. Lilly couldn't believe the way Henry looked. He'd aged 20 years, and his skin was yellow, sick looking. He had the worst haircut ever, and there was gray all around the edges. Most of all he looked and carried himself like a born loser.

"I'm in trouble. I owe my bookie almost $800. I need to have at least $300 as a down payment by Saturday or they're going to break my legs. I hate to ask but honestly there's no where else to turn."

Lilly sat back in her chair and shook her head. "I don't give money to pay off gambling debts."

She pushed the coffee cup forward and reached for her purse to leave.

"Now wait a minute," Henry bumped his voice up an octave. "This does involve Arthur. In fact, it affects both boys. If I can't pay, my ass is grass, and neither of the boys will have a father—a least not one with two good legs who can earn a living."

Lilly pursed her lips and settled back.

"Who'll take care of me when I'm crippled?" Henry asked, the familiar whiny tone creeping into his voice. "Who's going to push the wheelchair, put me on the toilet? Those boys are the only family I have. For a lousy $300—which you'll never miss—you can spare all of us a lot of trouble."

Lilly remembered the days she waited on this guy hand and foot while he recovered from the burns on his feet. He'd been about as pathetic and needy as anyone could be.

"Don't drag the boys into your mess. You're such a weasel, damn you! Here's $200. That's all I have."

She threw the bills across the table where a couple of twenties fluttered to the floor. When Henry bent over to pick them up, she stood and walked toward the door.

On Saturday, Henry skimmed a double-sawbuck from the cash register, added in his paycheck, and Lilly's $200, and paid Mac the $300. He was broke until the next pay-day.

Instead of being grateful, Henry was furious. Lilly had humiliated him and treated him like dirt. They had a history together. He couldn't get her out of his head. She hadn't heard the last from him.

Sometimes the heart sees what is invisible to the eye.

–H. Jackson Brown, Jr.

Chapter 32

Lilly held the white card in her hand, the fancy cursive style type announcing the high school graduation of Paul Lee Goodwin on Saturday, June 4, 1956. The envelope also contained a personal note from Clara Bottman inviting Arthur, Henry, and Lilly to attend a pre-graduation party Friday evening at their home in Elk Point.

"Paul is so looking forward to seeing all of you," she wrote. "He's changed and is all grown up. We're so proud of him. Please plan to stay at our house. We insist!"

Lilly re-read the comment about Paul anticipating their visit, and tried to decipher the meaning. She wished Paul had sent the invitation himself with a hand-written note. Clara's note seemed to say the boy didn't object to her attending his party. Still, she felt uneasy and uncertain about what to do.

She stopped by her husband's office to seek counsel. Michael's office was like him—masculine, quiet, solid and confident. It also pleased her that the ashtray on his desk was shiny clean, no stubbed-out cigarettes. He glanced up from behind his large dark oak desk and smiled as she took a chair.

Behind Michael's desk, a wall-sized window, arched at the top, framed Grand Central Station, which loomed in the lower foreground. Beyond, the window opened to a panoramic view of downtown L.A., with the city's suburbs spreading in all directions. After dark, cars, trucks, and buses flowed like rivers of light on the city's jumble of streets and highways.

"I have a knotty situation that I hope you can help me unravel," Lilly said as she handed him the invitation, along with Clara's handwritten note. She fidgeted and waited as he read them.

Michael shrugged and said, "Looks pretty straightforward. What's the concern?"

"We haven't seen Paul in more than five years. Arthur would love to go. I doubt Henry has any interest in attending. He's such an ass."

She shook her head, at a loss for what else to say.

"I see Henry's invited," Michael said. "Does he know that?"

"Probably not. He moves around. I doubt Clara would have had an address for him. I'm guessing she expects me to contact him."

"Well, heck, look at this as an opportunity," Michael offered, waving the invitation in her direction. "We know Arthur's dying to see his brother. The kid's always pestering me to take him back to Nebraska. More than once I've been tempted to book airline tickets. It sounds like Paul's grown up enough to see things differently. A lot of water under the bridge, hopefully time to forgive and forget and to reunite."

Before they married, Lilly had told Michael about her fling with Henry. It wasn't a problem then and it didn't seem to bother him now, even though she soon might be traveling with Henry back to Elk Point.

"As for Henry? Well, he is what he is," Michael continued. "I know what I'd do. I'd call and invite him. He's part of the boy's family and should be there."

Squeezing her eyes shut Lilly said: "Going home to Elk Point has me all mixed up. There's no one left to see, no relatives, no close friends. Nobody's kept in touch except Paul and Arthur."

Then Lilly opened her eyes and straightened her back. She wore what had become her signature light-colored business suit, high collared white blouse, and plain and obviously expensive high-heel shoes. Her blond hair was back to being long, below her shoulders. She stared at her husband.

"I have to say there's a part of me that wants to go home, you know, take a walk down Main Street, saying my 'how-do-you-dos.' It'd be fun to show them what's happened to the chubby waitress who ran off to California with the town bartender and his kid." Lilly paused and asked. "Think that's silly?"

Michael laughed and reached for his pack of cigarettes, which weren't there. Instead, he popped a hard candy in his mouth. His body ached to light up a smoke.

"No, normal, I'd say," Michael mused. "Knowing you, I expect there's a lot more friends and well-wishers in that little town than you're giving yourself credit for. My advice? Go!"

He came around and sat down in a matching chair beside her. "You'll do just fine. And it's high time those two boys were reunited."

"Okay, I'll call Henry. It'll be a short visit—two or three days tops. I'll talk to Arthur and call his father tomorrow."

Arthur went bonkers when he read the invitation and Clara's note. "Does Paul know we're coming? Will it be a surprise? When do we leave?"

"In two weeks," Lilly said. Arthur's excitement was infectious. She was feeling better. "We'll fly to Omaha and arrive about mid-day Friday, rent a car, and drive to Elk Point. It'll just be a weekend. I need to be back here Monday."

Bracing herself, she dialed Kelsey's number. Henry picked up the phone.

"Kelsey's," he barked.

"You've been invited to Paul's high school graduation party in Elk Point," Lilly blurted out without so much as a greeting.

"I don't know," Henry hedged. "Nothing there for me. I'd love to see Paul. Do you think he wants to see me?"

"You're on the invite list." The line went dead for a few moments and she thought she'd lost him.

"Anyway," he said. "I've got to work and I sure as hell can't pay for an airplane ticket."

"You haven't seen your son for five years," Lilly urged. "I'm sure he wants to see you."

Then Lilly played her ace in the hole. "Margie would want you there."

"What about the wages I'll miss out on," Henry wheedled. Lilly couldn't believe he was angling for money. "I'm not rich like you. Make me square and I'll go along."

He made it sound like he was doing her a big favor.

"Fine," she said, exasperated. "Meantime get yourself cleaned up. You do have a suit, don't you?"

She called Clara and thanked her for the offer to stay at the house and suggested that it'd be easier if the three of them checked in at the new motel in town. When Clara objected, Lilly said, "Thank you, your hands will be full with all the party preparations. You don't need us underfoot. You're very kind to invite us."

After confirming the flight reservations, she and Michael talked again. "Well, we're set, except for one thing: I need you to say a prayer for me—a big one. I'll take all the help I can get."

"You'll do great, sweetheart. It's not the lion's den, only a family gathering. Want me to clear my schedule and tag along?"

"No, this is my doing. I'll handle it as best I can."

In all the world, there is no heart for me like yours.

–Maya Angelou

Chapter 33

In the early morning darkness, Henry dumped the bags with the skycap at Los Angeles International Airport and pulled a flask from his pocket and took a long pull. Lilly looked at her watch—5 a.m. By the time they boarded the flight for Omaha, he'd drained the small metal container. Once in the air, he ordered two bourbon and waters from the stewardess and quickly drank them. When he tried ordering two more, the young stewardess refused further service.

"I'm a paying customer. I have cash," Henry argued loudly. "You can't cut me off."

Her face flushed, the young woman leaned over and talked to Henry in a calming voice.

"No, damn it! Bring me two more drinks!"

Lilly whispered in Arthur's ear: "Pretend you don't know him."

Moments later, the pilot walked down the aisle and kneeled down on one knee at Henry's seat. Wearing a severe look, he leaned in close. Lilly could just barely hear the pilot's words. He spoke with a southern drawl.

"Now listen, buster. I'm saying this only once. I'm the boss on this plane and I look out for the safety and comfort of these nice passengers. I don't put up with any bullshit. Keep it up and the cops will be waiting for you when we land in Omaha. They'll lock ya up and throw the key away. You git it?"

Blurry eyed, Henry nodded. A few minutes later, Lilly glanced over and he was curled up in his seat, fast asleep.

After the plane landed, Lilly and Arthur stood on each side of Henry and guided him to the airport restaurant, where Lilly ordered two coffees and a Coke. She handed the Coke to Arthur and asked him to check on the luggage.

"I need to talk to your father." She could tell Arthur was itching to explore the airport on his own. Plus he wasn't any more comfortable sitting here with his father than she was.

She watched Henry slurp his coffee and saw a dark stream trickle down his chin and onto his shirt. She was about to reach over and blot it with the paper napkin then decided against it. It wasn't her business to keep him cleaned up.

Why had she so foolishly encouraged him to come on the trip? This reunion had all the markings of a train wreck, and they hadn't even left Omaha yet.

Unable to contain herself, through clenched teeth, she said, "Now listen to me, I'm only saying this once. You're the father of two wonderful boys and this is an important time for them. Sober up and stay that way or I swear you'll be on the next flight back to California."

"Shit, Lilly," Henry retorted, as he wiped his mouth with a napkin. "I had a couple of drinks to settle my nerves. So what? Don't get uppity with me, and don't tell me what to do. I'm not that sissy, rich-ass husband of yours. I can hurt you."

Jarred by this outburst, her first instinct was to reach across and smack him. Instead she took a long searching look at him. He was a mess: bloodshot eyes, tobacco-stained teeth, unshaven jowls, a flabby belly hanging over rumpled pants, and his boyish good looks now buried under deep creases. His skin was and blotchy and pale, like he hadn't been out in the sun in years. He looked closer to 50 than his actual 40.

While he'd always been a tough talker, she'd pegged him early on as a coward. In his current physical condition, soft as putty, he didn't seem much of a threat. Still, there was something different about him now—maybe desperation. Hard to tell what he was capable of doing, especially when he was pumped up on booze.

A lot of dismal things had to have happened over the years to bring the boys' father this low. Whatever had happened to him, she felt sure he'd mostly brought the trouble on himself. Right now, he was facing the pressure of meeting up with his oldest son, face-to-face. She understood his fear, how he wanted to run away. She had similar feelings. Henry had stranded Paul in Elk Point, while she had betrayed the boy after he'd put his trust in her. It wasn't a good situation.

At 1:30, she pulled the rental car into the motel parking lot in Elk Point and checked in. She walked out of the office and gave Henry his key. Arthur would bunk in with her. They were all due at Frank and Clara's at 6 p.m.

"Be at the car by a quarter till six or we'll leave without you," she said.

He pulled his suitcase out of the trunk and took the key without a word. Secretly, she hoped he'd pass out on the bed and sleep till morning. She'd tell people he didn't feel well, that the flight had made him sick. His absence would make things so much easier.

After depositing their bags next to the twin beds, she said to Arthur, "It's early. Let's take a walk downtown and look the town over."

They hadn't gone a block before Arthur said, "Geez, I remember this town being a lot bigger. Did it shrink?"

Touching the top of his head as though measuring him, she observed, "It's because you've grown bigger that the town seems smaller."

Their first stop was a walk-by of the house where Lilly had grown up. The new owners had updated the exterior—new paint, shutters, and roof. Everything looked sharp.

"Boy, this place looks nice," Lilly commented. "There's a swing set in the back yard. Isn't that sweet?"

It was sad seeing the two empty lots where the café and tavern once stood. The black-scorched brick foundations still overflowed with junk and weeds, some of the errant plants four feet high. Angled up through a thick layer of charred wood, shingles and other debris was the tavern's front door. Why hadn't the cook rebuilt the restaurant?

"See that big door there?" Arthur said. "The old brass door handle really sparkles in the sunlight."

"It's depressing," she said. "You'd think somebody would clean things up."

Once they reached the town square, Lilly recognized a number of people. The locals didn't seem surprised to see them. She guessed Clara had spread the word they'd be in town this weekend. Most simply nodded and smiled. However, Irma Lancaster, president of the garden club, made a point of stopping to chat.

"You're beautiful!" Irma gushed, as she snapped and unsnapped the clasp on her flowered handbag. "You're like one of those Hollywood movie stars."

Lilly remembered her as a regular at the restaurant. She and several members of the garden club ate lunch there once a month. She remembered them being snooty and barely acknowledging her presence. Irma also was the one who had organized the group of ladies to call on the Mayor to shut down Lilly's Tavern over the flap with "Sweet Tits." All that seemed so long ago.

A few steps farther and they met Norma Caldwell, secretary of the PTA. She'd lived here all of her life. She put her hands to her cheeks in astonishment. "And this can't be Arthur, so grown up?"

She reached over and touched his shoulder: "You know your big brother's the town hero. Why, he's put us on the map with his football playing. We're so proud we could bust. And handsome! He brought some excitement to our town and we'll sure miss him when he goes off to college."

"Thank you," Arthur answered politely, meeting the woman's stare head on.

They arrived back at the motel at 4:30 and promptly at 5:45 found Henry slouched against a front fender of the rental. Shaved and showered, he looked at least presentable in his rumpled dark suit, blue-striped tie and freshly polished shoes. His eyes remained bleary and red, though, and he wore the same haggard, woe-is-me expression.

"Sorry, too much whisky," he stammered. "I'm okay. I won't embarrass you guys."

He turned and belched and Lilly thought she heard a fart as well. Still, in his favor, he seemed to be trying.

Forgiveness is the economy of the heart. It saves the... waste of spirits.

–Hannah More

Chapter 34

Lilly had been rehearsing her "meeting with Paul scenes" since the day she'd received the invitation from Clara. Should she say: "Sorry, I had sex with your father—I promise not to do it again," or how about: "I apologize for how I acted back then. I was a horny, sex-crazed kid," or how about a simple, "Please forgive me?"

Their parting had been contentious, at least on Paul's part. Now it was crunch time. She'd be facing Paul in a few moments. The young man was inside Clara's house, and her mind was blank, a hopeless blank.

With the sound of rocks hitting the inside of the wheel wells, she pulled the car into the gravel driveway alongside Frank and Clara's two-story house with its traditional, farm-style, wrap-around front porch, a house much like the one in which she'd grown up.

Clara had invited her to park in the driveway. "We're reserving the driveway for honored guests," she had told her.

Frank was in the yard directing guests to park in neat rows along the edge of the front lawn. The sun eased in the sky with a quarter all ready moon beaming brightly overhead. Temperatures were in the low seventies—perfect party weather by Nebraska standards.

Most men wore white shirts, ties and dress slacks, not a jacket in the bunch. Henry stood out in his dark suit. The ladies sported new perms and floated around in colorful summer frocks. A southern boy named Elvis Presley sang "Blue Suede Shoes" over the speakers that Frank had hung around the front porch.

Arthur walked up to his former boss and poked him lightly on the arm "Hey Frank, this place looks super snazzy,"

Frank stepped back and took a good look at his former assistant. "Well, by gosh! Is that you, Arthur? You've grown, but seems to me you used to be a lot prettier."

"Ugh, boys aren't pretty," Arthur said, crinkling his nose. "It's really great to see you. How's the station doin'? Chuck and Smitty still giving you fits?"

Frank had put on a few pounds. His hair and beard were pure white, and so were his distinctive bushy eyebrows. He kept repeating, "Oh, my, how you've grown."

Lilly watched the two josh back and forth.

"Who's sweeping these days?" Arthur asked. "Betcha they're not doing as good a job as I did, huh?"

"I do it myself, and a heck of a lot better than you ever did. I never saw a kid push a broom as much as you did and end up with no dirt in the dustpan," he said, rubbing his knuckles over the boy's head.

"Hey, watch it! I just combed my hair. You want me to look nice for the party, don't you?"

Lilly stepped over the back-door threshold into the kitchen.

"Well, heavens to Betsy," Clara exclaimed, clapping her hands together. She embraced Lilly, and then Arthur. "How was the trip? And, Arthur! My goodness, you look so nice."

Henry stood a few feet back. Noticing his discomfort, Clara extended her hand and said, "Welcome. You must be Paul's father."

Lilly watched Henry's face. He blanched, and stood silent, like he didn't know how to react. He'd never met Clara, and had never thanked her for taking in his son. This was his chance. He just stood there.

When Arthur spotted Paul at the punch bowl across the room, he walked over and tapped him on the shoulder. "Hey, it's me."

Paul turned and his face broke into a wide grin.

"You're huge!" Arthur exclaimed as he threw his arms around his older brother. "What're they feeding you—oats?"

Arthur broke out laughing at his own joke.

He chattered on and Paul smiled, unable to fit a word in edgewise. Lilly could tell how much Arthur loved his brother and how much he had missed him. Finally, poor Paul managed to jump in and say a few words himself.

From the corner of her eye, she saw Henry leaning against the wall, out of the traffic, watching his sons' reunion unfold before him. He wore a sad look, like he was remembering better times, perhaps when Margie had been alive and he'd ruled the roost.

Once Arthur stepped away Henry sucked in a deep breath, pressed his hands against his coat jacket to flatten the wrinkles, and walked over to Paul. His son turned and had a startled look on his face when he spotted his father moving toward him. He offered a hand for a shake. With an unexpected tug, Henry pulled Paul into his arms. Nearly six inches taller than his Dad and twice as wide, Paul stiffened. They looked at each other with confusion, neither finding words to say. Finally, Paul broke the ice. "Hi, Dad. Thanks for coming. Good to see you."

What followed was an awkward exchange. She decided it was best to drift away and leave them to work things out as best they could. Later, she noticed Henry leaning against the wall, alone again, staring at his shoes, a glass of punch in his hand. He'd taken off his jacket and held it in his left arm.

Frank cranked up the music and a few brave couples and several little kids danced on the front porch. Lilly reminisced with two former high school classmates. Both girls were married and between them they had six children, which Lilly had trouble getting her mind around. As they talked and laughed, she glanced up and saw Paul standing next to her, within arm's length, politely waiting for a break in the conversation.

The two friends wandered away, leaving them alone. Lilly took a deep breath. Here it comes! She tried to recall the phrases she'd rehearsed. Nothing came to her. Glancing up, their eyes met and locked. Paul looked as helpless as she felt.

"How, are you?" Paul asked, his voice low and soft and friendly. "You look wonderful."

"Thankyou,andcongratulations.We'resoproudofyou." "Thanks for coming and for bringing Arthur."

He didn't mention his dad.

"Oh, believe me, it's entirely my pleasure," she said. Her words tumbled out. "It's so nice being back. Arthur's so happy and excited. He's hoping you'll come visit us in Los Angeles. My husband, Michael, wants to meet you. Arthur's been bragging you up for years."

"I definitely plan to do that," Paul replied. He stood unmoving, like he wanted to say more. Lilly sensed he was remembering the rancor he held toward her in the past. Would he ever be able to put it all behind him, to at last forgive her?

Lilly caught her breath. "I think you'll like Michael. You guys have a lot in common. He's crazy about football. In fact he loves all sports, especially golf and tennis."

"I've never seen Arthur so happy," Paul said. "You've done a wonderful job with him, a lot better than I ever could have done."

Lilly blushed. "Thank you, he's a special kid. Everybody loves him. As I'm sure you've noticed, he still talks a lot, like all the time." She laughed nervously.

"Yeah, I managed to squeeze in two or three words when he ran out of breath." Then the young man grew reflective. "It amazes me how much Arthur looks like our Mom. He walks like her, talks like her—even has the same facial expressions. And, of course, he has those eyes that see everything."

Lilly nodded. They remained quiet another moment before Lilly said, "Clara tells me several colleges are falling over themselves offering scholarships."

"My plan is to coach at the high school level and I still haven't decided where to attend college," Paul said, sounding like he'd made this same speech over and over. "The coaches at Lincoln want me to play at the University of Nebraska. I'm not so sure. I'm a small-town kid. Some of those lecture halls on the Lincoln campus can seat more students than we have enrolled in our high school. A small college in Iowa has put together a pretty good package. I'm seriously considering going to Des Moines."

"Wherever you end up, you'll do fine. Don't forget about visiting us in California, and the sooner the better. Arthur wants to show you off to all of his friends."

Paul shook his head. "Can't be this summer. Frank's short-handed and counting on me to help out at the station. Maybe I'll get out there over Christmas or next summer. Your husband, what's his name, Michael? He sounds like a great guy."

"It's a deal then."

Lilly reached up and touched his shoulder. He made a move like he was going to hug her but the moment slipped away. Instead, he said, "Lilly, I don't know how to say this, except I'm sorry for the way I acted before you guys left for California."

"I'm sorry, too," Lilly said, touching his sleeve, as tears streamed down her cheeks. "I wish I could change what happened. I can't."

This time Paul managed to give her a shy embrace. She'd never felt anything so good.

Go forth to meet the shadowy future without fear and with a manly heart.

–Henry Wadsworth Longfellow

Chapter 35

"No, thanks, just a Coke when you have a chance. No hurry," Henry said in a polite tone. The stewardess filled the order and rolled the beverage cart down the narrow aisle. Thankfully, she wasn't the young lady who'd served him on the first flight.

He sat in an aisle seat near the front of the plane, across from Arthur and Lilly. At the moment his youngest son was giggling and prattling on, pounding Lilly's leg for emphasis, with an impish grin on his face.

"Frank and Clara looked like Mr. and Mrs. Santa Claus, rosy cheeks and all," he gushed. "Then—and, oh, and this is sooo funny—remember how Clara pulled Paul out to dance? Man, I thought he'd die. Hilarious! A classic! I thought my big brother would roll over and die."

Henry rubbed his eyes as Arthur's sharp laughter rang loud in the plane's cabin, sending shards of pain into his tender, still hung-over brain. Did that boy ever shut up?

"Easy now," Lilly said as she dabbed the tears of laughter on her cheek with a handkerchief. She'd been joining in the fun. "Let's not disturb the other passengers."

"Oh, come on, we're having fun," Arthur replied.

As the plane approached Denver's Stapleton Airport for a 45-minute layover and crew change, a voice over the intercom encouraged passengers continuing on to L.A. to de-plane and stretch their legs in the terminal.

Henry chose to stay on the plane. He asked the stewardess, "May I take a seat toward the back? I'd appreciate some quiet."

"Certainly, sir," she replied. "I understand perfectly. The back six rows are unassigned. Select any one of them."

Racked with self-doubt, exhausted and with a splitting headache, Henry let out an involuntary groan as he eased himself into a window seat four rows from the back. His life was a total screw up. He had to find a way to start over. He needed a second chance—and right now.

The trip had been a disaster. He shouldn't have gone. First he had gotten piss-eyed drunk and made a fool of himself. Then Paul, in effect, had brushed him off. And really who could blame him? He'd made promises and never delivered. He'd ditched Paul in Elk Point and when

Gladys wiggled her backside he'd signed papers giving Lilly guardianship rights to Arthur. What would Margie think? He'd treated the kids like baggage that he didn't want to carry.

Returning to the moment, Henry watched a stream of passengers file onto the plane and take seats. Soon, the twin-prop engines roared and the plane rocketed down the runway.

The first step was to find a new job. He was through with Kelsey's. A couple of weeks earlier, Mac had offhandedly mentioned that Dutch planned to take on a couple of new field men to run numbers. The bookmaking business was booming. The mention of a job opening caught Henry's attention even though he didn't say anything to Mac at the time. He hesitated because he couldn't see himself as bookie. For one thing, it was illegal; a guy could go to jail. When he expressed concern, Mac had pooh-poohed the possibility.

"Every month Dutch delivers an envelope stuffed with cash to the cops. He has the authorities in his back pocket, bought and paid for. Think about it. When's the last time you heard of a bookie getting roughed up by the L.A. police? Doesn't happen in this town, take my word for it."

Henry carefully eased his way down the steep steps from the plane to the tarmac. The headache was gone but he felt unsteady on his feet. Drawing a deep breath, he nearly choked on the City of Angels' diesel-fuel tinged air.

Picking up his bag he gave a half-hearted goodbye wave to Lilly and Arthur and grabbed a cab to Kelsey's.

His first piece of good luck was walking through the door and finding Mac seated at the bar, dressed up in a suit and tie.

"Just the guy I was hoping to see!" Henry called out. "I've been out of town for a few days on a family thing."

"So that's where you were. I came by Saturday night wanting to show off my new girlfriend. Where were you: Iowa or Nebraska—some screwball place like that?"

"Yep, I had a great time with my boys." Henry then changed the subject. "A time back you said Dutch might be taking on some extra help. That still true?"

"Guess so. You interested?"

"Damn right. Business here is lousy. I'm working 60 hours a week and earning Mexican wages."

"Yeah, life's tough, especially when you have to actually work for a living." Mac said smugly, as at he continued rolling the shot glass in his hand.

"Can you put in a good word for me with this Dutch guy? I'd take it as a personal favor."

Mac hesitated long enough to make Henry feel uncomfortable. Then he looked him in the face, as if calculating whether he could measure up.

"Okay," he said. "What the hell? You'll probably do okay, what with your jokes and all. People seem to like you. If you mess up, it'll be on my head. A few guys have crossed Dutch over the years and it ain't pretty what's happened to them, if you follow my drift."

"I do. I've seen Lonnie eyeball to eyeball and smelled him up close. You were there. Remember?"

Mac's shoulders slumped. A while back, he'd half-assed apologized to Henry for what had happened that day when he came calling with Lonnie. The regrets didn't ring true.

"Sure, I'll put in a word for you. If Dutch takes you on, you'll owe me big time. Got it?"

"I appreciate it, buddy," Henry answered,

Mac called the next day. "Dutch says to bring you around. Clean yourself up, a decent haircut, a new suit and shine your shoes. Look sharp. I'll call tomorrow with the time and place."

Two days later Henry checked himself out in a full-length mirror. He'd borrowed and pilfered enough dough for a new suit, shirt and tie. His shoes were older but they gleamed from the good buffing he'd given them. He had a fresh haircut and a barbershop shave. He looked okay, other than he had aged terribly. He arrived at Dutch's place at ten on the dot.

The big boss made him stand while he sat behind his dark walnut desk. Finally, he pushed his flat, pug-nosed head forward. "Mac tells me you're a fancy story-teller, a bull-shitter of the first order. That true?" Dutch demanded.

Henry fought back the panic that raced up his spine.

"Can you make me laugh, right here, right now?" Dutch snorted, chomping on a half-finished unlit cigar.

Summoning his courage, Henry answered in a strong voice: "Hire me and I'll make you laugh anytime. That's a promise. I've got a million jokes. And, here's the best part. Take me on and I'll not only keep you in stitches, I'll make you a lot of money. I guarantee it."

"You got gonads, I'll say that for ya," Dutch snorted. "So let's hear one of those jokes that's gonna make me roll in the aisle."

Beads of sweat formed on Henry's forehead. He had one shot. He'd better unleash a corker or this was all over. He began:

A pirate walked into a bar, and the bartender said:

"Hey, I haven't seen you in a while. What happened? You look terrible."

"What do you mean?" said the pirate, "I feel fine."

"What about the wooden leg? You didn't have that before."

"Well," said the pirate, "We were in a battle, and I got hit with a cannon ball, but I'm fine now."

The bartender replied, "Well, OK, but what about that hook? What happened to your hand?"

The pirate explained, "We were in another battle. I boarded a ship and got into a sword fight. My hand was cut off. I got fitted with a hook but I'm fine, really."

"What about that eye patch?"

"Oh," said the pirate, "One day we were at sea, and a flock of birds flew over. I looked up, and one of them shit in my eye."
"You're kidding," said the bartender. "You couldn't lose an eye just from bird shit."
"It was my first day with the hook."

Henry looked into Dutch's face and the boss man returned the stare with depthless dark eyes. He was scowling, looked mad. Then after several seconds ticked by he slowly removed the cigar from his mouth and burst out laughing. Everyone in the room joined in the hilarity.

"That's a damn good joke," Dutch said, slapping his hand on the desktop. "All right. I'll think about it. Now get the hell out of here."

Within a week, Henry had teamed with Mac to learn the new job. Starting pay was $130 a week, nearly double what he'd earned at Kelsey's. Mac predicted he'd earn at least $250 once he got up to speed. As it turned out, it didn't take long for Henry to begin out-earning Mac, which didn't sit well with his fellow bookie. Henry wondered why he'd wasted all those years tending bar. This was the best job he'd ever had.

Shape your heart to front the hour, but dream not that the hours will last.

–Alfred Lord Tennyson

Chapter 36

Michael was concerned after Lilly had come to his office and reported on the threats Henry had made to her at the Omaha airport restaurant. "He's desperate. He'll do anything to get his hands on money, including bargaining with his son," she had told him.

Up until now, neither of them had taken Henry's bluster too seriously. In fact they considered him a blowhard, all smoke, no fire. This time, however, there was something in Henry's aggressive manner that had put a scare in Lilly. Michael saw fear in his wife's eyes as she talked. Maybe he wasn't as harmless as they had thought. After she left his office, he nervously drummed the eraser end of a pencil on the desktop. He picked up the phone and called his long-time lawyer, Frederick Vogel. Vogel was already in the process of reviewing and updating Arthur's guardianship papers.

""Hi, Fred, Michael said into the phone. "Hey, we're wondering where we stand on Arthur's legal papers. His father is making waves again. Lilly's worried."

"The documents should be ready in a day or so. I can tell you the attorney who drew up the original agreement did a decent job. Our people combed through all the details and strengthened provisions here and there. I'm confident the new language will stand up in any court in Los Angeles County, even on appeal, if it ever comes to that. Besides, we can always use the father's character as a compelling argument for the boy to remain in your custody. From what we've ascertained, this Henry fellow has a checkered past—and it's mostly all bad. For example, he's currently working as a bookie, which is criminal activity in this state."

"Good. Sounds like you're on top of things. We appreciate it. Meantime, please do me a favor. It's probably nothing. Henry has made some threats to Lilly. He was drunk at the time, but I guess you can never know what people are capable of doing. I'd like to keep an eye on him? It's probably nothing but we might as well some caution."

"Certainly, our firm works with several private detective agencies. I'll put a top person on it right away."

Michael's next call was to the security firm that patrolled his neighborhood. He asked for increased patrols near the house, and added: "A while back, one of your people reported this Henry Goodwin guy was in the neighborhood and he was acting suspiciously. You have a description of him and the license plate number in your files. I'd like you to keep an eye out for him in particular."

"We'll take care of it, Mr. Paulson."

He couldn't think of anything else to do at the moment, so he settled back in his chair and opened the bottom drawer to his desk. He reached under a stack of papers for his secret pack of Camel cigarettes. He lit up and luxuriated in the familiar smoke that calmed his senses. He had cut way back on his smoking, but every now and then he couldn't resist.

Marrying Lilly and taking on Arthur had been a honest-to-goodness miracle in his life. He'd never been happier.

He finished the cigarette, extinguished the end of the butt, and placed it in a matchbox where it joined the remnants of other secret smokes. He placed the matchbox in the drawer next to the package of cigarettes.

If Lilly knew he was having an occasional smoke, it'd break her heart, and Michael couldn't blame her. They'd had several visits to the physician, and he'd had dozens of chest X-rays. At the most recent appointment he and Lilly watched the doctor place the film in a wall-mounted light box. With a pointer, he indicated several dark shadows in his left lung, which the respiratory specialist described as "potential problem areas."

"I'm seeing excessive scarring, and enlarged air sacks, much larger than normal, here and here," he said, turning to look at them. "In my experience, lungs that look like these sometimes do progress to lung cancer.

"Right now you have a 30-percent diminished lung capacity in the left lung. Your right lung seems fairly clear. The lung disease you have is known as emphysema. It's why you're having trouble catching your breath, and why you are experiencing coughing spells. In my mind, there's no question this condition is mainly a result of your long-term smoking habit."

Michael looked at Lilly. She was close to a melt down. He took her hand.

"At some point, I'll probably recommend that we put a scope down into your left lung and collect a biopsy," the physician continued. "That'll give us a clearer picture of what we're dealing with. We'll hold off on this for the time being. I know this is a lot for you folks to deal with."

He looked at Michael. "I'm not here to unduly frighten you. However, it's important that you understand the seriousness of the problem. There's no cure for the chronic emphysema that you have. I can't fix it. No one can. As for lung cancer, we simply don't know. One thing you can do is quit smoking—and I don't mean tomorrow."

"He's already done that, doctor," Lilly said, swallowing hard. "He hasn't smoked for a long time, have you dear?"

Michael remained silent. He couldn't lie to Lilly's face.

After the meeting, he returned to his office. This time he had to take action. He threw the hidden pack of Camels away. He had to face the fact that he was mortal. Like a lot of people, he'd entertained the conceit that he was exceptional, that somehow his name had been left off the list. That was faulty thinking. He was an ordinary person, flesh and blood and, like everyone else. He would die. He didn't know the day, the hour, or the circumstances, but one day his number would pop up.

He'd all ready begun to put his affairs in order. He asked Attorney Vogel to re-write his will, leaving most of his estate, including Performance Arts, to Lilly. Working with an outside consultant, he began the process of putting in place a management plan to govern Performance Arts in the event he wasn't around to handle things himself. After all, his employees' livelihoods depended on the long-term success and profitability of the business.

Lately he'd been having trouble sleeping. He'd lay awake for hours, sometimes reviewing the events of his life, the good and not-so-good-times. A wry smile played on his lips as he remembered how his mom kept the household humming when he and his brother were kids in the New Jersey house.

His dad, William, a shy, reserved man did his part to bring home the bacon. As a lab specialist at one the country's leading drug companies, his father was responsible for testing an endless stream of experimental drug compounds for efficacy. He did the monotonous work with precision and skill, day after day, week after week, and year after year.

It was on nights, weekends and holidays that William immersed himself in his true passion, the study of insects, and not simply the common, every day variety of insects—even though he studied these, too—but the whole spectrum of insects indigenous to all corners of the planet. He did this work from the basement of the family's ranch-style house on 86th Avenue in Newark.

Bugs he catalogued came from apartment buildings in New York City, the great forests of Brazil, the vast deserts of Africa, the frigid lands of the North and South Poles, even the depths of the oceans. Daily, the postman delivered packages postmarked from exotic locales like the Island of Borneo and the ancient city of Timbuktu. After work, like a kid at Christmas, he'd take the cardboard boxes to the basement and lose himself in his bug studies.

Michael remembered the day in late 1956 when Bob and he arrived at the family home a day after their father's funeral. Mom had died two years earlier. They were taking a final walk-through to select a few personal items before putting the house and its contents up for sale. They found several boxes of family photographs, mostly taken by their father over the years. Michael volunteered to have the boxes shipped to his home in Los Angeles. When he had the time, he'd organize the photographs and share them with Bob.

"We'd better check the dungeon," Michael said as he flipped on the lights and started down the bare wooden stairs. "I haven't been down here in years."

Bob, three years older than Michael, was moderately overweight, with dark-rimmed glasses and thinning gray hair. With some reluctance, he trailed Michael as they made their way to the mysterious place where their father had spent most of his adult waking hours.

"When I was kid, I wouldn't come down here for nothing," Bob offered. "I was convinced Dad kept a live, 10-foot-tall tarantula running wild in here—or something worse!"

"I only remember being down here once myself, when Dad was here at his desk," Michael said. "Oh my God! Look at this! The brothers stood in awe as they surveyed the large, wood-paneled, windowless basement room—Bug World, in all of its glory.

No giant tarantula anywhere in sight; instead the cavernous room was filled with glass-fronted cabinets crammed with glass slides and small boxes containing specific samples of insect. There had to be hundreds of thousands of bugs in the room, mostly stored in the wall cabinets. Some were large as birds and hung from the ceiling on invisible wires, swinging to and fro in the air currents. Bob identified the music filtering through hidden speakers as "Flight of the Bumblebee" by Russian composer Rimsky-Korsakov.

"Appropriate," Michael commented.

Bob reached over and picked off one of the thick catalogs that crowded the bookshelves behind Dad's oversized desk, the top of which was covered with scales, microscopes and a half-eaten apple.

"Look at the detail," he exclaimed, as he paged through the loose-leaf journal. "The handwriting is tiny, precise, yet perfectly legible."

"Hard to imagine," Michael mused. "A lifetime devoted to insects. I'm guessing Dad had to be one of the world's leading experts on the subject."

"And yet he did all of this research in total obscurity, working alone," Bob added. "That's just like our good ol' dad, wouldn't you say?"

The brothers agreed to contact museums and entomologists to solicit interest in accepting their father's insect collection. Sadly the only place willing to take the collection was the biology department at a nearby New Jersey private university, located less than a mile from the family home.

Their father's lifetime of work was destined to be stacked in the backroom of an obscure science building, unnoticed, uncared for and probably one day forgotten entirely.

"Can't we do better than this?" Michael asked.

"It's either donate the collection to this school or send everything to the dump."

Neither could stand the thought of that.

Let your heart soar as high as it will.

–Alden Wilson Tozer

Chapter 37

Lilly watched Myrna open the hall closet, put on her coat and step out onto the front porch to wait for her husband to pick her up. Fifty-eight years old and dedicated to the bone, she had worked for Michael and the family for more than 10 years. She was one of them.

Lately, Lilly had been so busy at work, and concerned about Michael's health, she'd neglected her housekeeper and friend. Wanting to catch her before she departed, she hurried onto the porch and placed a hand lightly on Myrna's shoulder.

"Thanks for all you do for us," she said. "I don't know how we'd manage without you."

"Oh, phooey, you'd do just fine," she replied, the color rising in her cheeks from the compliment.

After the housekeeper drove away with her husband, Lilly returned to the problem of finding a reliable person to stay at the house with Arthur when she and Michael needed to travel out of town on business.

Earlier in the week, she'd asked Myrna if she'd stay over a couple of times a month. Immediately after having asked the question, Lilly regretted it.

"I'm sorry, Miss Lilly, but I have to be home nights," she answered, looking distraught. "I get supper for Joseph, and my daughter works nights and her three kids come over to eat. It's usually their only hot meal of the day."

Lilly apologized for putting her in an awkward position, and contacted an employment agency, which sent over three candidates. None seemed right.

The following morning, in her office, Lilly's gaze settled on the oak-framed Garcia family photo she kept on her desk as a reminder to stay in touch with Maria and the kids. In their last conversation several weeks earlier, Maria, who rarely complained, had stewed about her oldest daughter Sophia, who had graduated high school at the top of her class a year earlier. With no money for college, she now worked as a clerk in a department store and took night classes at a junior college, which put her on a slow path to one day earn her degree in elementary education.

"It breaks my heart," Maria said. "Sophia wants so bad to be a teacher. She's discouraged and unhappy. We can't afford to help with the other kids needing so much."

Staring at the photograph, Maria's words filled her mind. Sophia was a bright young lady, confident, attractive, and loaded with personality. When they first arrived in California, and moved in next door to the Garcia family, Sophia had babysat Arthur on several occasions. Lilly liked and trusted the young girl, and she and Arthur got along wonderfully.

Might Sophia be the answer to her problem?

Lilly called Maria and after the usual small talk asked, "Is Sophia still working at Bontels?"

"Yes. She can't find anything else," Maria said, an edge of disappointment in her voice. "She's so talented and smart. She speaks English better than most Americans, with no accent at all. Those big companies won't even let her in the door. It's hard for Mexicans."

Lilly explained that she was looking to find a responsible live-in person to look out for Arthur.

"Might Sophia be interested? She'd have her days free, and, if she wants, she could attend college full-time during the day. We'd help with expenses."

Maria drew in a deep breath. "Oh, Lilly! This answers my prayers. She'll do it. I'm sure of it."

When she informed Arthur about the plan, his reaction surprised her.

"Hey, I'm big enough to stay alone. I don't need a babysitter."

"This will help her earn money for college," Lilly explained. "We'll be helping Sophia achieve her dream to be a school teacher. You'd like to help, wouldn't you?"

Arthur grudgingly nodded. "All right, okay. If we're helping Sophia, I guess it's okay. She needs to know she's not my babysitter, or my boss. If anything, I'll be her boss."

"Right," Lilly replied, with a "there-he-goes-again" look on her face.

Sophia moved in with them in the spring of 1957 with plans to register as a full-time freshman at the University of Southern California in the fall.

For as he thinketh in his heart, so is he.

–Proverbs 23.7

Chapter 38

The first summer after Sophia started her live-in duties at the big Hollywood Hills house proved to be a major disappointment to Arthur. A lot of the regret he felt was due to his older brother. Paul had finished his freshman year in college and rather than spend the summer working in Elk Point, he'd accepted Lilly's invitation to spend three months in Los Angeles with them, which included working mornings at Performance Arts as an intern. Arthur had big plans to do a lot of catching up with his brother. It hadn't worked out that way.

What he hadn't counted on was the way Sophia became all giggly and foolish whenever his big brother walked into the room. The young lady was always at

Paul's elbow, gazing up at him with those moon-shaped eyes of hers. And Paul didn't discourage the interest.

If Paul wasn't with ding-a-ling Sophia, he and Michael were off playing golf.

"Golf's an old man's game, not even a real sport," Arthur complained, as Paul hoisted his borrowed clubs into Michael's trunk. In his mind, it made no sense whatsoever for someone to choose golf over tennis.

"Don't knock it if you haven't tried it, brother. How's the saying go: Different strokes for different folks?"

As the summer wore on Arthur began feeling like a fifth wheel. Michael was busier than ever at Performance Arts, and had little time for playing tennis with him. Paul and Sophia spent hour after hour splashing around the pool in the afternoons, taking long walks and, after dark, hanging out alone on the patio—doing who knew what! When he complained about Sophia hogging his time, Paul told him to back off. "I've got a girlfriend at college in Iowa named Nancy. Sophia and I are friends, nothing more."

One evening at dinner, with Paul and Sophia off to a concert, Arthur listened to Michael brag about how well Paul was fitting in at the office as a summer intern. "Paul's really interested in the business," Michael declared. "I'm feeling good about all of this. The department heads and I are meeting in the morning to consider establishing a new Performance Arts department to focus on professional sports figures. I've asked Paul to sit in on the discussion.

With his background in sports, and since he's about the same age as many of the young sports pros we're talking to, I figure he can be a big help to us.

With excitement in his voice, Michael continued: "I'm amazed, Lilly. Some of these sports stars are earning millions of dollars a year. Advertisers, like the Wheaties cereal folks, are lined up to pay the athletes big money to endorse their products. The players need help sorting out the contracts and making certain everything's up to snuff."

"Sounds like a nice opportunity for the agency," she replied, as she turned to Arthur. "I'm sure your mom would be so pleased to see what's happening to you guys."

"Yeah, Mom would be happy," Arthur said in a subdued tone.

"It's a shame your dad isn't paying more attention to you boys, or, on second thought, maybe it's better that he isn't," Michael added.

Arthur remained silent. Later, after thinking about it, he wasn't sure Michael should have said a thing like that about his father.

The next evening the five of them gathered around the pool for a light dinner. Everybody was talking, except for Arthur, who uncharacteristically didn't seem to have much to say.

"After our meeting at the office, I took the crew out for an afternoon of golf," Michael was saying. "You should have seen the looks on the guys' faces when Paul stepped up and drove the ball 265 yards straight down the fairway."

"I was lucky," Paul responded. "Besides, you beat me by four strokes."

"Only because I out-putted you. I'll wager a steak dinner in a year or two you'll be a better putter than I am. I'm thinking one day you could turn pro. Trust me on this. I know golf," Michael said, wagging his head.

Arthur had heard enough. He excused himself and walked over to the deserted tennis courts. It was all about Paul! Paul! Paul! Sophia tripping over her feet around him, and Michael raving about his golf game, like that was some big achievement. This is my house, my family! Paul's a visitor. He should go back to Des Moines and stay there.

* * * * *

It was during this same summer of 1957 that Michael's health issues roared to the forefront. He sat in his office, rubbing the back of his neck and running a hand through his gray hair. He couldn't feel them or see them, but those damnable dark spots on his lung loomed over him like demons from hell. No question, the threat of cancer was the dominant, all-consuming issue of his life. He felt like he was on hold, simply going through the motions—eating, sleeping and working—while waiting for something to happen—or the ax to fall.

He and Lilly hoped and prayed for intervention, even as they recognized that with his condition it wasn't possible he'd one day wake up and miraculously find his lungs had cleared on their own.

Only the week before they'd met for a follow-up review of his most recent chest X-rays. They were terrible, or at least that was Michael's gut-wrenching response to the doctor's assessment. The doctor now pressed to go forward with the scope biopsy.

Doctor Herbold was an older gentleman, almost 60, with an impeccable record in his specialty. Self-possessed, he had a friendly, easy-going manner. He gave Michael and Lilly confidence that they were in the best medical hands possible.

"There's been some change," the doctor said, using a pointer to indicate new growth. The biopsy will give us a clearer picture of what we're dealing with, and how to proceed from here. I want you to know my overall prognosis of your condition remains stable. There's plenty of room for optimism."

Michael glanced at Lilly. She was near tears.

Michael left the office, his mind in a dismal fog. Extremely upset and red-eyed, Lilly clutched his forearm so hard the knuckles on her hand turned white.

He and Lilly had attended too many funerals and buried too many friends and clients. There was a deep sense of foreboding hanging over them as they drove away. He felt like he'd fallen into a deep mine shaft without even a foothold to give hope that he could climb to safety. Lilly kept her eyes averted, like she couldn't bear to look at him.

"Let's not say anything to the boys," Michael said, easing the car into a parking place outside the office. "The doctor is fairly positive. And, when I have my head on straight, I believe everything will turn out okay. You believe that, don't you?"

"Absolutely—with all my heart," she said, touching his cheek.

That evening, in the darkness of their bed, they lay in each other's arms, weeping quietly, saying nothing, their tears intermingling. The following morning, over break-fast, they made small talk about everything except the X-rays. They stood, kissed and drove to work in separate cars to begin the new day.

Michael hated it that this health trouble had come at a time when all the stars had seemed so perfectly aligned. Mostly it hurt like blazes to see Lilly suffering.

He'd never put much stock in taking bad news and sugar-coating it into something it wasn't. Yet, in this instance, a tiny voice kept saying there was always a chance. Maybe he'd be that one in a hundred, or in a thousand, or ten thousand who beats cancer. Everyone has his own Waterloo; some have many. Everyone lives on the razor's edge. He remembered his mother's words, repeated often in her matter-of-fact manner: "In this life you don't get to choose when you're born or when the

Lord calls you home. But you do wake up each day with a fresh opportunity to choose how you live this day."

Mom had it right. This day was all he had. He could decide.

A kind heart is a fountain of gladness.

–Washington Irving

Chapter 39

It was Saturday morning in mid-January 1959. The weather in Southern California had been unseasonably mild since New Year's Day. Even though Lilly had advised against it, Michael was keeping a promise to play tennis with Arthur. Paul was back in classes for his senior year in Des Moines. Sophia was off at her parents' house for the weekend. They'd played only 15 minutes when Arthur rushed into the kitchen yelling that Michael had fallen and couldn't catch his breath.

"I pounded on his back and tried to help him to his feet. He won't get up," Arthur shouted. "He's coughing and hacking, and there's blood all over."

Lilly's eyes widened. She reached for the phone just as the back door swung open and Michael stumbled in, his face white, the front of his shirt covered in blood. He held a blood-drenched handkerchief to his mouth. He struggled for breath.

"Oh, my God," Lilly cried out, rushing to him. "What happened?"

"It's okay," Michael managed to say. "Not as bad as it looks. I bit my tongue when I fell. Help me to the sink." Blood gushed from his mouth as he talked.

"Arthur, honey, call an ambulance, and the doctor."

"No, don't do that," Michael protested. "I'm fine. I fell. That's all."

Working together to apply cold compresses, Lilly and Arthur managed to staunch the flow of blood. Then they helped him up the stairs where he went to bed and slept until dinnertime.

"I guess it's cold soup for supper," Michael said, his words slurred. He offered a weak smile as he edged his way carefully down the stairs. He was trying to make light of the matter. Lilly wasn't buying it. He'd scared her good.

"You have to take better care of yourself," she said, helping him to a chair at the kitchen table. "Give up tennis, at least for a while." He shook his head at her.

By Sunday night his voice was almost normal as he packed a bag and gathered papers and stuffed them into his briefcase. He'd be catching a Monday morning flight to New York City for two days of business meetings. He also planned a side trip to visit Bob in Boston. He wanted his brother to look over the latest set of X-rays. He planned to hand-carry the film onto the plane in an oversized manila envelope.

After dropping him off at the gate with a kiss and an embrace, on an impulse Lilly called Thelma from an airport phone booth.

"Sorry to bother you at this early hour. I'm at the airport. Can you possibly join me for coffee before work? I know it's a lot to ask." Her voice trailed off and she fought to raise the volume. "I just dropped Michael off. I'm worried sick." Now she was nearly shouting.

"I'll be at our little café near the office in 45 minutes," Thelma said. "Meantime, calm down, please, and be especially careful as you leave the airport. Traffic is terrible. We don't need you having an accident."

Lilly sat in a back booth, as far as possible from the crush of customers and noise that filled the front of the tiny, square-shaped City Café. Thelma waved to her as she pushed through the crowd.

"Thanks so much, you're such a dear," Lilly said, as her best friend threw her coat, briefcase and purse into the booth seat across from her. "The world's all topsy-turvy, spinning away from me and I can't set it right. I love him so much. I'm afraid I'm losing him."

She related the story about the Saturday morning incident on the tennis court.

Thelma listened intently. Lilly kept brushing her hair back. She'd gone into the restroom to freshen up when she'd arrived at the cafe. She was shocked. Her eyes were bloodshot from crying and lack of sleep. She'd finally fallen asleep in the early morning hours, and when the alarm sounded she left the house for the airport without even putting on lipstick. Her clothes were a mass of wrinkles. She'd planned to return home from the airport but instead had called Thelma.

Looking quite the opposite, Thelma arrived bright-eyed and decked out in a dark blue business suit, fresh makeup, and sporting a stylish new hair-do, with every strand of hair in place. Lilly breathed easier. Her mere presence lifted her spirits.

"The directors' meeting is at eleven, and with Michael away I'm in charge. I sure don't look very business-like, do I?"

Thelma gave her a critical look. She leaned over and brushed a tear from her cheek.

"Don't worry about your looks. You're surrounded by people who love you and understand what you and Michael are going through."

The waitress brought coffee and Lilly held the cup with both hands as she tried to control her shaking. Bracing her elbows on the table, she lifted the cup and took a tentative sip. Her hands had stopped shaking but now under the table her legs began to wobble. After watching the coffee drama unfold, Thelma stood and moved over to Lilly's side of the booth. She pulled a makeup kit from her purse. "Relax, honey. This will take just a few minutes."

Lilly closed her eyes and surrendered as her friend's competent hands restored her face.

"You'll be fine," she said, snapping her purse closed. "You're a trooper. Now, let's hear what's causing you all this distress. Tell me everything."

Taking a deep breath, Lilly began: "You remember how excited we were about Michael's set of X-rays two months ago? Well, we have newer ones and they aren't nearly as impressive. Nothing is going as we had hoped, even though the doctor says we shouldn't be discouraged."

Thelma kept her eyes glued on her friend.

Lilly took another sip of coffee. Her legs had stopped trembling.

"I begged Michael to cancel the New York trip. He said he had to go to the business meeting. And he didn't want to miss out seeing Bob in Boston about the X-rays."

"Bob's a cancer doctor, isn't he?" Thelma injected.

Lilly lifted her eyes to her friend and nodded, as she pushed her empty coffee cup in a circle. She looked into Thelma's eyes. "I'm at the end of my wits. This lung disease is tearing at Michael's spirit. He tries to remain positive but he's wearing down and I can't help him."

She took Lilly's hands in hers. "You're helping, honey, more than you can ever know. Keep in mind you need to take care your needs, too. He's counting on you."

"I'm trying, Thelma, really trying."

Thelma straightened, her face businesslike. "Let's look at the facts. Michael took a tumble and cut his tongue. He's okay. It was an accident. Your doctor says his lungs are about the same, or at least no significant change. That's really good news. If you don't believe me, ask someone's whose cancer is out of control!"

"You're right, of course," Lilly said. "This is exactly why I love you. You know how to right my fragile ship when it's close to sinking."

Thelma put on a grim look and leaned in close so Lilly could hear her words over the noise of office workers angling for a take-out coffee and Danish: "Every damn day in this town someone is either diagnosed with cancer or dies of the disease. Who wouldn't be frightened? Cancer's a fucking plague in Hollywood. It doesn't care who it takes next."

Thelma began searching in her purse.

Lilly watched in amazement as her friend removed a pack of Lucky Strikes and a lighter. Thelma lit up, took a deep drag and rocketed a thin, white stream of tobacco smoke from the corner of her mouth to above her head, in a polite attempt to keep the smoke away from her booth companion.

"Soon as we get to the office, I'll help you get spiffed up for the day," she said, as she tapped her cigarette on the edge of the coffee saucer. "You still keep a spare set of business clothes there, don't you?"

Lilly nodded, as her eyes focused on the smoke coming from the tip of her friend's cigarette. It curled and twisted and rose like a poisonous snake toward the nicotine-stained ceiling.

If your heart is in the right place, you can go for it, and do it.

–Heidi Klum

Chapter 40

Paul lay in agony, flat out on his back in a hospital bed with his left leg straight out and covered from knee to ankle with a heavy cast. In last Saturday's game against Wallburg College, a 250-pound linebacker blasted his knee with the crown of his helmet, snapping his anterior cruciate ligament like a rubber band. Today that knee throbbed from yesterday's surgery.

Nurse Megan appeared in the doorway and said, "Did I hear cussin' coming from in here?"

"Damn it!" Paul yelled, his face burning with anger. He jammed the eraser end of a pencil under the tight edge of the cast.

"Jesus Christ! There's an itch that's driving me nuts," he fumed, and then put down the pencil and took a fork from the breakfast tray.

"Hold on partner, that won't work," Megan said. "You'll hurt yourself. I can't allow that while you're under my care."

"What the hell do you suggest? I'm going crazy. You stand there with a stupid grin on your face!"

Nurse Megan couldn't hide a smile. "Sorry. It is kind of funny."

She walked around the bed with a serious look on her face. She was a born flirt with an infectious smile. To clear the air, she had early on told Paul that she was happily married with two kids.

She'd been the single bright spot since they'd hauled him off the football field. However, this morning even her cheerfulness and good-natured teasing couldn't make him feel better. Paul was 21 years old and in his junior year in college in Des Moines and feeling like a lot of the plans he'd made were slipping away.

"Do something, will you?" Paul snapped as he dropped the fork noisily onto the metal breakfast tray.

She nodded. "At the nurse's station there's a rubber stick designed to reach pesky itches. Be right back."

She was almost out the door when she looked back over her shoulder, "Be good, or I'll give you a spanking."

Megan returned and handed him the stick. "It's a beautiful day. Should I open the blinds to let in the sunshine?"

Paul was so busy poking around inside his cast he didn't reply. Finally, he emitted a long pleasurable ahhh when he reached the spot.

Nurse Megan gazed out the window at the fall morning.

"Open the blinds," Paul said. "I forgot. Coach Sumter plans to drop by so I won't be taking a nap."

Even though he tried to stay awake, Paul drifted into dreamland.

"HEY THERE, PAUL! HOW YOU DOIN'?"

Paul jerked awake. Coach Sumter was screaming in his ear.

The pot-bellied man reached over and gave Paul's hurting leg a nudge.

"Cripes," Paul said, pushing his hand away. "That hurts like hell."

"Sorry, son. Say, the entire team wants me to say howdy for them. Dagnabit, we're real sorry about what's happened."

"Thanks, Coach. It's nobody's fault, really. Hazard of the game."

"I'm not so sure. It looked to me and the other coaches like that kid was trying to knock out our star quarterback. And it didn't surprise me that the official didn't call a penalty. That SOB's got a real hard-on when it comes to Winthrop College. Thinks we're a bunch of sissies, rich kids, and he's pissed that you're our quarterback. Anyway, the surgeon tells me you're definitely out for the rest of the season."

"That's what I figured," Paul answered.

"He says you probably shouldn't play next year, either," he continued, his voice low and almost apologetic.

That was news. After an awkward silence, Sumter rambled on, turning a "got a minute" into fifteen.

"The good news is that your athletic scholarship continues through graduation, whether you play or not. The college president has a fund he taps in emergencies. He wants me to convey our appreciation for all you've done for our football program—runner-up and a championship over two seasons. Pretty damned good, I'd say."

"Thank him for me."

So this was the reason for the coach's visit. He was broken and Coach Sumter was dumping him. No problem, he thought. That's the way sports work—and the world. If you can't cut it, hit the road, jack!

"Soon as you get on your feet the team wants you on the sidelines cheering the squad on," Coach said, actually misting up a little. "They love you, son, and so do I."

He backed toward the door and stopped abruptly when Nancy Bain, Paul's girlfriend, leaned her head into the room. After sex with Nancy in Omaha, and breaking up with Annie, he and Nancy had played house all through their senior year in high school. When Paul announced plans to attend Winthrop College in Des Moines, much to his surprise Nancy declared she'd be going there, too. At first, he felt blindsided. She hadn't asked him if it was all right. There wasn't much he could do. Now, with nearly three years of college life under their belts, Paul was getting tired of the same ole', same ole', but he could never could come up with a good reason, or the courage, to break it off with Nancy. But something needed to be done soon. There was a girl named Sophia waiting for him in Los Angeles.

"Oh, Paul. You have company. I'll wait here in the hall, honey," Nancy said.

"No, No. Come on in," Paul said, relieved to finally say goodbye to Sumter.

Nancy, if anything, was even more a beauty in college than in high school. Today she wore a tight, pale yellow pullover sweater that emphasized her sizable girls, as she liked to refer to them. Her black pleated skirt rose at least four inches above the knee, and her light-colored bobby socks contrasted nicely with the expensive black patent-leather shoes on her feet. She had gone sorority girl to the hilt.

Coach kept hanging around.

"Well, Miss Nancy," Coach Sumter said, his eyes shifting over every inch of the young girl's body. "Did I ever tell you how much the coaching staff appreciate the terrific job you cheerleaders do?"

"You're very kind, sir," Nancy answered, laying a big smile on the old man. She leaned back and swung her long hair in a wide circle.

Coach finally gave Nancy a parting wink and left. Paul was surprised he didn't reach over and give her a pinch.

Nancy bounced over and pecked him on the lips, and put on a caring look. "You doing okay, honey?"

"Yeah, except the news isn't good. Knee's shot, so football's over for me."

"That's what I heard. I don't care what they say, you'll heal up and be back playing real soon."

"Don't count on it."

"Any wise, sweetie, I dropped by to talk about the big Sorority Ball. It's this Saturday. Looks like you'll have to miss it."

Paul's eyes narrowed. He saw what was coming.

"Do you think, sweetie, it'd be all right if I asked Timmy Grogan to accompany me to the ball?" Nancy said, curling a finger and tracing a line along the cast. "It'd be like he was doing us a favor. Not a date or anything. The cheerleaders want this dance to be really special. They're counting on me being there, you know, to support them."

"By all means, go to the dance," Paul said. "And thank Tim for helping us out."

Nancy's face brightened. "Well, ta, ta, I've got lots to do before Saturday. Thanks for understanding. Soon as you're back on your feet, give me a call, you hear?"

Paul allowed her to stretch over and scrunch the girls against his chest. Then she skipped around the corner and disappeared down the hallway.

Well, it had been a busy morning. He was officially off the football team and his girlfriend had moved on and not a tear had been spilled.

Funny thing, neither of these events bothered him in the least.

Even before the injury, he had decided to give up on being a high school coach. He'd worked the past two summers at Performance Arts. Michael said there'd be a full-time job waiting for him after he graduated, if that's what he wanted. As he stared at his busted up knee, he knew the last thing in the world he wanted was to coach football. After college, he'd work in the entertainment industry, and he'd live in sunny and warm California. Michael had presented him with a terrific opportunity. He'd be crazy not to take advantage of it.

Soon as the hospital released him, he'd turn in his football gear and switch majors from Education to Business Administration. After graduation, he'd make a permanent move to L.A. He felt much better. Along with everything else, Sophia's face kept popping into his head. He hadn't realized how much he missed her.

Paul stared at the battered knee in the cast. The injury could be the best thing that had ever happened to him.

Life is art. An open, aware heart is your camera.

–Ansel Adams

Chapter 41

Three weeks had passed. The telephone rang at the house in Los Angeles and Arthur nearly tripped over himself rushing to pick up the receiver.

"Hello?" he shouted.

"Hey brother! How you doin'?" It was Paul calling from Des Moines.

"Good. How's the knee?"

"I'm on crutches and expect to get the cast off next week."

"You're coming for Thanksgiving, aren't you? Lilly says she'll pay for your airline ticket. Sophia's family is coming over. You should see Myrna. She's running around like a chicken with its head cut off. The kitchen looks like an Army mess hall, ready to feed a hundred people. My assignment is to put the 22-pound turkey in the oven early Thanksgiving morning."

"Whoa, slow down, buddy," Paul laughed.

"OK, OK," Arthur replied, "I will. Sorry."

"That turkey is a major responsibility. You up to it?"

"Oh, yeah, unless I oversleep. I have this new alarm clock, a big one. It'll wake the dead. Course I've slept through it twice."

"Wish I could be there. Clara called and wants me to spend a few days with them in Elk Point. Frank's not doing so well—something about a cold or flu that he can't shake. He drags around all the time."

"Jeez, hope he's okay. Be sure and tell him hello for me." Then Arthur got excited again. "How about Christmas?"

"You bet! I'll be there. By then I should be dancing in the street."

"You dancing? You hate to dance."

"That's true. I have enough chances to make a fool of myself without getting on the dance floor," Paul admitted.

As they chatted, Paul told Arthur that Christmas would be a better time for him to visit in Los Angeles. "Over the year-end holidays, I'll have two full weeks to spend with you guys.

Sophia walked in while Arthur was on the phone.

"Is that Paul?" she asked.

"Shhh! I'm trying to talk."

She hung on Arthur's shoulder, trying to catch his brother's every word. He pushed her back. She leaned in even closer to hear. What is it about girls? Arthur thought. No understanding them! Shoot, he'd probably see even less of Paul over Christmas than he did last summer.

"Christmas?" Sophia asked. "Paul's coming for Christmas?"

"Is that Sophia talking in the background?" Paul asked. "I'm late for my next class. Please tell her I'll call her soon, maybe this evening."

Three days later Paul packed a bag for the long Elk Point weekend. He rose early on Thanksgiving morning and after a breakfast of cold cereal and toast in the nearly deserted college cafeteria, he was on the road by 6:30, driving the first car ever titled in his name, a two-door black 1955 Dodge sedan, a gift from Lilly. He loved the car. It was a slick buggy that ran like a new one, in spite of having a lot of miles under its fan belt. It didn't hurt that his buddies said he looked cool behind the wheel.

The day started cold and sunny. By the time he reached the bridge over the Missouri River at Sioux City, it was breezy and heavy clouds blocked the sun, casting a pall over the bare branches of the cottonwoods, oaks, maples, and scrub trees bunched along the river. He rolled down the window and the heady scent of dead leaves and river water floated through the car. The water-starved Missouri now consisted of a series of tiny streams snaking around giant sand bars. It would remain low until the snow-pack in Minnesota and Canada began to melt. Then the Mighty Missouri would evolve into a wild, ice-chunked terror.

Crossing the bridge, Paul rolled into Nebraska, home to the University of Nebraska Cornhuskers football team. Briefly, he wondered where he'd be today had he accepted the scholarship in Lincoln.

Only an hour or so from Elk Point, he pictured a dozen of Frank and Clara's relatives and friends gathering at the house for the traditional family Thanksgiving celebration. He was certain the dining room table was spread with extra leafs, the top draped with Clara's finest damask pink tablecloth, and set perfectly with her best china and silverware. His stomach growled with thoughts of turkey and all the trimmings. That little breakfast he'd had in Des Moines was long gone. He was starving.

At the next intersection, he spotted a sign with an arrow pointing up river to Belleview, the town where he and Arthur had been born. It was 32 miles away. He was surprised at the strong feelings that flowed over him. His first impulse was to take the sharp right-hand turn. The years in that farm town had been his happiest, the times when his mother had been at his side. His last visit to the little river town was to attend Grandmother Lucille's funeral. She had suffered a massive stroke only two years after Mom had died. She'd lived those two years in a nursing home, like a vegetable, unable to talk, unable to feed herself. One morning she didn't wake up. When Clara told him of her passing, he choked up momentarily. But with all that had gone before, he soon resolved her death in his mind. Just another crappy thing to add to a growing list, he thought. Why should he be surprised?

At the time, he never said a word about Grandma's passing to Arthur. No sense stirring up unhappy memories for the kid. Still, with the passage of the years, now it was time to tell everyone—including his father about Grandma Lucille, even though he knew Dad had had differences with her.

He rolled past the Belleview turnoff and punched the gas pedal, a swirl of crinkly, dried-up leaves billowing in his rear-view mirror. If he wasn't in Elk Point by noon, Clara would worry. Belleview could wait for another day.

He swung his eyes back and forth as he passed Bottman's Standard and the courthouse. The town looked clean and well taken care of, which didn't surprise him. Folks in Elk Point took a lot of pride in their hometown. Someone had even cleaned up the two burned-out lots. Approaching the house, he spotted four kids playing touch football in Frank's front yard, and saw two of Frank's son-in-laws talking and smoking on the front porch. One waved and then turned and yelled, "College boy's arrived!"

Paul stepped in through the back kitchen door just as Clara came in from the front room wearing a bright red-and-white-checked apron. He'd left his crutches in the car. She looked and smelled wonderful, as she kissed his cheek and hugged him. In the front room, Frank lurched up from his favorite armchair and encircled him in his giant arms. Paul could feel the man's enormous strength as they swayed back and forth in a tight bear hug. Strong as ever. He couldn't have been too sick. Clara later told him that Frank was down for more than a week with a virus. It had caused her quite a worry.

"Come see my new car. I'll take you for a spin."

"What? Well, I'll be darned!" he hooted. "The big-time college boy has his own wheels. Ain't that something?"

"Turkey's almost ready so don't be long," Clara said. "Fifteen minutes till we carve. Be here or we'll eat without you!"

A kind heart is a fountain of gladness.

–Washington Irving

Chapter 42

On December 21, 1959, Paul stepped off the airplane at Los Angeles International to swaying palm trees, sparkling sunshine, and temperatures in the mid-seventies. Finally, his Christmas vacation had begun. After the knee incident, and the terrible Iowa weather he'd experienced for the past three weeks, he was tempted to kneel down and kiss the ground.

Michael and Arthur hailed him from the open doors leading into the terminal building. Even after a long flight in a cramped seat, Paul barely limped. The knee was healing fast.

After shaking Michael's hand he gave Arthur a brotherly slug on the shoulder.

"Great to see you," Arthur responded. "Knee okay?"

"Much better, thanks. I ditched the crutches—more trouble than they were worth. Still working out at the gym every chance I get."

The two Californians wore tennis togs, white shorts, collared white pullovers, and, of course, gleaming white tennis shoes. Arthur looked tanned, fit and energetic while Michael had dark bags under his heavy-lidded eyes and appeared worn out.

"You guys just come from the courts?" Paul asked. Despite Lilly's warnings, Michael was back to playing tennis, although, with his diminished energy level, his play wasn't anything like it used to be.

Arthur piped up, "Yeah, we don't play too hard, though. This old guy has trouble keeping up." Michael grimaced and chose to ignore the boy's insensitive comment.

"You hungry?" Michael inquired. "This boy has been pestering for food. I had to put him in a headlock or he'd have stormed the airport restaurant."

"Oh c'mon! How could a snack have hurt?"

"I've been dreaming of Mexican food ever since I boarded the plane," Paul said. "Can't find it in Iowa. Believe me, I've looked."

Michael clapped his hands. "It's your lucky day. There's a new place I've been meaning to try, and it's getting rave reviews. It's right on our way. Okay with you, Arthur?"

"I'd eat burritos, rice, and black beans every day if I could," Arthur declared.

The benches in Chelitos waiting area were full of customers. Michael returned from the hostess station and said there'd be a 20-minute wait.

"I'm starving and now we have to wait?" Arthur snipped. "Forget it! Let's go someplace else."

"Oh, settle down," Michael soothed. "We'll have our table before we can drive to another place. Besides, I want to try the food. Supposed to be very authentic."

"Forget it!" Arthur yelped. I'm not putting up with this. I'll walk down the street and see what else is around here."

The childish outburst was a side of his brother he hadn't seen for quite a while. Michael had been right. The kid had turned into a pain since he'd last seen him—a first-rate annoyance.

"Come on, little brother," Paul urged. "Don't be difficult. The food smells great. It's only a little wait."

"Oh, all right," he said, taking a seat on one the benches and crossing his arms, a dark scowl on his face.

After lunch, Michael drove up the driveway to the garage. They spotted Lilly and Sophia stretched out on lounge chairs poolside in their swimming suits.

"Where have you guys been?" Lilly asked. "We expected you an hour ago."

Michael flopped down on a chair next to his wife. "We stopped for a bite at that new Mexican place. It was great, wasn't it, Arthur? Tacos to die for."

Arthur nodded grudgingly and disappeared into the house.

Paul caught Sophia's eye and gave her a wave. When Sophia realized the others were watching her cheeks flared. Paul hadn't seen her since last August. She looked especially beautiful, and sexy, stretched out on the lounge chair in a bikini.

How come you're here on a weekend, Sophia?" Michael asked, before realizing he should have thought before he spoke.

"Sophia's part of the party," Lilly stepped in to cover for her husband. "We're all five going out for dinner tonight, my treat, to celebrate Paul's arrival and to welcome him home."

"Thanks for including me," Sophia said, regaining her composure. "This is a nice break." Lilly traditionally gave Sophia two weeks off over Christmas to spend with her family. With Paul coming, she'd asked the young lady to join them for dinner. She knew Paul's homecoming was a big event for both of them.

As it turned out, instead of fighting the crowds to go out for dinner, Michael grilled hamburgers by the pool, and Lilly and Sophia threw together a great tossed salad. They kept the meal simple. After dinner, Michael announced their Acapulco plans.

"We're off for five days between Christmas and New Years," Lilly said, reaching over to cover Michael's hand. "Myrna is off so when you guys choose to stay in for meals, you'll need to take turns on kitchen duty."

Paul leaned forward and asked, "Do you have plans, Sophia?"

"Disneyland with my brother and sister," she said. "I've been promising and it's time to deliver. I haven't seen Mickey, Goofy, or Snow White in years."

"Hey, mind if I join you?" he asked. "I've never been. I'll help you keep the ruffians under control."

"That'd be great!" Sophia gushed. Then she lowered her voice. "Can you join us, Arthur?"

"Naw, thanks. I have tennis lessons almost every morning and a bag full of schoolwork to catch up on. Give Minnie a kiss for me." He maintained his petulance.

Everyone scattered except for Paul and Sophia, who cleaned up the kitchen and did the dishes.

"Did I hear you switched majors midstream?" Sophia asked. "Something about a business curriculum rather than teaching and coaching."

"Football's over for me. What I'll miss most are cheering crowds and all that attention, especially from the girls," he said teasingly. "Michael's offered me a job after I graduate. I'm going to take it."

"That's wonderful, Paul."

"How about you? How's school going?"

"Sticking to teaching," she answered, pride in her voice. "It won't make me rich but it's a lifelong dream. I love seeing the light go on in a kid's head when he or she suddenly understands. Lilly and Michael have been so good to me."

"Know exactly how you feel. Before Lilly took us in, Arthur and I were homeless ragamuffins—a scruffier, needier pair you never would have seen! Whenever things got tough, she was there to bail us out."

Paul dried the last plate. "Um, I wanted to ask you something. Michael looks like he's lost weight. Is he feeling all right?"

Sophia hesitated. "I found Lilly crying in the kitchen one day. She said his lungs are infected with something. I know Michael has quit smoking, thank goodness, but you still have to worry about lung cancer. I'm so happy you don't smoke, Paul."

"Wow, cancer?" Paul said, a shocked look on his face.

"I don't know for sure what Michael has. Lilly worries all the time. This trip to Acapulco is a good idea. They need time away to relax and enjoy themselves."

"Well, let's hope for the best." He reached down and took her hand. "It's wonderful seeing you. Care to take a walk? This weather is such a treat, so much nicer than all the snow and ice in Iowa."

* * * * *

From their upstairs bedroom, Lilly and Michael watched them stroll hand-in-hand down the long, curvy driveway from the house to the street, then make a right turn and disappear in the direction of Sunset Park.

Although small, the half-acre park featured dozens of evergreen trees, mainly spruce, and a few towering deciduous trees, as well as a clear running, spring-fed creek and a scattering of park benches. It was a favorite place in the neighborhood.

" Love is in the air," Lilly said as she rested her head on Michael's shoulder.

The heart, like the stomach, wants a varied diet.

—Gustave Flaubert

Chapter 43

It was the spring of his sophomore year at the Los Angeles Academy and Arthur had found a girl-friend—Mandy Fishman—or rather she'd found him. He was 15, and itching to get a driver's license when he turned 16 in August. She was already sweet 16. Mandy arrived on a bus at the Academy with dozens of other girls from a nearby all-girl private high school for a "mixer" dance with the Academy boys. A couple of Arthur's buddies had dared him to attend. So here he was.

The girls bounced through the gymnasium door and scattered like billiard balls. A tall, gangly one with fizzy hair and dark curls and wearing no makeup marched right up to him and put her face inches from his.

"Hi, I'm Mandy," she said in a deep voice. "Let's dance."

He hesitated so she grabbed his hand and yanked him onto the dance floor. After that first meeting, Mandy commandeered all of his free time. Without even asking, she declared him her new boyfriend and he was hands-off to the other girls. He didn't protest, even though he felt like a gigged frog when Mandy got overly bossy. He considered it cool to have his own girlfriend. She wasn't the most attractive girl around, and she dressed atrociously, with mismatched clothes and colors, and she wore boots with hiking socks up to her knees. She walked like a boy and went for weeks at a time without shaving her legs. An odder girl he'd never seen.

Mandy was an honest-to-god rebel. She didn't take any crap from anybody. Man, how he admired that spirit. What he didn't like so much was she looked down her nose at everyone, ranging from parents to classmates. God help anyone if they disagreed with anything she said or thought.

She was also the most aggressive and fearless girl he'd ever come across. If she wanted to make out in a booth in crowded café, well he'd better go along with what she wanted to do or else she'd fly into a rage. When they were alone, she'd encourage him to paw all over her body. Her breasts were hardly more than nubs, which proved to be a disappointment to him.

Then Mandy started feeling him up, and it made him uncomfortable. Sure, it was time for adventure and exploration but this was going too far. He'd have quit her right then except he took perverse pleasure in the fact that Lilly and Myrna couldn't stand his new girlfriend. He supposed the women in his household had gotten so used to him toeing the mark all the time, they didn't know what to do when naughty Mandy stood up to them, even sassed them to their faces. He enjoyed standing back and watching the fireworks.

"What do you see in her?" Lilly asked one day. "She's so unlike you."

"Hey," he sputtered, "she's my girlfriend. You don't have to like her!"

Arthur made a point of inviting Mandy to the house. Before long, the forward young lady began coming around even when Arthur wasn't home.

When he suggested that they spend time at her house, she growled, "You don't want to hang around my parents. They're peasants! This is a nice place. I like it here."

They'd been a couple all through the summer and were still going together in October. Arthur now had his license. One afternoon after a tennis match, he returned home to find Mandy sprawled out on a couch in the living room fast asleep, the television set droning in the background, something she claimed she never watched.

Myrna appeared at the doorway and pointed out to Arthur that Mandy had logged a lot of hours staring at the mindless lighted box. "She's always underfoot and leaves a trail of messes. The queen-bee expects me to clean up after her."

Word got to Lilly and she cornered Arthur.

"She has to go!" Lilly said, shaking her head in disgust. "She's wrecking our house and Myrna isn't putting up with her anymore. Neither am I."

"Now wait a minute," Arthur protested. "She's my friend. If she goes, I go. Besides, Myrna works here. I'm her boss."

"You're nobody's boss, young man!" Lilly fired back, raising her hand in a threat to slap him.

"You can't tell me what to do. You're not my real mother!" Arthur stormed out of the room.

What's happened to our Arthur, Lilly thought?

In truth, Arthur had to admit Mandy had become a big problem, even if he did gain a lot of satisfaction seeing her torment Myrna and Lilly. The last straw was when Mandy began demanding that they engage in sex.

"Come on," she coaxed, trying without success to put an arousing look on her face. "We're both virgins. We'll figure it out as we go. Heck, most of our friends have already done it, dozens of times. Don't be such a killjoy. I've read up on it. I'll show you how."

Arthur took strong offense to Mandy's insistent demands. He was the guy; it was up to him to decide when and where to make the moves.

"What if I knock you up?" Arthur asked, looking for an out.

Mandy waved him off. "I'm taking precautions. Don't worry about it."

Well, he did worry. Mandy told a lot of lies, in fact, sometimes he felt she didn't have it in her to tell the truth. For example, she'd told him that her parents treated her like dirt, and that her mom had more than once slapped her around. "Dad just stands by and lets her."

Arthur couldn't imagine any of this was true, though he could appreciate her mother desiring to lay one on her daughter's smart mouth. He'd met Mandy's parents and they were good, gentle people. Adding to the situation, Mandy swore she'd never had sex with anyone. He knew at least two guys at school who said they'd screwed her, and he had no reason to doubt them.

One classmate claimed after he'd plunked her, Mandy threatened to tell his parents if he didn't do it again.

"I called her bluff, and got the hell away from her," he told Arthur.

The only sensible thing to do was to break up. How to do it was the question Mandy had a super hot temper. One day, she ranted on about the virtues of Communism, and when he had the nerve to pipe up, "Every Communist state is a totalitarian regime. No one has any freedom. Everyone knows that!" her eyes grew large at his insolence. She swung at him with the back of her bony hand and busted his lip open. Blood covered the front of his shirt and his lip stayed swollen for a week. He told Lilly some guy had caught him off guard with a fast tennis ball.

If he was going to break up with her, he needed to do it in a public place, surrounded by a crowd. She wouldn't dare try anything then. Leastwise, he hoped she wouldn't.

He drove his troublesome girlfriend to a drive-in restaurant for a hamburger. In his pocket were tickets for a Lettermen concert at the Hollywood Bowl. The show was a sell-out, thanks to The Lettermen having two hits on the current Top 20, "That's My Desire" and "The Way You Look Tonight."

He steered the car into Haley's Drive-In and rolled down the window. A tall, long-legged carhop in a tight top and short skirt rolled up the to driver's window on skates.

"What'll it be, Mandy?" Arthur asked.

"A Haley burger with the works, and a Coke. No fries. They make me fat."

"Two Haley burgers with everything, two Cokes and one fry," Arthur said to the carhop, who jotted the order on a pad of paper.

"And hurry it up," Mandy called from across the seat. "We're running late."

Arthur saw the pretty girl's face drop. Why did Mandy have to be so rude? He was tired of it. He was going to tell her right now.

"While we're waiting, I need to talk to you about something," Arthur said, turning toward her.

"Well, good," she snapped. "Lately you haven't said shit to me. I carry the whole goddamn conversation. Then you give me on of those funny looks, like I'm crazy."

"I've been thinking," Arthur said, his voice starting out low. "You and I are awfully busy. I'm wondering if we should think about slowing down our relationship, you know, not seeing each other so often."

"You what?" Mandy screeched. She punched him hard in the right shoulder and raked her nails across his cheek. Damn—it hurt like hell.

He leaned away, crouching against the driver's door and put his hands up to protect his face, and used the steering wheel as a wedge between him and her.

The carhop returned and, seeing trouble, made a quick turn on her skates. Too quick. She tumbled to the ground, landing with a sickening thud and spilled the tray full of food. Several of the carhops and nearby customers rushed to her aid.

"Oh, gosh," Arthur yelled, feeling helpless. "I'm so sorry."

He reached over and roughly pushed Mandy away from him. He had to get out of here. He gave one of the carhops five dollars, offered another "sorry" and backed the car out of the parking slot.

"You, you prick! There's another girl, isn't there?" Mandy said, her voice loud and threatening.

He reached the main street and turned in the direction of his girlfriend's house. No way was he taking her to a Lettermen concert.

He saw the murderous look in her eye. She wasn't about to take this lying down.

"Darn it, Mandy, of course there's no one else," he argued, trying to keep his voice friendly and measured so as not to rile her up even more. "It's just…er…we argue, and you get mad and I don't know what to say or do. It's mostly my fault."

"Oh really. That's bullshit! We're a great couple. You love me, and I love you."

"Please keep your voice down," Arthur said, rolling up his window.

"Fuck them!" she bellowed out her open window.

"We'll talk, but not here," he said, pressing down on the accelerator."

"Screw you and screw everybody," she went on. "You're my boyfriend. I've been nice to you; let you do anything you wanted, no matter how disgusting. You remember? What will my friends think?"

Arthur pulled to the curb in front of her house.

He tried another tack. "Honestly. I just need space. Maybe we can get back together again one day, you know when we're not so busy with school, and stuff like that."

Her face brightened. Ding, ding, ding, he thought, maybe she's finally ready to calm down.

In a blink, she morphed from raging bull to purring kitten. Wearing a conciliatory smile, she slid across the seat and nearly climbed into his lap.

"Oh, sweetheart," she cooed. "I'm so sorry about the scratches."

She brushed a finger against them and continued. "That's a great idea about a short little break. I love you so much. We'll get together this weekend, say Saturday night. I'll come over to your place. Okay, sweetheart?"

"Sure. That might be possible," he answered.

She gave him a deep, passionate kiss, and seemed ready to settle in for some heavy necking. Instead, he pulled back as gently as possible, opened his door and hustled around to the other side.

This act of gender politeness threw her off. Confused, she stepped out of her door without protest. On the porch, he gave her a peck on the cheek. She threw her arms around him and ground her body into his.

Her kiss was hard and she forced her tongue inside his mouth.

Wobbling backwards and feeling nauseous, he mumbled "see you later" and jogged to the car, gagging from the saliva she'd left behind. When he got the car moving, he rolled the window down and spit until his mouth went dry.

It was the last time he ever saw Mandy Fishman.

Home is where the heart is.

–Pliny the Elder

Chapter 44

Mandy had been a mistake, no question about it. Still it was his mistake! He grinned inside—she'd been interesting. The driver's license in his pocket, and Michael providing him with an old car to drive around in, had gone a long way toward making up for the loss.

What still ticked him off, though, was how Lilly and Myrna had stuck their busybody noses into his first-girlfriend relationship. He'd dug in his heels and told them to mind their own business. Now it was like the cold war around the house. When Lilly asked about his day, he'd reply in a single word and leave it at that. He noticed Lilly and Myrna tried to make nice, like they were sorry for the way they'd treated him. Well, he'd let them keep trying. It was high time someone paid him some respect.

He wondered: How might his "real mom" have handled things with Mandy?

A few things about his mother were seared in his brain—like her face leaning in close to him, her smell, the melodious sound of her voice as she read to him before bedtime, her kindnesses when he was sick, and the way she smiled and laughed, a laugh that started out low, almost a soft chuckle and progressed to a loud, full-throated celebration of life.

He had vague memories coated in thick layers of sadness of Grandma waking them up and leading them into Mom's bedroom the night she had died. The scene flickered like a broken film clip. Did he really see his mother dead?

What kind of life had Mom led? What was her relationship with his father? He was only six when she died and his memory of her, while good in some respects, faded in and out in other ways, like his mind was blocking out certain things. It was frustrating. During the few times he managed to be alone with Paul the past two summers he had peppered his older brother with questions about their mother. Paul tried to put him off. He kept at him.

Exasperated, Paul said, "Hey, she was a good person, she loved us. She was nice, fun, and that's all I want to say. Now, get a life, and leave me alone."

He wouldn't let go. He had to know more about the woman in the billfold-size, creased black and white photograph that he now carried everywhere in his wallet. He had studied every detail of the tall, elegant woman, and shared the photo with Paul.

"What you can't see in that old photo are her bright blue eyes," Paul said, his voice growing soft. "You have those same eyes, you know."

"You'll think this is weird, Paul. I've been dreaming about Mom. It's like she's out there in front of me, close, but I can't really see her. I have the feeling she wants to tell me something. I wake up and she's gone."

"I miss her, too," Paul said. "And here's a scoop: I always thought you were her favorite."

Her favorite? Now he had to learn more. The only other person he could turn to was Dad. He hadn't seen him since the trip to Paul's graduation party. He had promised to stay in touch but the years rolled by and neither of them had made an effort. Now that Paul was finishing college and preparing to move to Los Angeles, he wondered whether the three of them could be more like a family, not necessarily live together but be a family of sorts.

A while back, Lilly said she'd heard Dad had left his job at Kelsey's and was working in a new place. She didn't know what kind of a job he'd taken. After going back and forth for a couple days, Arthur called Kelsey's and talked the replacement bartender into giving him his father's current number. He steeled his nerve and picked up the phone. He had no idea how Dad would react. Maybe he didn't want to hear from him ever again.

He didn't mention his plans to Lilly. He was 16, with a driver's license and a car that he drove to school every day. For crying out loud, she didn't need to know everything he was doing.

"Hi, Dad. Guess who? It's Arthur."

The other end of the line was quiet except for breathing sounds. He tried to picture his dad's face. He'd looked terrible the last time he'd seen him. He heard a throat being cleared.

"Say, Dad, Paul and I have been talking about Mom. He remembers her in some ways, but he's sketchy on the details. I'm wondering if we could talk. I'd like to know more about her."

The phone went quiet. Arthur forged on.

"Paul can't remember a lot. You're the only one I can rely on to provide more details about her, you know, to fill in the blanks. Would you mind? Would that be okay?"

Arthur realized he was talking fast and sounding desperate. He decided to shut up and wait for his father to speak.

"I guess so," Henry finally replied. "It's good to hear from you, son. Then, out of the blue he demanded, "Does Lilly know about this?"

"No. It's just between us. I haven't said a word to her. How about breakfast at that little family restaurant at Westmar and Boone. Say at 10 o'clock Saturday? I'll buy."

"Sounds good, Mr. Moneybags. I know the place."

Arthur was all ready in a booth when his father entered the café. As he walked toward him, he looked different—a lot better. He had a confident air about him, upbeat, almost cocky, like he'd done something special and wanted everyone to know it. "Hey, kid, how you doin'?" Henry called out, as he gave his youngest son the once-over. He was smiling. Arthur shook his hand and smiled back.

"You ever going to stop growing? You'll be as tall as your mother one of these days. She was taller than me. Of course your brother is out of sight. What is Paul now, six-three?"

"Probably," Arthur said, heartened by his Dad's upbeat mood. "I really appreciate your meeting with me."

They ordered breakfast: bacon, eggs and toast for the two of them, coffee for Dad and a Coke for him.

"Hey, I'm sorry I haven't been in touch," he said. "Meant to call so many times. I've had a lot on my plate. Started a new job and all." He smiled again. "I haven't forgotten you guys. There's a special place in my heart for you boys."

"Its okay. Paul and I understand. We're all real busy."

"So, I suppose you and Lilly are living high on the hog in the mansion? I'm sure Lilly's doin' just great."

"She's fine. Works all the time. Sometimes I hardly see her. She's out of the house early and back late."

Arthur noticed a small frown creep over his father's face at the mention of her name, like he held a grudge toward her.

Then without any prodding from him, Henry started talking. "A day doesn't pass that I don't think about your mom. She was the best thing that ever happened to me, and she was a great mother to you boys. Fact is, she took care of all of us real well."

The waitress brought their food and refilled Henry's coffee cup.

"I'm wondering what she was really like, you know, as a person," Arthur said. "Was she content with her life? Was she happy? Was she doing what she wanted to do? I understand she was an extremely capable person."

Henry pondered the questions. "Happy? I suppose so. Most days. There were times she'd get a faraway look in her eye. I guess we all feel like that sometimes, wondering if we'd gone this way instead of that way at a particular time how things might have turned out differently. Overall, though, I'd say she was happy—exceptionally happy, really."

He noticed his dad's face softened when he talked about her.

"She was bright as a penny, that's for sure. And she could do anything. I always thought when you kids got older she'd go back to school and be a schoolteacher, like your grandmother.

"Oh, sure, sometimes there's be tears in her eyes, and I'd ask, 'What's wrong, honey?' She'd look at me and say everything was fine, and that would be the end of it."

Arthur nodded, silently urging his father to continue.

"I wonder if your mother somehow knew she wouldn't live long enough to see you boys grow up. Maybe that's what made her sad. She had a sixth sense, like she could see the future. She understood things that I couldn't begin to figure out."

The first two times they met for breakfast went fine. His father was friendly and chatty, went out of his way to answer questions, really made an effort. He was patient and courteous, like a real dad would be under the circumstances.

However, on this Saturday morning, the third meeting, Arthur sensed something had changed. He was irritable, on edge. It was like he didn't want to be there, and couldn't wait to get away. "Anything wrong?" Arthur asked.

"Had a piss-ass week at work. Lot's of problems. What do ya' want to talk about? I'm in kind of a hurry."

Henry grabbed his orange juice glass and promptly drained it.

"Well, I'll hurry along then," Arthur said, placing a lined sheet of paper on the table before him. "I jotted down a few questions so I wouldn't forget."

Henry sighed. "You brought a list? How long will this take?"

"I've heard different stories about how Mom died. Were Paul and I in the room with her? Paul seems to remember being there. I'm not so sure I was. I can't remember."

"She died of influenza, or at least that's what the doctor said. I think it was something far worse. One day she came down with a cold. She ended up in bed—and never got up again. I always thought the doctor could have done more, put her in the hospital or done something else to help her.

"She died early in the morning. Just as the sun began to come up. You guys were sleeping. Your grandmother wanted me to bring you into the bedroom. I put my foot down. You were too young to see a dead person, especially your own mother! I learned later she went ahead and took you kids into the bedroom anyway. That was just like her."

"Were you there when Mom died?"

"Sure, along with your crazy grandmother and Doctor Mullen."

Henry tapped his fork on his plate. He hadn't touched his eggs. "Your grandmother and I never got along. I put up with her to please your mom."

"What ever happened to Grandma?" Arthur asked. "Why didn't she come to see us, or even write?"

Henry's fork clattered on the plate. He looked perturbed, ready to bolt.

"Hell, I don't know. After leaving Belleview we traveled around a lot. Then we moved to California. Maybe Lilly or Clara kept in touch. Ask them."

Just a couple more questions. "Did Mom like me more than Paul?"

Henry tossed his napkin on the table and growled. "Now what kind of a dumb-ass question is that? I've had enough."

Arthur pulled back, startled. "She was my mom. All I have are two photographs, one of her alone and the other of the three of us. I'm a baby in her arms. Paul looks to be about seven or so. Mom's looks really happy."

"Yeah, she loved you guys. Both of you! Truth is, you kids were all she had time for, far as I could tell. She sure didn't pay much attention to me."

A silence fell between them. Breakfast was over and Arthur realized there would be no more Saturday meetings. He stood and extended his hand. "You've been a big help." As he made his way to the restaurant door, he began processing all the new information he now had about his mom. People said he was a lot like her. He had her eyes, the ones that seemed to see everything, like she could tell what a guy was thinking even before he did. Now he knew she loved him. He was certain of that.

Share from your heart. Your story will touch and heal people's souls.

–Melody Beattie

Chapter 45

Attorney Vogel called Michael with intriguing news. "You're probably not going to like this. Henry and Arthur have met on three occasions on Saturday mornings in a small restaurant near your house. The surveillance team reports the meetings usually lasted an hour or so."

"Any indication what they talked about?" Michael's asked, going on full alert.

"No way to know that." The private detectives report everything seemed friendly enough, amicable, like a father and son catching up."

"Hmmm. That's strange. Henry hasn't shown any interest in meeting with Arthur in the past several years.

I wonder if this is the start of another attempt to shake down Lilly for money. He may be trying to use his son to get to her. Or, on a more positive note, it may be that Henry is simply trying to reconnect with his youngest son."

Michael thanked Vogel and asked him to continue keeping an eye on Henry's activities. After hanging up, he settled back in his chair. What the hell is this all about? Did Henry ask Arthur to meet with him? If so, why? Michael could understand Arthur's interest in his father. It was natural for a boy to be curious about his dad.

Why hadn't Arthur said anything to Lilly? She must not know. If she did, she'd have told him. She'd never withhold such information from him. They were both too wary of Henry and his shenanigans to keep any news from each other.

He glanced at the clock. It was nearly eleven and time for a scheduled morning briefing with his wife. She entered his office with her arms loaded with papers and files. Michael helped her arrange them on the front of his desk.

"We closed on the CBS contract," Lilly said, pushing a file across to him. "The network is willing to sign a three-year deal to continue the TV show with our client. She couldn't be happier and, why not, she's making millions."

"That's good. I saw the ratings, and the audience for the redhead's show is already out of sight, and growing by the week. You did a great job helping her hash out the contract details. She can be very demanding."

As they talked, his eyes lingered on the tiny lines around his wife's eyes. She'd been worrying about his health, and now he was about to drop the news that Arthur had been meeting secretly with Henry, which would only add to her stress. Still, she had a right to know what was going on.

For the next hour, they methodically reviewed projects. When they finished, his wife gathered her papers and prepared to leave.

Michael cleared his throat and placed a light hand on her arm. "I hate to bring this news to you: Do you know Arthur's been meeting with Henry?"

"What!" Lilly's eyes widened and her face paled.

He regretted delivering the news so abruptly.

Lilly slumped in the chair. "Why in the world would Arthur do such a thing? And why didn't he tell me? He hasn't been right since that girlfriend."

Michael reached for his cigarettes. Instead his hand found a jar of jellybeans. Damn it, he wanted a smoke in the worst way.

"Don't know. According to the people I hired to keep tabs on Henry, they shared breakfast three consecutive Saturdays at a neighborhood cafe about a mile from our house."

"What did they talk about? Why would Henry…oh, God, is he after money again? Won't he ever leave us in peace?"

Michael twisted the lid off the jar and then retightened it. "We can't forbid him from seeing his own father. I wonder if Paul knows anything. The brothers spent a lot of time together last summer, and they talk on the phone. Should we call him in Iowa?"

"You do it," Lilly said, her voice breaking. She massaged her forehead. "I can't deal with it."

Michael stood up. "I'll try this evening. And please, honey, don't worry. I'm sure there's a good explanation. Arthur's a teenager and spreading his wings. It's normal for him to test the boundaries. He's got a good head on his shoulders. We need to trust him."

Michael made the call at 7:30 that evening, knowing it was 9:30 in Des Moines. "Hi, Paul, this is Michael. Hope I'm not calling too late. We think about you all the time. Hard to believe you'll be graduating in only a few months. Can't wait to have you here working at the office."

"Plugging away. I'm enjoying the business and marketing classes. Feel like I'm in the right place."

"That's wonderful but leave some time for fun. Say, I don't want to put you in awkward position but Lilly and I are concerned about Arthur."

"Really?" Paul responded. "What's he up to now?"

"He's been meeting with your dad on Saturday mornings for breakfast. Problem is he hasn't said anything to either of us. Lilly feels shut out. She doesn't want to confront him. He has a right to meet with your father anytime he wants."

"Geez, what's the kid's problem? Lilly's done everything for him, for Christ's sake. He owes her the courtesy of knowing what he's up to, especially when it involves Dad."

"Yes, I agree. But he's a teenager now, and who knows what's going on in his head."

"I'm guessing he's talking to Dad about Mom," Paul said. "Last summer he drove

me nuts with questions about her. There's a lot he doesn't remember." Paul paused. He didn't want to talk about Arthur behind his back, and betray any confidences, but, heck, this was Michael. He kept going.

"He told me he'd been having dreams about her, said she comes to him at night. He wakes up and feels like Mom's trying to tell him something. I told him I dream about her, too. That's normal, don't you think?"

"I'd say so. Anyway, thanks for shedding some light on this. I'll pass it on to Lilly. It'll relieve her mind. Henry's been a pain in her backside for years. He's badgered her more than once for money."

"Yeah, I can understand why she'd feel like that. Dad's always trying to finagle something for nothing. Please assure her that I believe it was Arthur who initiated the breakfast meetings. That kid can be persistent, almost to a fault!"

"I'll do that. Meantime, let's keep this conversation between us. He and your dad seem to have broken off the meetings. I'm thinking it's best to forget the whole thing. Let sleeping dogs lie. I'm sure Lilly will agree."

Life will not break your heart. It'll crush it.

–Henry Rollins

Chapter 46

"**W**e gotta meet," Mac said, alarm in his faltering voice. "Don't tell anyone."

Henry sensed Mac's chilling fear through the telephone wires. Something, or someone, had scared the shit out of him. His fellow bookie's voice was so low Henry strained to hear the words.

"What's with all this cloak-and-dagger stuff?" Henry asked, trying to sound tough.

"I'll tell you tomorrow. Just know this, we're both in big trouble."

Henry had spent Thanksgiving Day with his new girlfriend, and it was his best holiday in years. So far, the new job was going well. He now earned nearly three times what those sing-song Filipinos at Kelsey's had been paying him. Things were finally looking up in his life.

Now this.

Henry walked through the door at Kelsey's and squinted in the half dark. Mac was in a back booth in the shadows, crouching down low, like he was hiding. Taking a seat across from him, he watched the man nervously play with his half-empty shot glass, rolling it in his fingers.

"Christ, man," Henry said. "You look like your puppy got swept up by a street sweeper. You okay?"

"No, I'm not. We've got a problem, buddy, a serious one, maybe even life-or-death."

Henry stared at the flickering tick in Mac's left eyelid. That was new.

"Tell me everything," Henry said, leaning forward and giving Mac his full attention. It wasn't like Mac to be so dramatic.

"You've heard about the East Coast gang trying to muscle in on Dutch's territory. It's not a rumor. It's for real."

Mac's eyes jumped around as he talked, like someone was out to get him.

"Two goons visited Dutch last week and offered a good price to buy him out," Mac continued. "He threw them out. A day later a package arrived on the boss's front porch. His wife opened it and found her cat inside. Dead! She nearly pissed her pants. A note inside warned Dutch if he valued his wife, kids and grandkids, and his own ass, he'd better reconsider the offer they'd made for the business.

"Christ, what kind of sick bastards are they?" Henry said, fear grabbing at his lower gut.

"Word is they're from New York. Apparently, the top mob dons have dispatched a guy with a suitcase full of money and half a dozen soldiers to establish a beachhead here in L.A. I heard there's another bunch pressuring Las Vegas casino owners."

Mac had let himself go: food spots on his tie, checkered suit wrinkled and shiny, and his normally crisp and expertly pressed white shirt banded at the collar with a ring of sweat and dirt.

"All this crap stems from the Feds turning up the heat along the eastern seaboard, and the rats are scurrying into our backyards," Mac kept going. "That Kennedy guy—the one who's the Attorney General and the president's brother—is cracking down in Boston, New York, even in Kansas City. They say he's trying to make a name for himself. He's also the one who's supposedly screwing Marilyn Monroe. They say Brother John, the president, is bopping the blonde, too. Ain't that something? They're keeping it all in the family."

"Shit! Dutch isn't going to roll over, is he?" Henry asked. "He's got a lot invested here. He needs to tell those guys to go piss up a rope. They'll need a bigger army than six." He put on a brave face and looked Mac right in the eye.

"Watch out what you wish for," Mac said. "If there's a fight, people will get hurt, and that could include us. My guess is Dutch will buy his wife a new cat and take the money and head for a Mexican beach."

"Where's that leave us?"

"Speaking Dago, I reckon. After Dutch is gone, the Italians will probably bring in their own boys—those spaghetti eaters stick together. They're all kissing cousins. Can you believe gangsters going around kissing each other? There's no way you and I are going to fit into that bunch. Trust me, brother, if you're smart, you'll put together some dough and be ready to blow this town at the drop of a dime. That's what I'm doing. And start watching your back. I've got a feeling I'm being followed."

Mac polished off his drink, stood and shook Henry's hand.

"Thanks for tipping me off. God, why is it when things are going so well, something always comes along to foul them up?"

"Yeah, know what you mean. See you around, pal" Mac said, as he moved unsteadily toward Kelsey's front door.

Henry lingered, twirling the ice in his glass of Coca-Cola. These days he confined himself to nothing stronger than soda or coffee during working hours. In this new job he needed his wits about him at all times. So far he'd kept the promise, though at the moment he was sorely tempted to down a couple of strong bourbons.

The timing of the Mafia trouble couldn't have come at a worse time. Until a few weeks ago, he'd squirreled away just under $3,000. Now, that dough was gone and he had maybe $500 in his pocket; and the outlook for future paydays was not good.

Crystal Favor, his new girlfriend, was a knock out and he was dancing on cloud nine. He'd met her at one of the bars on his bookmaking route. It was off the beaten track, a neighborhood joint for factory working stiffs. She worked the tables there and wore one of those skimpy outfits designed to show off just enough to gain attention. Actually, the outfit should have been retired years ago. It was dirty, torn in places and way too big for her. It sagged in the seat, and when she bent over, she revealed a lot more than she wanted to show off. She kept tugging at her front, trying to cover up. At the moment, he was at the bar talking to the bartender, a guy he'd gotten to know pretty well. From the corner of his eye, he watched the cocktail waitress moving around the room. She didn't look happy

He guessed her at five-foot-four. She was soft spoken, with reddish hair and blue eyes and straight white teeth. Even under the oversized outfit, he saw a killer figure. He took a seat at one of the tables. She came by for his order, and treated him like she did all of her customers—rudely snapping, "What'll you have?" and stood on one foot impatiently waiting for the order. When she brought the drink, he handed her a dollar tip. A big smile broke over her face and she thanked him profusely. As he passed her the buck, he touched her hand. She didn't pull away.

From the bartender, he learned Crystal came from a large family in the Midwest. Her old man was a drunk who wouldn't keep his hands off of her. Her mom had to contact the cops to put a scare into the SOB and keep him at bay. It was also up to her mother to raise Crystal and her four brothers and sisters with what she earned working her buns off in a beauty shop.

Crystal grew up pretty enough that after high school her boyfriend encouraged her to enter the Miss Kansas Contest. She came in third. One of the other losing contestants talked her into going to Hollywood with grand plans to break into the movie business.

Three discouraging years in Hollywood had left the Kansas girls disappointed and disillusioned. Crystal had taken up smoking, and these days spent a sizable chunk of her wages on straight shots of whiskey. She'd let her looks go, too. Her hair was greasy and pulled back in a ponytail with a cheap rubber band around it. She had creases in the corner of her eyes and little lines on her upper lip. Still, Henry sensed there was something very special about this young lady, a diamond in the rough, for sure. He was interested.

He made her laugh with his jokes. One evening when the bar was nearly deserted, she sat down and let her guard down and told him her all-too familiar story about how Hollywood hadn't turned out to be the place she'd dreamed it'd be.

"My girlfriend and I had been in L.A. for a while and before long we were broke and hungry. The rent was due. We dropped by a corner bar to try to pick up a couple of guys, who'd spring for drinks, maybe even buy us something to eat. This guy bought me a drink, which was fine. He was good looking, well dressed and flashed a nice roll of cash. With my figure and looks, he said I'd be a shoo-in to break into the movie business. He claimed to know how to make it happen.

We dated a couple of times and I moved into his place. He had a spare bedroom I could use. You know how that sort of thing goes. At first he treated me real nice.

"He told me I needed professional photos for a portfolio so he could make the rounds of talent agents in the town. 'Nobody gets ahead in Hollywood without first-rate photographs,' he told me."

Oh, boy, Henry thought. I've heard this story before.

"Honestly, Henry," Crystal continued, sincerity in her voice, "the guy seemed to know what he was talking about. I was thrilled. Finally a break! I borrowed $50 from my Kansas friend, who was making good money as a stripper at a men's club. I had my hair done, nails, facial, the works, in preparation for the photo shoot.

"I was at my wit's end. Nothing was happening. I was considering returning to Kansas with my tail between my legs. The photo shoot seemed like my one last opportunity to make it out here."

"He took me to an old house in a rundown neighborhood where this guy with black hair slicked back so you could see the comb marks in it, had lights and cameras set up in a smelly back room painted all black. At first it seemed all right, then the guy behind the camera asked me to take off my top. He smiled and acted nice, and talked like what he was asking me to do was fairly routine, even said I could fold my arms across my chest, you know, so not much would show.

"My friend, the one who promised to find me an agent, stepped forward and said what I really needed was a full-frontal pose in the nude, standing tall, hands on my hips, with my legs spread, the kind of picture Marilyn Monroe had done early in her career, to give the agents an eyeful."

"That's bullshit," Henry sputtered. "I'd like to get my hands on that guy."

"The photographer started egging me on. I gathered up my clothes and said I was leaving." Her voice broke and she started crying. Henry knew the tears were genuine. He put an arm around her shoulders.

"I was shaking so hard I could hardly button my blouse. The photographer just stood there, his arms folded, an asshole grin on his mug, like he could care less. My boyfriend grabbed my arm and said he'd spent a bundle on me and I'd better cooperate.

"I started bawling and screaming. He backed away and I got the heck out of there. I walked nearly a mile before I found a cabbie who'd stop for me."

Before parting that evening, Henry asked Crystal for a date. She accepted and he took her to the snazziest restaurant in the neighborhood. He bought her presents, clothes, jewelry, and beauty treatments. He spent nearly all of his savings. He didn't care. He'd tumbled hard. Within a month, they were a couple. They now lived in a larger apartment, filled with new furniture. He was on top of the world.

One thing Henry didn't mention to Crystal was that he'd given her name and her friend's name to a cop buddy who'd run them through the system. He learned Crystal had been picked up once for prostitution, and her Kansas girlfriend had been charged with soliciting, not once but three times. The girlfriend, the one now stripping for a living, had spent 30 days in the county jail for rolling a drunk who'd passed out next to her in a rundown flophouse that rented rooms by the hour.

What the hell, Henry thought, we all have our little secrets. Crystal was down and out, probably broke and hungry. He understood how things happen. It didn't matter. He loved her.

"Hey, I make plenty of dough," Henry declared one night after they'd made love. "You don't need to work in that dive. Quit and you and I can start really enjoying ourselves. It kills me seeing those guys in the bar pawing all over you and you having to act nice to them."

She quit the job and he felt like the luckiest SOB in the world. She looked great on his arm, like a movie star. Mac drooled when Henry introduced Crystal. She was classy and smart as a whip and she cared about him, he knew that. It was like the sky finally had opened up and the sun was shining through.

Henry began thinking that he and this new girlfriend might one day get hitched. But now with the hoods pressuring Dutch, his savings gone, and his job in jeopardy—well, shit, the dream seemed to be taking flight right before his eyes.

He had to do something. He needed to get his hands on some money, and a lot of it, and all in one big pile. He didn't have much time.

The heart of another is a dark forest... no matter how close it has been to one's own.

–Willa Cather

Chapter 47

Henry stood at the foot of the bed at Los Angeles County Hospital and looked down at Mac. He laid flat on his back in a rumpled, blood-splattered hospital gown, as close to being dead as anyone can be without actually croaking. A sick feeling swept over him. Mac's lips and cheeks were stitched and bruised, and a white-gauze patchwork covered his face. His left eye was swollen shut and he was missing at least one front tooth, maybe two. The guys who'd worked him over had done a damn good job of it.

Poor Mac. He'd said someone was following him; now here he was. The Mafia gang had told him to pass the word to Dutch to sell out or he'd get a dose of the same medicine.

Struggling to move his lips, Mac gulped in shallow pulls of air, the words fragmented and tortured: "I'm hurtin' real bad, Henry. I...I...eh...don't think I'm going to make it. They wouldn't stop. I begged them, 'no more, please...please,' but...but they jus' wouldn't lay off."

"Christ, buddy," Henry managed. "I can't believe this."

Mac groaned as a wave of pain swept over him. A torrent of spastic tremors followed. "The doctor says if I'm lucky, I'll keep my leg. I'll be on crutches the rest of my life. Oh shit! It hurts so damn much. What's going to happen to me? Who's going to help? Can I count on you, Henry?"

"You bet," Henry said. "You name it and I'll be there."

Like hell he would. Henry knew it could just as easily have been him in that bed. Like Mac, he wouldn't have seen them coming. They'd have dragged him into a back alley, stuck a rag in his mouth, and beat him till he looked like Mac did right now. One of them would have finished up by taking a sawed-off baseball bat to his knee. He cringed as he imagined the crack of the bone breaking.

Looking at the crying man, he knew goddamn well Mac wouldn't have given him the time of day if the roles were reversed.

Mac had no right to ask for help. He'd been the one who'd brought Lonnie into Kelsey's that afternoon and turned the monster loose on him. He'd found a way to pay off his gambling debts, otherwise he'd be in wheelchair today. In a real sense, Mac had this beating coming. He'd spent years putting the hurt on other guys. How's the old saying go? What goes around comes around?

A grim, overweight nurse, wearing a rumpled white uniform and a stained white hat, and looking like she hadn't slept in a week, walked into the dreary, bare-walled hospital room and, without a word, jammed a thermometer into Mac's mouth. He winced as the cold glass rod passed through his battered lips.

With Mac gumming on the thermometer, Henry ducked out without even a "see you later, pal." He needed fresh air and time alone to shake off the awful feelings that enveloped him. Everything had been going so well. Now he had to find a way out of this mess, and at the same time keep Crystal happy.

How would Crystal react if the goons had beaten him up? She was a great gal, with a loving heart, and she liked him—he hoped loved him. But, hell, there was no way a beautiful, bright girl like her would spend her life taking care of a cripple. She'd no more be a nursemaid to him than he'd be to Mac who, as far as Henry was concerned, was strictly on his own.

Two days later, Dutch called a meeting and informed Henry and the other book runners that Mac had died from the injuries, and that the mob from out east was putting more pressure on him to sell out. Hemming and hawing, Dutch finally got out the words that he was taking the offer. He and his wife were leaving Los Angeles for good.

"Far as I know you fellows still have jobs until you're told differently. If anything changes, you'll get the word from the new owners. I expect to be around for a few days, showing them the ropes."

Turning his head so no one could look him in the eye, and with his shoulders slumping, Dutch made a quick exit. The boss had spent a lifetime building the business, starting when he was a skinny 10-year-old on L.A.'s tough streets. As he advanced to take over much of the book-making in Los Angeles, he'd been ruthless—some said murderous—in battling his way to the top. Now, it was clear there was no fight left in the man. He was bowing out while he still could. He had plenty of dough and was getting out clean. In Henry's mind, it was a smart move; he envied the old guy.

What about him? Lately, he'd experienced an over-whelming desire to reclaim the life he once enjoyed in Belleview. Those were the best years of his life. People loved him, loved his stories. He had a solid family; the Co-op job paid well. He was respected. What he'd give to roll into Belleview in a fancy new car, take a stroll down River Street with Crystal on his arm. Maybe he'd buy the Riverfront Tavern. He'd be a leading citizen. Could he get it all back?

Who's not sat tense before his own heart's curtain.

–James Russell Lowell

Chapter 48

Seated at an oak library table at the Glenwood Public Library on Stadium Drive, about a mile from the house, Arthur was surrounded by stacks of physics, geometry and chemistry books. He scribbled notes on a yellow pad of paper. His current course load included everything from studies on Shakespeare to advanced physics.

Like all of the juniors at the Academy, 17-year-old Arthur was studying for finals. If he scored well, he had a chance to nail down letters of admission to Harvard, Yale, Dartmouth, Brown, Stanford, Cal-Tech, and a handful of other prestigious colleges.

The tension was sky high and competition was ruthless. During finals week even best friends scarcely acknowledged one another as they passed in the hallways.

Arthur's goal was Stanford, an undisputed academic pioneer in the emerging field of computers. Early in his junior year, he'd visited the Palo Alto campus and was impressed with the enthusiasm and commitment of Stanford's faculty and students in the promise of this new information-age technology. Stanford all ready had established an Electronics Lab and was working with the Federal government and private companies like IBM and NCR to advance the development of the solid-state transistor.

A Stanford freshman exchange student from China named Mai Ling showed Arthur around. She stood before him, hands on hips and stared him down. "You wait. What is happening on this campus will one day change the world," she declared in flawless English.

Pretty and with a dazzling smile, Mai Ling had a fire in her eyes and a passion for her studies unlike anyone he'd ever encountered. He decided then and there that Stanford was where he'd go to college—and he'd study computing. He also vowed to stay in touch with this young lady from China.

The physics formulas swam before Arthur's eyes on the page in front of him when a janitor tapped him on the shoulder: "Sorry, young man, we're closing. I'll have to walk you to the front door and unlock it to let you out."

Carrying a canvass satchel stuffed with books down the stairs, Arthur stepped out under a dark, wide-open night sky. Keys in hand, he walked slowly to his car, which was parked in the nearly deserted library parking lot. He was dead tired and didn't notice the car parked next to his until he was almost upon it. The hood was up and a man with a flashlight peered at the engine.

"Anything I can do?" Arthur asked, hoping he'd say no. He'd been up since five-thirty. All he wanted was to go home and climb in bed.

"Darn thing won't start. Guess I've ground down the battery. You wouldn't happen to have a set of jumper cables, would you?"

"Sorry. I can call a garage for you. I'm only a few minutes from home."

He was a big guy, maybe six-two and rugged looking. Arthur guessed him in his forties. The question flickered in his bushed brain: strange, what was this guy doing in the library's deserted parking lot?

Suddenly, a second man stepped up beside him and the big one grabbed him and pinned his arms painfully behind his back.

Panicked, Arthur shouted, "Hey! What's going on? Let me go!"

The second man covered Arthur's mouth and nose with a cloth. From chemistry classes he recognized the smell: chloroform. They were trying to knock him out. He raised his legs and kicked hard against the car, pushing backwards with all his might. He heard an "oomph" come from the second man. He couldn't fight them off; they were bigger and stronger. They shoved him into the back seat of the car where he sat, disoriented, his head woozy and spinning. The smaller man jumped in with him and forced him to lie flat on the seat. The last thing he heard before slipping into unconsciousness was, "Quit fighting, kid. Nobody's gonna' hurt you."

As the men crept away from the parking lot, they didn't see a second car pull out from behind a small grove of pine trees and follow at a discreet distance, far enough back to go unnoticed. Ten minutes later his abductors parked the car in the driveway of a small, one-story bungalow on West Alito Avenue. They carried the unconscious Arthur through the side door. With its headlights off and the motor running, the other car remained until the lights came on in the house.

Then it slowly pulled away.

If it were not for hopes, the heart would break.

–Thomas Fuller

Chapter 49

The grandfather clock on the wall bonged 10 times. Lilly sat at her desk in the home library and was reading through a long, detailed report that had been on her desk at work for more than a week. The overly detailed and not particularly interesting outline of a marketing plan was important to the person who wrote it, so she had pledged to read every word.

She paused, removed her reading glasses and rubbed her temples. Maybe she'd get up early and finish the report in the morning. It was late and Michael had all ready retired, complaining of a headache.

Where was Arthur? He should be home from the library by now. The sharp ring of the phone snapped her into alertness.

"Hello? Is that you, Arthur?" she asked. "Where the heck are you?"

"No, lady, this ain't Arthur." The voice sounded gruff and raspy, like the man was trying to disguise it.

"Who is this?"

"Never mind. All you need to know is the boy's safe, and he'll stay that way as long as you do exactly what I say. Understand?"

"What? Who are—?"

"I'm telling you, lady, we have Arthur. You'll get him back when you pay us $250,000. We want it in small bills delivered to us early tomorrow night. I'll call at 10 o'clock in the morning with drop-off instructions, including the precise time. Do not call the police, or something not so nice will happen to the kid."

"This is crazy!" Lilly exclaimed. "Let me talk to him. If this is a joke, it's not funny."

"I'm going to put him on the line. Don't say anything. Just listen."

Then, in the background, Lilly heard the man say, "Here, kid. Read what I wrote down, and don't say another word, or else."

"Lilly, it's me." Arthur's voice sounded scared. "I don't know what's going on. They've taken me to some place I don't know. You're to do as they say and I'll be okay."

She heard the man yank the phone out of Arthur's hand and someone roughly pull Arthur away.

"Think I'm serious now?"

In a trembling voice, Lilly answered, "Yes, I under-stand. Please don't hurt him. He's only a boy—a good boy. We'll do whatever you say."

The phone went dead.

Stunned, Lilly stood with the receiver in her hand. She couldn't feel it. Her fingers were numb; her whole body was numb from the shock. A sick feeling crawled up the back of her throat. She sat down, the receiver beeping in her hand.

She and Michael had discussed the possibility of something like this happening. A while back the world-wide news media reported the kidnapping in England of an eight-year-old boy whose parents had won a one-hun-dred-thousand-pound lottery prize. Kidnappers grabbed their son off the street and held him for ransom. Police found his partially decomposed body weeks later. They never caught the criminals.

Now strangers had taken Arthur. The feeling finally returned to Lilly's vocal chords and she screamed. "Michael! Michael!"

Lilly listened in on the extension as her husband talked to Attorney Vogel. "You must call the police, Michael," Vogel was saying. "Make certain the cops understand the importance of keeping this quiet." His voice was calm, kind, and competent. "We don't want a whisper of this in the morning newspapers."

He said he'd rush right over. "I know this is hard, Lilly, but I need you to write down every word and detail you can remember about the call. Any background sounds, accent or unique way of saying words. We'll get your family through this."

Michael offered to write down whatever she could remember about the telephone call.

"Do you think that crazy ex-girlfriend of his, Mandy, had anything to do with this?" Michael asked. "She was something of a nut, and Arthur was scared of her, that's for sure."

"I can't imagine. She's only a child, really," Lilly said. "But in this world, anything's possible. I'll mention her name to the police."

"I've called Paul in Iowa. He'll be on the first plane out of Des Moines in the morning and should be here late tomorrow afternoon," Michael said, as he tried to absorb Vogel's calmness. "He's very upset."

Michael and Vogel greeted the two plain-clothes L.A. detectives at the door. She watched as the fat one lumbered ahead of his associate, who was the taller and the younger of the two. He was the one with the crew-cut haircut that stood straight up and looked like it'd been trimmed with a lawnmower.

The fat one glanced up at the foyer's high ceiling. "Man, this is a hell of a place." Then, under his breath, Lilly heard him say to his partner: "Rich bastards get…" and she couldn't make out the rest.

The tall detective pulled out a pad and licked the tip of his pencil. "So, is it possible the boy just hasn't come home? Did you check with his friends? Maybe they're playing a joke on you."

His tone was abrasive, rude. "It's happened before. You know college pranks, that sort of thing. Have you had a falling out with the boy? A disagreement?"

The fat detective kept circling the dining room, looking over all the furniture, glancing into the adjoining rooms, not paying any attention whatsoever to what the other detective was doing.

"Maybe there's a girlfriend involved. The kid shacking up with anyone?"

Vogel had heard enough. He stood and said, "All right, gentlemen. The boy has been kidnapped. A ransom demand has been made. This woman has talked to the boy. There's no question this is a criminal act. It's time you began taking this case seriously."

"Who the hell are you?" the fat guy asked, poking his face inches from Vogel's nose.

"I'm Frederick Vogel, the Paulson family attorney, and you owe them a lot more courtesy and professionalism than I've seen displayed here so far."

"We're doing our job, mister, so butt out," chimed in the other detective.

Without a word, Frederick turned and walked into Michael's home office where he made a call. He returned and indicated to the older one that he was wanted on the telephone.

Who in hell is calling me?"

"Police Commissioner Wellington would like a word with you."

"The Commish. What's he want?"

"Ask him."

The senior detective talked on the telephone for a moment, then returned to the front room and told the other detective they were off the case. "We're supposed to wait here until other troops arrive."

Thirty minutes later, the house swarmed with half a dozen local police officials, plus two agents with the FBI. The first two cops had departed. Technicians fitted phones with listening devices and a team of officers interviewed Lilly, probing for every detail of the kidnapper's phone call. They asked about Arthur's whereabouts that evening, whether he had followed a normal routine or schedule, and if he'd mentioned anything about people following him, or if they'd seen strangers in the neighborhood. Had there been anything out of the ordinary around the house or his school lately? They sent a team to look for Arthur's car in the library lot.

In a tremulous voice, Lilly related everything she knew, which wasn't much. Then she joined Michael and Vogel behind a closed door in the library.

"I suggest you wake up your banker and start the wheels moving on putting together the quarter-million dollars," Vogel advised. "I'm hoping we won't need the money, still we need to be ready. Police departments, especially the Los Angeles crew, have a dismal record in solving kidnappings. We may be mostly on our own here. If it's all right, I'd like to bring in some of my own people."

"Do whatever it takes. All we care about is getting Arthur back safely," Michael stated. "We'll pay anything."

He went to Lilly and put his arms around her.

"Henry's behind this. It's him! I know it," Lilly said, her face in anguish.

"I wouldn't be surprised," Vogel said. "He's tried stunts like this before. Still, this seems extreme even for him. I mean, kidnapping his own son?"

"He might have hired other people to do it," Michael suggested.

"You may be right," Vogel answered. "I'll talk to the captain and have the cops pick him up. If he knows something, he'll talk to the police; otherwise they'll beat it out of him with a rubber hose. I'll also ask the police to check on this Mandy person."

Lilly grimaced. Michael looked gray. It was nearly two in the morning. The night was taking its toll on her husband.

"I can't believe Henry would be so reckless as to put his own son in danger," Michael offered.

"There's nothing to do until the kidnappers call back," Vogel commented. "Let's all try to get some rest. Meantime, the police and my private investigators will go to work trying to come up with some answers. The captain already has people on the way to pick up Henry."

The battleline between good and evil runs through the heart.

–Aleksander Solzhenitsyn

Chapter 50

The front door to the apartment crashed open, sending splinters of wood and the door handle flying against the inside wall. Three policemen charged in. Henry bolted upright in bed. Crystal screamed and pulled the covers to her naked breasts.

The overhead ceiling light blinked on as a uniformed cop yanked Henry out of bed, pushed him to the floor, and placed a heavy boot on his back. In a pair of boxer shorts, Henry twisted to see the burly police officer standing over him.

"What's going on here?" Henry grunted. "You guys got a warrant?"

"Yeah we do, Henry, ole' buddy," said a plain-clothes detective, an older guy, standing next to the wall. He appeared to be in charge. "You and your little sweetheart are going downtown with us. And while you're away, my men are going to tear this love nest apart like Sherman marching on Atlanta. If you're hiding anything, you damn well better tell us now."

Henry tried to tell them that Crystal was an innocent bystander; they shouldn't drag her into this. The cops wouldn't listen. She stood there sobbing, hysterical, a sheet wrapped around her body.

The uniformed cop jerked Henry to his feet and handcuffed his hands behind his back.

"Honey, honey, don't cry. It's going to be all right. This is a big mistake," Henry called out to her. He wanted to take her in his arms and comfort her. He'd never felt so helpless.

"Get some clothes on, lady, we're taking a ride," said the detective. He was one who'd pulled her out of bed and gotten an eye full. He seemed eager to do some damage if necessary. He was young, and looked like he kept himself in shape, as opposed to the other detective, the older guy who'd gone to seed. "What the hell's a good lookin' babe like you doing with this loser?" he said. "Believe me, honey, you can do a lot better."

At the main station a policewoman led Crystal away, while she looked back at Henry with pleading eyes. Henry, now dressed in a rumpled white dress shirt, a gray suit and no tie, stumbled as the young detective pushed him roughly into a small interrogation room. The one in charge was Richard; his partner was Don. It was Don who pushed him into a straight-back chair and beamed a hot, bright light directly into his face. Henry kept telling himself to keep his cool, watch what he said or these two would railroad his ass to jail. The older cop popped Tums like candy, and burped a lot. He started talking, nice at first, trying to make Henry feel comfortable. Don was showing off his muscle and kept cuffing him on the side of his head with the palm of his hand. It hurt like hell.

"Hey, knock it off. I'm a citizen of this town. I'll sue your ugly ass," Henry said.

"Yeah, right," the young guy answered, snapping his gum. "You and the mayor are best of friends, eh? Quit fucking around and tell us where the boy is."

"I don't know, I swear."

Henry smelled the sickly sweet scent of spearmint gum as Don leaned in close to him. "What the hell kind of a father are you anyway, kidnapping your own son?" he said, as he followed up this question with another cuff to Henry's head.

"That's not true. I don't know anything about this." Henry turned his eyes to Richard. "I love Arthur. The first I heard about a kidnapping was from you guys."

They held him in the small room and hammered at him for what seemed forever, At 6 a.m., with the first signs of morning light sliding in dull and gloomy through a small window high overhead, Richard suggested a break. "You look beat. You probably could use a little rest. I know I can," he said, popping another Tum. "We'll put you in a cell for a couple of hours. Eggs, sausage and coffee sound okay for breakfast? The food's pretty good here. Eat and rest up. You'll feel like a new man."

The other cop dumped his gum in a wastebasket. "Our street sources tell us it was Walter Brink and his sidekick, Joey, who grabbed your kid. You know those guys, don't ya?"

Henry was taken aback.

"If you know who did it, go arrest them and free my son," Henry murmured defensively. "You're wasting time questioning me. I had nothing to do with this. And I sure as hell don't remember ever meeting anyone named Walter, and that other guy, either."

Lilly had to be the one behind the cops picking him up, Henry thought. What a bitch! These cops were on a fishing trip, trying to coerce him into implicating himself. He wasn't going to let that happen.

"When you teamed up with Walter, I'll bet you didn't know the kind of person you were dealing with," Richard jumped in to say. "He's a real hard ass and he's been involved in several killings. And he's a lucky bastard. We've never been able to get enough evidence to put him away. He cleans up after a job; never leaves a live witness behind. Trust me, Henry, if that madman has your son—and we're convinced he does—you can kiss him goodbye."

Don tore open another piece of spearmint gum and jammed it in his mouth and raised his hand like he was going to slam him again. But Richard waved him off.

"As a father of three myself, I'm asking you to do the right thing," the older cop said, in a soft, cajoling manner. "Tell us where they're holding your boy and we'll go get him. We don't want him to get hurt. I'm sure you don't either."

"Honest to God, I don't know." Henry said. "Believe me. I wouldn't put my son with a killer like that."

"Okay, we're through here for now," Richard said. "Put him in the tank to think things over."

Don sidled over. "Keep in mind, Goodwin, when we bring you back here we won't be so nice. Time's running out. Think about what's happening. You could be facing the gas chamber, right along with Walter and Joey."

Henry went limp. Two uniformed cops had to pull him out the door. The gum-chewer trailed behind as they moved along a long, dark hallway and down a noisy iron stairway to the jail cells. Their footsteps rang out on the metal stairs, the cold indifference of the steel sending a chill to Henry's very soul.

Henry demanded: "Hey, the law says I get a phone call. I want it."

"Give him one call," instructed the detective. "Nothing else, no visitors—nothing except a little breakfast. I'll be back for him in a couple of hours."

Instead of the promised hot eggs and sausage, they brought him cold oatmeal, stale toast and the worst coffee he'd ever tasted. Henry dialed the number of the lawyer Dutch kept on retainer in the unlikely case one of his boys got tangled up with the law. He hoped the guy was still working for Dutch. Maybe he hadn't heard about the changes. The phone rang several times.

"Branard Law Offices. Bill Branard here."

"Yeah, hey, this is Henry Goodwin, one of Dutch's boys. I met you once, remember? Cops got me down here at headquarters. I haven't been charged with anything. I'm locked up. Can you help?"

"Crap, I'm still in bed. I'll see what I can do. Sit tight, and enjoy that delicious breakfast the city serves." Branard chuckled like he'd made an inside joke at Henry's expense. Then he hung up. Henry figured the barrister and the older cop must have had first-hand knowledge of how crummy the jail food was in this place.

An hour later, a day jailer came on shift and the night jailor went off. Another 20 minutes passed and the front-desk cop walked down the stairs and told the day jailer Henry Goodwin had made bail.

"Let him out, and I'll take him upstairs for out-processing," he said.

"Ain't no skin off my butt," said the jailer. He unlocked the cell and motioned to Henry to step out.

"You've made bail. Go with this officer."

When the younger detective, Don, learned Henry had been released, he cut loose with a string of obscenities and rushed upstairs to report the screw-up to his boss.

By then, Henry was in a cab headed for the downtown bus depot. At a wall of lockers, he removed a small key from a secret pocket in his billfold and opened locker #27. He removed $300 in cash and a loaded Smith & Wesson .38 Special, along with a nearly full box of cartridges. A couple of months earlier Dutch had provided his boys with revolvers as a precaution in case the Italians tried to cause trouble. Henry went to a firing range once, to make sure the damn thing fired. Then he put it in the locker and forgot about it. The cash and bullets went into his left pants pocket and the revolver into the right. He tightened his belt another notch as his pants sagged from the weight.

He caught another cab and gave the driver the address of Crystal's former apartment. Her rent was paid till the end of the month and he still had a key. He sure as hell couldn't go to his apartment. The cops would be all over the place.

Henry gazed numbly out of the cab window. He'd lied when he said he didn't know Walter or his sidekick Joey. They both had spent time at Kelsey's. Later, after he'd gone to work for Dutch, he'd taken bets from them. There wasn't much to like about either one of them. Could Walter really be a killer? Or were the cops blowing smoke? He didn't know. What he did know was that Walter owned a pair of the meanest eyes he'd ever seen.

As the cab driver pulled up to Crystal's three-story apartment building, Henry expelled a deep breath. He had to face the truth. Arthur was in grave danger, and at this point he was the only one who could help him.

A good head and a good heart are always a formidable combination.

–Nelson Mandela

Chapter 51

Arthur's head pounded. He squinted one eye open; the clock on the table next to the TV read 9:50 p.m. He presumed he was still in Los Angeles since the two guys who grabbed him couldn't have gone far in an hour. He remembered being on the phone, saying something to Lilly but he couldn't quite recall all the details. Cripes, only an hour earlier the janitor had practically pushed him out of the front door of the library, and then two guys had grabbed him in the dark parking lot.

Finally, his eyes cleared and the room came into sharp focus. He remembered everything now. He was in a small house that looked a lot like the rental house they'd moved into when they'd arrived in L.A. The big guy was saying something to him, telling him how once the ransom was paid, they'd let him go. He nodded even as a warning sign flashed red in his brain. The two men kept calling each other by their first names. The big guy was Walter and he called the other one Joey. They made no effort to conceal their names or their faces. Something was wrong but his foggy brain couldn't pin it down.

"Shouldn't be more than a day or so," Walter assured him, his voice friendly and comforting. His appearance was in direct contrast to his words. Walter had thick, mutton-chop sideburns and a faded tattoo of a coiled serpent on his right forearm. It was the toothpick that bobbed up and down out of the side of his mouth that gave Arthur the willies. It was like a ticking time bomb, up, down, up, down. When would it go off?

The small guy, Joey, didn't say a word. He watched TV and cleaned his gun, occasionally pointing the .45 caliber pistol at Matt Dillon's face on the tube and pulling the trigger. Arthur flinched. All he heard was a dry click. Seeing the shock on his face Joey grinned, revealing a row of tiny, discolored teeth. His black hair was slicked back in a Wildroot ducktail.

"Hell, we're glad to see you looking so well," Walter said, the toothpick bobbling. "You didn't look so good when we carried you in. Your color's back now, kid."

Once again, Arthur tried to shake the fuzziness from his brain. He had to think straight. These guys are trying their best to convince me that they're my good-time buddies. None of this rings true.

"You remember the conversation we had with Lilly, don't you?" Walter asked, his voice soothing. "You were out of it. You did fine, though. Sorry I had to talk so rough to her. It was important she understand about getting the money."

The guy smiled around the toothpick but there was something about his eyes, something dark and sinister. It was an empty smile. "Now all you gotta do is remain calm and everything will turn out just fine. You'll be home sometime tomorrow."

"I'm scared," Arthur replied. "I'll do whatever you guys say." Until he figured things out, he was going to be their good, obedient buddy.

Walter's manner was friendly, easy going, and there was no doubt he was in complete charge of this kidnapping. "After I pick up the suitcase, I'll haul the money back here to check it out. Bet you've never seen a quarter million in cash in one pile, 'eh, kid? You seem pretty smart. Maybe I'll let you help count it. If the money's okay, this little caper will be history and we'll drop you off on a street corner with a dime to make a telephone call. Meanwhile, help yourself to a Coke and whatever you want to eat from the fridge."

Arthur rattled the handcuffs that encased his wrists. Walter was trying to convince him he was a guest in his house. With what was going on, he wasn't falling for it.

"A little later Joey will make you comfortable for the night in one of the back bedrooms," Walter continued. "After a good night's sleep, we'll all wake up nice and refreshed and put the finishing touches on this little deal, then we'll go our separate ways, no hard feelings. It'll be like this never happened."

"Yeah, I'll be glad to be home," Arthur said as he took in the modest front room, the shades pulled over the two windows and the TV now blaring the late-night news summary. There were two large stuffed chairs and a couple of lamp tables. With his hands cuffed in front of him on the couch, Arthur wriggled around until he sat upright, which gave him a wider view of the house.

An open doorway led to a small kitchen where he caught a glimpse of a stove and refrigerator. He couldn't see it but he guessed the kitchen had a back door. If this was the same design as his old house, the hallway to the left led to two small bedrooms and the bathroom. No way out in that direction.

His eyes narrowed as he spotted the double-barrel shotgun leaning in a corner of the front room. Walter and Joey had removed their jackets, and each wore brown leather shoulder holsters filled with high-caliber handguns. There was a lot of firepower in the room for what Walter had predicted was to be a proverbial walk in the park. Then it came to him with a thud. Once they had the money, hell, maybe even before, Walter would put a bullet in his brain and dump his body in a ditch somewhere.

He wasn't supposed to get out of this alive.

The hot flush of panic welled up from his belly and his breathing came in short and shallow gasps. Calm down! He struggled to control his breathing as he offered Walter a sheepish smile. Best not to let them know he was wise to their plan. His life depended on finding a way out of this house.

"Mind if I use the john?" Arthur asked.

"Sure. Everybody's got to take a piss."

Walter pointed his toothpick at his partner. "Hey Joey! Escort this young man to the bathroom."

"Well, uh, I've got to do more than urinate," Arthur said with embarrassment. "It'd be nice to have a little privacy."

"Okay, kid. Joey will…"

Joey was already half way down the hall to the bathroom. "Hey Joey! Listen up! Stand outside and leave the door half-open."

Walter looked back at Arthur, "Want a magazine or something?"

"Thanks, I appreciate the offer. I'll be quick about it."

Arthur's mind raced. This might be his only chance to put a plan in motion. He'd read that people with handcuffs in front of their bodies had the best chance of slipping out of the restraints, especially if they were young and flexible like him. Harry Houdini had proven his skill at maneuvering out of handcuffs time after time in his stage acts, thanks in part to using lubricant on his hands and arms. No magic to it, just keep wiggling and moving. At one time, Arthur had been enthralled with the master escape artist; he'd read everything he could find in the library about him. All I need is a bar of soap or some lotion, he thought, as he dropped his pants and sat on the stool. Right before him on the bathroom sink was a full bar of soap.

Exactly what he needed!

What if Walter or Joey noticed it missing when they used the bathroom?

Cigarette smoke curled through the cracked door. Joey called out, "You done in there? My favorite TV show's on next."

"Be out in a jiffy."

From the stool, Arthur pulled back a corner of the pink plastic shower curtain and there within easy reach was a sliver of soap sitting on the edge of the tub. He reached out and it was dry and hard. When he was ready, he'd have to use his own saliva to slick it up. He considered shoving the soap into one of his socks. There'd be a bulge and Walter might notice. Not much got by him.

Arthur shoved his hand into his pockets. Nothing. They must have emptied them while he was knocked out. With his fingers he found a small pouch sewn inside his right pocket that held coins to keep them from jiggling when a fellow walked. He slipped the scrap of soap into the pouch. He stood, buckled his belt and looked down. No bulge.

After Walter and Joey finished watching the news and were satisfied there was no word of the kidnapping, they guided him to one of the back bedrooms. While Walter watched, Joey handcuffed his ankles and then unlocked his left hand. He locked his right hand to a metal rung in the headboard.

Joey tossed the key up and down in his hand. "This way you'll have one hand free to scratch your nose, or balls, or whatever." He laughed.

Arthur jingled the cuff against the metal rung. "Thanks a lot," he said, trying to make himself sound upbeat about his situation.

Actually, Joey and Walter had done him a big favor: first, by allowing his hands in front of him and, second, by cuffing only his right hand. Generally, big guys with big wrists were screwed—no matter how much soap they used. For a skinny kid like him he had a chance.

A half hour after they'd left him with the door cracked, Arthur realized there was no way to get out of the cuffs on his ankles. Even removing his size ten shoes and soaping up his ankles wouldn't help. When the time was right he'd either have to hop or crawl his way to the back kitchen door.

Walter and Joey had left the hall light on, which provided enough illumination to see the hands on the bedside clock click along at a frustratingly slow pace. When the national anthem played on the TV, signaling the station was signing off, Arthur lay still, hardly moving for what seemed an eternity. All had been quiet in the front room for at least an hour. He hoped his captors had fallen asleep.

He brought the sliver of soap to his lips and licked it like a thirsty puppy at a water bowl. It didn't taste too bad and soon he had the sliver good and soapy. He rubbed the soapy mess on his wrist and hand and in less than a minute of tugging and pulling, his right hand was free. He pulled away and the metal cuffs jangled as they bumped against the steel rung on the back of the bed. He held his breath. Nothing.

He waited another half hour, and then lifted his legs and placed them on the carpeted floor. He waited some more. Trying to jump with his cuffed legs would be noisy, so he'd crawl. On his belly, he inched his way down the hallway to the front room where the TV sent out a silent flickering gray light. Walter was sprawled out on an overstuffed chair, feet propped on a footstool. Joey snored on the couch, a pillow under his head.

Arthur belly-crawled to the kitchen door. He turned and looked back. Nothing. He struggled to his feet, the cuffs clattering a little. He waited a minute and tugged at the door handle. Locked! He reached with his left hand and twisted the door lock to the open position. It squeaked. Arthur held his breath, not daring to move.

"Why, you sneaky little sonofabitch!" an angry voice boomed. A huge arm with a serpent tattoo wrapped around his neck and jerked Arthur backward. "Think you could get away?"

Arthur tried to break out but the man's hold was rock-solid. He struggled for air and flailed his arms, certain he was about to die. Then Walter's arm relaxed and the big man spun him around and drove his fist deep into his stomach. Arthur collapsed to his knees unable to catch his breath. It felt like the blow had ruptured his spleen.

"Joey, get your ass in here and turn on the light," Walter growled. "We've caught ourselves a little minnow here."

Joey brought Walter a length of white clothesline and the big man pulled Arthur's hands behind his back and roughly wrapped the rope several times around his wrists. Then he pulled his legs up behind him and looped the rope around his ankles. He was hog-tied with no possible way to escape. All the soap in a supermarket wouldn't help him now.

"Let's see if the shithead can get out of that," Walter said, giving the rope a yank. Arthur cried out. Walter's toothpick bobbed as he admired his work.

They threw him on the bed like a bag of dirty laundry. He spent the rest of the night in excruciating pain, tied up in such a way that every joint in his body screamed for release. Every time he moved the rope dug deeper into his skin. It was like someone was taking a dull hacksaw to his wrists and ankles. As the night dragged on, the coppery stench of drying blood from his wounds made him nauseated. He was thirsty, so thirsty.

The clock read 10 a.m. sharp when Arthur heard Walter talking to Lilly on the telephone.

"It's me," he was saying. "Get a pencil and write down these instructions. No screw ups, you understand?"

It was silent for a few moments. "Got it? OK. Put the money in a leather suitcase, one of those new ones with wheels on it. It's going to be heavy. Deliver the bag to Jim's Tobacco Emporium at 826 W. Seventh Street in downtown Los Angeles at 6:25 this evening—not a minute early, or a minute late. The store will be closed. Walk into the vestibule that leads to the front door. On the left side of the door there's a tall wooden Indian holding a fist full of wooden cigars. Behind the Chief there's space to place the bag so it can't be seen from the sidewalk. Push the suitcase all the way in there. Then leave."

A pause. Then Arthur heard Walter continue: "Yeah, that's a good gal. Do exactly as told and the boy will be released within the hour."

Another pause, and then Walter snapped, "No, you can't talk to him. I know the cops are listening in and you're trying to keep me on the line. You think I'm stupid. Time's up."

Walter placed the phone on the cradle and said to Joey: "Let's eat. Eight hours to kill till I pick up the money."

It is hard to contend against one's heart's desire.

–Heraclitus

Chapter 52

A moment later, Walter appeared at the bedroom door, his toothpick bobbing a mile a minute and sporting a wide grin.

"Sleep good, kid?" Walter taunted. He looked with disgust at the bed where the boy was still trussed up like a pig. The sheets were tangled and blood stained.

Arthur twisted his neck and winced as he gave his tormenter a pitiful look.

"You sure as hell have made a mess, kid."

Walter untied him, removed the ropes and escorted the limping, whimpering kid to the bathroom where he watched him scrub the blood from his wrists and ankles and gulp down two glasses of water. Then he fed him a breakfast of milk and corn flakes at the kitchen table.

As he watched the boy devour the cereal, Walter got to thinking he was a good kid, a likable sort, a young fellow filled with all kinds of plans for life. A shame he was caught up in this. Bad luck for the boy, good luck for him. He was going to cash in big time.

Following breakfast, Walter cuffed Arthur's hands in front of him, shackled his ankles and perched him on the couch next to Joey, who was staring blankly at the TV.

What followed for the next several hours was an endless litany of soaps—*The Edge of Night, Search for Tomorrow, As the World Turns*. Walter wondered out loud how housewives handled this crap. It was the game shows that really stuck in Walter's craw. *The Price is Right* and *Truth or Consequences* were bad enough, but *Queen for a Day* took the cake.

"Can you believe it?" Walter said to no one in particular. "The women pour out their sob stories and an applause meter measures the audience's response to the saddest tribulations. Now Jack Bailey's awarding the crown to a woman who needs an iron lung for her old man. Then they bring out her family, and parade 'em around and everybody starts bawling. I say get a life!"

He noticed the kid just sat there and stared at the screen. He expected him to do something, maybe break down crying. He was a cool cucumber. He watched the boy's eyes darting around, like he was planning another break for it.

At 5:30 p.m., Walter scratched his belly and announced: "I'll be back in an hour and a half, Joey. After I'm gone, cuff the kid's hands behind his back. Take the cuffs off the ankles. We may have to move fast when I return and I don't want to have to carry him. Understand? He might try to get away again, so be on guard. He's a game little bastard."

"Yeah, yeah," Joey said, reaching up and touching the handle on his pistol. "Just bring back the money."

Walter started up the blue sedan he'd stolen from a garage. The owner only used it to run errands on weekends so Walter didn't expect the guy to miss it until Saturday at the earliest. By then, he'd have dumped the vehicle and set it on fire, destroying any evidence that might link him to it.

He glanced at his watch and calculated Lilly was on her way to the drop-off point with the suitcase of ransom money. She'd drop it off at exactly the right time; he was certain of that. The cops were all ready at the scene, concealing themselves on rooftops, in the back of service vans, and in storm drains. It was all so expected, and so predictable.

They're stupid, he thought. Like I'm going to walk up to the Indian Chief, take the suitcase, and then let them pile on me.

Idiots.

At 6:20 p.m. he pulled the Ford to the curb and stepped into a public telephone booth three blocks from the pick-up area. He dropped in a coin and dialed the fire department.

"Los Angeles Fire Department. What's your emergency?" barked a deep, masculine voice.

"Yeah, this is Ben. I live in an apartment across from Smith's Warehouse at the corner of 7th and Santa Fe. Smoke's pouring out of the top floor. I see flames too. Christ, it looks like a big one. Better get here fast as you can."

"Repeat the address, and stay on the line. What's your name?"

"Ben Frazier. The warehouse is at 7th and Santa Fe. The fire's spreading like crazy. Looks like it could take out the whole block."

"We're on our way."

Walter hung up the phone. So far so good.

A week earlier, he'd called in a similar false alarm and used a stopwatch to time exactly how long it would take the firefighters to load up and travel the 10 blocks along 7th to pass directly in front of the tobacco shop at precisely 6:32 p.m., with their lights flashing and sirens blaring. They had procedures, and Walter knew the firemen would follow the same pattern and the same schedule this evening.

He returned to the Ford and drove down 6th Street, a one-way. At Broadway, he took a hard left and pulled into a nearly deserted underground parking lot at the corner of 7th and Broadway. Sweaty and hyped up, he shut off the Ford and ran to a concealed side door. He had three doors to open before reaching the tobacco shop. He opened the first with one of three duplicate keys that a locksmith had made for him from wax impressions of keys he'd stolen earlier from the stores and then returned so they wouldn't be missed. Now he hustled through the first store, past carousel racks of women's dresses in the Fashion Perfect ladies shop, and opened a second side door, this one accessing an adjoining RCA Radio/TV store. He had to hurry. The third key opened the door to Jim's Smoking Emporium. The sweet scent of pipe and cigar tobacco teased his nostrils as he stepped inside. His watch read 6:31 p.m. He opened the front door just as the nose of the first fire engine arrived with its siren screaming, its red bulk blocking the view of the vestibule.

Keeping his back flat against the inside wall, he waited until a second engine roared past on 7th, then he extended his right hand behind the Indian and wrapped his fingers around the suitcase handle. Yanking the heavy bag into the store, he closed the door a scant second before the second fire truck flew by. He took a moment to catch his breath.

With the suitcase rumbling behind on its wheels, he retraced his steps through the two adjoining retail stores as the wail of sirens began to fade. In the dark underground parking area everything was quiet. No cops; nothing moving.

He wrestled the suitcase into the back seat, got in behind the wheel and whipped the car onto Broadway, heading north, never taking his eye off the rear-view mirror. No one followed. He estimated it would take the cops at least 15 minutes to discover the money missing and 10 more for some genius to realize that they'd been had by the oldest trick in the book, a diversion, and a simple one at that, involving the city's own fire trucks.

Walter drove toward the house with the loot. He hummed a tune from *The Edge of Night*. Damn, he hated that show. Now he couldn't get the theme song out of his head.

The plan had come off like clockwork.

Two days earlier he'd dug Arthur's grave in a secluded wooded area near a city dump, a location he'd used before. He also dug a second grave next to the first, this one for Joey. He'd take care of the kid's old man later, when things cooled down.

Walter loosened his grip on the steering wheel and reached behind him and caressed the leather bag. Christ, he thought, I've done it. A quarter-million in cash—and it's all mine.

A runner must run with dreams in his heart....

–Emil Zatopek

Chapter 53

Even as he had suffered in the bed from the rope cuts and the terrible discomfort of being bound up, Arthur never once believed anything truly bad could happen to him. He wasn't going to end up dead in this little house. He'd find a way to outfox Walter and Joey and escape. He'd return home triumphantly.

With all his heart, Arthur believed in happy endings, even as he had to admit things didn't look too good at the moment.

After Walter left to pick up the ransom, Joey unlocked Arthur's ankle cuffs and roughly positioned him on the couch with his wrists handcuffed behind his back. The metal cuffs felt cool and smooth on his damaged, chafed skin, a welcome relief to the torture he'd endured overnight.

While he sat cuffed on the couch, his captor paced back and forth in the front room, jumping up at every sound.

Arthur's mind raced. The clock next to the small television read 6:37 p.m. Walter was due back in 23 minutes. There had to be an escape path. He needed to find it. Maybe when Walter came back and he and Joey began counting the money he'd find a way to make a break. Would they really take time to count all that money?

"May I have some water?"

"No, kid. You may not! Keep your mouth shut."

Joey continued pacing back and forth. He pulled back the shade on the window overlooking the driveway and peered out. He returned to the chair, sat briefly and tapped his foot, then was back on his feet again, stalking like a caged tiger, back and forth, back and forth.

Arthur eyed the shotgun leaning against the wall. He was closer to it than Joey, but with his hands cuffed behind his back, there was no way to grab, aim and fire it before Joey pulled him back. If his abductor went to the bathroom or to the kitchen for a glass of water, he might make it out the front door and scream for help. Maybe a passing car would stop, or a neighbor would see him in distress and call the cops. Joey seemed intent on pacing. He wasn't leaving the front room. The clock was ticking off the minutes.

A knock on the front door startled them both.

"What the hell?" Joey said, as he pulled the pistol from the holster.

"Don't say a word," he hissed. He positioned himself on the left side of the front door. With no peephole in the door, Joey couldn't tell who was standing on the front porch. He chewed his lower lip and clicked the safety off on the pistol.

"Yeah, what do you want?" Joey called out. "Is that you, Walter?"

Beyond the door came a muffled response. "It's Henry Goodwin, Joey. Let me in. The cops are on to you and Walter. We need to talk."

It was Dad! What was he doing here? Didn't he know these guys were crazy?

Joey struggled to figure out what to do. Finally, he unlocked the door, back-pedaled and ducked behind an overstuffed chair. He rested his revolver on the top of the chair back and pointed it at the door.

"Door's open! Come on in. Keep your hands where I can see them."

Henry walked into the room. He wore the same droopy pants, and the rumpled suit jacket. While his face looked strained and grim, he also seemed calm.

Joey stood up from behind the chair and aimed the pistol at his father's chest.

"What the fuck are you talking about?"

"I'm telling you the cops have Walter in custody," Henry said, his voice level and confident. "They know you guys kidnapped Arthur. They picked me up and grilled me at the police station. I didn't say anything."

Arthur was amazed at how cool his dad was, standing there with a gun pointed right at him.

"Say, Joey, can you please put that gun down? You're scaring the crap out of me," Henry said, keeping his voice friendly.

Joey hesitated. His dad kept talking to him, like they were the best of buddies, like he was looking out for the guy's welfare. "You need to run, and do it now! The cops are on the way."

Joey looked uncertain. Then he shook his head no. "I'm staying right here till Walter comes back. Why should I trust you?"

The gun trembled in his hand. He reached up with his other hand to steady it.

"Don't you get it, Joey? Walter's not coming back. The cops arrested him. He's in a cell all locked up. You need to leave. Now."

Joey's brow furrowed. The pistol dropped to his side, as if he couldn't think and point the weapon at the same time. Unconsciously, he returned the gun to his shoulder holster.

"Walter told me to wait here. He's bringing the money."

"That may have been true an hour ago, but I assure you Walter's in jail at this moment. He's not coming back. There's no money."

"You a hundred percent sure?" Joey asked. He pulled aside the curtain, as if almost willing Walter to appear. "It doesn't sound right."

"I'm sure. There's a cab waiting around the corner. Take it and get out of here and leave the boy with me."

Joey's eyes widened as he came to a decision. "No fuckin' way! The kid's my insurance. I'm not leaving without him."

Joey reached for his gun but Henry already had the .38 pointed right at him.

"You're the one who's not going anywhere," Henry said in a quiet, measured voice, a voice Arthur had never heard before.

Joey seemed to have forgotten the pistol in his holster instead he dived toward the shotgun. Henry's eyes opened wide and his lips tightened across his front teeth.

Arthur yelled. "Cripes, Dad! Shoot! He's going for the shotgun."

BAM! Smoke and the acrid smell of gunpowder filled the small room. Henry's first bullet flew past Joey's head. Stunned, he stopped and turned toward Henry. The .38 exploded again, the second bullet tearing into Joey's right hip just below the waistline.

"Goddamn you!" Joey screamed, dropping to one knee. His hand touched the shotgun as his father steadied the .38 with both hands.

BAM! BAM! BAM! BAM!! Four more bullets tore into Joey's body. The gun was empty. Joey slumped to the floor and blood pooled around him. He twitched once and stopped moving.

A dazed Henry looked over at Arthur. "You okay, son?"

"Yeah, Dad. I'm fine."

The front door swung open and banged against the inside wall. Walter stood in the doorway with a .357 Magnum in hand. He scanned the room and spotted Joey on the floor.

Henry fumbled to reload his pistol as Walter turned toward him as calm as can be.

"Well, I'll be damned," he muttered.

With a casual flip of his wrist the Magnum went off and the big-caliber slug hit Henry squarely in the center of his forehead. His father's face registered disbelief, as if this couldn't be happening to him.

The powerful blast lifted Henry's body off the floor and slammed him against the wall. A round crimson stain formed on the white plaster wall where the back of his head had exploded. Then, slowly, the body slid down the wall, leaving a stark trail of bright red blood.

"Well this is a fine kettle of fish," Walter remarked, as if he'd just swatted a fly. "I'd shoot you, too, you little prick, but I may need you as a bargaining tool."

He shut the front door and took time to gather up a few things that might indicate he'd been in the house. He put on gloves and used a towel to wipe down anything he might have touched. Then he grabbed Arthur by the handcuffs and forced him to stumble ahead of him through the front door. On the dark front porch, with no moon or nearby streetlight, Walter paused to allow his eyes to adjust. Suddenly, like flashbulbs going off in rapid-fire succession, headlights from a half a dozen police squad cars popped on, the light beams pointed directly at the porch.

"Drop the gun, Walter, and let the boy go," the police captain ordered through a bullhorn. "You're not going anywhere!"

"Can't do it," Walter responded. He pushed Arthur in front of him as they inched down the steps. When he reached the sidewalk, Walter yelled: "You cops clear a path for me and this kid to get to my car and drive away. Do it or the boy dies, right here, right now!"

It was now or never. Arthur flexed his knees, slumped, and coiled his body, and then with all his strength he catapulted straight up, aiming the top of his skull at Walter's chin. His captor's head snapped back, and for an instant, Walter's iron-tight grip on the cuffs loosened. Arthur slithered down as a canon-size BOOM exploded next to his ear. Walter had fired wildly. A sharp, stinging pain slashed through the right side of Arthur's head.

His ears rang like tuning forks, as three shots cracked into the night. Walter flew backwards from the force of the police sharpshooter rifle bullets that hit the man simultaneously in the head, chest and neck. He curled up on the ground as other cops began indiscriminately blasting away.

"Hold your fire," commanded the captain. "This is over."

Everyone was in motion at once. Medics carried Arthur to an ambulance and pressed bandages to the side of his head to slow the flow of blood from the wound.

"It's nothin', kid," the medic assured him, yelling into his good ear. "The bullet shaved a quarter-inch off the top of your ear and you've got a burn from the flash of the gun. If the bullet had been a half-inch closer you'd be dead."

Arthur couldn't stop shaking—too much adrenalin and that awful ringing in his ears. Then the image of his dad's body hitting the wall, along with the smell of gunpowder rushed back. He saw Joey and his father's blood pouring out and mingling on the threadbare carpet.

His father was dead at age 44.

Suddenly, a surge of pride flowed through his body. Dad gave his life to save him. He'd stopped Joey from reaching the shotgun.

The heart forgets its sorrow and ache.

–James Russell Lowell

Chapter 54

The police car pulled up and Michael and Lilly jumped out. Lilly breathed in sharply and Michael's face went white when they saw the body sprawled across the porch steps.

"Oh, my God!" Lilly cried. She rushed forward. Michael grabbed her and held her back. "It's Arthur!"

The police captain stepped forward. "No, it's not, ma'am. The boy's all right. Just a slight flesh wound. He's on his way to the hospital."

A few moments later a detective stepped forward and announced that a Henry Goodwin had died in the house.

"Someone put a bullet in his head," the cop said, "and it wasn't a police bullet."

Henry dead? Lilly's mind whirled at the thought. She turned to Michael and choked back tears. Her entire body quivered. The captain called for a squad car. "Take these folks to Cedars-Sinai. Keep the press back."

Police pushed through a crowd of reporters and photographers to allow Michael and Lilly to enter the hospital front door. Arthur sat on the edge of a hospital bed in the emergency room while a doctor and nurse worked on his right ear.

Lilly ran to his side. "Arthur, honey, are you all right?"

He turned his left ear toward her. "I think so, but I can't hear out of my other ear."

The emergency room doc was a young, good-looking guy, maybe 30. He handled himself like an old pro.

"He's darn lucky," the doctor said. "The bullet raked across the top of his ear and he's lost some blood. He's also got a powder burn. Looks worse than it is. Far as I can tell, there's no permanent damage to his eardrum. That's really something. A .357 Magnum going off next to a guy's ear usually does a lot of damage. Count your lucky stars, buddy."

"Lilly, Dad's dead," Arthur said, his eyes watering. "Walter shot him. It was horrible. He tried to save me. I'd never seen Dad so brave."

Lilly and Michael stayed at his side while the doctor and nurse finished cleaning and bandaging the wound. An attendant brought a clean cotton hospital smock to replace his bloodied shirt.

The family waited outside as the police finished taking Arthur's statement. A little after midnight Paul arrived. His plane had been delayed. The three drank coffee and waited. An hour later, the captain came out with Arthur at his side.

"This is a fine young man you have," the captain said, nodding to Arthur "He kept his cool under some very trying circumstances, and he acted decisively at exactly the right time."

On the way home the wounded Arthur sat in the back seat with Lilly as Paul drove and Michael rode shotgun. Arthur looked like a mummy, with a large white bandage bulging over his ear and the top of his head swathed with bandages. A police car escorted them. Lilly clutched the kid's hand so tightly he finally had to pry her fingers off.

"Please, you're cutting off my circulation. I'm okay, really, I'm okay."

TV trucks, newspaper reporters and curiosity seekers crowded the driveway outside the gate to the house. As their car approached, two squad cars blocking the drive parted and a cop waved them through. Emotionally exhausted, the house on the hill never looked so welcoming and safe.

"Does your ear hurt?" Michael asked.

"No, everything's numb, just a throbbing feeling. They gave me some pain medication. I want to crawl in bed and sleep a week."

"A good idea, son."

Lilly picked up on Michael's use of "son", the first time in her presence he'd referred to Arthur that way. She and Michael followed the boy up the stairs. Paul said he'd stay downstairs in case someone came to the door or the telephone rang. "I'm all wound up anyway. I won't sleep until I can sort this out in my head."

Lilly undressed, put on a gown and began removing her makeup. She gazed into the mirror and was shocked. She looked drained, and like she'd aged 10 years. Her bloodshot eyes reflected a mixture of fright and blessed relief. She brushed her teeth and slipped into bed alongside Michael, who was already asleep. She mercifully slept through the night. She dreamed of Henry. He was behind the bar at the tavern in Elk Point, working the crowd like a comedic maestro. He looked young and strong. His eyes blazed with excitement. He was in his glory.

The next morning, still in the gown and wearing a white robe, she went downstairs to make coffee. She was the first one up, though it was almost nine.

As the coffee perked, she pulled back a curtain and saw two patrol cars still blocking a cluster of cars and TV trucks at the end of the driveway. This isn't over yet, she thought. Those reporters will have a long wait if they're hanging around expecting to hear anything from her family.

She sat down at the kitchen table and nearly spilled her coffee when the wall-mounted pink kitchen phone rang.

"Hello," she answered cautiously. Had some inventive reporter sniffed out their unlisted phone number?

It was Mr. Vogel. After apologizing for calling so early, he got straight to the point. "The L.A. police commissioner and the county attorney want to talk to you and Michael at police headquarters at three this afternoon. It's about Henry. I can meet you there."

"What about Henry?"

"They didn't come right out and say it but I suspect they're considering identifying Henry as a co-conspirator in the abduction. There are complications, however. Apparently, the case against Henry isn't as clear-cut as they had first thought. In addition, the press is complicating things by labeling him a hero based on comments that Arthur made to the police after the shooting. Someone leaked the information to the press."

Vogel paused. "If the DA names Henry as the person behind the abduction, it can get messy, lead to public hearings, that sort of thing. The police commissioner is concerned."

"Oh, for God's sake, can't we just let it be?" Lilly said, irritation in her voice. "Arthur's safe and that's all that matters. Let the boy believe what he wants."

"I agree. Still, the police have a job to do. It's their responsibility to tie up the loose ends, one way or the other. I sincerely believe it is in your family's best interest for you and Michael to attend this afternoon meeting. We can hash things out in private, away from the press."

"Oh, all right. I'll talk to Michael when he wakes up. If you don't hear from us, we'll be at the police station at three. Do they want Arthur there?"

"No, just the two of you."

After hanging up, Lilly opened the front door a crack and retrieved the morning newspaper. Sure enough, the 60-point, front-page banner headline read:

Father Gives Own Life to Save Son

Reliable sources report that the boy's father, Henry Goodwin, somehow learned where the kidnappers were hiding his son. After reporting the address to the police, he took a taxi to the small house at 359 Alito Avenue, gained admittance and shot one of the abductors. He was in the process of fleeing with his son, when the second kidnapper appeared and shot Mr. Goodwin to death.

Police and other officials are hailing Goodwin for his bravery in giving his life to save his son.

She set the newspaper aside and went upstairs to wake her husband.

Imagine, she thought. The world wakes up this morning to learn Henry Goodwin is a hero. This, she decided, could only happen in Hollywood!

High rank...may not always belong to a true heart.

–Anthony Trollope

Chapter 55

Smartly dressed District Attorney Gary Phipps smiled when Lilly walked into the commissioner's office with Michael at her side. It was a condescending smile, one you'd see on the face of an office-seeker when he knows a photographer is about to take his picture. In his early forties, the DA's hair was gray at the edges and he wore a dark blue blazer, gray slacks, white shirt and a red bow tie. There was no question he considered himself in charge of this get-together.

Dressed considerably more conservatively, Attorney Vogel was already seated at a large round table with Phipps and Police Commissioner Wellington. Lilly and Michael shook hands all around and took a seat on either side of Vogel.

"Thanks for taking the time to come here," Wellington said. Lilly took an instant liking to this man. The commissioner had a courteous, respectful manner He chose his words carefully, and when he spoke he looked her directly in the face.

"We appreciate all the work the police did," Vogel stated. "Now, we want to let the family members put these distressing incidents behind them. How can...?"

"If I may," the DA interrupted. "There's a problem regarding this Mr. Henry Goodwin, the boy's father. Some in the press are calling him a hero. Our investigation indicates he may have orchestrated the whole affair. I wonder, Commissioner Wellington, if you'd update us on what we now know."

"Glad to," Wellington said, obviously embarrassed with the DA's pompous behavior. Unlike the DA, the Commissioner kept his seat as he spoke, and he adopted an unhurried and smooth conversational tone, which helped put the room at ease.

"Our senior detectives have sifted through the available information and we are, at this point, uncertain of Mr. Goodwin's level of involvement. We strongly suspect he tipped Walter and Joey off that his son would be in the library parking lot the night he was abducted."

"Yes, we've had similar suspicions," Vogel said. Lilly and Michael nodded in agreement.

"We do know Mr. Goodwin had knowledge of where Arthur was being held," Wellington continued. "We also suspect it was Henry who called the police and provided them the address of the house where the boy was being held. The question is: how could he have this information unless he was involved? From what the boy told us at the hospital, during the confrontation in the house, the father seemed to know the kidnappers on a first-name basis.

"We also found this newspaper clipping in Mr. Goodwin's wallet," Wellington continued, as he picked up the clipping and handed it to Michael. "It's well-worn, like he had carried this press report around with him for a considerable length to time.

"As you can see, it describes the abduction of a young man in Chicago. The details of this incident are eerily similar to Arthur's kidnapping, right down to the amount of the ransom—a quarter-million dollars. Why did Mr. Goodwin carry this clipping around in his pocket? Coincidence? We don't think so."

The DA interrupted: "Now, just so you folks know, all of the items the commissioner has reviewed to this point are what we in the legal profession consider as circumstantial evidence. If I may," he said, clearing his throat and dropping his voice an octave, "I'll take a moment to explain the precise legal meaning of the word *circumstantial*."

"That won't be necessary," Vogel said, cutting the man off. "We're well aware of the meaning. Let's proceed."

Phipps lowered his head and glanced up like he was about to offer a stinging rebuttal then backed off. "Very well, the root of the matter is that while we have strong suspicions about Mr. Goodwin's complicity, the fact remains, with all three of the men now deceased, and no corroborating witnesses, there's no way to conclusively prove this Goodwin fellow's guilt or innocence, at least not in a court of law."

"So where are we?" asked Vogel impatiently.

"Well," the Commissioner stepped in, "at this point, it depends on whether the family is intent on pursuing the matter further. I could put a dozen detectives on the case to try to dig up hard evidence. I doubt we'll find anything new."

"Or we can do what?" Vogel asked.

"Or we can end this right here. Three men have paid the ultimate price for the crime. There's no one alive to implicate or clear Mr. Goodwin. We may never know whether he was a good or a bad guy in the matter."

"What are your feelings?" Frederick said, turning to Lilly and Michael.

"I'll defer to Lilly," Michael said.

She took her time before speaking. "I truly believe Henry was up to his eye-teeth in this kidnapping. But Arthur wants to believe his father is a hero. Considering everything, it seems to me, as you pointed out, Commissioner, there's little to be gained in pursuing the matter further."

After the meeting broke up, Wellington instructed his aide to organize a press briefing on the steps of the Los

Angeles County Courthouse. He also arranged to have the ransom money returned to Michael and Lilly.

The next morning, Commissioner Wellington read a prepared press release that offered congratulations to city and county law enforcement for an outstanding job of tracking down the kidnappers and successfully rescuing Arthur Goodwin.

"Yeah, but what about the boy's father?" yelled a reporter. "Our sources tell us he was involved in taking the kid. Was he or not?"

"All I can say is that Mr. Goodwin entered the house to rescue his son and, on his own, shot and killed one of the kidnappers, a man named Joey Holloway. The second kidnapper, a person named Walter Brink, shot and killed Mr. Goodwin. We have no evidence that Mr. Goodwin was involved in the kidnapping and, in fact, at this time we consider his actions heroic and self-sacrificing. As far as the police and the boy's family are concerned, this matter is closed."

"Hold on a minute," shouted out another reporter. "I know for a fact this Goodwin guy knew the two men from when he tended bar at this place called Kelsey's. We've heard on good sources he hired the two to do his dirty work."

"That's all I have to say," Wellington said, as he gathered his papers and stepped from the podium.

Later came accusations of a cover up and even an editorial in the newspaper calling for an investigation of the police department. Without any hard evidence, the story faded to the back pages and soon vanished entirely from the public eye.

After dinner that evening, Lilly talked to Paul about the meeting at the police department. Arthur was upstairs studying.

Even though she'd never say a word to Arthur, Lilly told Paul she remained convinced Henry was behind the kidnapping.

"Yeah, I think he did it," Paul agreed. "But to Dad's credit, when he learned of Walter's history of not leaving any witnesses alive, he did do the right thing."

"You're right," Lilly responded. "He stood up to those horrible men, and he did save Arthur's life. Still, it's ironic, don't you think, that your father will be remembered as the brave man who gave his life to save his son when, in truth…well, you know."

"I know," Paul said, shaking his head. "But, really, what we have here is a pretty good ending when you consider all the things that might have happened, like Arthur being seriously hurt or maybe killed."

"Of course. And just so you know, the police did check on Arthur's former girlfriend, Mandy. From what I heard, the quick-tempered lass practically waylaid a cop when he tried to question her about Arthur's disappearance. In the end, she was cleared, too, which, as you say, is not a bad ending."

The next day, Michael drove Paul, Arthur and Lilly to the funeral home to arrange for Henry's burial. From the back seat, Arthur complained about press reports that implied his father was in partnership with Walter and Joey.

"They weren't there. I was. Dad shot Joey," Arthur said defiantly. "If that doesn't make him a hero, I don't know what does. I should go to the newspaper and straighten them out."

"That'll just stir things up," Paul injected. "Newspapers thrive on controversy. It sells papers. Isn't it enough that the police have cleared Dad's name? Let it go. It's time we forgive and forget and move on."

"Amen," said Lilly.

Chapter 56

One question remained to be answered.

Arthur stood before the door to Apartment 3-C, uncertain whether to knock. He'd read in the newspaper that his father's girlfriend, Crystal Favor, lived here. He'd driven by the three-story apartment building several times since his father's funeral.

He didn't have the courage to stop.

The police had kept her in jail until the day after the shootout. Eventually, she was cleared of any involvement in the crime.

She'd meant a lot to his father. At one of their breakfast meetings, Dad told him he was thinking of marrying his new friend. Arthur had seen Crystal's picture in the newspapers. Who was she really? And why was such a pretty young girl like her interested in his father?

What weighed most on Arthur's mind was learning the truth about Dad's involvement in the abduction. He hoped Crystal could provide some answers. It nagged him that his father was on a first-name basis with both kidnappers. And how did Dad know where he was being held? He squared up and rang the doorbell.

"Who is it?" called out a wary voice from behind the door.

"It's Arthur Goodwin. You knew my father, Henry."

"Are you alone?" she asked, her voice soft and tentative.

"Yes."

Two locks clicked and the door opened to reveal an ashen, slender young lady wearing a bathrobe, her thick auburn hair uncombed and her complexion as pale and pure as the inside of a seashell. There was no lipstick. There were bruises under her eyes the color of plums, like she'd spent the last week crying.

Crystal was the polar opposite of Gladys, the scary lady his Dad had come calling with that night when they lived in the small house just off Sunset Boulevard. He remembered Gladys as rude and loud, and wearing lipstick as red as a wound. Crystal was different. Even though she'd been crying, and he had the impression she hadn't been out of the apartment in days, there was a simple and honest beauty in her manner and looks.

"You're Arthur, his youngest son, aren't you?" Crystal inquired. "You look like him, except for those eyes."

She searched his face. "Your dad told me you have your mother's eyes."

She stepped aside and allowed him into a spare, modest apartment.

"I apologize for the mess. I had to come back here after the police busted up the apartment I shared with your dad. The police even tore into the walls. It'll take weeks to repair and the landlord was very upset. He wouldn't let me stay. I can't blame him."

"It wasn't your fault," Arthur began.

"The landlord was kind enough to allow me to return to gather my clothes," she said modestly.

He looked over at her two open suitcases on the floor, clothes spilling out. Arthur had heard that when the police surprised Henry and Crystal in bed, all she wore was a sheet that she had wrapped around herself.

"I can offer a cup of tea. Would you like one?" Crystal asked as she showed him to a seat at the kitchen table.

"Sure," Arthur replied, uncomfortable that he was intruding on her at a difficult time. He cleared his throat. "I had breakfast with Dad a while back and he talked a lot about you. He said you're an actress, and that you were very talented and prettier than most of the female movie stars. He was right."

Crystal opened a cabinet and Arthur noticed that the cupboard only contained two plates, two glasses and two cups. She placed the two cups on the counter then turned to the sink and filled the metal teapot with water and set it on the stove.

"At one time I wanted to be an actress. I'm over it now," Crystal said. "I don't have what it takes to make it in this town. I can't fight for everything, and I don't want to play all the games. Right now, with all my heart, I want to go home and I hope to do that within the next few days." She lit a match, turned on the burner and held the match until the gas flared.

"Dad was certain you could make it in Hollywood."

Crystal cocked her head toward him, her lips parted and her white teeth showed through. "That's what I admired about your father. To him, I could do anything. You're surprised, aren't you, that your father and I got together?"

Arthur nodded. "He was a charming man when he wanted to be."

"He was a good man," Crystal said. "So funny, and I felt comfortable and safe with him. He talked about getting married. I miss him, and I'm so sorry that he's gone." A vague sadness and a faraway look crossed her face.

Crystal placed her hand on Arthur's. "I know you lost your mother, and now your dad, too."

"Yeah," Arthur answered. "Dad and I didn't see a lot of each other over the years. I can see what he saw in you."

She blushed.

The teapot started singing and she walked over and turned off the burner. "Sorry, there's no lemon or sugar. I haven't done much shopping."

"That's okay, plain is fine," Arthur said. He wanted to keep her talking.

He took a sip and asked, "I'm hoping you can help me clear up some questions that are floating around in my head."

"Try to."

"The newspapers are saying Dad was involved in the kidnapping," Arthur said, warming his hands on the cup. Suddenly, he felt chilled. "I don't think it's true. He saved my life."

"I read the same reports. They're ridiculous. Your father loved you boys He'd never put you in danger. He was proud of you and wished he'd been a better father."

Crystal sipped her tea. "He talked a lot about the days when you kids were growing up in Nebraska. After your mom died he told me he almost went crazy. She was the anchor in his life, and his years with her had been the best of his life. He hid his sorrow because he had to be strong for you guys. Maybe that's why he didn't visit you much over the years."

Watching her, Arthur understood how much Crystal had cared for his father. It was too man that things hadn't worked out for them. With Crystal, his dad finally had something good going for him.

"Henry told me he wished he could do a lot of things over with you boys."

Arthur placed his cup on the table. "Yeah, Dad had trouble expressing his feelings, that's for sure. Truth is, I didn't know him, never really had a clue about what made him tick, or even what he thought of me as a person."

Her eyes wandered. "I could have made him happy. He understood me as only an older man can."

They talked for almost an hour and shared another cup of tea together. Finally Arthur stood and thanked her. As he reached to shake her hand, she brushed it aside and embraced him, releasing him with a light kiss on the cheek.

"Never forget that your father loved you boys," she said, her eyes sincere and caring.

Arthur was at the door when, almost as an after-thought, Crystal said: "You know, a few days before he was killed your father told me that he was quitting his job. He wanted to leave Los Angeles and move back to Nebraska. He talked about having you boys at our wedding—Paul as best man, and you standing up with me. He was working on a deal, one that would bring him a big pile of cash to pay for a new start. He was excited to escape this town."

Arthur froze. There it was, the clincher! Dad had told Crystal he expected to come into a lot of money real soon—and all at one time.

It had to be the ransom money.

Without realizing it, Crystal had revealed what he hadn't wanted to hear. The newspapers had it right. His father had conspired with Walter and Joey and put into motion events that ended in three deaths, and almost a fourth—his!

With a lump in his throat, he walked to the car. Dad wasn't the first guy to fall for a pretty girl, and when things took a wrong turn, to make a desperate, high-stakes bet to turn things around. Dad had lived a frayed life, plagued with missteps, mainly of his own making. Yet, when it really mattered, he'd abandoned all of his personal dreams and stood bravely like a man—and a father. In his mind, Henry Goodwin would forever be an honest-to-god hero!

"I must do something or I shall wear my heart away...."

–Charles Dickens

Chapter 57

It was 1966. More than five years had passed since Henry's funeral. Lilly sat at the kitchen table with the day's newspaper and her morning coffee. It was a comfortable ritual. The family was doing well. Arthur was a graduate student at Stanford University and living on the Palo Alto campus. He had a delightful girlfriend, a young Chinese lady who was also a student at the university. Paul had his own apartment and worked for Performance Arts in the Sports Division. He and Sophia were engaged. They hadn't set a wedding date, and didn't seem in any hurry to do so. Sophia taught third grade in one of the best public schools in Los Angeles.

Lilly flipped over the paper and read a bold headline, just below the page-one fold. It reported that Walt Disney, one of the most loved and successful studio owners in Hollywood, had died at age 65. Over the years, she and Michael had worked on charity events with Walt and served on several voluntary boards. Walt and his family were good friends of theirs.

There were reports that Walt had been a three-pack-a-day man, which meant he smoked even more cigarettes than Michael did before her husband finally managed to quit. Lilly couldn't remember a single time when they'd been together with Mr. Disney when he didn't have a lit cigarette going. It was said he kept smoking right up to the very end. He died of acute circulatory collapse only one month after undergoing surgery for removal of a lung tumor.

Feeling terrible, Lilly stopped reading. She knew Michael would take the loss of another dear friend very hard. He entered the kitchen and poured a cup of coffee.

"It's Walt Disney," Lilly said, in a somber voice. "He's gone."

Michael frowned. He sat down with his coffee and picked up the newspaper. A moment later, he glanced up. "Don't look so stricken, honey. Heavens, I'm getting used to friends dying off. Truth is, sometimes I feel guilty for still being alive."

Lilly looked at him. "Oh, honey…"

"It's tragic for Walt's family," Michael sighed. "Those damnable cigarettes! If it wasn't for you and the doctors, I'd be in the same boat, or should I say, the same casket. I only wish something could have saved him."

Lilly could appreciate Michael's words. Six months earlier, the surgeons had removed most of his left lung after she and his L.A. oncologist, in consultation with brother Bob, had urged her husband to move decisively to eradicate the cancer that was growing in his lung.

"It's your best chance," they all had pleaded with him.

At first Michael dithered. Surgery, as he often reminded Lilly, was the final procedure employed after everything else had failed. In almost every instance the surgeons would open the cancer victim's chest, peer inside and announce that the cancer has advanced too far and there was nothing more to be done. They'd sew up the poor soul's chest and send him or her home to die an agonizing, inch-by-inch death.

"With Lilly's constant encouragement, and on-going pressure from the doctors, Michael, despite his reservations, decided to go ahead.

"What choice do I have?" he told Lilly. "If it were only me, I'd accept the inevitable, and skip the surgery."

"Then do it for us, please. If there's any chance at all, we want you to take it. We love you so much."

During the five-hour process, surgeons removed most of his diseased left lung, leaving the other lung, which appeared cancer-free, untouched. When he woke in the recovery room, Lilly and the boys were at his side, as were Bob and his wife. They watched as the head surgeon, with a bounce, stepped over to Michael's bed.

"I have wonderful news," he began. "The operation was a success. All of us on the medical team are optimistic." Michael looked up at the smiling man, dazed, not comprehending.

Lilly squeezed her husband's hand.

"It's okay, darling," she said. "You're going to make it."

"The best thing now is rest and plenty of it," the doctor continued. "We should have you on your way home in a few days."

Lilly sobbed in relief as she leaned over the hospital bed to hold him. The others in the room, including Michael's long-time oncologist, looked on with pure joy on their faces.

"We'll monitor you over the next several months, more X-rays, that sort of thing," his doctor said. "If all goes well, which I expect it will, you'll return every six months for a checkup. This routine will continue on a regular basis, likely for the rest of your life—as a precaution."

A month later Michael convened a special meeting of the Performance Arts board and executive staff. With his natural dignity and diplomatic skills on full display, he looked at each of them and offered a nod and smile.

Michael's gaze lingered on Lilly. "All of you have followed our battle with lung disease. You know the good news. It's difficult to express the deep appreciation we have for your steadfast support and friendship.

"There's no guarantee this good fortune of ours will continue. Still, we have reason to hope. During my many absences, each of you has done a magnificent job maintaining this firm's high standards of service to our clients."

The boardroom was quiet but for the tick of the clock on the wall. Every eye was on Michael.

"I love Performance Arts; it's my baby," Michael continued, his voice thickening with emotion. "Still, everything has to end, and with this new lease on life, I'm resigning as chairman and, effective today, I plan to devote the remainder of my days doing what I can to help others. I feel very blessed as I embark on this new path."

He looked again to Lilly.

"Lilly becomes Chairman of the Board, and remains as director of the Television Division. Each of you will continue in your current positions. I leave knowing that Performance Arts is in capable hands, and confident that our best days are still ahead."

Then he allowed his gaze to slide from one face to the next as he moved around the table, acknowledging each person by name and offering a word of personal thanks. After shaking the last hand, he turned and left.

Later, Lilly later reported that there wasn't a dry eye in the conference room.

I put my heart and my soul into my work, and have lost my mind in the process.

–Vincent Van Gogh

Chapter 58

One early evening during a visit to Sunset Park, Lilly and Michael, both with knife in hand, carved their initials alongside the ones Paul and Sophia had carved a few years earlier on the back of a wooden park bench.

"Isn't that lovely," Lilly said. "Two sets of hearts, side by side."

With Paul and Sophia now off on their own, Sunset Park had become Michael and Lilly's favorite spots to visit, with its bubbly, clear-flowing creek, trees, grass and gorgeous flowers. Whoever planned the flower gardens had done a remarkable job. No matter the season, when one variety died out and went to seed, another came into delightful bloom. "Sort of like life, wouldn't you think?" Michael said, smiling.

Lilly was working only three days a week to spend more time with Michael during his recovery. For the first time in their marriage, they enjoyed sleeping in, leisurely breakfasts at the kitchen table, and long walks. Michael even began working in the flower gardens surrounding the house. He'd always been a talker, if a quiet and measured one. Now the floodgates had opened and his most intimate thoughts and feelings flowed out of his mouth. He was unfailingly honest.

He surprised her by saying he was in the process of reading the Bible, from Genesis to Revelation.

"It's a goal I've harbored for years," he said, his eyes earnest. "I was always a little uncomfortable picking up the Bible. I'm discovering what a great book it is, with wonderful teaching stories. It's corny, I know. But I've never felt so content, or at ease with myself.

"I'm proud of you," Lilly said, "and I envy what you're feeling and experiencing."

As Michael's health continued to improve, Lilly began enjoying a kind of cat-in-the-sunshine sense of ease of her own. In some ways, she regretted she'd soon have to return to work full time.

In the meantime, she and Michael's favorite times involved quiet evenings at home, just the two of them. They'd sit on the floor for hours and sort and organize the four large boxes of family photos that Michael had had shipped to Los

Angeles from New Jersey after his father died. Compared to Michael's trove of hundreds, maybe thousands of photographs, Lilly had only one manila envelope with several dozen photographs, in no particular order, of she and her parents during their years in Elk Horn. Because Mom and Dad worked so many hours, the family rarely had the time or the energy to break out the Brownie camera.

"Dad was detail-oriented, and a darned good photographer," Michael commented, as he reached in a box for another handful of pictures. "When he wasn't photographing insects he'd turn the camera on the family. And when the prints came back from the processor, Dad would carefully write on the back the date, subject, circumstances, and who was in each photo, you know, from left to right."

Michael held up a print. "Sometimes he'd pen a personal comment on the back, like this one: 'A gorgeous day and a gorgeous family.'" Michael placed the picture back in the box. "It amazes me that Dad would express his inner feelings in writings on the back of photographs but I never once heard him express aloud his inner feelings to either of us boys, and certainly not to Mom. He seemed embarrassed, or too shy, to allow his feelings to show."

"Wish I'd known him better," Lilly said. "I only met him that once when we attended your mother's funeral. If I could, I'd give both your mom and dad hugs for bringing two wonderful sons into the world—and for preserving these photos. My God, they're a treasure."

Lilly swooned each time she looked at the picture of Michael in Army uniform, which was taken by his father. Turning it over she saw his dad had written that her husband was 28 years old when the photograph was taken "and a wonderful, thoughtful young man." She thought the photograph of Michael was handsome beyond description. He looked strong and confident, and oh that smile. She had it cleaned and framed, and placed it on the fireplace mantle in the parlor. Whenever she walked past it, she'd put a finger to her lips and touch the photograph, and be reminded how fortunate she'd been to find her Prince Charming.

One night as they sorted through the boxes, Michael started talking. "Lately, I've been thinking about where Bob and I came from, you know, our home life in New Jersey, and how those experiences molded us into the people we are today. For instance, for a long time I thought Mom was the dominant influence in the house. She set the agenda while Dad concentrated on his bug collection. Now, I'm wondering if it wasn't Dad who most influenced our lives."

"Wait a second. I thought you rarely saw your father, and when you did, you boys never got two words out of the man. Now you're telling me William loomed large in your lives. Are we talking about the same person?"

"That's what I'm saying," Michael said, nodding his head and smiling.

"Let me tell you a story…

"When I turned 16 and received my driver's license, it was a Saturday and Mom was running errands. Dad, of course, was in the basement. I wanted in the worst way to borrow the family's second car parked in the garage, a big, noisy Pontiac that he drove back and forth to work. I was determined to drive to my buddy's house and show off my new license.

"I didn't dare take the car without permission, and, as I said, Mom was out shopping. Dad was the only one I could go to. I cautiously edged my way down the basement stairs to the bug lair. He was peering into a microscope, totally absorbed in the work. Books were scattered everywhere. I faked a cough but he didn't even look up."

"Eeek, I can't imagine living in house with a basement full of bugs," Lilly said, rubbing her bare arms up and down, like tiny creatures were crawling on her skin.

Michael laughed. "Relax, the bugs were dead, or at least most of them."

Still, Lilly shivered and wrapped her arms tight across her chest.

"From half way down the stairs, I said something dumb like, 'Whatcha doin', Dad?'

"Glancing up, he smiled, not in the least surprised to see me standing there, even though it was the first time I could ever remember having ventured down those stairs while Dad was present.

'I'm looking for this gnat's heart,' he answered.

"Bugs don't have hearts," I countered with a confidence only a 16-year-old can put forth, "especially tiny insects like gnats. What would a bug need a heart for anyway? Most don't even have blood. Except maybe mosquitoes, after they bite a guy."

"He sighed and looked up at me. 'They most assuredly do,' he said patiently. 'Not necessarily red blood as we know it, but bugs are like all living things—they have hearts, and circulatory systems that carry oxygen and nutrients, maybe not exactly the way ours work, but along the same principle.'

"He told me every creature in this world lives from the heart, even the tiniest of insects. And we all share a heartbeat, or something very much like a heartbeat.

"He asked me to look through the microscope at a live ant that he'd placed on a slide. Then he stood aside.

'What do you see?' he asked.

"What am I looking for, Dad?"

'A beating heart,' he answered

"I do see it! Movement, something inside the body of the ant is pulsating. A heart?"

Dad could hardly contain his excitement. I saw the expression on his face, and it was like I was seeing him for the first time, as a person, a really special person."

"How wonderful," Lilly said.

"Then I asked him if could borrow the Pontiac and he didn't even blink. 'Sure,' he said. 'Go ahead.'

"Climbing back up the stairs, I looked down and he was at his desk, making notes in one of his catalogs, lost in his work. I drove to my friend's house. Later, Mom was ready to chew me out until I told her Dad had given me permission to take the car.

"She looked at me like I was nuts and didn't say anything, only shook her head like she'd never heard of such a thing.

"I'd like to say that after having made that connection in the basement, Dad and I spent more time together and grew closer. But nothing changed. We returned to our old ways."

"Your father's comment about the heart and all living things sharing a heartbeat is lyrical."

"Yeah, I know. The longer I live the more I understand what Dad was trying to tell me. The Bible is loaded with verses and teachings about the heart being the wellspring of life, the spiritual source of all goodness, compassion and love. And here's a tidbit I bet you don't know: the word 'heart' is mentioned 762 times in the Bible, plus 114 times more if you include the word 'hearts'. Know what else? There's not a single mention of the word 'brain' in the entire Bible."

"Well aren't you a fount of Biblical knowledge!" Lilly observed. "You know, I should probably read that book sometime."

There are strings in the human heart that had better not be vibrated.

–Charles Dickens

Chapter 59

"I've joined the Army," Paul said, his voice barely audible. He kept his eyes down on the plate.

Paul's matter-of-fact pronouncement ripped into Lilly like someone had reached into her chest and squeezed her heart.

Paul was at the house for dinner. He'd called the day before and asked to stop by to talk, without giving a hint of what he wanted to say. She invited him to come for supper.

"I've already signed the papers," he continued in a rush to keep Lilly from interrupting. "After I finish an eight-week basic training program, I begin helicopter flight training at Fort Walters in Texas. If I make it through the school, I'll likely deploy to Vietnam."

Stunned by the outrageousness of what Paul had said, Lilly leaned toward him. "What in the world are you thinking?" Her words came out like a shrill screech, like chalk on a blackboard. "Why would you do such a thing? It sounds so …so… preposterous." Her face twisted into disbelief.

"You know there's a war and people are getting killed," she continued. "Every night on the news they show body bags coming off the planes on conveyer belts. It's terrible. All those young men!"

She looked at Michael and turned back to Paul. "What does Sophia say?"

Paul continued to look down. The roast beef was untouched. "Actually, we're taking a break. We need space to figure things out."

He looked up as if he was about to say more. Instead, he folded his hands in his lap and kept silent.

"I'm sorry," Michael said. "I thought you and Sophia were doing fine."

"We're still, you know, close, very close," Paul said. "I love her and she loves me. It's, well, oh cripes, I don't know exactly how to say this. We decided to take a break."

"Oh, Paul," Lilly said. "Are you joining the Army because you and Sophie had a fight? Please, stop and think this through. Running off to war isn't going to solve anything."

"I have thought it through," Paul responded. "The war is heating up. There's a critical need for helicopter pilots. By joining I choose my own assignment. I've always wanted to fly. Besides, I've been fortunate that my draft number hasn't been called up yet."

Paul took a deep breath. "There's one more thing. Serving in the Army seems the right thing to do. Dad always bragged how he'd beat the draft, like it was a major accomplishment. Seems to me at least one Goodwin ought to step up and do his part. And, frankly, I'd rather it's me than Arthur."

"That's admirable," Michael said. "You know of course flying helicopters in a war zone in a tropical jungle is about the worst—and most dangerous—assignment you can draw. If you like, I'll try to pull some strings and secure you a better slot."

"Appreciate the offer. But I'm all set. I leave in two weeks."

After Paul left, Lilly and Michael sat wordlessly at the dinner table.

"I wonder if Maria knows about the break up," Lilly said to her husband. "The last time we had coffee we had such fun talking about the possibility of a big wedding.

"Call her and find out what she knows," Michael said. "It'll ease your mind."

Lilly picked up the phone and dialed her former neighbor's number.

"It's me," Lilly said, forcing cheerfulness into her voice. "I wonder if you have time for coffee tomorrow morning. I can come by."

"Sounds wonderful," Maria answered. "The kitchen re-do turned out beautifully, and I want to show it off. About nine okay?"

Lilly hung up, certain that Maria didn't know. Next morning her former neighbor greeted her at the door with a big smile but it vanished the moment she touched Lilly's hand. She collapsed into her arms and cried.

When she calmed down and poured coffee, Maria said, "After your call I got to thinking. So I called Sophia. She was upset and crying. I could hardly understand what she was saying. She and Paul had a fight."

Lilly took Maria's hands. "I'm sorry."

"Sophia blames herself. Apparently, the fight has something to do with Sophia's insistence that Paul convert to Catholicism. She won't marry a non-Catholic and insists that their children be raised in the church."

"Do you think that's *really* what's behind this?" Lilly asked. "I've never known Paul to have strong feelings one way or another about organized religion. It doesn't seem like a major deal to him."

"All I know is that Paul met several times with our parish priest," Maria said. "Things seemed fine, at least far as Sophia could tell, and then something must have happened, or something was said, because the priest asked Sophia to come in alone for a talk."

"What happened?" Lilly asked.

"I don't know," Maria replied. "Afterwards, she and Paul had this fight and now they're split up."

"I'm so sorry," Lilly said as she looked into the saddened face of her friend across the kitchen table. "Let's hope for the best."

Lilly picked up her purse and excused herself. She had an appointment at work. As she started out the door Maria called out, her voice breaking: "It's my fault. I raised my kids to be strict Catholics and to follow the church. Do exactly what the priests say, I told them. Now this happens. Sophia is so unhappy. It breaks my heart."

"Paul's suffering, too," Lilly said and then paused. She decided to tell her friend the news. "Do you know Paul has joined the Army? He leaves next week."

"No! And I bet Sophia doesn't know, either," Maria answered. "Will he go to that Vietnam place?"

"Yes, probably. He wants to fly helicopters, the kind you see on television."

"Oh, Hail Mary, Full of Grace, I'll pray for him every day."

"I'm praying, too," Lilly said, as she went out the door.

There is no charm equal to tenderness of heart.

–Jane Austen

Chapter 60

June 1998

The new, six-story Michael J. Paulson School of Mass Communications building towered above and behind the portable stage. Lilly sat in a straight-back chair in a long row of black-robed faculty staff and members of the Board of Trustees of Dartmouth College. The night before, Lilly, Paul and Arthur and their families had participated in the building's ribbon-cutting ceremony.

Today, under the bright June sun, Lilly, now a poised and gracious widow, listened to the college president read a long list of Michael's accomplishments and contributions to the growth and continuing success of Dartmouth College.

She glanced down at a throng of gowned young men and women seated in white folding chairs on the campus green as they waited to receive their diplomas.

Lilly heard her name introduced and looked over at the president's smiling face. Michael, this is your moment, she thought, as she rose to accept the Honorary Doctorate of Humane Letters degree in his name. At 69, with gray streaks in her hair and a slight limp from a recent hip replacement, Lilly was a strikingly beautiful woman who carried herself with serene confidence. *Hollywood Reporter* had recently named her one of Los Angeles' top female business leaders.

At the podium, she accepted the award and in a strong, resonant voice thanked the trustees, faculty and the new crop of graduates for allowing her a few moments during their special day. She pointed out that Michael served 10 years on the College Board of Trustees, including two years as chairperson.

Lilly continued, "My husband, a 1933 Dartmouth graduate, who passed away 16 years ago to this day, loved this school, and was extremely proud to be a graduate of an institution that can count among its many illustrious alumni Poet Robert Frost and New England favorite Daniel Webster."

The audience broke into applause at the mention of two of the college's most famous graduates.

"My sincere wish is that each of you could have known Michael. He lived his life in a way that can serve as an example to us all. A successful businessman, Michael cared, really cared for the people. He had a deep respect for every person, no matter his or her station in life. Although he operated in rough and tumble Hollywood where short cuts and ethical missteps are often the norm, he chose to conduct his affairs differently, and to treat clients with honesty and fairness, and always to put their interests ahead of his own.

"As new graduates looking to start careers, I hope your first boss will be someone like Michael Paulson. If so, count yourself very fortunate. On numerous occasions Michael rallied friends in Hollywood, including many of the best-loved actors and actresses in the world, to support programs that serve young people.

"Even though he didn't live long enough to see this building finished, and to be here on this beautiful morning, Michael's spirit is here. Through my voice he's asking me to extend best wishes to all of you graduates, your family members and friends gathered here."

Lilly gazed out at the sea of young faces. "Thank you very much, and congratulations to each and every one of you."

Polite applause greeted her words as Lilly returned to her seat. She understood. To most of the graduates, and the others in attendance, Michael J. Paulson was a rich dead guy whose name now graced a new building on the Dartmouth campus.

Her mind wandered as several hundred graduates of the Class of 1998 passed in a steady stream across the stage to receive their diplomas. Her eyes settled on a young woman who reminded Lilly of how she might have looked when she received her high school diploma back in Elk Point so many years ago. Overweight and with a bit of waddle in her walk, Lilly was intrigued with the alluring look on this young lady's face as she passed in front of her. Her eyes flashed with joy and excitement. She accepted her diploma from the college president with one hand and shook his hand with the other. It wasn't a simple shake and drop. She pumped the president's hand like she was drawing water from a balky well, and wouldn't let go. Sensing her pride and excitement, he pumped back, just as vigorously. The crowd roared its approval. It was one of those rare, rich moments when you can't help but feel good to be alive, when the thoughts in your head find a path to your heart.

Lilly's family was gathered in the VIP section near the front: Paul and Arthur with their wives and children. Arthur and Mai had recently celebrated their thirtieth wedding anniversary. Their girls reminded Lilly of two fragile porcelain dolls, but they were anything but—full of life with razor-sharp intellects.

Seated next to Arthur was Paul, with a cane leaning against his chair. He'd lost his left foot above the ankle when enemy fire hit his Huey medevac helicopter during a rescue mission in Vietnam. He received a Medal of Honor, the nation's highest military decoration, for guiding his helicopter, not once but three times, into a hot landing zone in Kon Tum Province. In the process, he saved the lives of 14 wounded American soldiers.

Seated next to Paul was his wife, Annie. It gladdened Lilly's heart to recall Paul and Annie's fairytale romance that started when they were barely teenagers at a church youth-group meeting in Elk Point. Upon hearing of Paul's wounds, Clara called Annie's mother to let her know what had happened to Paul and, as she had hoped, Annie's mom passed the news on to her daughter.

Though Annie hadn't seen Paul since the break-up kiss that night in Elk Point, she immediately asked for a leave of absence from her residency in pediatrics at a hospital in Maryland and rushed to San Francisco where Paul's was hospitalized. They were married two years later in a wedding ceremony in Elk Point. They had two boys in quick succession and named their first son Michael.

Frank passed away at age 77, three years after Paul and Annie's wedding. Clara lived four years longer than her husband.

Bob and Smitty tried to keep Bottman's Standard open after Frank died. Neither had much of an aptitude for business, and with the advent of high-tech electronics and sophisticated diagnostic equipment, the mechanical end of the gas station's business moved to the new-car and tractor dealerships in Elk Point. The Standard station's final death knell came when two shiny convenience stores opened, one on East Main and the other on West Main. The extended-hour stores offered discounted gasoline at the pumps, and pizza and sandwiches inside, along with milk and bread and other items of convenience.

Paul, 59 years old, now served as president of Performance Arts, while Lilly retained the title of Chairman of the Board.

From her perch on the elevated stage, Lilly picked Arthur out of the audience. With those sparkling eyes, he was easy to spot. He offered a thumbs up, and followed with their secret wink. She nodded and returned the favor.

At 53, Arthur was a full professor and department chair of Stanford's Computer Science Department. He and a handful of Stanford graduates were known internationally as the unofficial founders of Silicon Valley. Arthur, in particular, had an intimate part in the start up of several companies with strange-sounding names like Yahoo, Google, and Cisco. In the process, he was awarded generous stock options. When the companies went public, those stock options exploded in value and made him very wealthy.

These days, he and his family continued to live on his Stanford's professor's salary. The windfall stock-option money was in a separate account, and the earnings supported the *Arthur and Mai Lin Goodwin Better Life Foundation*, led by none other than Paul's wife, Dr. Annie Goodwin, who had once held the distinction of leading the junior high youth group at the Methodist Church in Elk Point, Nebraska.

The foundation's purpose was to hire and train medical personnel and disperse them throughout the world to provide life-improving medical assistance to the needy in places where such services were either unavailable or unaffordable.

Closer to home, and near and dear to Paul and Arthur's hearts, was a smaller foundation, supported by the brothers, the *Hearts That Matter Institute*. It provided financial and counseling assistance to young boys and girls with the potential to excel in the sciences and arts. Lilly loved the logo that Paul and Arthur had selected for the *Hearts* institute—a small, line-art drawing of two boys, bundled up, carrying a red fuel can, their heads bowed to the wind, as they trudged resolutely into a furious snowstorm.

The last graduate was awarded her diploma. In a burst of youthful exuberance, the happy grads flung their mortarboards skyward and pulled off their robes. Lilly clapped and cheered as her family joined in the celebration, laughing and swaying with the graduates, everyone caught up in the majesty of this beautiful, sun-filled morning on a grassy campus green in Hanover, New Hampshire.

How Michael would have loved all of this, Lilly thought.

Amid the clamor, she mouthed words softly under her breath: "Rest well, Margie. And sleep well my darling Michael. And thank you, Frank, Clara and Henry. Each of you touched my life, and the lives of two young boys in ways none of us could ever have imagined."

Made in the USA
Lexington, KY
10 December 2013